LONG LIVE THE KING

LONG LIVE THE KING
KAITLYN AND THE HIGHLANDER
BOOK NINETEEN

DIANA KNIGHTLEY

Copyright © 2024 by Diana Knightley

All rights reserved.

No part of this book may be reproduced in any form or by any electronic or mechanical means, including information storage and retrieval systems, without written permission from the author, except for the use of brief quotations in a book review.

❈ Created with Vellum

For Ean, for being such a great guy, and sometimes carrying such a heavy load, watching you turn into a man is an honor...

PROLOGUE I - KAITLYN

TAKES PLACE JUST AFTER TIME IS A WHEEL- LONG BEFORE LONG LIVE THE KING

Magnus was sitting in the sand, while Isla and Zoe splashed around in a tidal pool. I was crouched nearby sifting through shells looking for shark teeth.

Everyone else was under umbrellas: Jack napping beside Noah on a beach towel, Quentin, Beaty, James, Sophie, Hayley, Fraoch, Zach and Emma were on beach chairs. Ben and Archie were swimming with Lochie.

We had come down here for a day of fun because Ben and Archie told us we were "boring" and that all we did was "lie around and do nothing."

They were right, we had been resting from the shifting craziness of the last long, time shifting, terrifying months. We deserved the rest, it was only about a month since we kicked ass in 1557, since we were separated through time, losing memories, since the world had been shifting.

Everyone looked relaxed on their beach chairs, a little tan, laughing as we talked about little-nothings.

Magnus splashed a hand in the water of the tidal pool a few times, watching the ripples. "This is the life, we canna want anything else in the world."

Fraoch said, "Aye, tis the best place on earth. I am never leavin'."

James held up a bottle of beer. "Definitely. We should come out here every day and just do this, no more crises."

Quentin squiggled his toes into the sand, his eyes closed, his hands on his belly. "Amen to that, not doing anything but this from now on. We've earned it. I'm retiring." He pulled his hat down over his eyes.

Magnus said, "Ye arna goin' tae be my Colonel anymore?"

Quentin flicked the front of his hat up a bit. "I'm still your Colonel, but you're retiring too, we're all retiring, *this* is our new normal."

The rest of us raised our drinks. Zach said, "Good, retiring sounds great." Then he joked, "What does everyone want for dinner?" We all laughed.

Then we fell quiet. Lochinvar returned from the beach and shook, showering us, then dropped to the sand, getting it all over him. "What are ye talkin' about?"

Magnus said, "How much we are enjoyin' that we are restin'."

Lochie nodded. He opened the cooler, grabbed out a soda can and opened it, spilling some on his legs. He drank with big gulps then burped.

Hayley said, "Lochie!"

"M'apologies, Madame Hayley."

We grew quiet again. Then he said, "But we ought tae do *somethin'*."

Magnus nodded. "Aye, we ought tae... I hae been wonderin' does the path still go back past 1557 all the way tae 1290? Last we checked it did, and it bothers me that we hae such a long stretch of timeline tae protect... it weighs on me. But then with all the loops and shifts recently, and usin' the Bridge, it seems things might hae changed — we ought tae test how far back the time travel path goes."

Quentin flicked the front of his hat up. "I'm in. I'll test. James, you in?"

"Yep. I'm in, leave tomorrow?"

Quentin said, "Return the next day. Or someone comes to rescue us with the Trailblazer."

Fraoch said, "I am Trailblazer rescue team. Ye on m'rescue team, Og Lochie? I warn ye, tis a horrible experience."

"Aye, ye will need m'help."

Magnus said, "Och, for a bunch of men who were retired a moment ago, ye are all rarin' tae go now!"

So that was how we sent Quentin and James to use the vessel to test the timeline. They were going to go to October 28, 1557, first. If the timeline was open they would be able to go farther and farther back, we had a list of places and dates.

If the timeline was closed down, they would be stuck there without a vessel and wouldn't be able to get home.

If they didn't come home we would know, we would mount a rescue with the Trailblazer, using the dates to look for them.

This was the royal we, it was Fraoch and Lochinvar who would blaze the trail.

The following day we had stormy weather, big dark waves, howling wind, spraying sand, we waited, it was nerve wracking, and they didn't return.

The next morning at dawn, Fraoch and Lochinvar left to go rescue them with a vessel and the Trailblazer, headed to the first of the agreed upon dates.

. . .

I felt awful for them when they left, because the Trailblazer was notoriously awful to use. Fraoch said, "Maybe they will be there on the first date we check, maybe we winna hae tae use the agony machine."

Lochinvar said, "Twill be nothing."

I expected that I would feel the Trailblazer at work, a splitting headache and the electric feeling, but no, nothing.

It was another night of worry, but at dawn we heard Zach, "They're back!"

I got up, bleary-eyed, and pulled on a robe, following Magnus downstairs.

Magnus grabbed his keys and went to go pick them up from the beach.

All us adults were up, waiting. Zach made coffee. While he dumped spoonfuls of coffee into the maker, he said, "I've said it before and I'll say it again, we hope it's zipped up. I can deal with the eighteenth century, a bit of the seventeenth, I'm not a fan of the sixteenth, but fine, we can deal, but I don't like having the middle ages to contend with."

They returned a while later, wet and cold. We met them in the foyer, and wrapped them in beach towels. Quentin said, "Well, the timeline shifted back, we can't go past November 1, 1557."

James said, "It was an easy test, we went to October 29, and got stuck, first jump. We camped for three nights, woke up the morning of November 1, 1557 and Fraoch and Lochie were there."

Lochie said, "We dinna even hae tae use the Trailblazer, tis too bad, I was lookin' forward tae it."

Fraoch said, "Och nae, ye werna lookin' forward tae it. I ought tae hae let ye use it for a try, let ye see how God-awful tis."

Magnus dropped his keys into the bowl on the table by the door. "Except using the Trailblazer would open up the timeline again, nae we are glad tis closed."

James said, "November 1, 1557 is the end of time for our purposes."

Magnus said, "This is good news. There are centuries we daena hae tae think on, we are not responsible for them, we canna shift them or change them. We hae our timeline settled, our enemies vanquished, we are in a time of peace. Tis all good."

Quentin joked, "*Now* we can retire."

Magnus laughed. "Did I mention I ought tae go check in with Lady Mairead at my kingdom?"

We all groaned.

PROLOGUE II

Since we left off in Time is a Wheel a while back, here is a wee bit about where we left the family.

The rolling aspects of time had threatened to flatten them, people were missing, not just from their lives but from their memories. Even children. But Magnus and Kaitlyn used the Bridge and fixed the timeline.

Their children, Archie (8), Isla (4), and Jack (not yet 1) are with them.

Quentin and Beaty have Noah (almost 1).
Zach and Emma have Ben (7) and Zoe (3).
Fraoch is reunited with Hayley.
Lochinvar is there, growing lonely.
They have solved everything.
Peace reigns. They are in Florida.

Magnus's mother, Lady Mairead, is overseeing his kingdom of Riaghalbane in the year 2391. They believe they have almost all the machines.

These include:

Most of the twenty-six vessels (small handheld devices) for traveling through time. When the vessel is used it causes a storm. It is very painful to jump. They can go to the future indefinitely. Or they can go back in time to November 1, 1557. If a vessel attempts to go past November 1, 1557, it disappears and strands the person in the past.

There are two Trailblazers. (There might be more.) Magnus has one, Lady Mairead has hidden the other. The Trailblazer blazes a trail further into the past than 1557, so the vessels can be used there. It is very very painful to operate. The downside of the Trailblazer is the farther back one can travel, the more of history there is to deal with —shifts are more likely to occur. It raises the likelihood that history will be changed.

There is one Bridge. If the timeline gets screwy, our time travelers can use the Bridge. One of the descendants of the kings of Riaghalbane is needed to operate it. The Bridge must be taken to the time where the screwiness started (usually time shifts or overwrites or history ruining uh-ohs or oopsies). A thumb is pressed into the obsidian stone contained within a carefully made small box.

The timeline returns to the way it was before. If the screwiness involved a trail that the Trailblazer blazed, it would be sealed shut. The end of time travel would once again be Nov. 1, 1557. (We think, through trial and error.)

For slightly less painful time traveling, there are golden threads that can be fastened to the nape of the head, reducing the physical torment of using the vessels. There are only a few threads so they are saved for the children to use.

As of the beginning of this story, Magnus believes that he has all the machines, and that time has been sealed up, the shifts have been fixed. He believes the vessels can only be used back to the year 1557.

He believes the moment in November 1290, when he was crowned king at Scone, has been overwritten and it is like it never happened.

**At the end of Time is a Wheel, Magnus gave the auld warrior's horse to Archie and Ben, and one last thing was left undone, they needed to name him. They chose the name Mario.

Months have passed since that moment to this new story. There has been peace; life has been normal. It is now May, the two new bairns, Noah and Jack, are nearing their one-year birthdays. Magnus and the other men have taken the bigger kids to the Ichetucknee River to go tubing.

CHAPTER 1 - MAGNUS

ICHETUCKNEE RIVER - SPRING, 2025

I rolled the inner tube in front of us, carrying Isla in m'arms. She was thrilled by the prospect of riding down the spring, yellin', "Da! We go in the water!"

"Aye, Isla, we will go down the river."

"This going to be fun, Da!"

Ahead of us, Fraoch swung a big raft intae the river and strode in after it, plowin' through the water. He puffed because of the cold and yelled over his shoulder tae the boys, "Och aye, tis brisk as a Scottish loch on a spring day!"

The boys were standin' at the water's edge lookin' brave, but tentatively dippin' toes and shiverin', until Lochinvar ran up behind them, picked them both up, gigglin' and squealin', and jogged, splashin' into the water. Chef Zach was carryin' Zoe, and ran in after them. She blew air, as if she were going under though she dinna hae any of her body in the water. James ran by carrying two tubes. Slinging them out across the surface of the water, the current quickly took them. "Oh, shit! Wait, they're going...!" Fraoch laughed as James jogged into the water, his knees high, chasing the tubes and laughing.

I got tae the edge of the water as everyone was climbing

ontae their tubes and pushed our tube from shore. Isla put her hands on m'face. "Da, this is going be verra fun."

I plowed into the water. "Aye, Isla, twill be verra fun." But then she gasped as her toe touched the water, fed by a spring, a verra cold spring.

"Da! It freezing! Too freezing!" She climbed up m'waist scrambling up tae m'shoulder and perched there with her arms wrapped around m'head, knocking m'sunglasses askew.

She shrieked near my ear as I went deeper, and submerged m'self intae the water. She climbed so that she was standin' on m'shoulder.

I pulled the tube close. "Ye will hae tae get wet Isla, ye canna go down the Ichetucknee River and stay dry."

Archie said, "Isla, you can't stand on Da's head, you have to get in!"

"No! No!" She shrieked. Then looked at me earnestly. "Da, I will go in, I will have fun, I just not ready."

I hefted us onto the inner tube and sat in the center, while Isla squirmed around and sat on my chest, shiverin'. "This good, Da? See, we have fun!"

I said, "Yer bottom is on m'neck, Isla, tis uncomfortable." She scooted down a wee bit, makin' sure that not one bit of her was touchin' the water.

Zoe was perched similarly on Zach's chest, but her feet were danglin' in the cold spring.

Lochinvar was on a tube and was splashin' the big raft that Archie and Ben were in, rowin' along with the current.

James was farther down the river holding ontae a branch, waitin' for us tae catch up.

We floated down the river, playin' and splashin' in the water, kids swimmin' and jumpin' from the tubes intae the river — except Isla. She remained perched as far from the surface as she could be so when I wanted tae move I had tae pass her tae

Fraoch's chest tae ride while I jumped on the raft and rowed with the boys and jumped in the water and swam alongside.

Then Isla sat on Zach's chest with Zoe while Fraoch and I rowed on the biggest raft, playing a game of keep-the-boys-from-the-boat. Fraoch said, "Ye remember the last time we were on a ship, Og Maggy?"

"Och do I, ye had a fever and we were terribly hungry, twas a long and desperate voyage. The ship was much larger than this one, though, remember — tae meet that ship we had tae steal a smaller boat, much like this one."

Archie's eyes went wide, he whispered, as he swam alongside our raft. "You *stole*, Da?"

"Aye, son, I had tae, twas not tae enrich m'self, twas tae get home."

Fraoch said, "Then he saved m'life. So we ken God thought on it favorably." His eyes went wide and he asked the boys, "Dost ye think there are gators in this water?"

The boys yelled, trying tae scramble ontae the raft.

Fraoch pretended tae battle them off, saying, "If there are gators, we must feed them with boy-appetizers, so they winna be hungry for the men."

The boys swam tae the back near me and tenaciously held on, pulling their legs up.

Archie said, "Da is safe zone!"

Ben yelled, "No appetizers for the gators!"

Fraoch said, "Og Maggy, ye just goin' tae let the appetizers use ye like that?"

Then Lochinvar snuck up from under the water, yanked the boys off, swam tae the side, flopped ontae the raft, climbed tae his feet, and rocked us back and forth, dislodgin' Fraoch who slid off the raft tae the water. "Och, ye are too wily, ye stole m'raft!"

I held on, as Lochinvar kept rockin' until he capsized the whole raft, knockin' me intae the water as well. Lochinvar flipped the raft right-side up, climbed on, and yelled, "I am king of the river!"

He pretended not tae see us as Fraoch and I each hoisted a boy and flung them ontae the raft where they wrestled Lochinvar down until he slid off intae the water.

He said, "Och nae, the pirates hae taken m'ship."

Archie said, "It's okay, Uncle Lochie, I had tae take the ship, I needed tae save m'life." Sounding verra much like a young Scotsman.

Everyone laughed.

I swam away from the raft leaving it for the boys and climbed back on m'tube and pulled Isla over tae m'chest again, pretending for a moment that I might drop her in the water. She shrieked so loud m'ears rang.

"Isla! If ye scream ye will get tossed in!"

She clung tae m'arms, "Da, I am very sorry, I just not ready."

There was a cooler of fruit and snacks tied tae Zach's tube, floatin' along behind us. At lunch time Zach passed out sandwiches. While I was eatin' m'roast beef with pepper jack cheese, Isla remained perched on m'chest, havin' her peanut butter and jelly, and assurin' me that this was all verra fun.

We all grew quiet while we ate. Archie was sittin' on the big raft, with his sandwich on his lap, and his feet trailin' in the water. "How long have you been a king, Da?"

I said, "Och it feels like centuries — how auld are ye?"

Ben and Archie laughed.

Isla said, "You don't know how old he is, Da?"

"I forget, sometimes, Isla, as time is rollin' by and has blurred the details."

Archie said, "I'm eight years old."

Fraoch said, "Eight! Och, ye are nearly ready for yer first broadsword. How much ye weigh?"

Archie said, "I don't know."

Lochinvar said, "He is wee, he is the weight of a broadsword."

Fraoch said, "Ye ken it daena matter, the question is how much does he benchpress?"

Archie and Ben laughed.

Archie joked, "I can lift almost thirty."

Fraoch said, "Thirty! Och aye, in that case ye will be able tae swing a broadsword, easily, but it will need tae be made of flower petals."

Once the laughter died down. I said, "So, I've been a king for eight years, as the crow flies."

Isla said, "What does that mean?"

I said, "The crow flies in a straight line, if I follow its path it has been eight years, but if I truly recount how long I hae been a king, the path has been a big loop-the-loop — it feels as if I hae been a king for much longer. But I use Archibald's age tae mark it — eight years."

Archie took a bite of his sandwich and chewed thoughtfully. He and Ben were alone on the big raft and it was lackadaisically spinning. Then he asked, "How long do kings usually rule?"

I narrowed my eyes, "I daena ken, tis dependent on war and rules of succession and the length of time the king lives."

Archie said, "If I am going to be king does that mean you will be..." He whispered, "Dead?"

Fraoch was perched on a small tube, eating his sandwich. "Och nae, this conversation took a dire turn."

I watched Archie for a moment, tryin' tae decide what the turn of question meant, but answered truthfully, "Aye, Archibald, if ye are crowned king, I will be gone."

"That doesn't seem fair."

"I ken. Fortunately we hae decades tae go afore that happens, I intend tae hae a verra long life."

"Good." He looked quietly down at his sandwich. Then said, "Not sure I want to be king if you are gone."

I nodded. "Well, Archie, life is full of responsibilities, and this is one of them, someday ye will be king, and God willin', ye will be ready for the challenge."

Fraoch said, "Of course he will be ready, he already presses thirty! He canna weigh much over four stone, he lifts close tae half his weight. He is goin' tae be a king of power and glory who all will revere—!"

Lochinvar jumped from his tube ontae Fraoch's tube — the tube tipped, Fraoch spun his arms, pretendin' tae try tae save himself, but slid intae the water, holdin' his sandwich up above his head. "Saved it!"

Fraoch and Lochinvar both climbed back ontae their tubes and Lochinvar and the boys sang songs as we floated down the current.

A while later, Fraoch scrambled up, pulling his legs from the water and crouched on his tube. "Och!"

Isla said, "Too cold, Uncle Fraoch?"

He looked suspiciously down at the water and around in it in all directions. "Nae, like all good Scotsmen, this brisk temperature is perfect, if yer heart races and yer breath puffs, ye are certain ye are alive and that the summer is upon ye. I was just thinkin' on what is under the— " He startled, "Did ye see that?"

Ben said, "Uncle Fraoch, there aren't gators in the water, we told you that!"

"Aye, but I wonder, Ben, are ye just tellin' yer uncle a story? Ye ken how I feel about gators, ye might be lyin' tae me."

Archie earnestly said, "I would *never* lie to you."

"Ye hae stolen m'glorious raft right from under me!"

Archie and Ben laughed.

Fraoch was crouched and his tube was spinning. "Och nae!" He was frantically looking down in the water.

Ben said, "Uncle Fraoch there aren't any gators, tell him Dad!"

Chef Zach said, "Fraoch, I promise, there are no gators, you know why?"

"Because ye are telling me a story?"

"No, because it is too cold for them. They hate the cold. That's why they never build snowmen, right Zoe?" She giggled.

Fraoch grinned. "This is why the gators daena live in Scotland!"

Zach said, "Exactly, they don't want to live in Scotland and the gators damn sure don't want to eat a Scot. Too cold. They like a warmer, sweatier dinner."

"I always knew a proper Scotsman wasna meant tae live with those monstrous beasts." He relaxed and sank down on the tube, allowing his arse tae submerge intae the water in the middle of the tube. "All ye gators daena bite m'arse, tis a cold arse, ye canna hae any!"

The boys thought Fraoch was hilarious.

He said, "Isla, did ye hear? If ye want tae put yer arse in the water, ye can. Tis good tae taunt the gators with our primacy. We are the Scots, and this is cold water. If ye dangle yer butt and fart in the water the gators will feel sorry for themselves."

Isla said, "That's okay, Uncle Fraoch, I don't want to make the gators feel bad."

He feigned upset. "Isla! Ye take it back! Ye ken the gators want tae feel bad — they are monsters, they thrive on grumpiness."

She giggled and adjusted her weight, her heel digging into my rib. I pushed her a bit and she grabbed hold even harder. "You almost knocked me off, Da!"

I laughed. "Ye ought tae go in the water, Isla. Tae hae fun, ye need tae get wet."

She shook her head. "I am not ready, Da, these things take time."

At the end of the float downstream we bumped against the landing dock. We dragged our raft and tubes tae shore, climbed out, and began wrapping ourselves in towels.

Isla stood on the side of the riverbank with her hands on her hips lookin' verra disappointed with herself. I asked, "What are ye doin', Isla?"

"Nothing, Da," she huffed. "Just thinking about how much fun we had."

We wandered up tae the van tae get juice boxes from the cooler, and I watched her, as she jabbed her straw in her box, as her chin trembled.

I texted Kaitlyn on m'phone:

> How is Jack?

> His fever broke, he's all good, did you boys have fun?

I chuckled, thinking about how Isla was talking about fun.

Quentin and James tossed our towels intae the back of the van. Chef Zach passed out snacks tae everyone. Isla looked down on her juice box with deep melancholy.

I called Kaitlyn and said, "Isla wants tae tell ye about her day." I put the phone on speaker and held the phone for Isla.

Isla said, "Hi Mammy."

"Did you have fun?"

Isla burst intae tears.

I heard Kaitlyn's voice say, "Uh oh."

Isla wailed.

Kaitlyn said, "Let me guess, my love, you didn't go in the water."

Isla sniffled and said, "It wasn't the right time, Mammy."

"I have so been there, Isla, I also want to make sure the time is exactly right. I once waited a whole summer before jumping in the lake. I kept waiting for the right time. Are you sad about it?"

Isla nodded.

I told Kaitlyn, "Aye, she is disappointed."

Kaitlyn said, "Disappointed? You can't be disappointed, Isla, you were just waiting for the right time! This is important, ask your Da, is it important?"

Isla looked up at me.

I nodded.

Kaitlyn said, "Ask Fraoch, is it important to do something at the right time?"

Fraoch said, "Och aye."

Kaitlyn said, "I think your disappointment isn't that you were waiting, it's that the time is right, right now, it's there — are you ready?"

She set her jaw and raised her chin, a little like her grandmother. She said, "Aye, I'm ready."

"Perfect, there's no reason to be disappointed, this is the exact right time..."

But Isla was marching down the grassy bank and striding right into the water up to her waist.

I said, "Thank ye, mo reul-iuil, she has gone in."

Lochinvar, Fraoch, and James stripped off their shirts and jogged down the grassy bank, behind her. They all waded into the water.

Kaitlyn said, "Love you, see you in a few hours. We girls will have dinner ready."

I dropped m'phone on the floor of the van, took off m'shirt, and ran down the bank after them. The sun was behind a cloud, it was chilly in the air and freezing in the water, but we all waded in and stood there for a minute until Isla turned around, shivering, and marched out and up the bank.

She said, "That was the right time."

I followed her out and Archie and Ben met us, carrying down our towels, now already damp. I wrapped one towel around her, her teeth chattered.

Archie said, "Isla, it's okay."

She huffed.

Ben said, "You didn't miss anything, Isla, it was cold the whole time."

She glowered.

And in her eyes she continued looking disappointed.

Fraoch came up and stood beside her, a towel lookin' small wrapped around his shoulders. She had the same sized towel but hers dragged on the ground. The two of them looked out over the water. While the rest of us finished packing up our things and returned our rafts, they both stood quietly.

Then I heard Fraoch say, "Ye ken, Isla, tis a hard thing tae regret what ye dinna do."

She nodded.

He said, "But ye canna regret it if ye learned from it, did ye learn something?"

"Aye, Uncle Fraoch, I learned ye ought tae start at the beginning."

"That's a good lesson, and well put in a Scottish brogue." He put out a fist and she brought her fist down on it and they both turned and followed us tae the van for Quentin tae drive us all home.

CHAPTER 2 - KAITLYN

FERNANDINA BEACH - HOME

When Magnus walked up I pulled Jack from the sling and passed him over. Magnus held him and nuzzled into his neck, making his 'horse noises': neigh, neigh, spluttering and blustering. Jack giggled, his little pudgy hands holding onto Magnus's ears, his baby way of saying, "More!"

Magnus said, "Och ye feel much better, wee Jack, ye are not ablaze as ye were. Noah is good?"

I said, "Yep, their baby-fevers broke about the same time. And Sophie never got it, which is good."

"Aye, tis too close tae her time. She'll be deliverin' the bairn soon."

"We are going to have so many babies."

Magnus tucked Jack into the crook of his arm and said, "Och, Jack inna a bairn anymore, look at him, a big boy!"

Jack giggled again.

∼

Our days had settled into ordinary. We lived in Florida. Lady Mairead ran the kingdom in our absence. Magnus went there periodically, only missing a few days here and there. He had some pressing issues in Riaghalbane, but nothing like a challenge for the throne — he had frightened off all the usurpers.

He was strong, surrounded by good men. He wouldn't accept a challenge, he didn't need to. He had no need to prove himself.

He was a powerful king.

Quentin and James had tested the timeline again and discovered that, during the recent time shifts, it had contracted to its original length. We could not time travel further back than November 1, 1557.

This was a relief. There was less time to contend with, a lot less history that we might screw up.

I still remembered with clarity the year Magnus and I spent stranded in 1551 through 1552, but the shifts had made other memories of long ago centuries vague figments of our imagination.

Part of Magnus's strength was that the kingdom's succession was orderly: we had met the original king of Riaghalbane, Nor. Magnus, Fraoch, Quentin, and James had gone to Nor's time and helped found and establish the kingdom. Quentin had overseen the building of its military might, and had organized the coronation of the king, Normond I.

James had contracted the hell out of that castle compound.

We had been wary about helping, not wanting to screw anything up, but we had been successful and brought peace and prosperity to the kingdom.

Magnus didn't expect anything from Normond in return for his help, but... we knew he was an ally. We assumed that therefore his son would be an ally, his grandson, and on and on.

There was a list of kings, the master list, the kings that mattered, a direct line from Normond to Magnus, with nary a deviation. As I ran my finger down that list of kings we were confident that another ancestor we had met, Artair, was also an ally if needed.

But there was a second list, the footnotes of the throne's

history that cataloged all the arena battles; the cousin-usurpers; the kings for a short time; the time travelers who had disrupted the line of succession; me, who had murdered a king; and men who had tried to overthrow the royal bloodline. This inventory was three times as big as the other.

In Magnus's lifetime, alone, there had been Ian and Agnes, Samuel and Roderick, Ormr and Domnall, and...

But history was written by the victors. We were victorious. We wrote the list of kings.

We ignored the rest.

Except I kept my eye on the footnotes, mulling it over, wondering: Was this master list of kings the end of the story? Was history settled?

We rarely changed the big things, and kings were big, after all, about as big as it got.

But... it was in this time that a kingdom from history began to infiltrate Magnus's dreams.

CHAPTER 3 - MAGNUS

HOME

I woke up with a start. *Long live the king! Long live the king! Long live the king!* was echoing in my head... a massive crowd chanting... I had been standing on a stage, a crown placed upon m'brow. I had bowed my head, but now I looked up, out over the screaming hordes, at the timber walls, buildings with thatched roofs, flags fluttering above — *what flags?* I tried tae remember how they had looked against the sky.

But there was a darkness around the edges, the flags fluttering against a high blue sky had crisp edges but unformed centers.

I had forgotten becoming a king. Now, I remembered I had once been a medieval king.

Which came first?

I had acquired the throne, years ago, it had happened before I knew it had happened — a loop, an entanglement.

A long confusing time ago.

I had been a king.

Mag Mòr, crowned in the year 1290.

It had been the most difficult thing in the world tae be a king at two ends of time, tae be stretched by duty and honor well past my limits. With time shifting between.

CHAPTER 3 - MAGNUS

. . .

But now I wasna Mag Mòr. I wasna a king of the past. The shift of time had sloughed me from the line. Or wheel. As my auld friend Cailean had argued.

I had known him back then. How had I forgotten him? What caused me tae remember?

My experience had proven Cailean right, twas a wheel, I felt sure. And I had been thrown from that circuitous rolling. That royal role.

I was a king in the future, no longer king in the past.

It was scarcely even a memory anymore.

More like an echo, though twas inside myself, an echo that got m'heart racing, and filled m'gut with a cold dread.

I had been the ruler of a kingdom. Twas a great demandin' responsibility.

But it wasna real.

It had been real but now twas only an imagined past, echoing around inside m'being.

I had been dreaming. I was certain of it.

But this had seemed somehow new… it unsettled me and made it difficult tae return tae sleep.

I rolled over on m'side and placed a hand on Kaitlyn's stomach, soft and pouchy from bearin' my bairns.

I had forgotten that Jack had come tae sleep with us in the night. He looked over her shoulder at me and said, "Da!"

I chuckled, and pressed my finger tae m'lips. Then I held out my arms. He crawled across Kaitlyn's chest and climbed into my arms. I lifted him, carried him from the room, and down the stairs. We went tae the refrigerator and stood in the light of the open door. I pulled out the carton of milk, took down a mug, poured some milk in and chugged it down, leaving a bit of milk on m'upper lip. Jack giggled and put out his hands. "Me!"

I gave him the mug and he chugged. He gave it back, a grin on his face.

I said, "This is what we do, Jack, we drink from a mug in the light of the refrigerator in the twenty-first century. Next, we hae a verra important task, dost ye ken what tis?"

His face grew serious as if he were thinking this was a consequential thing.

"In every century, if we are up in the night, we ought tae go guard the house. Are ye ready?"

He nodded and sat up straight on m'arm. We walked across the living room, slid open the door, and stepped out on the back deck.

There was a light breeze, rustling the hair on his head. He wrapped his arm around my bicep and shivered.

"Aye, wee bairn, this is the cold of duty. Ye hae tae go out intae it tae keep yer family safe. Dost ye see the guard on the roof?"

We looked up on the roof tae see Sam, who had been with us for years. He raised a hand. Jack and I both raised a hand in return. Then we stood there, takin' in the beach, my eyes sweepin' up and down the sand dunes. Jack tucked his head tae m'shoulder. I stood there for a long time, relishin' the breeze on m'skin, the certainty of the ocean, even as it ebbed and flowed against our beach. Our house was a stronghold, even as the sand beneath it shifted under the foundation.

I breathed in the salt air and felt Jack grow heavy in m'arms, the weight bringing me comfort. A burden was a purpose and there was nae greater burden nor purpose than sons.

And thrones.

A man with burden and purpose wanted safety. Tae ken a certain peace. Life these days seemed tae be a quest for strikin' balance between the purpose and burden and peace, tae hae balance of all.

CHAPTER 3 - MAGNUS

I had achieved it, yet...

Long live the king, long live the king, long live the king, echoed still.

The shifting sands of time seemed tae be signaling that the balance was becoming dislodged.

I returned Jack tae his bed.

And returned tae m'own.

As I climbed in under the covers, Kaitlyn mumbled, "You're cold."

"Aye, I need yer warmth." I pulled her hips close, and settled m'mouth beside her ear. She woke up kindly, and warmed me mercifully, providin' the release I needed tae return tae sleep, m'arms around her in the darkness of our room. A guard stood on the roof, the bairns slept soundly down the hall. All was well, the balance of burden and purpose and peace achieved.

The following morn I was early in the gym, workin' out.

Fraoch, James, and Quentin came in a bit later, tossin' their towels on the equipment, using dumbbells tae warm up their shoulders. Lochinvar entered, "Everyone here already?"

"Aye."

Quentin sat down on the bench and put on gloves. "Did you guys feel anything weird last night?"

I was curling. I said, "Aye, I had fitful dreams, I was up more than I slept."

Quentin lay back and pressed 225 pounds for a few reps, with Fraoch spotting. Then he re-racked it, sat up, and toweled off his face. "It made me think of using the Trailblazer, same sensation, much vaguer, but still, the same..."

My brow drew down. "Anyone else notice that sensation?"

Lochinvar shook his head, "But what would I know? I slept

like a log, woke early for guard duty, dinna feel anythin' but a headache."

Fraoch said, "The headache is part of it."

"Tis? Then I change m'answer, aye, I noticed it."

James said, "I didn't notice anything, but Sophie said the baby was really active, she barely slept."

Fraoch said, "My knees ached."

Lochinvar said, "Because ye are auld."

"Tis not, tis because the weather is changin' and not the normal kind of weather, the weather of time."

James laughed. "That's still because you're old, young people don't feel weather in their knees."

"I am verra certain I am only a few years older than ye, James Cook."

Lochinvar said, "A few centuries beyond that..."

While they argued, a common practice while workin' out, I did more curls, up and down, up and down. Then I put the weights down and moved tae the bench. "I had a dream, where I was a king of an ancient land, and the people were chantin', 'Long live the king!'"

They all turned tae look at me.

Fraoch slid another plate on the bar. "An ancient land? Dinna that happen once afore?"

I nodded. "Aye, I feel certain of it. I was called Mag Mòr. I was crowned king at Scone."

James shook his head. "Don't remember."

I repped the weight three times.

Fraoch said, "Nice, that was 275, wanna go higher?"

"Aye, let's go tae 315."

He slid more plates on the bar, then said, "I vaguely remember when ye were crowned."

"Because ye were there, ye helped me acquire the throne. There is a shadow of it, a vagueness, but last night I *remembered* it, and this morn, by the light of day, I recognize it. I battled for the throne, and won it. I was a king of Scotland."

Quentin scowled. "Damn it. When I mentioned it felt like the Trailblazer had been in use, I really hoped you would tell me I was crazy."

I shook my head. "Nae, ye arna crazy, someone is usin' a Trailblazer tae go further back in time than 1557."

James said, "Remind me, how many Trailblazers are there?"

Magnus said, "I hae one in the vault, m'mother has one hidden in secret — we ken of two."

James said, "Dammit, I wanted you to know for certain, there might be more?"

"Aye."

Fraoch said, "We checked the timeline — the trail ended at 1557. What happens if the Trailblazer is used tae open up the trail *again* — will it dredge up the memories and all that we did?"

I shrugged. "Anything is possible."

Quentin said, "It's *all* possible, but also, note, *we* aren't using a Trailblazer."

Lochinvar said, "Och, I daena like the sound of that. Then who is?"

I said, "I will go tae Riaghalbane and see if we can figure it out."

Quentin said, "Who do you want to come with?"

I said, "Lochinvar and Fraoch will come, ye and James will stay. James has a bairn close, and I took ye last time. Beaty has been givin' me grief for it."

Quentin said, "You afraid of Beaty?"

"Och aye, she is a Scottish lass, tis best not tae upset them."

Our trip tae Riaghalbane was fruitful in many ways, I accomplished much, but there was naething tae discover about the Trailblazer. Lady Mairead and I both had possession of ours

— they werna bein' used. If one was in use, twas a mystery: who or how or why?

According tae the history of the world, I had never been king of Scotland.

At least not yet.

Twas a relief, as I dinna care tae be the king, but how else tae explain the dreams? They were comin' verra often now, in the deep night, a thunderin' *Long live the king!* Causing me tae shudder at the thought of all that would mean.

CHAPTER 4 - KAITLYN

MAY 15, 2025 - FLORIDA

One Spring night, we celebrated Zach and Emma's not-quite-wedding anniversary after a full day of celebrating Ben's birthday. They had chosen to celebrate a Fakiversary near the date when Ben was born, because, as Zach pointed out, that was when they felt like they got hitched. But also, as he pointed out, "There is too much going on in between Thanksgiving and Christmas, we'll *never* get a proper celebration!"

Ben was seven years old, give or take a bit of time because of time travel. Emma and Zach were celebrating their seventh Fakiversary.

Zach had said, when he was telling us the plan, "It's the itchy one!"

Emma smacked him in the arm. "Are you itchy?"

He laughed, "No, of course not, it's just what it's called!"

Fraoch said, "What does itchy mean?"

Zach said, "They call it the seven-year-itch, when you want to fool around — ugh, it was my poor attempt at a joke."

Fraoch's eyes went wide. "I am surprised ye survived it."

Magnus said, "I think we hae come close tae a murder, I am grateful Madame Emma inna the type tae carry a dirk."

Zach said, "I thought it would be funny, but in hindsight..."

She said, "What my husband is forgetting is that itchiness can go both ways." She scratched behind her ear and then her side.

He said, "Oh no, no, no don't tease me!"

She said, "He's also forgetting the true meaning of a Fakiversary, where husbands must lavish gifts upon their wives, especially long-*suffering* wives."

He joked, "So the thing I was already getting you...?"

She grinned. "Sounds like the only solution is you'll need to double it."

He said, "Yes, of course, anything you say, love of my life. Just, promise if you get itchy you come to me for the cream."

We all groaned, exaggeratedly. Zach said, "I know I know, humor is risky, again, poor joke. I will triple the size of the diamond."

Emma laughed. He kissed her on the cheek.

We had offered to watch the kids while Zach and Emma went out to dinner, but they had gone out the weekend before to a hotel for two nights, calling it the prelude to the Fakiversary, and so for the actual Fakiversary they preferred to have a dinner with all of us.

The kids were wiped out by the day, a bouncy house with a water slide, and cake and ice cream. The littles had been melting down, and had all gone to bed. Archie and Ben, already in their pajamas, were watching a movie in the living room with popcorn.

And we adults were out on the back deck, a long table decorated with a floral centerpiece, and takeaway from Zach's favorite restaurant. He had to sit there while we served it too, not helping, since he was part of the couple we were celebrating.

He gripped the edge of the table comically, pretending like it was hard to watch Fraoch pull boxes from the bags, popping the clamshell lids open, and peeking inside. Fraoch poked a finger in and licked it. "Och aye, tis garlic potatoes."

CHAPTER 4 - KAITLYN

Zach groaned. "It says it on the box! You don't have to put your finger in!"

"Aye, but ye canna trust everything, Zach, this is yer problem, ye are too trustful!" Fraoch grinned at Hayley. "Inna it true?"

"I disagree, his problem is he's *mistrustful*, look at him, he can't even trust us to open the boxes and put them in front of everyone." She pulled a box out of the bag, checked the tag taped to the side. "Short ribs, who ordered short ribs?'

Zach said, "Me!"

Hayley grinned. "Let me check first." She opened the clamshell and poked her finger in. "Yep, seems like short ribs!"

Zach groaned, put his arms around Emma's shoulders, and buried his face in her hair. "Don't make me watch! We should have gone out."

We got the boxes of food in front of all the places. I said, "I'm sorry we didn't open it in the kitchen and put it prettily on the plates."

Zach said, "I couldn't bear letting you do it out of my sight, or in my sight, I might have a problem — but kidding aside, this is perfect."

Magnus pushed his chair out and raised a glass of whisky. We all raised our glasses.

He opened a piece of paper and I could see his handwriting on it. He squinted at his notes in the darkness, "Och nae, tis difficult tae read, I have a good toast I wanted tae make..."

I turned on my phone's flashlight and held it over the page.

He said without reading, "We hae convened here, a light tae illuminate the words, a deck built from hearty trees, here in the present, with our gathered guests from so many different ages, one, our Sophie, carrying a bairn, bringing a future tae our family—"

Sophie smiled, "I am due with the next moon."

"Aye, twill be a blessing. And we hae spent the day with

bairns, celebrating the honor of them, and now we hae a toast from the past that I read upon the computer—"

Fraoch said, "M'arm is growin' tired."

Magnus said, "Och, ye are soft."

Fraoch shrugged. "I am not the one who has written out a blessin' tae read afore dinner."

Magnus ignored him and began to read: "Chef Zach and Madame Emma, may the blessin' of light be upon ye – light without and light within. May the blessed sunlight shine upon ye like a great peat fire so stranger and friend may warm himself in the flame. And may light shine from yer eyes, like a candle set in the window, biddin' wanderers tae come in from the storm tae bless them with yer fine meals and yer warmth. And may the blessing of the rain be upon ye, may it beat upon your Spirit and wash it fair and clean, and leave there a shining pool where the blue Heaven shines reflected..."

Fraoch lowered his glass.

Magnus grinned, and continued, "...*and* may the blessing of the earth be on ye, soft under yer feet as ye pass along the roads, soft under ye as you lie upon it, tired at the end of day." He raised his glass even higher. "And may yer love grow strengthened in the arms of our family. Slàinte!"

We all said, "Slàinte!"

Fraoch said, "I grew impatient but twas lovely."

We sipped from our whisky and then dug into the food, a loud cacophony of conversation and laughter as we ate. At one point Noah woke up, crying in his bed. Beaty said, "Pardon me, I must go see tae the bairn. He is all turned upside down from the party today."

Quentin closed the box covering her food. "...to keep it warm." She left the deck with Mookie following along behind her, never leaving her side.

. . .

Hayley said, "Man, I really like the ease these days, nothing happening, no worries, history is settled—"

James said, "Uh oh," and added, "Could we maybe wheesht and not tempt fate, because Sophie's due date is this week?"

We all raised our glasses to him and Sophie.

I tossed back a little more whisky. "Sophie, I cannot wait to meet your new baby, Jack and Noah are so old we need new babies around here!"

Everyone laughed, because the boys weren't even one yet.

James raised his glass, "Here's to the Irish triplets we're about to have in the house!"

I said, "One of the things I've liked is that the pregnancies take almost ten months, they're fairly constant, we can judge time by them. Even if you time jump, even if time shifts, your body is still growing a baby and it takes the amount of time that it takes."

Sophie said, "Och, I am ready for it tae be done though, the bairn has been kickin' up a storm, but aye, with time changin' around us, tis nice tae hae somethin' that follows the moon. The physician told me the bairn was due on the twenty-second day of the month, but I am inclined tae think he will be delivered tae our arms on the night of the new moon."

"That's lovely, we ought to drink to that." I raised my glass. "To the coming bairn on the night of the new moon and Sophie and James's waiting arms."

Everyone raised their glasses and we toasted with a bit more whisky.

Then Zach stood. "No one stop me. I know I'm not supposed to do anything, I must be waited on, but if we don't have a round of beers we're going to be drunk off my arse." He hiccuped, laughed, and went into the house.

Magnus shook his head. "How long did we keep him from the kitchen?"

Emma said, "It was a valiant effort, but lasted about an hour."

Fraoch said, "Tis where he is lord, he must rule over it."

We all raised our glasses again, but then Zach returned with a case of beer and a pitcher of what he called Party Punch, a nonalcoholic juice.

Hayley said, "Hey, how come you don't serve us Party Punch after a jump? Why go-go juice? Party Punch tastes much better."

"It's much better because it has mounds of sugar in it, go-go juice is specially made to be vitamin heavy and… gah!" He waved his hand. "Just drink your juice. Just accept that I have concoctions that are specially made and I know best. When I pass everyone a juice…" He popped a cap off a beer bottle and tipped it up taking a swig. "What do you say?"

Quentin joked, "Yes, sir. It tastes terrible, sir, thank you, sir."

Chef Zach said, "See, Quentin gets me!"

I said, "Now where were we…?"

Hayley said, "I said 'History is settled' and was told to wheesht and not to tempt fate, is that what you mean?"

I said, "I agree with the wheesht — no talking about the big scheme of things, not when everything seems good — it feels settled. We're surrounded by twinkly lights and barbecue, babies sleeping, a baby about to be born… let's not discuss the history of the world."

Hayley said, "I'm sorry I said it. Now, looking around at everyone, that seems like a downward turn, who wants that? Not me! I ate a fine dish of barbecue, let's just digest."

Lochie said, "But…"

Magnus groaned. "What Lochinvar?"

"Nothin', just daena like the idea of becomin' soft."

Fraoch scoffed. "We arna soft." He tried to pop the cap off a beer and accidentally nicked his thumb, winced, and sucked it for a minute. "Daena look at me."

Lochie said, "We canna be soft, we must keep aware of our surroundings."

Quentin nodded. "Totally agree."

Lochie said, "We hae tae keep a clear eye when we look

CHAPTER 4 - KAITLYN

around at the timeline, make certain we arna missin' something."

Magnus exhaled. "Aye, tis true. We must always be watchful."

Hayley said, "Well, that's a downer. I notice no one told *you* to wheesht."

Beaty returned, holding Noah.

I asked, "Did Jack wake?"

"Nae, he's fast asleep."

She sat down with Noah in her lap. Quentin kissed her cheek and the top of Noah's wee head. Mookie dropped down to his side by her chair with a grunt.

I asked, "What would be a good way to keep aware of our surroundings?"

Lochie said, "Since Magnus has had the dream about becoming a king—"

Magnus said, "They are recurring, and I am nae *becomin'* a king, I *am* the king. I am rulin' over people in a long ago past."

Lochie waved his hands toward Magnus, "See? Since those dreams started, I hae been thinkin' on the line of succession of the kings..."

Fraoch said, "Och nae..."

Lochie said, "What dost ye mean, 'Och nae'?"

"Nothin' good comes from ye thinkin' on the kings, first ye speak on it, next we are riding intae battle somewhere."

"What is wrong with ridin' intae battle? If ye are needed tae ride, ye ought tae ride. This is what I am sayin', ye are grown soft..."

Fraoch waved his fists. "I will show ye soft, ye want an arse-kicking?"

Hayley said, "You boys have to stop arguing. Fraoch you are definitely not soft, you don't need to prove yourself, we all know it—"

Fraoch said, "I fought him in an arena, not... how long ago was it?"

Hayley patted his arm. "Not long ago, you aren't soft, Lochie is just teasing to get his way."

Magnus said, "Aye, this is a pattern with ye, Lochinvar, tae get what ye want ye abuse us — dost ye want tae sit at the table with the men and enjoy a fine meal or dost ye want tae sit at the children's table with the bairns?"

"I want tae sit with the men. I am verra sorry, Fraoch, ye arna soft, ye could probably fight me without becomin' too winded. I would win, but then again I am much younger than ye, tis not yer softness but yer age."

Magnus chuckled. "Has this made it better, Fraoch?"

"Aye, that was a wonderful apology from a young lad, barely auld enough tae wipe his own arse."

Magnus chuckled more, then asked, "By the succession ye mean the list of the kings of Riaghalbane, not of Scotland?"

"Aye, why...?"

"Because lately I wonder if we are goin' tae see m'name appear on the list of Scottish kings."

Fraoch said, "I daena ever think it could be so easy."

Lochie said, "I will start with the list of Riaghalbane kings."

Magnus said, "I think Kaitlyn can get it for ye, right, mo reul-iuil?"

"Got it right here." I pulled my phone from my pocket, opened my note app and the document, *Kings*. I placed my phone on the table in front of Lochie.

Everyone leaned in.

I explained, "So we have Normond, then his son, then Artair's father, then Artair, then... couple more, then Magnus, but notice this is the official record. This is the one that is set. We have probably overwritten a lot of history, but we don't have that; it's lost to time—"

Lochie said, "So this is the real, true history."

"Yes."

He asked, "And Magnus is a direct descendant, right?"

"Aye, I am direct."

Lochie asked, "But what of all the arena battles?"

I said, "There are probably a lot of those that were overwritten but the ones we know about we have on another list. I have a copy of it in my office."

I picked up the phone. "It has more kings, regents, and a couple of interim managers, a usurper or two — during Magnus's reign there have been many arena battles, Samuel took the throne for a hot minute, then there were Fraoch's brothers, and..."

Lochie said, "This is what I was thinkin' on, none of this is on the main list, so I am ponderin' what else has been omitted and do we ken?"

Fraoch said, "Usurpers daena get tae stay on the official record or it looks like we are weak. I am usin' the 'we', that means the royal we."

Hayley laughed. "I'm impressed you used it correctly."

Lochie said, "So ye will rewrite history just so ye daena hae some men upon the list?"

Magnus said, "Aye, because they are unimportant. Tae the victor go the spoils."

Fraoch said, "If they couldna hold their throne, they daena get the honor of our pen writin' their names upon our list."

Quentin said, "This means there's a lot of turbulence we're overlooking."

Magnus said, "Aye, or ye could think on it this way — we arna overlooking it, there is just an official list and then there are the footnotes. There are many more footnotes because of overthrow and battle, a few years here and there, tis a mess. There is a long history, whole books hae been written about it."

I said, "I've got a few of the official history books upstairs too..."

Lochie said, "Do the books include all the battles?"

Quentin said, "Yep, unless they are overwritten by time travel, they're there. I've looked them over, it's chilling."

Magnus said, "Kaitlyn will be sure tae get ye a copy of the

list and some of the books, Lochie, ye can look them over. Tis funny though, ye haena been interested in the kingdom's history before. M'mother is always studyin' it."

Lochie said, "She is a wise auld crone."

We all groaned.

Beaty said, "Daena let her hear ye call her a crone, Lochie. I like ye, ye are a part of the family. I would miss ye when she feeds ye tae the dragons."

He chuckled. "I would never say that tae her face, I am a warrior — I am not foolhardy." He wiped barbecue sauce off his hands. "I am glad there is a good list... I wonder if there are repeating names, maybe a branch of cousins who are particularly troublesome."

Fraoch said, "Haena we dispatched all the cousins yet?"

Magnus said, "If we haena gotten them yet, we will." They clicked their beer bottles together.

Lochie said, "But this is a good example, all the enemies ye hae fought, Og Maggy, yet when we look down at this list none of them are mentioned. Ye daena want tae give them the honor of bein' on yer list, but without their names it looks as if yer throne has been easy tae keep."

Magnus nodded in agreement, "I suppose ye are right, Lochinvar, it belies the bloodshed we needed tae maintain the throne."

"Aye, and ye will want tae see the names tae see the way they might be connected. What if there is a cousin who plans tae avenge his brother?"

Magnus said, "Och, a revengin' cousin is the worst of them."

Quentin said, "We dismissed second and third cousins as insignificant, but maybe we do need to see a full list for the patterns."

Magnus nodded. "My mother has spoken tae me on something similar. She mentioned some of m'second cousins, insignificant relations, yet.... She said, she was keeping her eye on them."

Lochie said, "Wise auld crone, as I said."

We all groaned again. I said, "Please, *please* don't say it to her face, but yes, I'll give you the list and the books, all the stuff I have about the lines of succession."

Lochie tipped the beer to his mouth, with a grin. Then he put the beer bottle down and said, "Nae one is goin' tae ask me about m'readin'?" He looked down at Emma, "Madame Emma, I hae been talking about the list for ten minutes and nae one mentioned it!"

Beaty said, "I will ask, Lochie, how are yer reading lessons?"

"With Madame Emma's tutelage I hae learned tae read, verra proficiently."

We all applauded.

I said, "That is great, Lochie, I'm really proud of you. I'm sorry I didn't mention it. I didn't think you wanted to talk about it."

"I dinna much want tae talk on it but now I can read most everything!" He leaned forward, "Frookie, ye ought tae get Emma tae teach ye—"

Fraoch said, "Och nae, I asked Archie tae read tae me *one* time! I needed help with the instructions — the letterin' was verra small! I can read! Och nae." He waved his hand at Lochie. "I am nae speakin' tae ye anymore, ye are givin' me indigestion." Then he said, "Most every night I read, daena I, m'bean ghlan?"

"Yes you do."

Lochie said, "What dost ye read?"

"I am readin' right now about a man who came tae the world from another planet. Tis verra entertaining. There are paintings but I daena hae tae use them, I read the words upon the page."

Lochie said, "He came from another planet? How did he get tae the world, through the air?"

"Aye, he can fly."

Zach covered his mouth with a napkin so no one could see him laugh, his shoulders shaking. He took a big swig of beer, pretending to do something besides listen. Hayley, James, Quentin, and I were all glancing at each other bemused.

Lochie leaned back in his seat, as if he were mulling that over. Then he leaned forward. "Does he hae wings?"

Fraoch said, "Nae, he has a cape and the power tae fly with his arms out, swooping through the air."

Lochie said, "Och, I would like tae do that."

Fraoch said, "Aye, tis verra good, he is verra strong as well — ye would like him. I can loan ye one of the books, I hae collected many of them."

"Och aye, I would like tae read it now that I can. Dost ye ken tae read, Og Maggy?"

"Aye, I was tutored in London when I was wee, I also ken how tae speak other languages and tae perform maths, as well."

Lochie said, "I guess that's why ye are a king."

Magnus grinned. "That and the bloodline and the kickin' arse in an arena." Then he said, "Ye learnin' tae read because of the young lass?"

"Aye," he sighed, "she is a beauty."

Hayley said, "You met someone, Lochie?"

"Nae." He shifted in his seat uncomfortably.

Fraoch said, "He haena met her *yet*, but he has looked upon her with awe."

"Aye, I *will* meet her, I just canna... not yet."

James said, "Is this Ash, from the Palace Saloon?"

Lochie nodded. "What kind of name is Ash, dost ye think? Tis the same as the Ash tree?"

I said, "I think it's short for Ashley, a nickname, like Lochie."

"Ashley, but they call her Ash, like the tree," he nodded. "Makes more sense."

James said, "I'll go down there with you next week and introduce you, I used to know her dad, and we all know the bartender, Don, we went to school with his older brother."

Hayley said, "James, you can't go to a bar next week, you're about to have a baby."

"Oh right."

Magnus checked his watch, then said, "Beaty and Sophie, will ye watch the bairns? The rest of us will go tae the Palace and see if we can introduce Lochie tae Ash, the maiden."

Lochie's eyes went wide. "What are ye... nae, not now... ye canna, we daena..."

Magnus stood. "Nae blusterin', Og Lochie, ye hae learned tae read and ye did it tae meet the maiden, ye are proud of yerself, aye?"

Lochie nodded.

Emma said, "I am very proud of you, Lochie, we ought to go to the Palace." She stood and jerked her head to Zach. "Come on, Babe, up and at em."

Hayley said, "Quentin and I will drive! Come on!"

Lochie shook his head, gripping the edge of the table, looking frightened.

Magnus said, "Lochinvar, we are goin' tae go tae the Palace Saloon, we will see if she is working. She might not be working, ye ken. If she is, James Cook will introduce ye. Ye will ken her name and she will ken yers."

Lochie said, "Nae one will mock me in front of her? I daena want her tae... ye winna talk down tae me?"

Magnus said, "Nae, Lochinvar, we all ken the importance and the dignity of the moment, we winna mock ye in front of her."

Fraoch said, "But if ye do something stupid I reserve the right tae insult ye in the truck after."

"I would expect it." Lochie took a deep breath.

Magnus said, "We will go, we will buy a round of drinks, we will introduce ye, and then we will come home. Twill be painless, Lochinvar."

Lochie had gone pale. "Tis the most excruciatin' thing in the world."

Fraoch clapped him on the back, "Come on, Og Lochie, throw on yer cologne and meet us in the car."

Lochie sniffed his armpits and said, "Aye, I will meet ye in the car."

He pushed his chair from the table and headed to the house.

I stood, "We're doing this?"

Magnus said, "Aye, we hae tae help the lad find a lass or he's going tae start a war."

I said, "What makes you think he wants to start a war?"

Fraoch straightened his kilt. "Why else does a young lad want tae see a long held list of usurpers tae go over the history of a kingdom? He's lookin' for trouble."

Magnus said, "Aye."

We all went into the house to gather our things to go.

CHAPTER 5 - KAITLYN

MAY 15, 2025 - PALACE SALOON

The bar was crowded so it took a minute to find a table, but then the bartender, Don, pointed us to one as a group left. We couldn't find enough chairs, so Magnus, James, and Fraoch stood against the wall taking in the scene, while the rest of us took seats at the big round table. Lochie was very nervous. He kept his eyes directed at the table in front of him, until James nudged him. "That her?"

Lochie glanced, our eyes all followed his. He gulped. "Och aye, she is a bonny lass, is she nae?"

She was very pretty. Petite, with strawberry blonde hair, cut in a cute shorter style, pale blue eyes, freckles. I leaned toward Hayley and Emma and said, "She looks like Meg Ryan!"

He was so smitten, whenever he glanced at her his eyes went all soft. Then he would quickly look away, looking in all directions, awkwardly, up at the ceiling, behind us, under the table. He was squirming in his seat looking uncomfortable.

He ran his hand through his hair, a redness rising up his cheeks.

The young woman approached our table. She was wearing an olive green shirt with a star on the front and a long khaki cargo skirt, covered in pockets, with elastic cords pulling up the side. A pair of dark combat boots. She was fit and cute. "Sorry, y'all, we are packed, did someone take your order?"

James said, "Not yet, we can go to the bar—"

"No, it's fine, just took a hot minute, Jess called in sick, so I'm swamped." She smiled, showing off the dazzling dimples on her cheeks. "What can I get you...?"

I thought Lochie might faint, luckily she didn't notice his reddening cheeks at all.

James ordered for all of us to keep it simple. Then said, "Your name is Ash — you're Jim McNeil's daughter?"

She blew hair off her forehead, then yelled across the table, trying to be heard over the raucous bar. "Yeah, you know my dad?"

"Yeah, I'm a contractor, worked with him a couple of times, he still around?"

"What?"

"Your dad still live here?"

"No, he and mom moved to North Carolina!"

He said, "I'm James Cook, hey, can I introduce you—?"

"No, sorry, really gotta get the order in!"

James said, "Okay cool, maybe when you get back."

She buzzed off and James said, "Well, someone else needs to try next, or she's going to think I'm hitting on her."

I said, "Got it. When she comes back, I'll talk."

Lochie pulled at the collar of his shirt. "Och nae, I daena ken if I can bear it. What if I wait out in the truck while ye finish yer drinks?"

Fraoch said, "She's going tae come back in a moment — what, ye are not brave enough tae meet her?"

"Ye said we would just come and see if she is here, now we ken. We can go home and come back on another less crowded night—"

The big table of rowdy hooligans beside us all got up and left, leaving a noticeably emptier bar.

Magnus joked, "And suddenly, tis not so crowded."

CHAPTER 5 - KAITLYN

Lochie leaned back in his chair looking defeated.

Ash came over carrying a tray with our beers. She blew her hair off her forehead again as she put them all out. "I'm sorry, first chance to breathe since eight."

I stood up to help. "That's fine, let me introduce you while I pass them out. The Coke is for Hayley and Quentin, class of '11. You already met James, he's class of '11 too. How about you?"

She said, "I'm class of '20."

I joked, "Damn, now I feel old." I placed beers in my place and in front of Emma and handed beers to Magnus and Fraoch. Then, the last beer...

I said, noting a thin trail of sweat rolling down the side of Lochie's temple, cold dread on his face, "And this is our friend, Lochinvar." I passed him the beer. "He's visiting from Scotland."

"Pleasure to meet you— wait..." She turned to me. "You're Kaitlyn Sheffield? *The* Kaitlyn Sheffield who was a YouTuber?"

"Well, yeah, many years ago, I'm Kaitlyn Campbell now. This is my husband, Magnus."

"That was *horrible* what he did to you."

"Yeah... um—"

Hayley jumped in, "So, Ash, class of '20, huh? Lochie is younger but—"

Her eyes narrowed. "How young is he? I didn't card him."

Hayley said, "Oops, not what I meant, fine upstanding citizens, he is old enough to be in a bar." She muttered, "We're pretty sure."

Lochie drew in a deep breath, pushed back his chair, and stood, tipping the chair over. It almost crashed except Fraoch grabbed it just before it hit the ground.

Meanwhile, in the commotion, Lochie's sporran tipped a glass over on the table. Beer splashed everywhere. Hayley quickly righted it, but the front of his kilt was soaked. Lochie said, "Och nae."

Ash rushed away, "Let me grab a rag!"

Lochie said, "She will think me an imbecile. We ought tae

go, I hae ruined m'chance." He ducked his head and tried to escape, but Fraoch yanked him around and clasped his arms, keeping him from leaving. It was Fraoch style, gentle enough, but because he and Lochie were both so big and as one struggled and the other grabbed, it seemed a wee-bit violent — chairs made scraping noises on the floor. Magnus, also big, had to back to the wall to get out of the way. All eyes turned to us, and Emma, Hayley, and I had to jump from our chairs to clear some room.

Ash rushed back, "I have the rag... but... the table over there needs their tab closed out." Her eyes swept over our table's disorder and that we were all awkwardly standing around. Magnus and Zach stepped together to block her view of Fraoch forcefully holding Lochie.

I grabbed the rag. "No worries, sorry, we didn't mean to make a mess..."

I mopped the beer up while James and Quentin both kind of waved at the remaining customers, mumbling, "No worries... just a friendly disagreement, sorry, didn't mean to bother you..."

While Fraoch sternly held Lochie near the wall, reprimanding him in a whisper, "Ye canna leave, I winna allow it."

"Ye saw her, she is the most bonny lass I hae ever laid eyes upon, and I was made a fool."

"Ye arna made a fool, Og Lochie, but och, ye are a coward!"

"I am nae!"

"Ye are, ye will fight in an arena but ye winna look a lass in the eye?"

"I looked foolish in front of—"

"Ye made a mess — tis just a spill. Ye simply mop it up. I hae seen ye mop the back deck, ye are capable enough."

Lochie's mouth turned up on the side. "Ye hae seen me do much more than mop a deck, ye hae seen me beat yer arse in the arena."

Fraoch put his hands on Lochie's shoulders. "That's a good lad, ye are insultin' me, ye are almost yerself again. I canna abide by a weak and cowardly Og Lochie, that is not the usual way of things."

Lochie straightened his back and stood taller.

We all resumed our seats and tried not to watch, but it was fascinating. Fraoch said, "She is going tae come back over here and what are ye going tae say tae her? Ye hae tae say something good."

Lochie gulped. "I daena ken, I suppose I will ask her if I might speak tae her father about a marriage cont—"

I exclaimed, "Oh no, that's not—!" I winced at Emma.

Hayley bit her lip to suppress her laughter.

But Fraoch straightened the collar on Lochie's shirt. "Nae, ye winna ask tae speak tae her father *or* about marriage. Ye will ask her if ye can talk tae her after she is done workin'."

Lochie ran both hands through his hair. "What will we talk about?"

"I daena ken — while we wait for her tae finish workin' we will come up with some ideas." He clapped his hands on Lochie's shoulders. "Dost ye understand? Ye are goin' tae behave with wisdom, I ken twill be difficult for ye, but with bravery ye can handle yerself. Can ye? Because we arna leavin' until we see ye talk tae the maiden. I canna go home after witnessin' this sorry business, I hae tae see ye be brave or m'opinion on ye might be irredeemable."

"Ye would think me cowardly?"

"Aye, I would think ye a coward and all the brave things ye hae done will be overwritten by this moment, daena let it happen, Og Lochie, ye hae a reputation ye must uphold in m'eyes. Daena disappoint me."

"Aye." Lochie's Adam's apple went up and down in his throat with his gulp. "Aye, I will."

Fraoch passed him his beer. "Good, now stand here with yer beer in yer hand and look competent or I will take all the cookies from ye for a full week."

Lochie mock-gasped, "Ye are goin' tae threaten a grown man with nae cookies?"

"Aye, if the grown man is gonna act like a bairn, then aye."

"I winna. I will speak tae the maiden."

"Good."

They both stood shoulder to shoulder.

Magnus grinned at me.

Did you see Fraoch father him...?

Aye, he is an auld softie.

Ash returned to our table, blew at her hair on her head, dazzled us with another smile and asked, "Where was I? Your table is clean — I am so sorry! Usually I'm much better than this, but my shift is almost done, what a night..." Her eyes, for really the first time, scanned the men, and settled on Lochie. "I don't think we met yet, I'm Ash." She put her hand forward.

He took it and bowed over it, a red curl brushing her wrist, his lips hovering above her knuckle. "Pleasure tae meet ye." He kissed it and raised his head.

She said, "Oh, shoot, that was... *wow*."

He said, "M'apologies, mistress, I am Lochinvar, brother of Magnus the First."

"Oh.. double wow, and you're from Scotland? I've never been to..."

"Aye."

She fanned herself, not in mockery, but because she had been working. But it was also clear that his steamy swoony brogue had caused her to heat up more.

She said, "My friends call me Ash, and um... yeah, I live um, here, grew up here."

He asked, "Are ye named for the exalted Ash tree?"

She shook her head. "The Ash tree? No, that's interesting, no one has ever asked that before, they usually mention ash, like from a fire."

He chuckled. "Dost ye mean the ash from a fire would come tae mind first and not the noble tree, renowned for its protection? The Ash Tree is the Tree of Life! Ye canna tell me that is not the first thought?"

"It's true, I've never had someone mention the tree first. My real name is Ashley McNeil."

"Och nae, I winna understand modern man." Then he added, "M'friends call me Lochie."

"Like Lucky?"

"Aye, like lucky, I am the luckiest man tae be speakin' tae ye."

Hayley dropped her head to the table.

Zach sprayed his drink. He was laughing so hard he had to leave to go to the bar.

She said, again, "Wow."

Emma nudged him, "You had a question for her...?"

He drew his eyes away from Ash's face. "Och, I did... the one about her father?"

Fraoch said, "Nae, Og Lochie, ye were going tae ask if ye could stay after tae speak tae her."

Lochie ran his hands through his hair. "Och, aye, Mistress Ash, would it be permissible for me tae wait for ye tae finish yer work. We could... um speak with one another...?"

She watched his face intently then glanced at all of us. We all averted our eyes as if we weren't hanging on her decision. She checked her watch. "I was early shift, the bar is still open, but I finish in twenty minutes. Would you want to wait? You could wait out front."

"Aye, I will wait."

She smiled her dazzling smile, and said, "Great, but I have to get back to it." She asked James, "You need anything else?"

He said, "Just the check."

She wandered off and we all played it cool until she was in the back, out of earshot, then Fraoch clapped him on the back. "I knew ye could do it!"

Lochie was even paler than usual. "Did I do it? I canna remember a moment of it, I think it all went black."

Magnus said, "Ye must remember tae breathe, and yer statement about bein' lucky was verra good."

Lochie said, "Good, I felt twas a good thing tae say. Dost ye think she liked me?"

Zach said, "If the girl you're talking to says 'Wow' like that over and over, that's a pretty good sign."

James got the check and paid for our drinks.

And we divided up, Quentin driving Zach, Emma, and James home. Magnus and I waited with Fraoch and Hayley in the truck parked a few spots down. We had a view of the front of the Palace Saloon, even with the fog rolling in off the river.

There were park benches, a lone tree sprouting up beside the sidewalk, and Lochie sat on a wall, his feet on the bench, his elbows on his knees, nervously watching the door.

Hayley joked, "Our boy is growing up."

Magnus and I were sitting in the back seat of his truck, he held my hand on his knee. I said, "I can't believe he was going to ask to speak to her father — we need to give him *way* more instructions. Is that how he thought they were going to date?" I said to Fraoch, "I'm glad you convinced him to talk to her."

Magnus said, "I forgot tae tell him something." He climbed from the truck and approached Lochie, stood beside him and they talked for a few moments, mostly Magnus speaking, with Lochie nodding.

Magnus returned to the truck, climbed in, and took up my hand again.

"What did you say?"

"I reminded him he shouldna brag about killin' in the arena, or that I am a king, that he needed tae act as if he is from this time and tae not tell her about time travel."

My eyes went wide. "Oh no, would he do that?"

"Aye, it came tae me that he would try tae win her by tellin' her he fought in the arena, and he was plannin' tae — when I told him 'nae' he asked, 'Then what will we talk about?' I told him he ought tae think of somethin'."

CHAPTER 5 - KAITLYN

Fraoch groaned and opened his door.

Magnus said, "Where are ye goin'?"

"Tae go give him some ideas. He canna think on this himself or he will be talking about cookies or video games the entire time. He will be lost." He strode over and spoke to Lochie at length.

When Fraoch returned to the front seat, Hayley asked, "What did you tell him?"

"I told him tae ask her questions, tae listen more than he speaks, and if she asks him about himself tae tell her about living in Maine with all of us, and when she asks about Scotland tae tell her about the landscape and how much he likes fishing and hunting. Lassies love it when men speak about how they will provide for them."

Hayley sighed. "You are almost completely correct, my love."

"I ken I am, I won ye over by feedin' ye, tis the one truth of the world, practiced through the centuries. I will provide ye food. Tis what love is, tis romantic."

We went back to watching Lochie, his shirt stretched across his shoulders, rounded as he hunched, his red curls on his collar, his knee jiggling from nervousness, waiting.

CHAPTER 6 - LOCHINVAR

CENTRE STREET - IN FRONT OF THE PALACE SALOON

Finally the door opened, Ash came out, and called over her shoulder, "See ya later, Don!"

I stood as she walked up. She had a bonny smile that lit up the night. I looked down on her, she was verra beautiful, makin' it difficult tae ken what tae say.

She said, "You waited for me, I wasn't sure you would."

"Aye, I waited, I said I would."

"Cool, cool." She nodded looking up intae m'eyes, renderin' me speechless, still.

There was a long awkward pause then she said, "So was that group of people, your um... family?"

"Aye, Magnus and Fraoch are m'brothers. We are all in the same clan."

Her eyes squinted. Then she said, "I heard he was really rich."

"He is a ki— a laird, aye, he has a great deal of wealth and much land, aye."

She walked over to the wall and put her bag down on it, placed her keys beside it, and leaned there.

"And what do you do, Lochie?"

CHAPTER 6 - LOCHINVAR

"Dost ye want tae sit down? Ye must be worn from the work."

"Yeah, actually, yeah." She perched on the wall and I stood in front of her.

"I work for m'brother..." I searched for a way tae express what I did without sayin' I fought in the arena for him, I said, "I help him keep his lands."

"Like a groundskeeper, or an assistant?"

"Aye, I assist him, if he needs me... I do what is required."

"Do you go to Scotland a lot?"

"Verra often, tis a beautiful land — hae ye seen it, Mistress Ash?"

"No, I've been a few places in the US, but never overseas, and nowhere as beautiful as that — you know, you can just call me Ash if you..." Her voice trailed off.

I shook my head.

She said, "I do kinda like it when you call me 'Mistress Ash', it makes me feel fancy, and... yeah, I could use the boost, it's been a tough year."

"Och nae, what has been tough on ye, Mistress Ash?"

She smiled up at me, lightin' a blaze in m'heart. "It's nothing really, I was in the army—"

"The army...?"

"Yeah, the military and—"

"Ye were a soldier? I daena understand..."

She squinted. "Lochie, yes, I was a soldier, I mean, I was in the military, my job was—"

"Ye fought in a war?"

"No, I worked on a base."

"Oh."

She said, "Have you ever met a woman soldier before Lochie?"

"Nae, never."

"There aren't women in your military in the UK?"

I shook my head, then because I wasna certain I said, "At least I hae never met one."

She grinned. "Now you have. I'm out now, a reservist, I can get called up if a war starts, but I'm out, so I came back here, started a job, but you don't want to hear about all my dramas..."

I said, "I do, I want tae be the one who ye share yer dramas with..."

"Oh."

There was a long pause. I was unsure what tae say.

Then she said, "I ought to go home, I had a long night."

"Och, aye... of course, I..."

She pulled her phone from her pocket. "What's your number?"

"Och nae, I daena..."

"You don't have a phone?"

I said, "I daena hae it on me."

She dug through her bag, uncapped a pen and wrote upon a small scrap of paper, 'Ash' and then a string of numbers. She passed it tae me, saying, "This is my number if you want to call."

I looked down on the page. "I would like that verra much." Then thought tae ask, "Do ye work tomorrow? I could come wait for ye again at the same time?"

She said, "I would like that."

I picked up her hand and bowed over it and kissed her knuckles.

She mumbled, "Wow."

"I will see ye on the morrow, Mistress Ash."

"I will see you tomorrow, Lochie."

She picked up her bag and keys and walked away down the sidewalk tae her car.

I went tae the truck, and climbed in the back beside Kaitlyn, sittin' with the scrap of paper still in my hand.

She asked, "She gave you her phone number?"

"Aye, she said I might call her, but I was also given permission tae see her on the morrow — here at the same time."

"Well done, Lochie!"
He grinned. Then his face fell, "I will need a phone."
"Yep, it seems like time."

CHAPTER 7 - KAITLYN

HOME - MIDDLE OF THE NIGHT

It was very late when we got home. I crept into Isla's bedroom, kissed her, tucked her in, and whispered that I was home now. She mumbled, "Good," and was back to sleep in a moment.

Jack was still sleeping, having completely worn himself out just being around a bouncy house and waterslide that he was too little to use. I pushed his hair back from his forehead and kissed his temple, sniffing in that lovely 'still a wee bit of baby' scent, it was glorious.

Archie and Ben were still slumber partying in the living room, but wearying: eyes heavy, lights dimmed, the movie flickering, the volume low, their sleeping bags dotted with spilled popcorn.

I whispered, "Where is everyone?"

Archie said, "Da and Uncle Fraoch went out on the deck with Uncle Lochie."

Ben said, "My mommy gave them an old phone from the drawer, they're showing him how to work it."

I watched out the back windows: Magnus, Fraoch, and Lochie in a circle of deck chairs, their knees almost touching. Magnus holding the phone, they looked like they were confer-

CHAPTER 7 - KAITLYN

ring how to put her phone number in. "Funny that Fraoch and Magnus are the ones who are showing him..."

"Mammy, does Uncle Lochie have a girlfriend?"

I smiled, "I think he does, now you mention it. Sort of."

Magnus put the phone up to his ear. I wondered about going out to help, but I was entranced by the memory of a million years ago, when Magnus didn't know how to work phones, and here he was, being a mentor to his young brother. It filled my heart with love.

It spilled over to his son, and how lucky he was to have such a father, and gratitude to his older brother Sean for the modeling he must have done, and the nature of his sister, and actually even a little for his mom, who, although she was a first-rate bitch, would never want her offspring to not know how to get through life. She would make sure they were prepared for what comes or she would fight her ass off to protect them. And Fraoch, who was a great brother to Magnus and had taken on the role of big brother for Lochie and these men cared for him and were going to help him win Ash.

I kissed Archie and Ben goodnight and went quietly up to our room to sleep.

A bit later Magnus went to the bathroom, brushed his teeth, and readied for sleep. Then crept to the bed and climbed in. I asked, "You helped Lochie?"

"Aye, he is verra nervous about her, but he has a phone now."

"He could send her a text, I could help him write a—"

He chuckled. "He already sent one." He pulled up the big comforter over us.

I groaned. "In the middle of the night? Without someone helping him spell? What did he text?"

"He texted 'it was a pleasure tae meet ye' and 'I will see ye on the morrow.' Then, because he had forgotten, he texted, "This is Lochinvar."

"I guess that's pretty good."

He pulled up alongside me and pulled me onto his arm and pulled my thigh up to his waist. With his lips against my forehead he said, "She texted him back."

I pulled my head up and looked at him in the darkness. "She *did*?"

"Aye, she said she had fun and looked forward to seeing him too."

"Wow, this is happening? Lochie is winning the girl? We are good matchmakers?"

"Aye, we are verra good, speakin' of… I hae a match I want tae make right now." He lifted my chin and began to kiss me with our wonderfully familiar deep kisses of desire and love.

∽

I heard him yell.

"Magnus? Magnus. Magnus!" I was up in the dark, nudging his shoulder trying to wake him.

Finally he said, "What…?"

"Wow, you were deep, that took a moment, you usually wake easier than that."

"I was havin' a terrible dream."

There was a faint light coming into our room from the moon, but it was the middle of the night, deep and dark. His yell had been unnerving, I took stock: Archie was sleeping in the living room. Isla was in her room. I could hear the sweet breaths of Jack in the monitor. I put my hand on the monitor to turn on the video to check. He was fast asleep.

I turned it off and lay down on Magnus with my chin on his chest. "What were you dreaming about?"

"The same, the chant. It seems tae echo in m'mind."

I nodded. He twirled his finger through my hair and

stretched out one of the locks and let it fall. "I ken the reasonable explanation is that I am rememberin' it, that I had forgotten it, and that now a time shift has caused the memories tae resurface, but yet... it is happening the way it did afore, mo reul-iuil. I am rememberin' it afore I have done it."

"It's like the deep past is different, the farther away we go into the past the more wonky it gets."

"What does wonky mean?"

"Like crooked or off-the-center. If time is a wheel, it's like the wheel has gone flat and is going flap-flap-flap and air is rushing out and the wheel is veering off the road. You ever been in a car with a flat?"

"Nae, but I hae seen a cart overturn because the axle broke in a rut puddle on a rainy market day."

"Yeah, just like that, *wonky*. But that's all this is. We've been here before, you are just dreaming of something you barely remember, it's been overwritten, you've got the echo of—"

"I haena been exactly truthful on it, mo reul-iuil. It has become more than an echo, the details hae grown verra intricate: the colors are lush, and when I am dreaming it I believe tis real, tis as if I can reach out and touch the leaves on the tree, as if I can feel the wind upon m'skin." He raised his head to look into my eyes. "I can see the flag as it flutters across the sky, tis mine, mo reul-iuil, in the colors of green and blue with the thin yellow stripe through the middle."

He lowered his head, looking up at our fan blades as they continued their very slow lackadaisical spin, like always, whatever the weather outside, our slowly turning bedroom ceiling fan was a constant, as constant as time.

"And tis as if the crown is heavy upon m'brow."

I tucked my head to his chest. "I am so sorry my love."

He said, very quietly, "Tis alright, mo reul-iuil. We will meet the day as it comes."

I tightened my arm across his chest and held on.

CHAPTER 8 - MAGNUS

HOME - THE SAME NIGHT

*I*n the dark before dawn there was a voice outside our door, "Da!"

"Archibald, all is well?"

"Nae, can I come in?"

"Yer ma is sleeping, I'll come, hold on." I climbed from the bed and pulled on a robe and opened the door tae the hall tae see m'son, his head bowed, his face grim. I whispered. "What happened?"

"I had a dream."

"Och nae, tis a hard thing, come with me." I led him downstairs.

We crept intae the room, picking a route past Ben who was fast asleep on the floor. I turned on the lamp at its dimmest setting, picked a comfortable place on the couch, and put out my arm. He sat beside me and cuddled against me, seeming frightened and needin' comfort.

I said, "Tell me about the dream."

"I call it a dream but it seems like, *real*. Like a video game, you know?" He grasped a bit of the front of my shirt in his fist and twisted it back and forth.

"Aye, I hae been havin' the same, they are verra detailed, the colors are crisp and I think I can smell it."

He nodded, quietly.

"What is happening in yer dream?"

"I'm up on a stage and there is large crowd yelling, 'The king is dead, long live the king!'"

I looked down on his face through the darkness.

He added, "You know what that means, Da?"

"Aye, I ken what it means."

"They're talking to *me*."

"Ye hae become the king?"

He nodded.

"Yer heart must be verra heavy from it."

He nodded again.

I tightened my hold around his wee shoulders, holdin' him close. "Dost ye hae a crown on yer head?"

"It pinches me, here." He pointed to a place right above his brow.

"It does the same tae me." I exhaled. "Is the crowd from the future, Archibald? Dost ye ken how tae tell?"

"It doesn't look like Riaghalbane, it looks like the cousin's castle."

"Balloch?"

"But even older. Because... I don't know why. It feels old."

"I see. I am havin' a similar dream, it is discomforting. But I find a wee bit of solace that ye are having them as well. I am not alone, does this comfort ye as well?"

"Aye." His wrenching grasp on my shirt let go, his hand relaxed.

"If we are both havin' the same dream then we are both there, that, in and of itself, is a good thing. I was once a king in the long ago past, we wrote over that timeline, but now I think the timeline has reemerged. I believe I am a king in the past. I am remembering it. Perhaps ye were standing beside me when I was crowned. Can ye tell how auld ye are in the dream?"

He shook his head. "I can't tell, Da, but it feels like it's big and I'm afraid."

"Well," I put my hand on his. "Ye might be verra young as ye are now, ye might be witnessin' the moment that I am becoming king, and ye are intelligent, ye ken the duty required, and ye ken that someday twill be yer duty..."

"Maybe."

"The thing is, Archie, tae rule a kingdom *is* big and it is grave, we carry a heavy burden, and someday, long in the future, ye will be crowned a king, but it winna happen for a verra long time. I am not goin' anywhere."

"Thank you, Da."

"Ye are welcome, son, dost ye want tae stay here for a bit? I can return ye tae yer spot once ye fall asleep?"

He nodded. I could feel his young body growing heavy with sleep.

I remained awake, thinking about the growing chant: *Long live the king! Long Live the King!* My dream dinna include: *The King is Dead!* Which made me conclude that our dreams werna the same. This was worrisome — was Archibald seeing the future, was he witnessin' my death?

Or was this nothin' but a dream? Did it mean nothing but the wisps and whispers of our minds when they ought tae be asleep?

I lightly tapped his shoulder — he was sound asleep. I lifted him and carried him tae his spot on the floor and tucked him intae his bedding.

Ben opened his eyes, "Is he okay?"

"Aye, he is well, goodnight Master Ben."

"Goodnight, Uncle Magnus."

CHAPTER 9 - KAITLYN

HOME - MAY 16

The following day Lochie was ready in the afternoon. He emerged from his room with his hair slicked back and a cloud of cologne wafting around him. He was wearing a clean shirt, laundered pleated pants, and a pair of shiny dark boots. He looked very handsome and a little vulnerable in that way of young men who are headed to prom with a girl they barely know, and get shined up for it.

Fraoch asked, "Why ye dressed so early?"

Lochie looked at his watch. "Is it early? I was thinking I would start out now."

Fraoch was incredulous. "Ye are goin' tae go *now* tae see her at ten? Are ye plannin' tae walk?"

"I thought tae."

"The walk would take ye three hours at the most, och, Og Lochie, ye canna be there hours early, she will think ye strange. We will give ye a ride at an *ordinary* time."

Lochie nodded. Then asked, "And I will sit out in the front tae wait for her?"

"Aye, just like last night, unless ye want tae go in and have a beer and tell her ye are waiting for her outside — ye could be a man who does regular things."

"I daena think I understand what regular things are here — did ye ken she is a soldier?"

Fraoch shook his head. "Nae, ye must hae misheard."

"She is, she told me plain. I asked again, tae make certain I had heard her correctly. She said she dinna go tae war though."

Fraoch and Lochie both went quiet, staring into space as if they were trying to figure it out.

I said, "There are lots of women in the military."

Fraoch said, "Is there? Tis an odd thing... for what purpose?"

I said, "Some women want to protect the country, they train, they serve."

Lochie and Fraoch both looked at me, nodding with their brows down, as if I were going to continue explaining.

When I didn't, Fraoch shook his head. "It daena make sense."

I said, "Fraoch, if Hayley could hear you! You're lucky she's out, what about all the viking women warriors? What about Joan of Arc? Haven't queens led their armies into battle?"

Fraoch nodded, "Aye, tis true, I suppose I just thought those lasses were not such... *lasses*."

I said, "Many young women join the military! If Ash joined the military that's great. And Lochie, I can't stress this enough, don't act surprised like Fraoch, or bad mouth it in any way. You need to be respectful."

"Aye, Queen Kaitlyn, but I was surprised at first— do ye think I ruined my chances?"

"She gave you her phone number *after* that conversation?"

"Aye."

"Then you're in the clear."

"And if ye think on it, tis verra courageous for her tae offer her life for her country. Tis honorable."

"Exactly."

Fraoch said, "This is true, and tis also true that I am an auld man and what do I know about anything? I hae tae remind myself all the time tae be a regular man."

Lochie said, "I daena think I ken how tae be a regular man."

"What would ye do if ye were at home in Scotland?"

"I would speak tae her brothers and ask her father for her—"

"Nae, we told ye, this is not how it works."

Archie and Ben were seated on stools by the kitchen island watching in rapt attention. Archie said, "You just have to be cool, Uncle Lochie."

Fraoch gestured, wildly, "Aye, ye just hae tae be cool! What if a young lass asked ye tae come tae the tavern in the evening, what would ye do?"

"I would walk tae the tavern, I would go tae the bar and order an ale, perhaps a whisky, and I would tell her that she is a bonny lass once I had the chance tae talk tae her."

"Exactly what ye should do in this instance."

Lochie said, "So I ought tae walk?

Fraoch said, "Nae, that is the one part ye canna do. This is a warm day, ye will be sweatin' like a fat mucag on butcherin' day in August. We will drive ye tae talk tae her."

Archie said, "You ought to ask her out on a date, Uncle Lochie."

"What is a date?"

Zach said, "You take her to dinner and dancing or a movie or something." He slammed the door of the oven closed.

Lochie's eyes went wide. "How would I… how do I… I daena ken what tae…"

Zach leaned on the counter. "Lochie, this is what you're gonna do. Wait for her after work. Talk to her, ask how her day was, then tell her you want to see her again. Ask her if you can take her to get dinner."

"Ask how her day was… want to see her… all right, I can do it."

"If she says yes, ask her if she has a favorite restaurant. Come back here, we will discuss and make a plan for you."

Lochie nodded.

"You got me, right? You know how to do it."

Lochie said, "Aye, I think so."

He sat down at the counter, beside the boys, asking for an afternoon snack.

And there Lochie waited all day. It grew to be evening. He checked his watch way too often.

Zach said, "She's probably not even at work yet, you don't want to get there before she does."

"I hae tae be cool."

"Yep, gotta be cool."

We ate dinner and Lochie kept checking his watch, having done really nothing all day but wait.

Fraoch said, "Och nae, I ought tae hae given ye something tae do!"

Lochie glanced at his watch again. "Like what?"

"Like a chore. Ye ought tae hae cleaned the trucks — idle hands cause ye tae bedevil yer family."

Lochie scowled. "I am bedevilin' ye just by checkin' the time?"

"Aye, daena do it again or I will send you from the room. We will tell ye when tis time tae go."

Lochie asked for another beer, then started to look at his watch, but stopped himself. A moment later he twisted in his seat to look at the clock on the oven.

Fraoch groaned.

Magnus shook his head, "Let the man check the time, Fraoch. He is goin' tae be on time tae visit the maiden and he canna drive so he is concerned he winna be there on time."

Fraoch said, "I ken, I ken."

James rushed into the room. "I think she started labor!"

CHAPTER 9 - KAITLYN

Emma stuck her head from her room. "Sophie...?"

James was on the edge of panic, "Of course Sophie, who the hell do you think?"

Emma said, "First, my apologies, my head was somewhere else. I'm cleaning out closets and wasn't thinking — also, no talking smack to me, don't be a jerk. How far apart are her contractions?"

He said, "I don't know!"

Emma and I followed him into the room, Beaty was already there. I said, "Hey Sophie, how ya doing?"

She smiled, then moaned, clutching under her rounded stomach.

Beaty said, "Twas quick upon the heels of the last, I think she be ready tae go."

I turned around to think, *what do we need?* to see James, standing at the door, keys in his hand, overnight bag on one shoulder, Sophie's purse on his elbow, a messenger bag on his other arm.

"I see you're ready."

"Yep."

Quentin said, "I got the van pulled up to the steps."

I joked, "Well look at us, all organized!"

Emma and Beaty helped Sophie up, and we all got her out to the van.

I called, "Hayley!"

She called back, "We got the kids!"

A big bunch of us rode to the hospital.

Then we sat in the waiting room. And waited.

CHAPTER 10 - LOCHINVAR

THE BAR AT THE PALACE SALOON

Magnus and Fraoch entered the room. Magnus scooped the keys from the bowl near the front door. Fraoch asked, "Ye ready tae go?"

I said, "Och nae, tis time? But we haena heard from James yet."

Fraoch said, "Nae, lad, ye get tae yer feet, tis time tae go. We hae phones, we can hear from James."

I followed them out tae the truck and climbed in the back.

We rode in silence tae Centre Street, except for once when Fraoch asked, "Ye ken what ye are goin' tae say?"

"Aye, I am goin' tae ask her how her day was, and then I will ask if I can take her tae dinner at her favorite restaurant."

Fraoch said, "But make it sound more natural, less planned, ye hae tae be—"

"I ken, I need tae be cool."

Magnus said, "Fraoch, I think ye are more nervous than Og Lochie."

Fraoch said, "I think ye might be right."

We were in the truck driving tae the Palace when Kaitlyn called. Magnus asked, "Did the bairn come?"

Then he listened and said tae us, "Not yet, but all is well..." He listened tae the phone again then said, "Fraoch and I are drivin' Lochinvar tae meet the lass."

He listened more then said goodbye and put the phone away. "Kaitlyn says tae be yerself."

I thought on that for a moment, then asked, as we pulled up in a parking spot down from the Palace, "What is *that* supposed tae mean? I am not supposed tae tell her I am from the sixteenth century. I canna tell her I killed men in an arena. I ought not burp after the ale... I daena understand what she means."

Magnus turned off the truck, then turned around and said, "I think we hae advised ye too much — ye ought tae ignore us. Dost ye think she is a bonny lass?"

"Aye."

"Then go talk tae her, talk about what men hae always talked tae with lasses all through history. The weather."

Fraoch laughed. "And if ye run out of weather conversation tell her she is beautiful."

I opened the door, climbed from the truck, and said through the window, "Talk of the weather and tell her she is bonny, daena talk of the arena, just be m'self, yet not a braggart, and daena speak of home as twill be confusin'."

Fraoch and Magnus chuckled.

Fraoch said, "Tis simple."

Magnus said, "Aye, tis... tis simply meeting a maiden, men hae been doin' it through time. This is what Kaitlyn meant, ye hae it within ye, daena listen tae the rest of us."

I said, "Call me as soon as ye ken of James and Sophie's bairn."

"We will."

***

I headed tae the door and entered.

Twas less crowded than the night before. I glanced around

and dinna see her at first, but then I spotted her across the room. She was waiting on a table, talking and laughing with the men there. I felt a pang of jealousy but then her eyes rose and fell on me, her smile was enchanting, and she crossed tae me. "Hi Lochie, you came!"

"Aye..." I took her hand, bowed, and kissed her knuckles.

"Oh, wow, that's... um...you want to come sit at the bar?"

I nodded and she led me there. I sat upon a stool and ordered an ale from the bartender, while she excused herself to rush around from table tae table. I sat at the bar and pretended not tae watch her. The bartender asked, "You friends with Ash?"

"Aye."

He chuckled. "Does her boyfriend know?"

Ash walked up then, put her tray on the counter, and said, "Phew, that was a rush, but after that order I can hang out for a moment." She looked from my face tae the bartender's. "What are you boys talking about? Lochie, did you and Don meet?"

"Aye, we did." Don and I shook hands across the bar.

Don jerked his head back, and asked Ash, "I was just asking your new friend here if he had met your boyfriend."

She said, "Buck and I aren't together anymore, and why don't you butt out, Don?"

He grinned. "Not really my style. Also, come on, Ash, he's got an accent, he's not from around here. You want him to know about your boyfriend before Buck unleashes his wrath on a tourist."

I shrugged. "I am nae usually concerned about a man's wrath, I can handle m'self."

Don raised his brow at Ash.

She huffed and turned her attention tae me. "Lochie, I had a boyfriend, *but...*" She gave Don an irritated look, then resumed, "I broke up with him, we broke up months ago, there is no reason why—"

Don's eyes drew up to the door. "Uh oh."

Ash followed his eyes and turned pale.

A large bearded man, wearin' leather strolled in.

I glanced back at Ash. "Tis him?"

She nodded. "I need to go speak to him, hold on."

She stalked over toward him and they looked immediately adversarial, but the music was so loud I couldna make out their loud whisperin'.

Don said, "You seem like someone who doesn't want that kind of trouble—"

I took a sip of m'ale and passed him the bottle. "Can I hae another?"

He pulled out a bottle, popped the cap off it, and passed it tae me. I glanced at Ash and the big fella. And asked Don, "What dost I 'seem' like? I daena seem like someone who can handle that man?"

"Nah, he's edgy, man…" He picked up a glass and began drying it with a bar towel. "Look, I think Ash is great, but that dude, he's a real ass, don't know how she got messed up with him, girls can be dumb as hell some— wait, here they come."

I tipped the beer to my lips as the big guy sauntered up tae the bar. "Don, give me a beer."

He purposely stared straight ahead and dinna look at me. I noticed Ash had drifted away tae one of the tables and was takin' an order for more drinks, givin' us nervous glances.

Don handed the man a beer and he took a sip, put it down, then slowly turned tae me. "What ye starin' at?"

"Tis a fine coat ye are wearin', tis the workmanship of the Codman John Taddoch?" I grasped his shoulder of his coat, yanked it closer, and eyed the stitches. Then I let go with a wee push. "Nae, I see, tis not the same stitch."

He was shocked that I had touched him. Tae unsettle him even more, I rose tae m'feet, put out m'hand, and said, "I'm Lochinvar, from Dun Sgathaich on the Eilean a' Cheò."

He shook his head, as if confused, and put out a hand. "I'm um… Buck."

"Where ye from, Buck?"

"Jax, born and raised."

I tipped my beer tae him. "Och, Jax is a fine place. I myself am from a bleak and blusterin' coast — I much prefer the summers here. Where I hail from the summers barely give ye a respite from the grey skies and the torrential rain — do ye ride...?"

He looked confused. "Yeah, I ride, a Harley."

I nodded, "Good, good," then I chuckled, shakin' m'head. "Apologies, I meant *horses*, do ye ride horses? I hae a Percheron by the name of Cookie."

"No, I don't..."

"Too bad, tis one of the great pleasures tae ride a horse." I took another sip of m'beer.

Buck asked, "Who the hell are you?"

I feigned incredulousness. "We werna introduced yet? Here I am speakin' tae ye like we are auld acquaintances. I thought I had said it already! I am Lochinvar—"

"I know your name, but how are you here, in Fernandina Beach, at this bar?"

I drank from m'ale and looked around. "I think this is a public beer house, inna it? I live here on the island—"

"Why are you messing around with Ash?"

I looked at her across the room.

She met my eyes.

The bartender was watching us.

There was a long pause where I considered what tae say. "Because she is a bonny lass and I want tae make her smile. The question I want answered is who are ye? And why are ye messin' around with Ash?"

Buck stood up from his stool. "She is my girlfriend!"

I remained on m'stool and shrugged my shoulders. "That is not what I heard."

He shoved me on m'chest. I saw the move comin' and had m'feet positioned so that it wouldna cause me tae react, I stayed still.

CHAPTER 10 - LOCHINVAR

Don yelled, "Buck, take that shit out of here! Don't make me call the cops!"

A big man came over. He was wearin' a shirt with the words Palace Saloon Security on it, and he grasped Buck's elbow. "Out."

Buck shook his hand off.

I put m'drink down on the bar, pushed it from the edge, and stood up, so we were chest tae chest.

He was furiously angry.

I had grown calm.

He was overpowered and dinna ken, he thought he would hae the better of me, but he had already lost the battle with the shove. He couldna control himself. I would hae him on the ground in... 30 seconds, but...

I wouldna want him tae look too weak, and though I kent four ways tae drop him I would allow him tae stand so the crowd wouldna turn.

I had learned much when I was battle-training in the courtyard of Dunscaith, that keepin' the audience on yer side was part of the fight. They would want tae root for ye, the victor, but not if ye were too cruel.

Buck and I glared at each other, the rest of the sounds grew quieter, though in m'periphery I could see the man trying tae pull Buck outside. Don was tryin' tae talk sense. Ash was pleading...och nae.

I snapped out of m'fury tae hear her sayin', "Buck, don't hurt him! Please!"

I scowled, sighed, and then chuckled and said tae Buck, "Clearly ye daena ken who I am."

CHAPTER 11 - KAITLYN

THE HOSPITAL

We waited and we waited and waited.

Doctors and nurses came and went, at times people bustled around the room where Sophie was, and we would stand and hover nearby hoping to hear what was happening. They rarely told us anything.

Other times it would be quiet and we would all return to our seats in the lounge, glancing through magazines, scrolling through our phones.

Beaty spent much of the time in the chapel, but had come to the waiting room because, as she said, "I am certain tis near time."

And then, around 10:15 pm, Emma said, "You hear that?"

I said, "Yeah, she's begun the howling."

Beatty said, "The bairn will be here afore the owls take flight."

Emma said, "Yep."

I said, "Absolutely."

And we stood together watching the door, waiting, mentally praying, until finally a nurse came out and said, "I'm happy to tell you that mother and baby are fine."

Then James strode out. "It's a boy!"

CHAPTER 11 - KAITLYN

We hugged and rejoiced. "Sophie's good?"

"Sophie's great, she and the baby are perfect."

We hugged more, remarked how quickly it had gone. Then we all went to make phone calls to tell everyone that James and Sophie had a baby.

His name was James Andrew Cook II and James wanted to call him Junior. We all loved the idea. It fit him.

CHAPTER 12 - LOCHINVAR

THE PALACE SALOON

"Who are you?" Buck was growling, spittle flingin' from his lips — I wanted tae kick his arse so badly, but he was just a bully and a weak man. From Ash's face I could see he frightened her and I dinna want tae cause her anymore alarm.

I said, "I am Lochinvar, and where I come from we fight *and* we recite poetry, sometimes at the same moment. Dost ye like an epic poem, Buck?"

He said, "What the fuck are you talking about?"

Ash said, "Lochie, maybe you can wait outside?"

I shook my head. "Nae, this is a public bar, I am nae goin' out, I am not causin' trouble. I hae never met this man in m'life, and I hae never heard of him — what is yer surname, Buck?"

"Buck Foster, what are—"

"Ye ken Ian Foster? I ran across him in Ord, back in '88?"

"No," he shook his head.

"How would I hae heard of ye? I am fairly new around here. I haena met many people, but ye hae barely introduced yerself and yet ye are botherin' me. Ye put yer hands on me..." I looked around, "Ye all saw it, dinna ye?"

People nodded in agreement.

CHAPTER 12 - LOCHINVAR

I continued, "I am wonderin' by what rights ye started a fight? Ye hae nae claim tae the room, tae the people inside, these are yer lands?"

"What the—?"

"How would I ken ye?"

"I was um... Ash is my girl—"

Ash said, "*Was*, Buck, we broke up months ago. You were sleeping around. Come on, stop causing trouble."

I smiled. "That is it, tis all of yer reputation?"

"I played football in school."

I raised my ale. "Och aye, good on ye! That is wonderful! I am new tae the game but I do like tae watch with m'brothers and we play a bit on the beach. Tis a fine game, ye were good at it?"

"Yeah, I was good."

"Has a poem been written about ye?"

Buck shook his head, "No, of course not, that's—"

I said, "I hae had a poem written about m'own exploits, tis by Sir Walter Scott. Ye heard of him?"

Buck said, "Yeah, but... what?"

I looked around at the room and boomed over the music, though I dinna need tae get their attention, many of the patrons were watchin' us already. "Hae ye heard of Sir Walter Scott?"

A lot of people nodded and said, yes.

I raised m'glass, "The poem is called, 'Lochinvar,' see, tis about m'self — dost ye want tae hear it?"

Everyone nodded, a few people cheered. I stood on the rungs of the stool tae raise m'self, because by this time most everyone was watchin' my performance. "It goes like this, 'O young Lochinvar is come out of the west,' this part means the Isle of Skye in Scotland, but Sir Walter Scott used the direction of west tae hae a better word tae rhyme." I continued, "'Through all the wide border his steed was the best; And save his good broadsword he weapons had none, he rode all unarm'd, and he rode all alone. So faithful in love, and so dauntless in war, There never was knight like the young Lochinvar!'"

My phone rang, vibratin' m'pocket. "Och nae, the poem is interrupted, I must answer m'phone!"

A man said, "Don't answer a phone in the middle of a poem!"

"I hae tae, it might be good news!" I put down my beer and fished the phone out. Twas a call from Magnus. I held up a hand, and pulled the phone tae my ear, "Aye?"

Magnus said, "The bairn has come, James is goin' tae call him Junior."

"Sophie is well?"

"Aye, they are both doin' well. How is yer—?"

"I canna talk now, I am brawlin' and in the midst of recitin' a poem!"

Magnus said, "Och nae Lochinvar, daena brawl, ye will get sent from the bar. Be more neighborly, ye can buy a round of drinks, I will—"

"Thanks, Og Maggy!"

I hung up the phone and raised m'ale even higher and boomed, "M'mate, James Cook, has had a bairn! Delivered just now by his wife, Sophie, tis a boy! His name is Junior! I am an uncle again! A round of drinks for the bar!"

Everyone cheered.

I climbed off the stool, shaking hands all around.

Don shook my hand, "Congratulations, and you're certain about the drinks? Orders are coming in." He put out his hand.

I looked at it blankly, "What?"

He had to lean forward and yell over the commotion. "Your card for the drinks!"

I looked at him blankly again. But then there was a clap on my shoulder. I turned around, Magnus and Fraoch were standing there. Dripping wet, unzippin' their raincoats because it had begun tae pour outside.

Magnus said, "Ye causin' trouble, Lochinvar?"

CHAPTER 12 - LOCHINVAR

"Nae, nae trouble at all."

Buck had taken one look at Magnus and Fraoch and moved down the bar, pretending not tae be botherin' me. Twas a wee bit irritatin' that he found m'brothers more dangerous than me, but they were auld and big, a dangerous combination.

Fraoch asked, "Who ye brawlin' with?"

"Nae one, tis long over, and the poem is finished anyway, I got tae the best part."

Don said, "He offered to buy the bar a round of drinks but doesn't seem to have the money."

"He has the money, he meant it." Magnus pulled out his wallet and pushed a card across the bar.

Ash sighed, "I guess I better go start taking orders."

I said, "Och nae, I dinna think of that, canna they all come tae the bar?"

"Nope, I need the tips. But you'll still be here when I'm done?"

"Aye, Mistress Ash, I will remain." I bowed over her hand, brushin' my lips on her knuckles, then looked up.

She smiled, lightin' up, and fanned herself. "I could definitely get used—" Another waitress rushed by, "Ash, come on, your tables are grumbling."

"See you in a minute, Lochie." She disappeared intae the crowd that had pressed up against the bar tae order their free drinks.

Magnus asked me, "Tis all right if Fraoch and I stay for a round?"

"Aye, ye are buyin' rounds for the bar, ye ought tae hae one for yerself."

People came up tae the bar tae place their orders, saying "Thank you," as they passed.

I nodded. "A bairn is a blessin', it ought tae be celebrated."

Magnus caught Don's eye and held up three fingers and gestured toward my ale.

Fraoch kept his feet wide, forcin' a space so the other patrons had tae press taegether at the end of the bar. He looked all around the room and said, "I see the man ye were brawlin' with, he looks as if he has been bested."

At the far end of the bar, Buck was scowling. He finished his drink and pressed away through the crowd. My eyes followed him as he stopped beside Ash and they spoke for a moment. I couldna tell what they said, but from his face it looked as if she were tellin' him tae leave. He left.

I said, "If ye guessed the 'sweaty carbunkle squeezed intae the poorly stitched leather' ye would be right."

We all chuckled.

Fraoch said, "From the looks of it ye bested the man *and* won the lass."

Don slid our three ales in front of us, then went back to making the complicated expensive drinks everyone else had ordered.

We all picked up our ales. I said, "Tae James Cook's bairn!"

Magnus said, "Slàinte!" We all drank.

I said, "I finally had a chance tae recite the poem of 'Lochinvar,' ye ken — it has been a good night."

Fraoch chuckled, "Ye hae been searchin' for the good moment since ye first heard it."

"Aye, twas perfect, he wanted tae brawl with me—"

Magnus shook his head. "Och nae, he has never seen ye fight."

"He shoved me in the chest."

"We are fortunate he lived."

"Aye, twould hae been easy tae beat him, I wanted tae, but I dinna want tae frighten her." My eyes traveled across the room and settled on Ash.

Fraoch said, "Och, he is smitten with the maiden. That is usually a way for a young man tae lose his head, but she has caused ye tae take heed and keep yer composure. This is a good thing. I think I speak for all of yer family when I say we are proud of yer newfound thoughtfulness, we ought tae raise our glasses tae Og Lochie not bein' a complete arse in front of the bonny lass."

We all raised our glasses and said, "Slainte!"

Magnus teased, "Perhaps ye ought tae grow yer beard out, Lochinvar, down tae yer mid-chest, so they winna think ye such a weak and incapable lad."

I joked, "I tried, if ye remember, Madame Hayley winna let me."

Fraoch said, "Tis because yer beard is as patchy as the shadow-side of a moor, she was tryin' tae make ye bonny for the lasses."

Ash glanced over at us, I nodded, she smiled and waved.

Magnus said, "It seems tae hae worked."

We finished our ales.

Magnus said, "I ought not hae another as I am the driver. Dost ye need us tae wait for ye?"

"Nae, I will remain. I hae a maiden tae speak tae."

Fraoch clapped me on the shoulder. "Good lad, Og Lochie. Call us when ye need a ride."

I said, "Or I might walk. Tis a fine night."

We looked at the windows of the Palace where there was rain pouring down outside.

Fraoch said, "Spoken like a true Scot."

Magnus spoke tae Don and signed for the drinks.

Then they took their leave.

CHAPTER 13 - LOCHINVAR

THE PALACE SALOON

The night began wearin' down and Ash was less busy. She came and pulled up a stool beside me. "Just one table left before I can go."

I said, "Mistress Ash, I apologize for the turmoil I caused ye earlier."

She said, "That wasn't your fault, that was Buck, he always causes trouble." She looked at me intently. "I just want you to know... we used to date. I don't date him anymore, I don't know why I ever did. It wasn't for long, he was my first boyfriend when I graduated and when I came back we went out for a bit. I thought... he was comfortable. I didn't have to think about anything, and I thought he was the good kind of trouble, like fun. One thing you might want to know about me is I like an adrenaline rush, but I realized he was the bad kind of trouble. The kind that upends your whole life..."

I said, "The kind of trouble that upends yer life, like what?"

"You know, like fighting, like being edgy—"

Don, who had been busy at the end of the bar, overheard our conversation. He added, "You're forgetting to mention that he's a lying cheater too."

"Yeah, I think seeing him behave this way tonight got me

CHAPTER 13 - LOCHINVAR

past the whole 'he cheated on me' bullshit. I'm remembering how bad he was overall, in every single way. But this is… that's a lot to dump on you. I just want to say, I am very impressed at how you handled him."

"Twas naethin' much, I had been lookin' for a chance tae recite the poem and there twas."

Don and Ash both laughed.

Don said, "That was pretty epic."

"I dinna even get tae the best, most heroic part. Tis a love poem and a tale of heroism, first he wins the maiden and steals her away—"

Ash said, "Tell us that part."

I considered where it started, then recited: "'One touch tae her hand, and one word in her ear, when they reach'd the hall-door, and the charger stood near; so light tae the croup the fair lady he swung, so light to the saddle before her he sprung!' That is them gettin' on the horse, ye ken, then he says, 'She is won! we are gone, over bank, bush, and scaur; they'll have fleet steeds that follow,' quoth young Lochinvar."

Ash applauded.

I said, "*Then* the other men chase, but the poem finishes with, 'There was racin' and chasing on Cannobie Lee…' They never do catch him. Then it finishes, 'So daring in love, and so dauntless in war, Have ye e'er heard of gallant like young Lochinvar?'"

Don said, "I'm not big on poetry but I can see why you'd memorize that one."

"Aye, tis a fine poem, but ye daena like poetry, Master Don? Ye hae poets recitin' tae ye, comin' from the speakers all around ye right now."

"I guess that's a little different."

I shrugged, "Where I come from the line between poem and song is verra thin, and in the evening, around a fire in the Great Hall, a man recitin' poems is likely tae break intae song."

Ash said, "Scotland sounds a lot different than I thought."

"Aye, tis a lifetime of difference between these places, but some things are all the same, like men who want tae start trouble, and laughin' barkeeps, and maidens with a bonny smile."

She said, "Lochie, are you saying my smile is bonny?"

"Aye, it lights up the rainy night."

She smiled and said, "Don, did you hear it?"

"I did, Ash, he's hitting on you."

I said, "What does this mean? I wouldna hit her, I daena...?"

Ash said, "Don means you're trying to ask me out on a date."

"Och aye, I would like to take ye tae dinner, Mistress Ash, tae yer favorite restaurant."

"I don't think I've ever gotten to pick my favorite restaurant before, um... what would I like..?" She said, "What's your favorite food?"

I chuckled. "I am verra fond of cookies, it has made me verra popular with m'nieces and nephews."

Then Ash said something that won m'heart completely. "I love baking, my aunt runs a bakery, not here, in Atlanta, but she taught me to bake."

"Ye bake, ye love tae bake...? Yer aunt runs a bakery...?"

"Yes, I love it, my favorite things to make are pies."

Twas all I could do tae keep from droppin' tae m'knees right then. I ran a hand through m'hair. "I verra much like cherry pie."

"I don't have cherry, but I have a peach pie, most of one, on my kitchen counter right now. Would you like to come have a midnight slice?"

"Aye, did I mention peach pie is m'favorite? I would like it verra much."

CHAPTER 14 - LOCHINVAR

ASH'S ATTIC APARTMENT

We rode in her car and she pulled up in front of a large two-story house on a tree-lined street, verra close tae downtown. She explained twas an easy, safe journey, and she usually walked alone, even at night, but she drove if it were goin' tae rain.

I looked up at the house. "Tis a verra fine house, Mistress Ash."

"Oh yes, it is, but it's not mine. I rent an apartment on the top floor. Which reminds me..." She turned off the car and dropped her key into her bag. "We have to be very very quiet when we climb the stairs. My landlady is asleep and she's old as the hills and wakes up.... let's just say, *irritated*."

"I will be quiet as a mouse."

She flashed her bonny smile and said, "Good, follow me, mouse." We climbed from the car and she led me up tae the house and unlocked the door. We crept verra quietly up the stair, nae small feat as the boards creaked. I whispered, when a tread creaked under m'weight, "Tis somethin' a hammer and nail might fix."

She giggled.

I whispered, "Wheesht, we will wake the—"

A feeble auld voice called up, "Is that you, Ashley?"

Ash froze on the step. "Yes, ma'am, coming home from work. Sorry I woke you."

"Are you alone? Don't be bringing strangers home."

"I have a friend who's come for a piece of pie, he's not a stranger. You can go back to bed, I'm sorry I woke you."

She began walking up again, and gestured for me to follow as the voice behind us said, "Try to keep it down, you sound like an elephant clomping up the steps."

I whispered, "Och nae, I tried tae be verra quiet."

She whispered, "Don't worry about it, she says that almost every night, there's no way you were going to be quiet enough you're twice my size — speaking of, low ceiling."

She tapped it, and I had tae duck at the top of the stairs where we came to a small door. She unlocked it and we entered.

Her apartment was in the attic, and down the middle of the room I was able to stand, but the ceilin' sloped down on both sides. There was a wee kitchen near the front door, a small table and chairs, an over-stuffed chair on the opposite side with a table and lamp beside it, and a bed under a small window at the far end.

She said, "You don't have to worry about sound up here, landlady sleeps on the bottom floor, thank heavens, it's only the stairs that wake her."

She pulled out a chair at the table so I could sit without needin' tae hunch. "I am sorry it's so small, it's... I love the location. It's probably much smaller than you're used to, your brother is a lord and all."

"I dinna ken him much of m'life and grew up an orphan, without much at all. So I am used tae livin' spaces where the chairs are near the bed, when I was lucky enough tae hae a bed tae sleep in." I sat down in the chair.

"An orphan! I'm so sorry."

"Tis fine, tis what made me who I am, and m'brother found me when it mattered, afore I got m'self in too much trouble."

"You don't seem like someone who gets in trouble. You seem... like not that type at all." She pulled out a dish and began slicing the pie. "Do you like ice cream with it? I have... Oh! I have cookies and cream."

I grinned. "M'favorite."

She scooped ice cream onto both slices. "Not the best flavor choice together, but we got what we got." She put a plate in front of me and one in front of her chair and then usin' a can sprayed foamy whipped cream on top of both. She passed me a fork and a spoon.

Then said, "Want a beer? You're not driving..." I nodded and she popped two cans and put them in front of of us, then sat down. She picked up her fork.

I said, "Dost ye mind if I say a prayer afore we eat?"

"Oh, um, sure..."

I folded my hands. "Bless this verra fine pie, made for me by m'new acquaintance the terrifically bonny Mistress Ash who has invited me intae her home tae share her bounty of peach in a flaky crust with cream whipped upon it and cookies crumbled within iced cream, thank ye for yer grace upon us, amen." I grinned.

She said, "Do you always pray before your meals?"

"Most meals, aye, I used tae hae tae work tae eat and so I am always grateful for a meal, but now I pray because somethin' delicious has been set in front of me. I canna allow it tae pass without mention. I had tae thank God for the meal, and of course ye for offerin' it."

She said, "You haven't even tasted it yet."

I scooped up a big bite, put it in, and chewed, moanin' with pleasure. "Tis yers? Ye made it, truly?"

"I did — did you know, Lochie, that back a hundred years ago a farmer's wife would make ten pies a week?"

I took another bite. "I always knew I ought tae go tae that time. Ten pies..." I chewed and swallowed. "Actually that is not so much... now I think on it if I were the farmer, a life of toil and hard work, especially a century or more ago, I could easily eat two pies a day. What would I eat on the rest of the days?"

She laughed and ate some of the peach pie. "So how long have you lived in Fernandina?"

"I canna say as I come and go... tis hard tae explain—"

"You also live in Scotland?"

"Aye, but it haena been long since I was united with m'brother, and now I live with them."

"Why don't you drive?"

"I daena ken. I would like tae learn, but I live with a big family, we always hae guards and drivers, someone is always drivin' — I haena done it."

I chuckled at a thought, and she said, "What?"

I told her, "I am always stuck in the back with the bairns on long drives, but I canna complain, my nephews, Archie and Ben are great conversationalists and if ye daena sit near m'niece, Isla, ye will miss all the fun."

She laughed. "You really love your nieces and nephews."

"Aye, they are good people."

"I'm an only child and I'm alone a lot. My mom says I'm overly independent, but I like doing stuff for myself. I like to prove myself."

"I do as well, but I like tae prove m'self in front of m'family."

She chuckled. "I do think my version gets lonely sometimes. My only friend right now is Don, and he's just a work friend."

"This is what's good about a large family, all m'friends are m'relations." I finished my pie, ran my finger across the surface of the plate, and licked the last bit.

She laughed again. "Would you like more?"

"Tis possible? I daena want tae be a bother."

"You are not a bother. I don't see how you could possibly be." She took the two steps tae the counter tae slice me another piece of pie.

I said, "Och nae, Ash, I can be a huge bother, ye ken, I am

rarely *not* botherin' my brothers, they hae tae find things tae keep me busy."

"Like what?"

"Magnus makes me muck the stables when I am a'botherin' him. Fraoch makes me fish, I tell ye, I hae had m'fill of fish. I ken I told ye I would take ye tae yer favorite restaurant, but I would like tae ask for it tae nae be fish, I greatly prefer a steak."

She laughed. "I like steak too."

"Ye hae a beautiful laugh, Mistress Ash."

She said, "Do I? I sometimes think people don't think I'm serious. When I enlisted everyone thought I was too cute to do anything. I had to work my butt off to prove I was more than cute and..."

"Ye hae a laugh that sounds like when tis a summer day and the waves are lappin' against the planks of the dock on the lake in Maine and the bairns are runnin' along on the lawn behind me, squealin' in joy."

"Bairns are children?"

"Aye."

"Are you saying I sound like the squealing bairns?"

"Nae, ye sound like the summer day, yer laugh sounds like the feelin' I get when there is warm sun on m'face and all is well in the family."

She sank down in the chair across from me and put the new piece of pie in front of me. "I don't know, Lochie, if anyone has ever said something so beautiful to me."

I grinned. "If me comparing yer laugh, Mistress Ash, as bonny as ye are, tae a summer day, is the first good compliment ye hae been given, then ye are surroundin' yerself with the wrong sort of people."

She laughed again and said, "You can say that again, you met my ex, you've *seen* my wrong sort of people."

I shoveled in a big bite of pie. "Och aye, he was an arse. He canna be yer choice of people."

"He's not, he just sort of happened, you know? Then I had to figure out how to make it not happen."

"Aye, I ken, we used tae hae many such stories back at the, um..." I had almost said 'castle' and now I couldna think of what tae say instead so after an uncomfortable pause I finished, "When I was growin' up, when young men and women are choosin' each other, tis a time that is fraught."

She raised her beer. "To a time that is fraught, and old, dumb exes and new friends."

I clinked m'can tae her's and said, "Slàinte!"

"What does that mean?"

"Tae good health!"

"Slàinte!" We clinked our cans again.

I finished eating my pie and pushed the plate away.

I drank some more beer, then asked, "What is your favorite thing tae do besides bakin' delicious pies?"

"Well, let's see, I love to go to the beach with a chair and a book and dig my feet down into the sand and sit and read." She gestured toward the wall down near her bed, twas lined with books. "Those are just some of my favorites. I have stacks of books in boxes at my parents' house, some in storage, I just can't fit them all."

"That is a great deal of books. What is the subject of them?"

"I read fantasy and dystopian, fairies, princes, the occasional dragon."

"Aye," I said, though I dinna really ken. "Tis like fairytales? For the bairns?"

"Kind of, but a lot darker, some romance, you've never heard of Divergent? You've for sure heard of Twilight, right?"

I shook my head.

She said, "Scotland seems like a distant world... so what do you like to do? You're done with fish, you like your nieces and nephews, what else is your favorite thing?"

"I daena ken..."

"If you get to relax, what do you do?"

CHAPTER 14 - LOCHINVAR

"I play on the PlayStation with the nephews."

She laughed. "Well, *that* is familiar."

I said, "Earlier ye called me yer 'new friend', we are friends?"

"Yes, definitely, though we just met — I can't really explain it, but I like you, you make me feel safe."

"Tis good, I like ye as well, Mistress Ash."

"And the fact that you call me Mistress Ash, that's awesome. Should I call you something fancy?"

I joked, "Ye could call me 'Lord Lochinvar.'"

"That sounds medieval, I might have to stick with Lochie. I like that it sounds like lucky."

"I am very lucky because—"

"Because you get to spend time with me, I know, you also have a smooooooth tongue."

"What does this mean?"

"You are complimentary, some might say to 'get your way'."

"Or some might say I am *romantic.*"

She said, "Some might say that men are romantic to get their way as well. So I wonder, Lochie, are you trying to get your way with me?"

I grinned, "I am uncertain what 'gettin' my way' would be, dost ye mean am I tryin' tae win ye? Did I see ye were a bonny lass with a dimpled smile and a lovely laugh and I thought tae m'self I would like her tae be mine? Aye, tis what I thought."

"Oh my, Lochie, you want to win me? That is very old fashioned."

"I am verra auld fashioned, tis true, but daena doubt for a moment that modern men feel the same, and now I hae met ye, and spoken tae ye, and tasted the pie ye baked for me—"

"Oh, I baked it for *you?*"

"Aye, peach pie is now m'favorite. Ye knew my mind before I did."

She laughed.

"And there is yer laugh again, bonny Mistress Ash, ye sound like sunshine and I never want it tae rain."

She looked at me shaking her head. "But I barely know you. Tell me something else about yourself."

I relaxed, and leaned back in my chair. "Ye already ken all about me, I like tae hang out with my nieces and nephews, not all are related by blood, ye ken, but they all call me Uncle Lochie, and I like tae play, I like tae eat dessert—"

"You have such a light, easy personality, I feel safe around you. It's hard to jibe that with the fact that you were an orphan and had such a hard upbringing."

"Twas difficult."

"Was it an orphanage situation or like foster homes?"

Once more, without sayin' castle, I wasna sure how tae answer — I shifted in my seat, and tried tae be vague about the details. "I lived in a big place, with lots of people."

"Were people mean to you?"

"Aye, but…I daena think we ought tae talk about it." I meant because twas certain tae catch me up in an unusual story, but she took it another way.

"Oh I'm sorry." She pouted, as if she were feeling sorry for me.

It bothered me tae hae her feel sorry for me. I wasna pitiful, but I couldna tell her of m'real life, twas verra confusing. "Twas not all awful, I made the best of it, and I gained a good reputation for… I was good at competitions. I like tae win and I was verra good."

I drank the rest of my beer, feelin' pleased with my answer.

"Cool, what kind of competitions? Like track? Or I've seen those Highland Games on the Discovery Channel — do you mean like that?"

I dinna ken what the Highland Games on the Discovery Channel meant, but I guessed the fights in the castle were similar, I said, "Och aye, tis just like the highland discover channel games." I ran m'hand through m'hair. I was growin' confused by her questioning and needin' tae keep m'answers vague.

She said, "Want another beer?"

CHAPTER 14 - LOCHINVAR

"Aye, twould be good."

She stepped to the refrigerator. "What was your favorite event? I seem to remember that they throw rocks and tree trunks, did you do that?"

She was speaking on the caber toss, we would do that in the courtyard and out in the fields, also we would fight and battle with lances and swords. I assumed if she had seen the caber toss she had seen all of it, even the horrible bloody violent parts, so I smiled and got comfortable. "Och aye, I was good at the caber toss. And when I was young I liked tae spar in combat, I like tae compete and see if I can best a man, and I really like tae win."

"Spar... like fight, you... how do you mean, like martial arts, hand to hand — like MMA?"

I had seen Mixed Martial Arts on the television before, so though twas far removed from what I meant, I nodded. "Aye, much like MMA."

Her eyes narrowed, she chuckled, shaking her head. "So what you're saying is I thought you were safe and chill and you're actually kind of violent?"

"Nae, not exactly—"

"But you like to fight, MMA style, and you like to win, you must have a lot of violence running through you, right? Do you ever draw blood?"

I ran my hand through m'hair tryin' tae think of what tae say.

"Do you ever fight with weapons?"

"Ye mean duel? Aye, I duel some—"

She scoffed, "With *weapons,* like *guns*?"

I found m'self leaned forward, my hands clasped between my knees. I said, "Swords."

"Swords? Wow, that's wild, *swords!*" Her face was scrunched up, thinking it all through. "So I thought you were somehow the one in danger with Buck, but you're the dangerous one?"

"Aye, I ken how tae fight."

"Yet you didn't fight him."

I took a deep breath. "Because a man who kens how tae fight tae the death, ought tae do his best not tae. Tae fight is tae lose control, tis dangerous, and I dinna want tae frighten ye."

"Oh, to the death, huh?" She crossed her arms, chewing her lip. "I'm a soldier you wouldn't frighten me," but she did look frightened.

She added, "Except that you're in my house."

"I dinna mean... nae harm would come tae ye."

"So you duel with weapons and have drawn blood? You said, 'to the death,' have you killed someone?"

I gulped.

"More than one?" Her eyes went wide.

My brow drew down.

"Lochie, you've killed people, you fight to the death...? Have you been in jail?"

"Nae, I..."

"I've been in the military, and I've never killed anyone — am I in danger?"

"Nae, of course not, ye are not in danger. I would never cause ye harm." I scowled, "Och nae, the conversation has gone verra far past..."

"Past what, letting me know that you're dangerous?" I saw her fingers near her phone, she looked tae be itchin' tae use it.

I leaned forward with m'elbows on my knees. "Och nae, Mistress Ash, tis not like that, I hae only fought when m'brother Magnus needed me tae protect him."

"Magnus, the big guy — he needs you to fight? Why on earth would your brother need to fight? He's a grown man with kids!"

I shifted in my seat, "He is not so much bigger, only by an inch, but... can we speak on somethin' else?"

Her brow was drawn down. "I don't know what else there is to talk about, and it's late and—"

"I dinna mean tae frighten ye—"

"I'm not frightened, I just need to go to sleep."

I nodded. "I hae kept ye up long past a regular hour, m'apologies, Mistress Ash — might I ask ye tae join me on the dinner we spoke of...?"

She stood. "I'm really tired. Maybe you could call me and we can plan it then."

I stood up and knocked m'head against the ceiling. She said, "Oh! Are you okay?"

I was seein' stars. "Och nae... aye, I am fine..." I rubbed my head. "I daena fit."

"How are you going to get home?"

I rubbed the sore spot, stepping toward the door. "I will call m'brother or walk."

"It's raining out, you can wait on the porch, until—"

"Nae, tis fine, I will call ye." I opened the door and began walkin' down the steps, whackin' m'head against the ceilin' with a loud thud.

She whispered, "Oh no, are you okay, Lochie? That sounded—"

"Aye, I am fine."

I went down the top flight and by the time I got half down the second the landlady's voice came from the back room. "Is that you, Ash? You're carrying on, like to wake the dead! How am I supposed to sleep with your wild ways at all hours?"

Ash's voice called down, "I'm sorry, my guest is leaving—"

The landlady grumbled, "You keep hooker's hours."

I opened the front door and stumbled outside, standing on the porch, taking deep breaths.

I had somehow won the bonny lass and then with m'talk of fightin' had lost her in the same night.

CHAPTER 15 - MAGNUS

TAKIN' LOCHIE HOME

I pulled up beside Lochinvar, the truck wheels splashin' puddle water on his legs. Fraoch and I laughed. He yanked open the door and climbed in, his expression was dark and stormy.

Fraoch tossed a towel tae him, "What happened with the lass?"

He said, "I daena want tae talk about it."

Fraoch said, "Och nae."

I drove us home with none of us speaking.

Near the house Lochinvar said, "The new bairn is well?'

"Aye, he is sleeping, they are all well."

"Good."

I pulled the truck up tae the house, we all climbed out, but then Fraoch and I headed tae the front door while Lochinvar hung back at the truck in the rain. "Ye comin' in?"

"Nae, I need a moment."

We went inside.

. . .

CHAPTER 15 - MAGNUS

In the foyer, putting up our wet coats, Fraoch asked, "What dost ye think happened?"

"I daena ken, but it dinna go well."

"Och, the poor lad, I canna believe he messed it up this badly. She looked on him as if he were the answer tae her dreams, how could she hae changed her mind?"

I peeked out the window. In the dim glow of the garden lights, Lochinvar was sitting on a chair on the porch.

"I daena ken, but he is achin'."

The house was quiet, the kids were all fast asleep, Fraoch and I went tae our rooms.

I climbed intae an empty bed because Kaitlyn was still at the hospital.

CHAPTER 16 - KAITLYN

THE PORCH AT HOME

It was late, I was almost asleep when we pulled up to the house. Lochie was slumped in a chair on the porch.

Quentin got out of the car. Beaty and I pulled our babies from their car seats and rushed up the steps through the rain to the house. Emma went up to the door. "Lochie, are you good?"

He nodded. "Just thinking."

I went into the house and put Jack into his crib. He shifted for half a minute, but then fell fast asleep.

I turned on the baby monitor and crept out and down the hall to the foyer, and peeked out the window. Lochie was still out there, alone in a rocking chair. The rain had slowed, a shower instead of a downpour, but it was the middle of the night and he was on the porch looking out at it, the embodiment of melancholy.

I went out to join him.

"How's it going, Lochie?"

"Tis fine." He looked down at his hands.

I took the chair beside him and began a slow rock, watching

the rain fall. "I love it out here, this porch is one of my favorite places. You can see all the comings and goings of the family. It's like a different world from the back of the house, the sand dunes and ocean. This has trees and feels like somewhere else. It's also an in-between, connecting the outside and the house, it's protected from weather and..." My voice trailed off.

He understood, and he was quietly rocking, not talking.

We sat there for a while then he said, "I am an in-between."

"I'm really sorry about that."

"I daena ken how to be here in Florida doin' the things that men must do. I need a wife, a family, and I could go tae the past, but where and when?" The side of his mouth went up. "And how would I live in the past without bein' able tae play Fortnite?"

"Yes, that would be a tragedy."

"I am used tae this time, growin' used tae it, but I am just a visitor."

"Maybe think of yourself as an immigrant. You want to become a modern American... you know, now that I think on it, now that you can read, you could take the citizenship course and test, if you wanted. That might feel good to have that win."

He said, "And a driver's license."

"Yeah, that's a good idea, we'll get that started. I just wasn't thinking about it."

"Nae worries, neither was I, until I met Ash. I believed I was a modern man and I hae learned a great deal about m'failings."

"Lochie, I have never heard you say such a thing, what happened?"

"I got invited tae her house tae hae a slice of pie."

"This is not a euphemism? Are you saying pie to mean something else...?"

"Like what?"

"Like um... *sex*, Lochie."

"Och nae, ye canna..." He looked shocked and shook his head, "She is a modest and chaste lass, Kaitlyn, and I hae only begun tae... ye canna mean it. Nae, she baked a pie and served me a slice with cookies and cream ice cream on top."

"That sounds like your dream come true. Forget I said anything about 'pie' meaning something more."

"Twas nothing more but a slice of pie. And then we began tae talk of our lives and I told her I play with m'nieces and nephews, twas goin' well. But then I couldna keep m'mouth shut, I was tellin' her I like tae spar and next thing I ken we are talking on dueling and weapons and swords, fightin' tae the death, and I couldna get control of the conversation. I could see the fear in her eyes and I left."

"She had invited you into her home and then you exposed your dangerous ways."

"Aye, twas verra dire."

"You barely knew her, maybe she wasn't right for you."

"Ye ken, Madame Kaitlyn, how ye just know someone? And tis easy tae be with them?"

I nodded.

"But tis also difficult because ye canna function over yer mind running through its mutterin'?"

"Your mind mutters, Lochie?"

"Aye, tis verra noisy, unless I am at work or battle tis always goin', tellin' me what tae do and while I was with Mistress Ash, twas tellin' me that I was goin' tae misstep and say somethin' that would expose m'self, and then I did."

"That really sucks."

"Aye, and we were meant tae be taegether, ye ken why?"

"Because of the pie?"

"That and because she said her favorite thing tae do was readin' and I just learned tae read, it means somethin', ye ken?"

I nodded. "Yeah, it does seem to."

"Hae ye heard of Twilight, dost ye think I could read it?"

"Probably, and yes, we have a copy around here, somewhere. She likes Twilight? Then she's good with a little moral ambiguity about murder."

His brow drew down. "I believe we are meant tae be." He sighed. "I canna tell her about the kingdom, about time travel, about livin' in a castle, and growin' up in the sixteenth century. What can I tell her? I am made tae lie, and if I lie what good is it? If I tell her the truth she might think I hae lost m'mind and how can I involve her in this life? Tis tae ask her tae take on a great deal of danger."

"Don't I know it. But here's the thing, Lochie, I wouldn't change anything, I would marry Magnus, always."

"Did ye ken of the time travel afore ye married him?"

I shook my head.

"I dinna think so. Women are too weak tae want tae face this danger."

I sighed. "Lochie, you are such an ass, sometimes. This is not the takeaway from the situation, that women are weak, yikes, she's a soldier! She's not weak and she's ready to face danger."

"She daena want tae face unknowable danger, the kind of danger that twists time. Tis too disorderly for women. Women follow the moods of the moon, ye ken. There is an order, and she has never heard of the real fact of time travel—"

The front door of the house opened and Magnus came out, wearing his pajama bottoms and a t-shirt, his hair sticking up on the side. "I realized ye hadna come tae bed, and wanted tae check — all is well?"

I said, "Yeah, but Lochie has some heartache we are talking over, want to join us?"

Magnus drew up another chair. "What happened with the lass, Lochinvar?"

"I spoke of duelin' and frightened her."

Magnus said, "But she is a soldier? She must hae tae fight sometimes."

I said, "It's one thing to sign up to face danger and another thing to invite it into your home in the middle of the night. I've grown used to hearing about your battles but I married you first."

Magnus teased, "And ye arna like most women."

Fraoch opened the door and said, "Ye helpin' Og Lochie?"

Magnus said, "Join us, Fraoch. Lochinvar was tellin' us he frightened the lass when he spoke of his battles."

Fraoch leaned n the rail, "Och nae, ye canna speak on it, Og Lochie, women daena want tae think about war. They daena want tae face danger."

I sighed. "I was trying to tell Lochie that this isn't true about women—"

Fraoch shrugged. "Depends on what ye are meanin' by women. Are ye speaking on Campbell women? If we are speaking on our Campbell women, they will readily face danger, but most women winna."

I said, "I'm sure Ash, who signed up for the *military*, has plenty of courage, just like the Campbell women. Thank you for the compliment by the way, Fraoch."

"So why did she grow frightened?"

"Because Lochie was in her kitchen. It's one thing to be in the military, another to have a stranger bragging about his prowess in battle while standing in your kitchen."

Magnus nodded. "Aye, ye were within her walls."

Lochie said, "Aye, I frightened her by speaking of fighting, she thought I was dangerous."

Magnus asked, "Tis how ye left it?"

"Aye, she fed me pie and—"

Fraoch said, "Ye mean somethin' else or a dessert?"

Lochie groaned, "I mean dessert, och nae — she is a fine lass, ye canna think she would invite me home and... is everyone in on the joke, does pie mean somethin' more?"

We all nodded.

He screwed up his face then shrugged. "Tis funny, she does hae verra fine pie. I think she might hae the finest pie in the modern world, and ye can find it amusin' all ye want, but m'heart is sore and ye ought tae stop mocking me and advise me instead... she fed me dessert. We talked and drank a beer and even toasted once or twice and twas a fine night, but then I ruined it by speaking on fighting and she grew frightened and I left. What am I tae do?"

Magnus said, "Ye like her?"

"Aye, I do."

Magnus said, "There is an easy situation tae solve, she is a new woman tae ye and she is tryin' tae discern one thing, are ye goin' tae bring danger intae her life, or will ye be keepin' danger away."

I nodded. "That's well put."

Fraoch said, "Aye, she wants tae ken are ye goin' tae frighten her or protect her."

"I frightened her."

Magnus said, "Tis because ye dinna tell her ye would protect her."

"I should hae fought Buck?"

Fraoch said, "Nae, ye proved ye could protect her by not fighting him."

"I daena ken what tae do then…"

I said, "Think of it this way, she is a red-blooded American girl, and a soldier, she's brave, but the only danger in her life right now is if she gets called up to fight. On the day to day, she has her ex, he's an ass, but you proved that you could disarm him with charm. That's a win, but now she sees you as dangerous. That's a loss, *but,* you can fix this, Lochie, because a lot of young red-blooded American girls like a strong protector. Did you tell her you were in Magnus's military?"

"I dinna think I could talk about it."

I said, "I think you have to, she's a soldier, you're a soldier too. You have that in common and she'll understand that. Even if she weren't a soldier she would like that. Girls will marry soldiers, there's a whole 'sexy-in-a-uniform' thing."

Fraoch said, "And a kilt."

I said, "True, but if you're wooing a young woman and she is trying to figure out if you're going to bring danger or protect her from danger, the best way to signify that is by wearing your uniform."

Lochie said, "Magnus, may I wear it here?"

"Usually I would think nae, it draws attention, might cause problems, but I will waive m'reservations, ye can wear it. Yer dress coat *with* the kilt."

I said, "That should do it."

Magnus grinned. "All I hae tae do is put on m'dress coat and kilt and Madame Campbell is reminded that I am her master and protector."

I laughed and rolled my eyes. "That is not true, Lochie, half of what they're telling you is bull-hooky."

Lochie laughed, "What part is the half?"

Magnus said, "She will say the wrong part is that I am her master, she is probably right. But I remain convinced that if I am wearing m'royal uniform she wants tae please me."

I said, "Now I suppose *that* is true." Then I asked, "So, Lochie, how did you leave it with her?"

"I rushed out intae the rain, canna remember if I said goodbye."

Fraoch groaned. Magnus grunted.

I sighed.

"Tis useless? I hae ruined m'chances?" He dropped his head back. "I will move back tae Dunscaith Castle and marry a farmer's lass, she will be dim but she winna hae many thoughts on me. I can tell her what to do."

Now it was my turn to groan. "There have been so many terrible thoughts on women here tonight, I can't bear another word of it. You're all monsters."

Magnus said, "But ye love me."

"True, I do, even with all your old fashioned notions, and it is not as dire as all that, Lochie. You don't have to live in a hovel in the sixteenth century."

Fraoch said, "I hae done it, tis terrible, Og Lochie, ye daena want it."

"I ken, it sounds terrible, but perhaps tis all I hae open tae me. I ought tae give up the time travel, move tae a long ago time, and find a maiden and live a simple life."

Magnus said, "Ye think ye ought tae give up bein' m'brother, the brother of the king? I daena think ye get tae decide it, Lochinvar, for better or worse, tis yer role."

"I lent ye m'sword and now ye winna allow me tae leave?"

"Ye dinna lend me yer sword, ye owed it tae me because I saved yer life and ye saved m'throne, and ye spared Fraoch and we are brothers. Tis not that I winna allow ye tae leave, tis that ye canna, ye must stay. Ye need us and ye are needed."

"Tis a terrible thing tae be such a great warrior. This is a verra dangerous life tae bring a bonny lass like Mistress Ash intae."

Magnus said, "Ye ken, Lochinvar, all of life is dangerous, tis all a trial and tribulation, and ye hae one purpose, tae honor God by livin' yer life well. Ye must love yer family, care for the bairns, protect yer hearth and home. This is yer life."

I nodded. "Our lives are very dangerous, and although it has calmed a great deal from the last evil turns of time, I am still on edge. But humans always have dangerous lives: they explore, they travel, they compete, and far too often they go to war. You are doing a disservice to decide for her that she can't handle it. She's brave. If you like her, she might like you, too. She deserves to decide for herself."

Magnus slapped his hands down on his thighs, "Tis verra verra late…"

I said, "Are you going to be okay, Lochie?"

"Aye, I will stay up for a wee bit longer, I will take the first watch."

Fraoch said, "We hae guards for that now."

"Aye, but I canna grow used tae it."

We all said goodnight and left Lochie alone on the porch staring out at the diminishing rain.

CHAPTER 17 - KAITLYN

THE KITCHEN

The following morning, I came downstairs for breakfast carrying Jack in a sling. He had woken up as soon as I had hit the bed last night and needed me desperately so I had brought him to our room.

Magnus, Fraoch and Lochie were animatedly talking around the kitchen island with mugs of coffee in hand. I said, "Good morning!"

Jack started leaning out trying to get a spoon off the counter. Then he tried to get a dishtowel. Then he wanted a mug. I handed it to him, and he swung it almost hitting me in the face. I passed him the spoon. He threw it down, then he wanted the salt shaker. I passed him the candlestick.

Zach said, "It's crystal!"

I pouted. "I don't know what else to do! I've been up for ten minutes and I'm already at my wits end."

Fraoch said, "He just wants his Uncle Frookie, tis clear." He put his hands over his eyes and then drew them away. "Keeky-bo!"

Jack giggled.

Fraoch ducked behind the counter, then hid behind the door, saying, "Keeky-bo!"

CHAPTER 17 - KAITLYN

Jack laughed and laughed and reached out for Uncle Frookie who drew him into his arms with much more patience than I had that morning.

I had been handed a cup of coffee but hadn't had a chance to sip yet.

It was cold. I drew some more from the BrewStation and added sugar and cream.

"How are you doing now in the light of the morning, Lochie?"

He said, "We hae come tae an idea."

"Good! What is it?"

Magnus said, "We are in need of a trip tae Riaghalbane, I need tae speak tae m'mother, so I am takin' Lochinvar away on urgent business."

I narrowed my eyes, "But, how does this help the situation with Ash?"

Magnus tapped his temple. "Because absence makes the heart grow fonder."

"I don't understand." I said to Hayley, "Do you get what's going on?"

"No, I just woke up, but the boys have been planning for hours."

Lochie said, "I daena think ye realize, Queen Kaitlyn, I will be wearin' my uniform. Twill be handsome."

I chuckled. "With the kilt?"

"Aye, my dress coat, m'finest kilt, with m'sword."

Beaty had come in with Noah and so now Fraoch had Noah on one elbow, Jack on the other, and was playing loud Keeky-bo with both, not hiding, but just saying it loudly, while the boys squealed with laughter.

He stopped playing long enough to say, "A uniform and a kilt, ye see, Kaitlyn, we hae thought of everything."

I bit my lips.

Hayley said, "So Lochie will be in a uniform with a kilt, what's that got to do with that waitress?"

Lochie said, "I will go tae the Palace Saloon wearing the uniform, this evening. Then she will see me bein' handsome in it. She winna be able tae resist me."

"This is the plan you came up with?"

Magnus said, "Aye, tis a perfectly well-laid plan, she winna be able tae resist him."

Zach slammed the oven. "Man in a uniform wins the girl."

Fraoch sat down on the floor with the boys, Noah began toddling around. Jack climbed onto Fraoch's lap.

I sipped my coffee and watched Fraoch and the boys play, then said, "You know, it actually is a good plan. If she's trying to decide if you're dangerous or a protector—"

Zach said, "Like all women, right baby?" He kissed Emma good morning.

She said, "I have missed all the conversation, who's the protector?"

"Me! Want a bagel before you go to the hospital to see the baby?"

"Absolutely." Then she asked, "How did your meet with the girl go, Lochie?"

"Not well, but I hae a plan, I will flash m'knees at her under m'uniform."

Emma nodded. "That will do it. Though I only have eyes for Zach's knees."

He laughed. "*My* knees? Mine look like bird knees — I know you're just trying to be nice, but even I know my knees aren't my best quality."

She said, "What do you think is your best quality?"

He grinned, "My winning personality and my tushie." He wiggled his butt, which was hilarious on such a tall, gangly guy.

I laughed, "So knees, huh? Are we women really so single minded?"

Most of the men in the room said, "Aye." Except Fraoch who said, "Nae, ye are verra complicated, but we can wheesht yer mind and direct yer thoughts with a glimpse of knee, tis not meant tae offend, tis true, right m'bean ghlan?"

"So true, no offense taken, the same can be said of you guys."

I said, "You can be directed and calmed with a glimpse of the flesh of a bosom peeking over a bodice."

Magnus joked, "Aye, tis why the men of earlier centuries are so calm and wise." We all laughed.

I said, "So you will go into the Palace and give her a glimpse of your knee and the sight of your shoulders in uniform and then what?"

Zach said, "Then he tells her he's been called away on urgent, important, dangerous business for Magnus, he's crucial and he must go now, he wished he didn't need to go, he would stay with her, but he must, because duty calls and the fate of the world rests in the balance."

Emma said, "Oh babe, you should write romance! But I totally get the idea now, he flashes his knee. She swoons. She says she is counting the days until he returns. He says, 'If I return,' because it is so dangerous and she swoons again, but says, 'Thank you for keeping us all safe.' He says, 'I do it for the bairns.' Make sure your voice is very low, Lochie. She swoons yet again—"

Zach said, "I think she might have a blood sugar issue. Better give that girl a cookie."

Lochie said, "I will carry some in m'pocket."

We all laughed again.

I said, "But Emma is right, this is a very good plan. She will rethink the whole conversation you had last night under this new information, you're a soldier, you have urgent duties. She will admire that. She will probably think she was overreacting. I know that's what I would think."

"Ye think twill work?"

"I think it's likely to, it can't hurt. She might not be interested in seeing you again, but *then* you can go move to your sixteenth century hovel."

Zach said, "Or find a different girl."

"I like Mistress Ash, I could live m'life making her smile. I hae tae try tae win her."

I said, "Then this seems like your best shot."

Lochie said, "So, tis time tae get dressed?"

Fraoch said, "Og Lochie, tis afore we hae even eaten our breakfast! Ye canna put on a uniform now, ye will hae it mussed afore the evening."

Lochie said, "I could just not move, stand verra still in the middle of the room."

Fraoch groaned. "We canna hae another full day of Lochie waitin' tae speak tae the maiden, he needs a chore. If he is idle he will drive me tae distraction."

Magnus said, "The horse stables need tendin', then ye hae liftin' tae do. Ye were goin' tae work on yer shoulders tae day." He raised his coffee mug. "And muckin' the stables was goin' tae by my chore, but I will give it over so that Fraoch inna driven tae distraction."

Fraoch said, from his seat on the floor, a baby boy sitting on each arm. "Then I will do this today, winna I boys? Wanna go tae the beach?" Fraoch stood and left the kitchen carrying babies, leading all the children down the walkway toward the beach.

Emma asked, "Have any of them eaten yet?"

Zach said, "Nope, not yet, there will be melt-downs in twenty minutes."

Emma grabbed a bagel with a smear of cream cheese. "Then this is the perfect time to go, who's ready to go see the new baby? He comes home today!"

CHAPTER 18 - KAITLYN

We were so excited for the new baby by the time James and Sophie came through the front door — they were nervous, exhausted, and beaming with happiness.

The baby was tucked in James's arms. Sophie was led to the couch, her feet put up, a blanket over her lap, the baby was placed in her arms, and all around her the kids gathered to see the baby. Zoe and Isla were speaking in loud, awed whispers, Archie and Ben acting very grownup and 'getting things' for Sophie when she asked.

And Jack and Noah being interested for about one minute then going about their business of crawling around and trying to demand all our attention. It wasn't working very well because a newborn is entrancing. We all just watched Junior sleep.

James was very proud. He fussed around Sophie making her comfortable.

Quentin looked around with his hands on his hips, "Man, this is a *lot* of kids."

Magnus smiled. "Seven, tis about right for us, daena ye think, Colonel Quentin? We hae reached the right amount."

I said, "Are you saying this is *enough*? I never thought you'd ever say such a thing."

He said, "Tis not enough, we can always hae more, but we hae finally got a good amount, tis not a crisis anymore."

We all laughed.

Zach said, "Magnus this is a lot of kids, can't believe you finally think this is a good amount."

"We hae three pairs and then a new one, he is a promise of the next one coming tae make it even — anyone else with child? We will soon need another!"

Lochie came from the back room, dressed in his dress shirt, dark coat, three medals pinned to his chest, a dark tartan kilt, long clean white socks with black flashes, and dress boots. He looked very handsome with his red hair combed back, his cropped beard accentuating his jaw.

Fraoch said, "I see ye are dressed three hours too early all the same."

"I cleaned the stables and lifted weights, I daena hae anythin' else tae do." He went over and gazed on the baby for a moment. "Och he is a fine boy, Master Cook, Madame Sophie, ye hae done well."

Then he stood, looking around, well overdressed for the afternoon. He turned to Emma, "Madame Emma, dost I still smell of stable?"

She sniffed. "Nope, you smell of cologne."

"Good, I scrubbed."

She adjusted his coat and brushed off his shoulder. "You look very good."

He said, "I wanted tae thank ye, Madame Emma, for helpin' me read — did ye ken that is her favorite thing tae do? Tis like we are meant tae be."

Emma said, "You're welcome, Lochie, I'm really proud of you. You have cash in your wallet?"

"Aye, I am ready for everythin'."

He sat on the barstool and sighed. Checked his watch, then tapped his fingers on the counter. He checked his watch again.

Fraoch groaned. "Och nae, I will hae tae go out and do something else or I will throttle the lad."

CHAPTER 19 - ASH

ASH'S PLACE - THE NEXT DAY

The day had been long and weird.
I had woken up late, but was still tired from being up all hours with Lochie. I lay in bed for a while googling the Tree of Life and Yggdrasil. Come to find out, it was Norse mythology, an ash tree that holds the world of humans and the world of the gods nestled in its branches and roots. Then I looked up what an Ash tree looked like, because I had never thought about it and it made me feel like a dumbass.

I have been in bed too long. I got up, made my bed, and then made a pot of coffee.

I cleaned up the kitchen, washing our dishes thinking about how much fun we had had — there had been an ease to our conversation... He was also very hot, but not in the normal way, he was a hot guy who didn't know he was hot, like he wasn't a player.

He reminded me a little of Tarzan, like he had been brought up somewhere far from civilization and didn't know how to judge or compare himself to anyone else.

There had been a look in his eye like he really really liked me. We hadn't talked much, we were just barely getting to know each other, but I had been comfortable enough to invite him home. There was something so amazing about the way he gazed at me, like he thought I was beautiful.

I had made a mistake inviting him home. What had I been thinking? I had been too trusting... This wasn't like me, usually I was a better judge of character and knew to keep dangerous guys at arm's length.

Except Buck. But Buck had happened because he was familiar, I knew him in high school, he had been easy. A pain in the butt, but easy.

I was better than that.

I prided myself on being independent. I didn't need anyone. So what was I doing inviting a stranger home...? But...

In my defense Lochie had seemed so lost and vulnerable, disarming the last of my good sense.

The way he had put Buck in his place with a sense of humor, he had seemed so competent, kind of badass and self-assured.

I sighed.

Then, when my defenses were down, he had started talking about fighting and had seemed like a whole 'nother person and before I could even decide what to think, he had fled down the stairs, just about knocking himself out.

It had happened so quickly I didn't truly understand what it had all been about.

I stacked the washed dishes, pulled a dish towel from the drawer, and began drying, thinking about how his eyes had looked — so haunted when he had said, 'I daena fit.'

I put the dried dishes on the shelves, closed the cabinet doors, and appraised my attic room. I loved this place in the morning — the eastern sun came through the window, my plants glowed green, the sunny yellow of my bed quilt looked cheery. I tried to decide what to do with my day: Errands? I needed to get some food, Lochie had eaten my whole pie.

I chuckled to myself, it was a funny thing to have done, to invite a boy I just met to my home to eat my pie.

And man, he had loved my peach pie.

I chuckled again, then sighed.

I could get some ice cream too, but why...?

It was almost like I wanted to get it for Lochie, but the way he left...? It seemed likely that he was not going to come around again. Why would he?

I had gotten weird, he was too hot to chase a weird girl and why would I want him to? He was a danger-boy. Hadn't I had enough of danger-boys? Between the soldiers and Buck, I had had *plenty* of it.

Too much of it.

Lochie was rich. A rich, handsome, danger-junkie. An MMA fighter. Sheesh. Why did I seek out violent dudes?

He wouldn't answer if he had killed someone or *many* someones. Why was I thinking about him at all?

I had promised myself after Buck, no more trouble. I wanted a nice, decent boy to take me out for pizza. To rub my feet when I had been on them all night. One who would speak fondly of his nephews like Lochie. Who would really like pie and would compliment it when I baked him his favorite and would be grateful when I served him a slice.

Drat.

CHAPTER 20 - ASH

PALACE SALOON

I was washing off a table and staring out at yet another rainy night. Don said, "Ash, if no one else comes in ten minutes, I'm sending you home."

I sighed. "I need the money."

"I know, me too. I'll share my tips tomorrow."

"I hate getting dressed, coming to work, and getting sent home."

"How'm I supposed to know in advance? I'm not a fortune teller." He said, "And how come you're so grumpy? How was your overnight with the Scot last night? He eat your pie?" He laughed.

"My sexual harassment case is going to be huge."

"It was just a joke."

"I know, and funny too, he did eat my real baked peach flaky round sweet dessert—"

"I bet he liked your dessert."

"Very funny, then he went home."

"No stay over? He seemed like the kind of guy you'd want to nail down. Get it, 'nail down'?"

"Yeah, and that harassment case just keeps getting *more* expensive."

He shrugged and laughed. "I've known you for ten years, if you haven't started the suit yet, you ain't going to."

"Yeah, I'm a lot of talk no action, last night was a perfect example of it."

"So what happened?"

"He's like a fighter, come to find out, like MMA and... he said dueling."

Don's face screwed up, "Like with guns? How is that even a thing?"

"Swords, and you've just blown past the idea that he's got a streak of violence in him. He said 'like an MMA fighter.' What is that even, like fight club? I knew guys who were 'fight club' kind of guys, not usually the kind of guys I ought to bring home."

"He didn't seem the type."

"Yeah, but I asked if he had killed someone and he basically admitted it, more than one."

"Basically admitted it... what do you mean?"

"He just admitted it."

"Has he been in jail?"

I shook my head.

"That's weird — he admitted manslaughter in your tiny little kitchen?"

"Yeah... it was weird — MMA is with an audience, right? It's not to the death — but then *sword* fighting?"

"Fencing is a thing you know..."

"Why didn't he say fencing? Why didn't he say 'I fight MMA'? He said *like* MMA. He said he duels with swords. When I asked if he had killed someone, he gulped and wouldn't answer—"

"How did you even get to that? I can't think of *any* conversation I've ever had where I asked, 'Hey, you ever killed someone?'"

"There was something about the way he was talking about it, indirect, like he was lying."

CHAPTER 20 - ASH

"You hate liars."

"Yeah, just be straight up with me, tell the truth, and it was like he couldn't be straight, like he had done things he couldn't tell me about, so I asked."

"I think you're blowing it way out of proportion — he's an MMA fighter. Maybe it's different in Scotland, different rules, you know? And he fences sometimes. He does things differently because he's from Scotland. He calls you Mistress Ash. It's weird, but not criminal. You were in the army, you must know plenty of dudes like that."

"Yeah, a lot of them were edgy. I just wasn't prepared for him being edgy in my kitchen…"

Don said, "He's probably in the Scottish military, probably killed someone — it happens. You know it happens. He just isn't allowed to talk about it."

"Has it happened to you, you ever killed anyone?"

He said, "That's not really something I can talk about." Then he added, "See?"

"Yeah, good point." I huffed. "So what you're saying is he might have very good reasons why he had trouble answering me, and I let my imagination get the best of me. You're saying I might have let a hottie who seemed to genuinely like me get away?"

"He also kissed your knuckles, I saw it at least once."

"Drat. I messed up."

He began wiping the bar again, from one end to the other, as was his habit when he was bored, polishing it to a shine. "How'd you end it?"

"He kinda ran from my place, because the conversation had turned so antagonistic, it was so awkward. We didn't make any plans to see each other or…" I huffed again.

He said, "You could call him?"

"Yeah…" I sighed. "But I don't want to come off as desperate, you know?"

He teased, "You should be better than this — a hottie kisses your knuckles, and you don't pin him down, much less invite him to stay the night? I thought you would have better instincts."

I said, "Ha!"

Then the door of the Palace opened.

The two tables of guests and Don and I all turned and looked as, out of the dark rain and wind, Lochie blew in.

"Oh," I said.

He waved at me from across the room with a sheepish grin, and wiped at the rain dripping down his long overcoat. He unbuttoned the front, swept it off, and hung it on the coat rack by the door.

He was so freaking hot. He was wearing a dark coat with silver buttons. There were medals on his left chest. He wore a starched white shirt and a dark plaid kilt, white socks up his calves, a pair of Doc Martens. There was a sword at his hip and a fur bag on his front.

Our bouncer hefted himself up from a stool and approached him. "Sorry, can't bring that in."

Lochie ran his hand through his hair. "What, the sword? Tis part of m'uniform. I canna take it off or I am not in m'dress."

"You can't have it in here, but Don can keep it behind the bar. And no trouble, *none*. If you get drunk I'm not letting you have your sword back." The bouncer sat back down on the stool.

Lochie unbuckled his belt and took off his sword as he walked toward me. I stood speechless because he was so handsome — Don behind me said, "Careful, close your mouth, you're drooling."

"Am not," but I wiped my mouth to be sure.

Lochie passed the belt and sword to Don. "Good evening, Don, will ye hold m'sword for me?"

Don said, "Sure, Lochie, welcome."

He said, "Tis verra quiet here this evening." Then he took my hand, bowed and kissed my knuckles. "Good evening, Mistress Ash, are ye well?"

CHAPTER 20 - ASH

I nodded.

He met my eyes and held them.

I said, "I wanted to talk to you."

"I wanted tae speak tae ye as well. I apologize for the way I left ye last night."

"It's okay, it was a misunderstanding, I think — this is your uniform, you're a soldier?"

"I am a captain."

"Oh... so when you said that you duel and you fight and you... You meant that you were in the military?"

"I fight for my brother, when I am asked. And now I hae been asked, I must go away on urgent business — ye winna see me as I will be gone for a time. I wanted tae let ye ken."

I nodded. "Oh, that makes more sense, but that's too bad, we were just..."

Don said, "We don't need you anymore, Ash. Clock out, go home."

I said, "Would you like to go get something to eat?"

He said, "I would like that verra much, Mistress Ash," and his low rumbling voice just about made me swoon to the ground.

CHAPTER 21 - ASH

A PIZZA RESTAURANT DOWNTOWN

While we were at the door pulling our raincoats on, I said, "So you said I could pick wherever I wanted?"

"Aye." He put his arm in his sleeves and pulled the coat on. "Anywhere at all, but... I am not a big fan of beans, all but beans."

I grinned. "Or fish, right? No beans or fish... They're easy to avoid, because my favorite is pizza — there's a place with a nice fireplace right around the corner." I picked up my umbrella. "We could run?"

"Sounds verra good."

We opened the door — the rain was a deluge. I said, "Ready?" as I opened the umbrella and we rushed out into the rain.

We ran down the sidewalk as rain came from all directions. He had his arm around me and was ducking under the umbrella and it was bonking us both in the head and not really keeping us dry as slanting rain came at us. We bumped and stumbled together as his sword knocked against my hip. We rushed, laughing, his laughter in his low tones, as he stepped, splashing in a puddle and I squealed, my laughs high and light.

CHAPTER 21 - ASH

We finally made it to the restaurant and under the awning. I folded the umbrella while he pushed on the door and we blustered into a mostly empty, warm, dry, inviting restaurant.

Everyone looked up as the handsome Scot and the drenched local-chick loudly entered. I apologized as we stifled our laughter, trying to have a measure of decorum. I propped our umbrella by the door and we took off our wet coats and hung them on a hook near the table closest to the hearth. We sat down.

Lochie passed me a menu and we opened them and looked them over, ordering two glasses of wine.

The waitress kept glancing at his sword, but ignored it. But when she returned a moment later with our glasses she said, "I have to ask, the sword is real?"

Lochie said, "Aye, but if I were tae fight I would prefer a broadsword."

She said, "And the kilt, it's... a costume? Like Outlander cosplay?"

His brow drew down.

I said, "It's a real uniform, he's in the military."

She said, "Oh cool." And went back to the kitchen.

We sipped our wine and looked over our menus. Then he lowered his glass. "Mistress Ash, what would be yer favorite pizza?"

I said, "I like all of them, so I'm the worst person to ask, but... you look like you're a carnivore, you like meat on your pizza?"

"I do, tis the best."

"Then we'll get this one, it's got pepperoni, sausage, bacon, all the things."

He put down his menu. "We are decided."

We sat there for a moment, looking at each other, until he

broke the silence. "Again, Mistress Ash, I apologize for causin' ye any upset."

"It's okay, I think I was mostly tired. It was late and I couldn't understand the most basic things: You're in the *military*. I'm kind of embarrassed. Why did my brain go to like a Roman gladiator or something? I think it was the word 'duel', that's my excuse. I hope you won't hold it against me, I'm usually much more realistic." I smiled.

He said, "Mistress Ash, yer smile upon me sets m'mind at ease. That is all I ask."

I'm sure I blushed, I said, under my breath, "Wow."

Then he asked, "May I hold yer hand?"

I put my hand across the table and he slowly touched it, and then wrapped his hand around it, sending an electric vibration up my spine. His hand was warm and big and encompassing, comforting. I put my other hand on his and he put his other hand on mine.

And we held hands, with his fingers trailing over the back of mine and my thumb grazing his until the waitress came up. "More wine?" We nodded, drawing our hands away. She poured more wine into our glasses.

And then she left.

Lochie looked at me and said, "I like ye a great deal."

"Do you? I like you too, and... though we barely know each other, somehow we can stare into each other's eyes and be quiet together."

He said, "And that is what I want tae continue doin'." He put his hand out again, palm up, I put mine on it, feeling his callouses as his palm enveloped mine — warm, sure, protective.

I sighed.

We each sipped some wine. Then I said, "But you have to go, how long will you be gone?"

"I will be gone for two weeks. Will I be able tae see ye when I return?"

"Yes."

"Now I hae eaten yer um... the dessert ye baked ...and now I hae taken ye tae dinner, we will hae tae come up with something new tae do with each other. I would like tae go tae the beach with ye. Tis yer favorite thing, ye said."

"Oh, that would be lovely. Do you have a favorite book?"

He said, "I am verra fond of How tae Train Yer Dragon. I read it tae m'nephews."

I grinned. "You like stories about dragons too! How about we can sit on the beach and I'll read to you from the book I'm reading, we can hold hands like this."

He nodded. "I would like that."

"And I bet we can come up with more fun things, and you've only eaten my peach pie, how about I make you cherry pie? You said it was your favorite. And I make a delicious cherry cheesecake pie with a cookie crust."

His eyes lit up. "What if ye made me all the pies ye ken how tae make and I will get tae taste them all? I will put them all around m'chair on the beach and eat pie while ye read tae me about dragons."

I grinned. "Yes."

"This will make the critical errand I must run almost bearable."

"Is it dangerous?"

He looked at me long and then shook his head, "Nae." Then he sipped his wine and asked, "What are yer plans for the coming week?"

"Looks like I'll be baking pies."

He laughed. "Ye arna goin' tae hae trouble with Buck?"

"No, I think he's got the message, you and your brothers, he's not going to embarrass himself. We have been broken up for a long time. I'm not sure why he acted like that, but he's not in my life. Not anymore."

"I am not certain I understand it, ye had married him?"

"Oh no, no I hadn't, no... he wasn't... I mean there was a moment where I thought it would be a good idea, but I'm relieved that very soon in I realized he was cheating on me with someone else."

"He married her?"

"No... I think that girl wised up too."

He looked like he was mulling it over.

I said, "...just so you know, I mean what I say... I'm fiercely loyal if..."

He said, "I ken ye are loyal, ye are named after the Ash tree. Tis the Tree of Life, ye ken, it carries all the best qualities, goodness, fertility, interconnectedness, ye couldna hae a bad quality with such a grand name."

I squinted, his fingers rubbing back and forth on the back of my hand. "Are we dating?"

He grinned. "What does this mean? We are on a date, eatin' a meal."

"I mean, we're talking like we're *dating*, like I'm waiting for you to get back and you're holding my hand, are we... you know?"

"I daena ken much about the culture of Amelia Island, Florida, but ye hae allowed me tae hold yer hand. This is an honor and I am certain it means we are datin'."

The waitress placed our pizza in the center of the table and I pulled a slice to my plate. Then because I had gotten a bit of cheese on my fingers and I figured I might as well continue, I picked up another slice. He raised his plate. I maneuvered the piece to his plate. He said, "Thank ye, Mistress Ash."

It had been a little like serving him but the 'Mistress Ash' made it worth it.

I took a bite of pizza then asked, "Where does that come from, calling me Mistress?"

"Growin' up we had tae use a title afore the name, tis habit, I suppose. Ye daena like it?"

"Oh I like it, it's very... what would I call you?"

His brow raised, "I would be called Laird Lochinvar, but ye daena hae tae, we are already on a first name basis."

CHAPTER 21 - ASH

"Laird Lochinvar... interesting."

He smiled. "Yet most call me by a shortened name — only Lochie. Laird Lochinvar sounds as if I am much aulder."

I said, "How old are you?"

He shrugged, then said, "I feel somedays as if I am hundreds of years auld."

"Laird Lochinvar sounds like you're hundreds of years old, so I will call you Lochie..."

He tilted his head back, "There is also a more personal way tae speak tae me..."

"What would that be?"

"M'laird." When he said it, he was unmistakably saying My Laird, but putting it together with a bit of a long A sound in it.

"My laird..." I tried it out, "m'laird...? I would call you that if we were close?"

"Och aye, ye would call me that if we were close."

"Good, m'laird." I smiled.

He said, "Och aye, Mistress Ash, ye ken the way tae m'heart."

I sighed, then shook my head as if coming out of a daze. "Hold on, now... What *is* this? We barely know each other."

He shrugged again. "We ken enough."

"I know literally nothing about you."

"Ye ken that ye like me, tis good enough, I like ye, that is verra fine, we will learn the rest over time."

I laughed. "You are so odd sometimes... the things you say!"

"Tis something else ye ken about me, I say odd things."

"And you are an orphan."

"Aye, and m'brother is Magnus. He has many responsibilities and I carry a sword for him."

"You serve in his military."

"Aye, tis a better way tae say it."

"... and you are really close to your brothers and your nieces and nephews."

"Aye, I am verra fond of m'nieces and nephews. Dost ye want tae see a photo of the new bairn?"

"I'd love to."

He worked on his phone for a moment until he pulled up a photo and turned it around to show me. "This is Sophie, holdin' him, we are goin' tae call him Junior. That is Master James Cook, he's the father."

"How is James related to you?"

"He is no relation, but the same clan. He was an old friend of Queen— I mean, Kaitlyn, they were in a relationship, now he carries a sword for Magnus as well. Though, daena tell him I said it, he inna good at the sword, he is far better at building."

I teased, "I guess building things is *almost* as good as sword fighting."

He said, "They are all necessary. If ye erect great buildings, ye will want tae protect them, ye canna allow yer enemies tae take advantage."

"And who are these enemies?"

"I daena ken now, we are in a time of relative peace."

"Good, I'm glad." I passed him back the phone. "The baby is perfect, I can't wait to meet him."

"Aye, I look forward tae when ye meet all the bairns. But enough about me, tell me about yerself, where is yer family? Ye daena live with them?"

"They moved to North Carolina now. They bought a house in the mountains, and rent out the house here that I grew up in, which makes me a little sad. I miss them, but I didn't want to go with them. I had gotten out of the military and Don offered me a job and I grew up here, you know? I didn't want to move to a new small town and start over."

"I'm sorry, tis a difficult choice tae make."

"Sometimes I wonder if I am just stuck here, for good."

He shook his head, "Tis unlikely."

I narrowed my eyes. "What makes you say that?"

CHAPTER 21 - ASH

"I want tae take ye tae see Scotland, and I generally do what I intend tae do. And tis clear ye intend tae go with me."

"And it's clear because...?"

"Because ye are holdin' my hand." He smiled.

I said, "I suppose that does sound good. I would like to see Scotland, it sounds really different from what I thought..."

He asked, "Do ye hae any brothers or sisters?"

"No, my family is very small."

"It sounds lonely, Mistress Ash."

"I am often alone. My dad used to call me Little Miss Do It Herself. He would give me a task and just leave me alone to get it done."

"I am rarely alone, on m'horse perhaps, sometimes, but the house is often filled with children and a loud ruckus. Did ye ken there is a dog and a pig that live with us?"

She said, "That sounds fun. Even though I don't mind being alone, it is getting a little old, and I have to be so quiet when I come and go at my house. As you saw the other day, my landlady is a nightmare."

"Aye, yer house with the verra short rooms. I daena fit under yer roof — twas disconcertin'. My head was ringin'." He sipped some wine.

I sighed. "That tugged at my heart when you said you didn't fit."

"I was bein' a great big bellyachin' bairn. Ye must forgive me for m'behavior, Mistress Ash. I was worried ye had turned against me and so I acted like an arse."

"I do forgive you, no worries, m'laird."

"Och, it has a nice ring tae it, nae one calls me their 'laird'. Ye are m'first."

We both finished our pizza, talking about our favorite movies and music, and then had an assortment of desserts, while talking about his favorite, the first Star Wars, and how he loved classic Rock. His tastes seemed stuck in the past. We determined that he had never seen Lord of the Rings and I promised to show him, because it was one of my favorites.

And then Lochie asked for the check while we finished our wine.

I said, "Lochie, um... m'laird, I left my car parked around the corner that way," I pointed over my shoulder, "but my house is just two blocks away from here... We could walk in the rain, do you want to come over?"

"I would like that, Mistress Ash."

CHAPTER 22 - ASH

ASH'S HOUSE

As we were getting our coats on near the door, he held mine for me while I put my hands in the sleeves. I asked, "Why don't you have an Instagram or anything like that?"

"Tis a security risk, we canna."

"Oh." I opened the umbrella as we stood at the door and looked out. I gestured, "We go that way."

Then he put his arm around me and we rushed out into the rainy-puddle mud-splattering night, laughing all the way down the street, bumping and jostling and splashing to the front of my house.

I closed the umbrella on my porch and pressed my finger to my lips. "Shhhhh."

He whispered, "I ken."

I unlocked the front door and we crept in and moved stealthily up the stairs. I pointed at the ceiling and he ducked low and we barely squeaked the floor at all. I opened the apartment door and led him in.

We placed the umbrella by the door and took our coats off. I asked, "Would you like a beer?"

"Aye." He ran his hands through his hair.

I popped the cap off a beer. I decided not to have one, because I had a bit of a buzz and this had grown serious — I had just invited Lochie home and not for dessert... it felt like he was about to stay the night.

He said, "Pardon me, Mistress Ash, I must call m'brother tae let him ken I winna need a ride home yet, or if tis late I might walk."

I said, "It's pouring outside."

"I am a Scot, we daena care about rain." He dialed his phone and held it to his ear as he swigged from the bottle. Then he said, "Aye, we ate at a verra fine restaurant... nae, ye can go on tae bed, ye are auld, ye need yer rest. I winna need a ride, if tis late I will walk... I ken tis five miles and I ken tis raining..." He smiled at me and drank a bit more beer. "...aye I winna see ye tonight, but will be there in the morn. Alright. Good. See ye then... Goodnight."

He put his phone in his bag on the front of his kilt. "Dost ye mind if I remove m'things?"

"No, go right ahead. Of course."

I went into the bathroom and ran a quick toothbrush over my teeth and applied a bit of lipstick and finger-scrunched my hair. I wanted to look pretty, but not unnatural.

I returned and he had placed his belt and sword against the wall, with his waist bag on the table. His dress coat was over the back of the chair. He took another swig of beer.

I put out my hand and he took it and pulled me slowly close to him. He put his beer down on the table and pushed my hair behind my ear. Then he leaned down, raised my chin and kissed me, just a press on my lips but oh... it was a sweet and delicious feeling.

I liked him so much. I wanted him. I was freaking out because I barely knew him — he was so old fashioned. I didn't want to be easy, but also... I really wanted him to be here. I didn't want him to go.

CHAPTER 22 - ASH

This internal monologue stirred around in my mind while my arms with a mind of their own, went up around his neck and his kisses pressed against my mouth, parting my lips, his tongue entering my mouth. Our kisses deepened and breaths quickened. His mouth moved up my cheek, drawing along my skin to my ear, his deep bullish breaths, warming my skin and vibrating my body.

"Are you staying the..." I asked, his mouth suckling my neck, "the um... night, m'laird?"

He paused, his forehead against mine. "I believe I must ask permission first."

"Of whom?" I kissed him again, a deep lingering kiss, our tongues exploring each other's mouths.

Then, long after I had forgotten what we had been talking about... finally he broke away. "I daena ken who... but...?"

Our lips found each other again, his arms tightening around me.

I breathed near his ear. "I'm a modern girl, the only permission you need is mine."

He pressed his mouth to my neck, suckling and kissing, his hands pressing against my back, pulling me into him. Then his hand settled on my front, his palm on my breast. He stilled and seemed to be struggling with an internal dilemma — he moaned. "Tis nae... tis alright?"

I said, "It's alright, m'laird."

His hand went up under my shirt and fondled my breast over my bra. His mouth settled on my jaw, by my ear, his breath even more bullish, his movements growing to what felt like desperation.

He lifted me and I wrapped my legs around his waist. My mouth settled on his, and, his hands under my thighs he carried me to my bed. He lowered me onto it, where it was near the window at the end of the room, tucked under the eave, and he banged his head. "Och nae!"

He still managed to get me down gently but I sat up. "Lochie, are you okay?"

"Aye." He stood there for a moment rubbing his head. "I daena fit, ye ken, yer roof is too low."

"I know, it's not good, it's—"

He reached under the side table and lifted it about two feet to the left under the window, then he reached under the mattress to the bed frame and dragged it out from under the eaves, looking up to make sure it was centered under the high point of the ceiling. I laughed as I rode the bed out to the middle of the room.

I flicked on the table lamp, then climbed from the bed. "I'm sorry I'm ruining all the effort you put into carrying me here." I rushed down the length of the room, turned off the overhead light in the kitchen, and then I returned.

He was sitting on the bed, looking nervous. I wrapped my arms around his head and looked down on his face. His chin tilted up.

"You nervous, m'laird?"

"Aye, tis momentous."

"Is it?"

"Aye, ye holdin' my hand was of great import, but allowin' me tae come tae yer bed has meant verra much more."

I kissed him and he put his arms around me and pulled me over him and we lay back on the bed. I was straddling him and could tell he was firm and hot and ready, as my friend used to say, 'his train was leaving the station, no going back.'

His hands went up under my shirt and fondled and I pulled off my shirt over my head and he kissed me as I pushed his shirt up and shoved it off over his head. Then I went back to kissing him, both our hands running over our fronts and arms and chests. He fumbled for a minute, but then unlatched my bra and he moaned with pleasure and fondled my breasts, his gliding palm over my skin, heating me and exciting me.

"We have to take off our shoes so we can actually get all the way on the bed."

"I will take off yers, if ye take off mine."

I leaned to the side, putting my feet up. He pulled my shoes off and tossed them away. I twisted on his lap, laughing, my head hanging off the bed, and untied his boots while upside down.

He re-righted me onto his lap and pushed his boots off and peeled his socks off and we went back to kissing. I drew my hands up and down his abs, feeling the roundness of his biceps, the width and strength in his shoulders, but then I grew frantic with desire.

I fumbled with the buckle on his kilt, getting it unbuckled, and climbed off his lap to pull my skirt off. He shoved his kilt off and yes, he was naked under it and absolutely gorgeously built. I said, "Wow, that is... you are amazing."

"Says the gorgeous maiden nude upon the bed, ye are breathtakin'."

"I'm not completely nude—" He drew my underwear down my legs and off, tossing them to the side. "Now I am."

We lay back, our feet still off the bed, holding onto each other, his fingers caressing and playing between my legs, me touching him everywhere. My desire and his desperation growing, we rolled to the middle of the bed and he lay down over me — he paused. He kissed me, deeply. We looked each other in the eyes and our breathing matched.

And there was a long moment where we waited, in sync, pausing before we leapt, deciding to hold on, and then he pushed himself into me... and holding onto me he pushed again and again, and I raised my hips to meet him and we built up a glorious friction, a rhythm, hot breaths and sweat misted skin, and deep longing kisses, and after a long but loving battle, we reached climax, first me and then him and then settled, heavy and spent, on the other side of the peak.

He was the wonderful kind of heavy — I felt completely held, comforted, protected. He moved his mouth to the place beside my throat, under my ear, pressing his lips to my skin. I could feel our heartbeats sync together as our breathing grew regular and slowed.

I tightened my grip around his back, holding him close.

And then I burst into tears.

He drew his head up and looked down on me. "Och nae, are ye well, Ash?"

I nodded. "I'm sorry, that was... it was overwhelming."

"Aye."

I looked into his eyes. "I didn't mean to spoil the moment, I just felt... like that was a *lot*. I can't put it into words. I really really like you."

He kissed the outer corner of my eye, wetting his lips with my tear. "I felt it as well, and aye, I feel the same on ye, Mistress Ash."

"Sometimes I am so caught up in how hard it all is, paying bills, going to work, and being kind of alone in the world, and wondering what the point is, but then you're here and I feel so safe."

"Aye, the world is a storm, but I think we can get through it taegether. I will protect ye."

I nodded and looked up in his eyes and we breathed together for some long moments while I gathered my emotions and calmed in his arms.

He rolled off me and patted his chest and put out an arm. I curled up alongside him. Rubbing my hand across his muscular chest, thinking to myself, again, *wow...* he held my hand over his heart.

Then he raised his head, giving me a long hot view of his neck muscles, and let go of my hand. "Here, do this." He put his thumb in his mouth. He laughed at me when I looked at him quizzically.

He pulled his wet thumb out to say, "Ye must do it as well."

I stuck my thumb in my mouth and slobbered on it while I mumbled, "What for?"

He pulled his thumb out again. "Because we forgot tae make a thumb oath afore I bedded ye, this is why ye are overcome. Tis important. Tis a promise so ye arna worried."

Then we pressed the pads of our wet thumbs together. He said, "Here is my thumb, Mistress Ash, I promise I will never beguile ye."

I frowned a bit. "I am not sure I know what beguile means...?"

"I winna deceive ye."

"Now I say it?"

"Aye."

"Here is my thumb, m'laird, I promise I will never beguile you."

We smiled at each other.

I asked, "You're going to sleep here with your duties coming up, you can?"

"Aye, how else can we copulate at least two more times?"

I laughed and sat up. "Then we need to get under the covers." We got up and loosened the sheets, and took turns in the bathroom. I loaned him a toothbrush. There was something awesome about watching his ass as he walked around my apartment in his majestic nakedness, and when I would glance at him he would be watching me with a look of awe. Then we climbed into bed under the covers, and I tucked my head to his chest.

He said, "Goodnight, Ash."

I raised my lips to kiss him. "Good night, Lochie." He pulled my thigh up to his waist and sighed, happily.

At first I was on edge, I had a man in my bed, listening to his breaths, hyper aware of his movements and sounds, and where his touch ended and my body met it, and then he slowly fell asleep and there was something so sweet about how this mighty man, so muscular and big, had grown so vulnerable beside me. I watched the side of his face, his pale skin, the redness of his beard stubble over a strong jaw, the planes of his face, angles. I kissed the edge of his jaw and snuggled my head to his shoulder and soon I was asleep too.

CHAPTER 23 - KAITLYN

LIVING ROOM AT HOME

Most of us were in the living room that night, some of the kids were already asleep. James and Sophie were in their room. Quentin and Beaty were in their own apartment. We had been fed, we were up talking. Magnus had an arm around me, his other hand petting the back of Haggis's head.

I asked Fraoch, "So what do you think Lochie is up to, has he won her back?"

"I daena ken, but m'guess would be he is ruinin' everything by running his mouth."

"He does have a way of doing that."

Magnus, Fraoch, Zach and I raised our glasses.

Emma said, "I don't know, five dollars says he's smooth, he's won her over with his combination of immature vulnerability and uncanny capabilities."

Zach said, "How would you know anything about that?"

She waved her hand around him. "Oh I don't know, what would I know of being with someone who is immature and also capable?"

Zach raised his drink to his lips. "Oh right, yeah, you're kind of an expert."

I said, "I feel like we sent him off on a fool's errand, he

doesn't know anything about modern women. Fraoch, did you tell him not to talk endlessly about Grand Theft Auto?"

Zach shrugged. "She might like that."

Fraoch said, "I told him not tae emit flatulence, nae braggin', I doubt he will listen on that one, and I told him not tae ask her tae marry him."

I said, "I told him to ask her questions, to let her talk."

Emma said, "And I did my best to explain that he shouldn't mention that he just learned how to read — that wasn't easy, he's very proud."

Magnus said, "Och nae, he will be fine, ye are all too worried. He will brag and he will crow and be uncivilized, and behave like men hae behaved through history, and she will be the same as all women hae always been — she winna hear a thing he says because she will be so smitten by the uniform as we talked of the other night, the cut of his jaw and the glimpse of his knee below his kilt. Ye will confuse him with all yer warnings and directions."

I scoffed. "You think women are so shallow?"

"I ken they are, ye hae told me so yerself, and ye dinna heed a word I said about danger afore we married. Ye married me anyway, twas because of… ?"

I chuckled. "Um… your knee, your jawline, your eyes when you smile… yeah, yeah, yet again, point taken."

Fraoch said, "Hayley was the same, she said, 'Fraoch, I love ye, here's a bar of soap tae stop yer stench, and I will marry ye.'"

Hayley joked, "Almost verbatim."

Magnus's phone rang. He looked down at the screen. "The lad is callin'."

Fraoch said, "Tell him Hayley and I will come get him." He pulled his shoes from the side and began putting them on.

Magnus answered his phone and asked, "Ye hae had a good night, Lochinvar?"

We all stilled trying to listen, though we could only hear Magnus's side. "Good, Fraoch is on his—" He listened and chuckled. "I am not that auld…" Then he said, "…tis a long walk, ye ken? Tis raining." He nodded, then said, "We meant tae go at dawn." He listened more. "Good, aye, we will go when ye return." Then, "Goodnight."

He turned off the phone and grinned. "I was right, Og Lochie daena need a ride home, he said twill be much later and we ought not wait up, he will walk if he needs tae."

My jaw dropped. "*Seriously?* Wow."

Hayley said, "What did he say, exactly?"

Magnus said, "He took her tae dinner and now he is stayin' late." His eyes twinkled, "He meant that he dinna hae tae do barely anything but show her his knee and she has invited him over. Tis exactly as I said."

I dropped my head back on the couch. "Now I have all new worries, I hope she doesn't break his heart."

Hayley said, "What of her heart?"

Fraoch said, "He winna break her heart, ye saw him. He is like a tuna on the baited end of the longline."

Hayley said, "What's that supposed to mean?"

"As good as caught." Fraoch took his shoes off again.

CHAPTER 24 - LOCHINVAR

ASH'S HOUSE

I had drifted off again that mornin' after havin' awakened with desire tae go another round with Ash. Then, finished, I had fallen asleep once more, with her comfortable soft breast under m'head.

But now I checked the time and had tae rise.

I kissed her, "Good morn, Mistress Ash."

"Good morn to you, Lochie, m'laird."

I climbed from bed. "I am called away." I pulled my shirt over my head.

"I know, but would you like some eggs first? I can whip them up, a cup of coffee?" She pulled a shirt over her head, givin' me a long last look at her chest as the fabric came down coverin' it, and then a shiftin' of her fine legs as she stepped intae an undergarment and drew it up her legs. Twas difficult tae concentrate watchin' it go.

I said, "Och nae, I canna bear it, I might cry."

She grinned. "Because I put on my clothes?"

"Aye, I am at yer mercy, give me a glimpse."

She lifted her shirt exposing a perfect pale breast.

I smiled and sighed.

She lowered the shirt, hidin' her breast once more, and I frowned. "Och nae, tis all the light gone from the world."

She raised it again. I smiled.

She lowered it and I frowned. "I canna bear the loss, I am inconsolable."

"Lochie, you are exaggerating, but also, that is awesome."

I pulled my kilt on and belted it, admirin' her arse as she stood in front of her dresser. "Ye are exquisite, from yer rounded arse and yer—"

She stepped into a pair of pants and pulled them up, hidin' the last of her nude form. "Och nae, will I survive it?"

She laughed, her smile was beautiful, the dimple on her cheek meanin' all was well.

She asked again, "Breakfast?"

I checked m'phone. I was due, but couldna bear tae go. "Aye, I would love some eggs and coffee."

CHAPTER 25 - ASH

ASH'S HOUSE

*H*e texted his brother to come. He was dressed and ready, except for his suit coat folded over the back of his chair. I was going to miss him.

"Two weeks?"

"Aye."

"And then you'll call, right?"

His head went back, in that sexy way he had. "Och aye, Mistress Ash of Yggdrasil, the Tree of Life, I will call and I will come see ye first thing."

"Good." Then I stood and went up to him and stood between his legs and hugged around his head, his arms went around my waist and we held each other like that until his phone vibrated. I let go.

He checked his phone. "M'brother is here."

"You won't forget me? I mean, wait, don't answer that, I don't want you to think I'm being too needy or clingy, I just…" No matter how I finished that sentence I would sound too needy. *Why couldn't I stop talking? I was going to scare him away.*

"How could I forget the bonny Mistress Ash of the soft breast tae lay my head?"

I shrugged. "You might."

CHAPTER 25 - ASH

"Seems doubtful now I hae tasted yer pie."

I grinned.

He said, standing to put on his coat, "And besides all the other things that make ye unforgettable, how could we forget each other? We hae pressed our thumbs taegether and recited the oath, tis unbreakable."

"We had sex, but the thumb thing was the unbreakable oath?"

"Aye. Tis how it is. Tis how it has always been, so I will see ye in two weeks Mistress Ash. I canna wait."

He kissed me. And then left my apartment and went down the stairs, the small sound of a bonk and a grunt as he lightly hit his head on the way.

CHAPTER 26 - MAGNUS

MAGNUS'S TRUCK

*L*ochinvar climbed intae the backseat of the truck. Fraoch said, "Did ye hae a good night, Og Lochie?"

"Aye, twas verra fine."

The edge of Fraoch's mouth twitched with a smile. He twisted to look over the back seat at Lochinvar. "Ye spent the night in her guest room? Twas uncomfortable? Ye look as if ye dinna sleep."

"I slept, and I am nae goin' tae talk on it, because she is a good lass and I winna allow ye tae besmirch her reputation."

"Yet ye spent the night with a good lass and ye daena think this will besmirch her reputation? I ken she is modern, but ye still must be careful."

"I daena hae tae be careful, we hae made a thumb oath. She is mine and I will come for her when we are done with this errand."

I looked in the rear view mirror and met Lochinvar's eyes. "What on earth is a thumb oath?"

"Tis when ye press yer thumbs taegether and promise not tae beguile her. I promised her, she promised me. We are as good as married, ye daena hae tae worry on us." He returned tae looking out the window as I drove him home.

CHAPTER 26 - MAGNUS

• • •

As soon as we pulled up in front of the house I said, "Ye hae thirty minutes tae eat and gather yer things before we go tae the jump spot."

He said, "Aye, I will be ready," and left tae go up the steps tae the house.

I looked at Fraoch. "What dost ye think?"

"We were worried he wouldna ken how tae behave but now he has won the lass and bedded her and…"

"I am still concerned he winna ken how tae behave."

"Aye, tis unlikely."

CHAPTER 27 - KAITLYN

HOME - AMELIA ISLAND

Emma and Hayley and I were milling around the living room with a view of the front door, so we would see Lochie as soon as he got back.

I had a million questions, starting with, *where did you sleep last night, with Ash?* And ending with: *How did you win her over?*

But he waved from the door and went straight to his room.

We all looked at each other. "What was that?"

Emma shrugged, "I have no idea."

Magnus and Fraoch entered and Magnus made his eyes big and chuckled. He came up to us and spoke low. "Lochinvar spent the night. He is smitten, verra desperately. And has assured me that I ought not be concerned as he has married her."

Fraoch said, "As good as married her."

"Uh oh." I said, "What are the odds she knows she has married him?"

Hayley nodded.

Emma said, "Yeah... poor Lochie."

Fraoch said, "Why wouldna she ken? She allowed him tae bed her! Either he is goin' tae marry her or he would run out on her, and she canna take him for a scoundrel. She ought tae be certain he inna a scoundrel!"

CHAPTER 27 - KAITLYN

Hayley said, "Fraoch, remember she's *modern*. She likely doesn't think about it that way."

"I feel certain we ought tae always ken it that way, or the world daena make sense."

Magnus checked his watch. "I ought tae go, I planned tae leave after breakfast. Quentin has the security shifts planned around our departure."

Fraoch said, "And I will be here, I hae it all under control."

Magnus said, "Kaitlyn, tis a fine day, can the kids come out tae say goodbye on the deck?"

I picked up Jack from where he was playing with blocks and asked Archie and Isla to follow us out, and we joined Magnus on the deck, looking out over the beach.

It wasn't until we stopped at the end of the deck, with a slight breeze against the seagrass, the small waves lapping, the high blue sky, that I looked at Magnus and that now familiar feeling hit me — he was leaving, again.

His face was beset with solemnity, Jack sitting on his arm — Isla had scaled the railing and sat on the top, with her head on Magnus's shoulder. Archie, being more grown up, stood stoically beside him.

Magnus saying goodbye to his children made my chin tremble and so I rolled into his arms hugging around him and Jack, and adding Archie and Isla so we were one big huddle, holding on.

Magnus murmured in our ears. "Tis a time of peace... ye daena hae tae worry on me... I ken I hae been having dreams, but nothing has come of them... I am goin' tae check on the kingdom, see if Lady Mairead needs anything, and then I will return... in a week, I ken it seems like a long time, but ye ken, twill be over afore ye realize it."

Archie said, "Uncle Lochie said he would be gone for two weeks."

Magnus said, "Aye, he will be, because he needs tae take more time afore he returns. I need tae get home tae ye sooner, because Jack still counts his life in days and weeks. I canna miss too many moments."

I kissed his cheek and then he kissed my lips. "I will see ye in seven days, mo reul-iuil."

"Goodbye my love, see you next week."

Isla said, "Da, do not forget my present."

"What will ye be getting for me?"

"Da, I am not going anywhere!"

"Ye will still hae a fine time — what I want for m'gift is a story. While I am gone I want ye tae decide what is the best thing ye did this week and when I return I want ye tae tell me the story of it. Good?"

She said, "Good, I already know what it will be, I am going on a surprise shopping trip with Beaty today."

"What are ye getting on the surprise shopping trip?"

"I can't tell you Da, because you won't like it."

He chuckled and muttered, "Och nae, Madame Beaty is getting another animal?"

Isla said, "Da, how did you guess?"

He sighed. Then said, "That *might* be yer best story, but ye never ken perhaps something even better will happen along."

She hugged his head. "Good Da, I will tell you the best story." Then she climbed down from the rail. But stopped on the bottom rung and lowered her brow. "But I want something *better* than a story."

"Of course, Isla, it goes without saying."

"What does that mean?"

"That means, I ken ye verra well, ye like a present."

"Yep, you know me perfectly." She jumped to the deck and bounded up the deck toward the house.

Archie gave his father a last long hug. Magnus pushed

Archie's hair from his forehead and gazed into his eyes, nodding, telepathically conveying something like, "I'm proud of you."

Then he kissed his head and Archie stepped aside so that Magnus could kiss Jack, who patted the side of his beard with a very wet slobber hand. "Da!"

Magnus said, "Aye, Jack, I will see ye in a week."

He passed Jack to me, and kissed me one last time and then turned and strode toward the house with Haggis at his heels, to go.

I looked up at the guard on the roof, stationed there because Magnus, Lochie, and Quentin were leaving to go check on the kingdom.

We had had calm for a long time, I was growing used to it, it... it frightened me a little, to be so at ease.

CHAPTER 28 - KAITLYN

WHILE MAGNUS IS AWAY

*B*eaty took the bigger kids off in the afternoon to go shopping while Jack and Noah were napping and returned with a new chicken. Archie carried it nestled in his arms.

Zach protested, "We have a coop with chickens right outside!"

Beaty said, "Aye, but this is a *house* chickie. I wanted her *especially* tae ride on Mookie's back."

I laughed. "To ride on Mookie's back?"

"Aye, I had a dream of a beautiful bird and it was sittin' on Mookie's back and Mookie said tae me—"

Zach said, "In your dream? He doesn't talk to you all the time?"

Beaty put her hands on her hips, "Mookie talks tae me all the time *and* he spoke tae me in the dream, Zachary! He said, '*Now* I feel complete.'"

Zach started laughing. "Well as long as Mookie is happy."

Beaty pulled the chick from Archie's arms and put him on Mookie's back. Mookie looked adorably at Beaty and then tried to turn to see the bird and then back at Beaty. She said, "See?"

CHAPTER 28 - KAITLYN

Though Mookie's expression was more like: *What now, with this thing on my back?*

The chickie lowered itself to sitting, comfortably. Beaty, Zoe, and Isla all folded their hands under their chins and said, "Aw!"

I said, "I guess this is a thing now, Magnus is just going to love it."

Beaty said, "I think we ought tae call her Saddle." Most of the kids applauded and cheered, frightening the bird, but they crowded around, patted it and petted Mookie until the bird calmed, sitting down on Mookie's back again — except Archie. He had an expression on his face as if he were trying to be excited but something was weighing on him. The expression looked a lot like the one Magnus wore when things were going wrong.

Archie stood in the outskirts as Beaty said, "I told ye, Mookie is finally complete with his Saddle."

Then he ended up standing right beside my seat on the tall kitchen chair.

I put my arm around him and asked the group, "What are you kids going to do with the rest of your day?"

Isla said, "Watch Saddle sit on Mookie."

I teased, "Sounds like you're 'complete' now too."

Zach muttered while he put a pan of sausages in the oven for our dinner. "Complete nut jobs."

Archie put his head on my shoulder.

I whispered, "How are you doing?"

"Okay... it's nothing."

I kissed his temple. "You sure?"

He nodded against my shoulder. "Just thinking about something."

"If you need to talk, I'm here."

He nodded again, and stood there for a long time, as all the other kids excitedly hung around with Mookie and Saddle, he clung to me.

I felt his forehead. *No fever.*

He said, "I'm not hot."

I said, "Just worried?"

He said, "Aye," sounding much like his Da.

Finally Ben turned on the Playstation and called into the kitchen, "Archie, come play!"

He said, "In a minute!" He looked at me. "Where do you think Da is right now?"

"He's in Riaghalbane, likely having dinner with your grandmother."

He nodded. "That's probably okay, he's got a guard there."

"Yes, he definitely does."

He called back to Ben, "Coming, Bug Man!" And ran off.

I asked Zach, "Why is Archie calling Ben 'Bug Man', or do I want to know?"

He laughed, "Apparently Ben accidentally ate a bug when we were going down the river."

I said, "A big bug?"

"Big enough we're watching to see if he gets super powers." Zach stood in front of the pantry door. "What goes with sausage?"

I laughed. "Aren't you supposed to plan the meals?"

Hayley said, "I just eat what you serve."

Fraoch was outside, checking on security, taking his job seriously. Sophie was sleeping with the baby. James was with us all in the kitchen while Zach cooked, when Hayley asked, "So what do y'all think about Lochie? Fraoch said he thinks they got married last night. Because of some thumb oath."

I pouted. "I'm worried she's going to break his heart."

Emma said, "I was thinking we go down there tonight after dinner and just 'check in'."

CHAPTER 28 - KAITLYN

Zach scoffed. "Check in? Are you going to interfere in his relationship? He's a grown-assed man!"

Emma said, "Yes, and I know I mother him, but come on, Zachary, he understands almost nothing about the contemporary world and even less about women. He's like a freaking caveman sometimes. I just want to get a feel for what she's thinking about him. I want to check in, but not in the *bad* way."

James said, "Look, you're overthinking this. He's a dude. He gets how to do this. It's not rocket science. Whether you're in the sixteenth century or now, you meet a girl and you try to sleep with her as soon as possible while the elders around you try to get you to marry her first. It's a dance as old as time. He's not stupid. I don't think you should interfere, what if you scare her off?"

Emma said, "If she likes him there's no way I scare her off. If she doesn't then shouldn't we know? We could advise him!"

I said, "I agree with Emma, we ought to go check in, see what she's thinking. We're not doing it in the bad way, in the *good* way. We can go tonight after dinner. Beaty, will you stay with the kids?"

Beaty said, "Aye, we ought not leave Saddle when she's new tae the house."

Zach said, "I'm not going. I'll stay here, that way when you screw it all up I can deny having any part of it."

Hayley said, "We don't need you anyway. This is a girl's mission."

James said, "Uh oh, the Campbell Women about to get all up in her business."

I joked, "It's what we do."

◈

Hayley, Emma, and I walked into the Palace Saloon and across the room I saw her, she was wearing a t-shirt with the bar logo on it, and another long khaki cargo skirt, with pull strings up the side, showing off her low boots. Her hair did look like Meg Ryan's in... really in *all* her movies.

I said, as we made our way to the table, "She's so freaking cute."

Emma said, "Yeah, no wonder he's smitten."

Hayley said, "She wears those long cargo skirts to work, he probably sees it as modest and traditional, instead of what we see — pockets."

Emma and I laughed.

We sat at a table with a different waitress, and ordered a beer, a glass of wine, and Hayley got a nonalcoholic mixed drink. Then as Ash walked by I caught her eye and waved.

Her brow drew down but then she said, "Oh, right, you're Lochie's um... family?"

I shook her hand and said, in a way that I hoped would sound cheery and not weird, "I'm his sister-in-law!"

"Right, cool, did you already place an order?"

Our drinks were delivered right then.

She laughed. "Looks like it." Then she asked, "Did Lochie, um... did he get off on his trip okay?"

I nodded.

Emma said, "They left before lunch, we just wanted to come by and say hello."

She grinned, flashing us her dazzling smile, then her eyes scanned the room. "Uh oh, um... table calling. I'll come back by in a bit." She rushed away.

Emma screwed up her face. "I can't tell, do you think she likes him?"

Hayley said, "I have no idea. She's just busy. What are you going to ask her when she gets back?"

Emma said, "Would it be weird if I asked, 'What are your intentions with our brother, Lochie, because if you break his heart I'm going to have to break you'?"

I said, "I doubt we need to threaten her. Maybe we can be more on the down low, right? No fighting, no breaking anyone."

Emma and Hayley jokingly scoffed.

Hayley said, "You're a fine one to pretend to be a pacifist. How many weapons you have strapped to you right now?"

"Two, but just because I've been *repeatedly* told I must. I don't intend to need either of them. No fighting, we're just here to find out what her intentions are. I'd also like to know if he told her about time travel..."

Hayley groaned. "I'm sure he told her everything. He does not strike me as the kind of guy who can keep secrets when he's sexing someone up. I think he was doing it and saying, 'oh, oh, oh, yes, yes, did I tell you I time travel?'"

I said, "Well Magnus gave him explicit instructions — he's not to talk about it. That's part of the reason why he was so destroyed the other night, because he didn't know what he could say... Damn it, I hope it's all okay—"

Emma said, "Wheesht, she's coming back."

CHAPTER 29 - ASH

PALACE SALOON

I was at the bar turning in a drink order and Don said, "See that table over there? That's Katie and Hayley, they went to school with my brother, weren't they with Lochie the other night?"

I smiled, "Yeah, Katie is his sister-in-law…"

"They here to see you? I thought you said Lochie was out of town…"

"He is."

Someone interrupted asking Don directly for a drink. I finished filling a soda glass, glancing over at the ladies, wondering why they were there…

Once Don was finished, he said, "I bet they're checking up on you."

My eyes went wide. "On me?"

"Yep, her little brother spent the night, they want to see if you're worthy."

"Like worthy, *how*?"

"Imagine it's your sister, why would she be here?"

"To see if I plan to break his heart."

"Whoa, I was just kind of kidding, there are hearts involved? You weren't just messing around? He seems like a big boy, and handsome — he's for sure a player, maybe they don't know he's a player...?"

"Nah, he's not a player and yeah, there are hearts involved. I guess I should go talk to them. Can I take a break? Will you cover my tables for a moment?"

"Sure."

I walked over to their table, and the three women abruptly stopped talking as if they had been talking about me. I sank into the empty chair. "So, hi."

They all reintroduced themselves, then the woman, Emma, said, "The reason why we came..."

I said, "My guess is you came to check up on me."

Hayley laughed. "Kind of, but not, you know, in the bad way."

Emma said, "Lochie's not... he's not from here, and he hasn't dated much, so... we were concerned that maybe...?"

Kaitlyn shook her head. "Now that we're in the conversation, I *totally* regret it. Why did we come?"

Emma said, "I have no idea, honestly, Ash. When we talked this out we thought it was a good idea."

Hayley said, "Yeah... and Ash, promise you won't hold this whole thing, *us*, against him?"

I said, "I won't hold it against him. I think he's really wonderful."

Kaitlyn smiled widely. "Yay! That's awesome, Ash, you're going to see him when he gets back?"

"Definitely. If he'll see me..."

Emma said, "That sets my mind at ease."

I said, "Phew, this was a little like an interrogation."

Hayley said, "Oh we have so many questions, we didn't even get past the first one."

I said, "If you need my back story, I was in the army, now I work here. I live nearby. I did well in school... is that pretty much all you needed to know?"

Kaitlyn said, "Yeah, again, really sorry that we bothered you." She took a sip of her drink and said, "I guess he told you all about Scotland?"

"Not much really, except...it's not at all what I expected Scotland to be like."

Kaitlyn nodded. "Good, yeah, perfect." Then she said, "Oh, I mean, *yeah,* Scotland is not at all like what you see in the movies. It's got a real ancient vibe to it."

I said, "I'd love to see it..."

Emma said, "Maybe Lochie will show you someday...?"

I said, "I would love that. He mentioned taking me, I hope he will."

All three of them leaned back in their chairs, smiling.

Emma said, "That's awesome. We're so glad. Thank you for not holding this against us."

I said, "Your family is really close, huh?"

Kaitlyn said, "Magnus has a lot of responsibilities, everyone works with him—"

Hayley said, "It's a family business, sorta."

I chuckled. "Almost like the mob?"

They glanced at each other then laughed.

Kaitlyn finished her drink and pulled a pen and paper from her purse. "I'm writing down my phone number. If you need anything, want to talk, if you want to ask when he's coming home, if anything goes down that's weird, you know... just call, okay?" She passed it to me.

I said, "Thank you, that sounds good. I'll call if I need to know anything." I tucked the paper in my pocket.

Kaitlyn said, "Please forgive us for intruding." She stood and jerked her head at Hayley and Emma. They all gathered their coats and bags. "Call me, if you need anything."

And then they left.

. . .

CHAPTER 29 - ASH

I returned to Don. "You were right, they were totally checking up on me."

I pulled the paper out of my pocket and laid it on the bar and pulled out my phone to key the number in: Kaitlyn Campbell (Lochie's Sister)

Don said, "Why'd she give you her number?"

I shook my head. "I don't really know. She said something strange about 'if anything goes down, that's weird.' What does that mean, you think?"

Don shook his head. "I don't know, that's super strange."

"Yeah, I agree. I asked if they were in the mob, they glanced at each other. Do you think he's in the mob?"

"A Scottish mob? Not sure that's a thing. But I do know Katie's husband is very rich... he owns that big house down on the south end, you know?"

"Yeah."

"Maybe they're just a close-knit family, is Lochie religious?"

"Yeah, he prayed before he ate my um... pie."

"I bet he did." Don laughed. "That explains it, they're just religious."

"Sure, yeah."

"You'll need to decide, do you like him enough to put up with the family?" He wandered away to fill a drink order.

I thought, *I do, I do really like him enough,* and put the phone in my pocket. Lochie flashed through my mind, his smoldering look when he would say, *Aye, Mistress Ash,* and my hand rubbing across his chest, the way he felt against my skin, the scent of his cologne... and the way he had looked when he pressed his thumb to mine and said, '*...I will never beguile ye...*' I finished serving the last tables, wondering where he was and what he was doing now...

CHAPTER 30 - MAGNUS

RIAGHALBANE

Quentin, Lochinvar, and I strode intae m'mother's office, with Haggis at m'heels. "Once again, ye winna deign tae meet in mine?"

Lady Mairead said, "Why would I, when mine is so much more comfortable, for *me*." She kissed us each on our cheeks and gestured toward her sitting room. "Must the dog be here? Daena he want anything else tae do? He could be off doing dog things?"

"Nae, he prefers tae listen in on meetings."

"Fine."

She and I took chairs, Haggis sat at my feet, Quentin and Lochinvar sat on the couch.

I said, "So fill me in."

"On what do you mean?"

"Ye haena come tae visit in a while, it usually means something is goin' on."

"No news is good news, I thought?"

"Tis not yer style — what is happening?"

"Nothing, not really, a lot of the usual, but... and I daena want tae worry ye, but there has been a challenge."

CHAPTER 30 - MAGNUS

"We hae never been stronger, tis ridiculous tae challenge us. Who is it, someone we hae heard of before?"

Quentin said, "I hate those cousins who just challenge you every year as if they are trying to build a name for themselves."

Lochinvar said, gruffly, "Aye, it shouldna be allowed."

Lady Mairead said, "Ye are correct, Colonel Quentin, tis another cousin." She waved her hand and brought up a video on the wall. A large man with his shirt off was on a stage, muscles ripplin' as he posed for the camera.

I sneered. Then the images shifted tae one of him wearin' a suit with his hand up wavin' at a crowd.

Lochinvar said, "He looks stupid."

"Aye."

Colonel Quentin said, "He looks as if he has worked hard on his surface. He's definitely in it for the notoriety and prestige. There's no way he could beat you, even if he wanted to. He can't even scratch his own back."

"Thank ye, Colonel Quentin, ye are a good friend for saying it. Where was this event?"

"A movie premiere."

"He is modern?"

"He was raised in the past, as is usual for our family, though as a cousin twas hardly necessary. His name is Dugal Denoon."

Lochinvar said, "Och, he grows even more tediously stupid."

Lady Mairead said, "I am only telling ye tae keep yer eye on him. We winna accept his challenge, I refuse tae even acknowledge it. Ye should ignore him, put it off as long as possible."

"Aye, but in the meantime ye must monitor him, make sure he daena cause any trouble..."

"I will. Speaking of, Magnus, hae ye been having more of the dreams ye mentioned last time?"

I said, "Aye, they hae grown more frequent and more realistic."

She sighed.

I added, "Archie is havin' them as well."

"Och nae, what sort of dreams is he having?"

"He is dreamin' that he is bein' crowned king, and the crowd is yellin' 'The King is Dead, Long Live the King!'"

"I daena like the idea of that."

"None of us do."

She smoothed down her skirts. "Well, the ChronoGuard has found a discrepancy."

"Och nae, ye are tellin' the story backward, Lady Mairead, ye ought tae tell us of the discrepancy first and the 'unimportant challenge we intend tae ignore' *last*."

"I will tell the story as I deem necessary, Magnus."

Lochinvar asked, "What is ChronoGuard?"

Colonel Quentin said, "It's a history monitoring software that tries to detect shifts, it doesn't find all of them, but—"

"How would it do it?"

Quentin said, "We have servers set at different points in time, they keep records, then the records are compared, any points in time that don't match are flagged. Then it's run through a deeper comparison."

Lady Mairead said, "We hae been developing it for years, it works verra well, considering, though last time Magnus visited he had concerns and it dinna hae anything new, but now... it has noticed a discrepancy *verra* far back, in the interregnum period at the end of the thirteenth century."

"Aye, when I was crowned king."

She looked at me quizzically. "Ye were crowned king...?"

I dinna answer because I wanted tae see what she would remember.

She thought for a moment, then said, "Aye... I suppose ye were... I had almost forgotten it, Magnus, twas well done, when was it...? I canna put m'finger on the full memory of it... We went that far intae the past?"

"Aye, yet ye daena remember it because the time shifts restored the timeline tae rights. Tis just as well ye daena remember, because it never happened, except I hae the scars

CHAPTER 30 - MAGNUS

on m'body and the wrinkles on m'forehead from the work of it."

"...I remember now, ye were crowned king, was it in 1290?"

I said, "Somethin' like it."

"Well, this clears up a great many mysteries." She picked up an ancient book and clutched it in her lap. "The discrepancy is near then, Magnus, 1296. I hae had it flagged, and then I hae had someone looking at it—"

"Someone ye trust?"

"Aye, he is a historian, he winna speak on the issue."

"Explain it then."

She asked the room's projection tae switch tae a marble sculpture, a man's head. Twas well done and in verra good condition. He was wearin' a crown.

She said, "There was an interregnum period beginning in 1296 in which there wasna a king, at least this is how we believe it went."

I nodded. "Aye, then Raibeart am Brusach came tae the throne."

"Aye, Robert the Bruce, correct, but ye see, Magnus, tis not what the record shows now. *This* man is listed as a king, and dost ye notice the newness of the statue? This is what triggered the flag — the sculpture daena seem as auld as it ought."

I asked, "What is his name?"

She snapped her fingers and an old record came up, it said: Asgall I.

"Ye ever heard of Asgall the First, Magnus?"

"Nae, and he sounds like an arse."

Lochinvar and Quentin nodded in agreement. Lochinvar said, "Like the bitter gall of an arse."

He and Quentin bumped fists.

She continued, "Thomas said—"

"Who is Thomas?"

"Thomas Innes, the historian, do try tae keep up, Magnus. I asked him tae look intae the period. In the beginning he found little about this king, a mention here and there, twas as if he had been barely studied, but when I visited recently Thomas had found a great many more records. There is a shifting tae it, I am certain. As I am farther along on the timeline, I will count the mentions of Asgall in history books, then I will go visit Thomas and he will tell me of twenty more mentions. I will return here and there will be fifty records. Therein is proof of time travel."

I said, "It does seem so."

"Thomas went tae Stirling tae further his research at the library, and found this ancient psalter." She showed me the book, embossed with an ornate M on the cover. "We hae determined the date tae be the late thirteenth century. Twas a mystery whose book twas but now I think I ken."

I raised my brow. "Ye think tis mine?"

"Aye, tis the book of a king. Dost ye recognize it?"

"Nae, and there are many different reasons for an M tae be on the cover of a book, why must ye assume tis mine?"

"I dinna until ye told me ye remember being a king, now it explains everything. Do ye recognize this photo we found stuck between the pages of the book?"

Lady Mairead pulled a photograph from the book, and also called out for the image tae be projected on the wall. "Ye might recognize the room?"

My eyes swept the projected photo, there were three men, who at first glance I dinna recognize because I was more taken with the familiar room. "Aye, tis one of the rooms at Scone. How am I familiar with it? I haena been there, yet... I recognize it, I am certain I sat there many a day." The memories flooded back, the battle in the fields outside the walls, the terraces, Kaitlyn in m'bed in m'chamber on the upper floor. "My memories must be from 1290, yet this room looks just as I remember it — Scone haena changed in eight hundred years?"

"It has changed a great deal. Because of the herald and other details in this photo we hae determined it was taken in the thirteenth century. As I said, Thomas found it stuffed between the

CHAPTER 30 - MAGNUS

pages of this psalter as if it were a bookmark, with nae explanation."

"What time period is Thomas from?"

"I hae asked for his help from the year 1708."

Quentin's eyes went wide. "I suppose he must be confused by what he's finding, especially photographs."

She waved her hand, indifferently. "He prays on it, he daena dwell on it. But we hae determined that the man in the center of the photo is Asgall, former king of Scotland."

While they spoke, I strode across the room for a closer view of the projected photo, focusing on the faces of the men. "The man on the left is m'auld friend and ally, Cailean, aged a few years beyond when I last spoke tae him. But tis him, I ken it. I remember him well."

Asgall was taller than Cailean, although not verra big, dark hair, a mustache and nae beard. I pointed at the man standing tae his right. "And this is William Wallace, I remember meetin' him. Dost ye remember — he stabbed me?" I scowled and pulled my collar away trying tae see my shoulder. I could remember getting wounded, but couldna remember if it had really happened or not. I had tae unbutton my shirt to pull it aside and look. *Aye, there was the scar from it.*

"Och, tis a relief, I was wonderin' if I lost m'mind."

She said, "The photograph is incontrovertible proof that there is time travel afoot."

I said, "Asgall has taken the throne during the interregnum period, as I did, during a time of great turmoil. Perhaps it winna change history much."

She raised her brow. "Think on the importance of Robert the Bruce, ye ken his name, he is *important* tae history."

Quentin said, "Is Robert the Bruce still listed there, as one of the kings?"

She asked the room tae project a list of the kings of Scotland. Robert the Bruce was listed after Asgall, beginning in 1325 until his death in 1329. "Do ye think tis right?"

I shook my head. "He was only king for four years...?"

Lochinvar said, "Is this the main list? Does it include the footnotes?"

Lady Mairead said, "This is a verra good question, Lochinvar, as the centuries hae passed, history becomes settled. The Scottish kings are set in stone."

He shrugged. "Except it sounds tae me like the history of Scottish kings inna set in stone..." His voice trailed off at her glare.

She sighed, dramatically. "This is the list of Scottish kings, the *main* list. This is all that is important."

Lochinvar said, "Aye, Lady Mairead, ye are correct in it."

She looked at the list and huffed.

I watched her looking at it intently.

Then she said, "It would be good though, if it would *remain* settled. Do ye remember how long Robert the Bruce was king?"

I said, "Nae, but four years seems a short time."

"Exactly! And throughout this time there would be malicious dealings by the king of England, Edward I, but he is barely mentioned."

I said, "Aye, I had many dealings with Edward, he was an arse. He wanted tae appoint the Scottish king, as if Scotland were his vassal state."

She said, "Tis clear that someone has applied pressure tae history and changed its course."

She asked the room tae project the photograph of Asgall and Cailean with William Wallace once more.

Lochinvar said, "Maybe it's a good thing, maybe history is better now."

Lady Mairead scoffed. "Those are the ravings of a bairn, not a serious insight from a learned person who can be trusted tae lead, Lochinvar. Yer past is how ye came tae be, ye canna change it without changin' yerself. Ye canna change yer ancestors without affectin' yer future."

CHAPTER 30 - MAGNUS

Lochinvar sat up straight in his chair. "Aye, Lady Mairead, my apologies."

She said, "Tis fine, Lochinvar, but ye ought tae grow more serious, when will ye be taking a wife?"

"I hae taken one. Her name is Ash McNeil."

Lady Mairead's eyes went wide. "What dost ye mean, Ash McNeil? Who is Ash McNeil? Why am I only now hearing this?"

I said, "Lochinvar has become enamored with a maiden."

Her eyes went wide, "Has she been properly *vetted*?"

I said, "Ye daena need tae worry, we *will* vet her, but he inna truly married either."

She turned tae Lochinvar. "Explain it tae me, Lochinvar, ye married without permission? Ye are the brother of a king, the uncle tae a prince — how can ye behave so irresponsibly?"

Lochinvar said, "I liked the look of her and I wanted her."

She sighed. "And how did ye convince her tae accept yer advances? Ye sound like an uneducated brute."

He said, "Ye once fancied this uneducated brute though, dinna ye?"

She glared. "Be *verra* careful, Lochinvar. This is yer future we are discussing."

He said, "I daena ken how I convinced her, I took her tae dinner, she served me pie. I like her a great deal. We hae made a thumb oath tae each other. I consider us betrothed."

She shook her head and muttered, "...served me pie..." Then said, "The fate of a kingdom rests upon yer ability tae battle and ye are goin' tae take a wife because she served ye pie?"

"Aye, twas peach." He grinned.

She threw up her hands. "Well, if twas peach, then of *course* it must mean twill be a good marriage."

She bellowed, "Show me an image of Lochinvar's wife and her file up to the date Lochinvar left." Then she asked, "Remind me her name?"

Lochinvar said, "Ash McNeil, she was in the military."

"Dear Lord, she probably has high ideas about women's abilities in running the world."

I said, "That is rich comin' from ye, Mother, high ideas! Ye run a kingdom!"

"I am a singular woman, there arna many like me."

"Thank God."

Lochinvar and Quentin laughed.

The projection on the wall showed a photograph of Ash McNeil. Then her files, listing her jobs and school and her military service.

Lochinvar said, "Can we see what happens in her future?"

I said, "Nae, ye daena want tae ken, Lochinvar, tis information that will only cause ye heartache and confusion."

Lady Mairead ignored us, reading, then asked the computer, "Please shew me a comparison between Ash McNeil, her family, her genetics, her history, and *our* family and all second cousins tae Magnus the First."

There came an answer: A zero percent match.

"That is a relief, but... ye are certain she has nae connection tae time travel, tae our kingdom, or our power?"

I said, "I daena think she has any connection tae us."

Lochinvar said, "She daena, she is innocent of it."

Lady Mairead said, "Well, this might hae been verra dire. Ye are sitting there dumbly, Lochinvar, as if ye hae not a care—"

She interrupted herself, and waved a hand toward him. "But ye are young, ye daena ken any better." She turned tae Quentin, "But ye, Colonel Quentin, I canna believe *ye* dinna vet her! Ye are ignoring it, as if we daena hae a care in the world?"

"I wanted to vet her, Lady Mairead, but we don't have access to all the information you have. I meant to ask you to look into her background, but we just got here—"

She looked at her watch.

I interrupted, "I think I speak for Colonel Quentin and Lochinvar and all the other men ye hae harangued in yer current mood when I say from now on we will vet *all* the maidens."

CHAPTER 30 - MAGNUS

"This is the *least* ye can do."

I said, "Are ye dating someone, Mother?"

"My associations are nae business of yers and daena distract me, we have enemies everywhere, and we must be on guard."

Colonel Quentin said, "Yes, ma'am." And glanced at me.

I winced and jokingly pulled my collar from my throat.

I said, "We will make certain tae protect ourselves, and I am sure Ash McNeil is acceptable. She is local tae Amelia Island and haena had any troubles or raised any suspicions before."

Lady Mairead leaned back in her chair admiring Ash McNeil's image. "Beyond the lapse of judgment, she looks verra handsome, and her gaze is direct, I admire that." She pulled up a book from the table and with a fine pen copied information from the projection. "I will hae my people look intae her further."

I said, "Back tae the matter at hand — *why* did Asgall put a photograph of himself intae a psalter?" I took the book up and turned it over, openin' it tae see the photo. "It seems messy, it inna keepin' history straight, and anyone could hae found it."

I asked the computer tae project it so that I held it in m'hand and had it on the wall as well.

"He is sendin' me a message."

She looked the projection over. "Aye, it does seem like it, and it shows verra little respect for history. And because he is with yer friend Cailean, it seems as if he mocks us." The corner of her mouth went up. "The *gall* of him."

Quentin said, "Unless he doesn't know about us."

Lady Mairead raised her chin. "That is highly unlikely. He is a time traveler. He has taken the throne a few years after twas Magnus's rear keepin' it warm."

I said, "I was there first."

"He is also standing beside one of Magnus's allies—"

"And one of m'sworn enemies."

"And putting the photo commemorating the moment within the leaves of yer book."

I asked, "Hae ye run a genetic test upon him. Is he related tae us?"

"I haena been able tae—"

Quentin cleared his throat and looked down at the watch on his arm.

I said, "This is usually the first thing ye do, the simplest thing. Tis crucial."

"I canna because he has been so reclusive." She stood and walked tae the back of her chair and gripped it. "I believe he is imitating ye, Magnus, ye were once crowned king in the thirteenth century and ye are the greatest king Riaghalbane has ever known in the twenty-fourth century. Ye are the first man in the history of time tae be a king twice over."

Lochinvar said, "Dinna Ormr and Domnall do it as well?"

Lady Mairead scoffed. "They are gone, mere footnotes. They might hae attempted it, but they werna a success. The only king tae hae a kingdom at two ends of time, *successfully*, was Magnus. It might hae been short lived, but that is only because we put history tae rights. This man, who is he, *Asgall the First?* This is not a king's name, tis ridiculous! He is mocking ye and I daena like it one bit."

Quentin said, "While I appreciate that the discrepancy was found by ChronoGuard, it bothers me that we found it *after* he was crowned. What else is he up to?"

Lochinvar sipped from a drink, leaned back in the chair, lookin' relieved that Lady Mairead's attention was off him. "I daena like the look on his face. He looks like he kens he is trouble."

I scoffed. "I am not afraid of him. What vessel dost ye think he has?"

Lady Mairead said, "It could be 17.A. That one is unaccounted for, but as ye ken we daena hae all of them."

She slid the photo intae a leather-bound folder wrapped in a ribbon and passed it tae me. "This is everything Thomas has collected about him. Tis not much."

"Can I hae the psalter as well?"

"Nae, tis mine."

My brow went up. "Tis yers?"

"Aye, I am going tae hae it appraised and placed intae the museum. Ye dinna even ken it existed an hour ago, Magnus, ye daena understand its worth. I think ye will agree tis best kept in my hands."

"Fine, I agree, and this is a place tae start." I stood. "It's been a long day, we ought tae get some rest. I'll look it over and we can discuss it on the morrow."

She continued, "…also, in the folder ye will find your speech for tomorrow's Dawn Address. Ye will need tae become acquainted with it…"

"Och nae, a speech tomorrow at dawn?"

"Aye, Magnus, tis a *must*. The speech is short, but an address tae the kingdom is crucial because ye hae been away. Yer subjects wake up in the morn and ye tell them that ye are here and in charge. Tis consequential."

Everyone stood and took their leave, but as we went tae her door I turned and asked, "Just tae be clear, my Trailblazer is still in the vault and yers is safe?"

She nodded her head. "I hae taken another inventory — if there is a Trailblazer at work it must belong tae someone else."

Quentin said, "Great, I just love knowing with certainty that there are more machines."

Lady Mairead said, "Tomorrow night we will hae a fine dinner. I expect all of ye tae be well dressed."

CHAPTER 31 - MAGNUS

BILLIARDS ROOM

*I*n the corridor outside Lady Mairead's office I said, "Should we go tae the billiards room?"

Lochinvar said, "I thought ye were tired."

"Tired of hearin' m'mother tell me about all the ways the history of the world is cocked up."

They laughed as I led them down the hall tae the elevator and up tae the top floor, servants rushing ahead of us tae ready the room afore we walked in.

The room was large with classical details, columns and gold frames, and long draping curtains on the windowed wall. The opposite walls were covered with paintings of our ancestors, and antiques and sculptures were arranged all around the floor. Twas verra much like a museum, Lady Mairead had a good eye, and her collection was priceless.

When I had first arrived in Riaghalbane, this was where I had first met with Donnan — the memory caused me tae wince. At the time, every square inch of floor space had been covered with m'mother's hoard, art and antiquities stolen from time, presented tae Donnan as a way tae purchase m'succession tae his throne.

The memories of how I felt, surrounded by m'mother's weakness and m'father's cruelties, turned m'stomach. It had been a dire time.

Quentin, at the change in m'expression, asked, "Something going on, Boss?"

"This room reminds me of when I first came tae Riaghalbane and the memories are not good."

"Want to go somewhere else?"

"Nae, I will force m'self tae endure it. This is a room that exists in my castle, I ought tae be comfortable here. Tis mine. And the memories come from long ago. Lady Mairead's collection has been pared down, the rest of her hoard moved tae her museum, Donnan is long gone, and there, at the other end of the gallery, is the billiard table. I will grow more relaxed with a drink and a game. We ought tae play."

I tossed the leather-bound documents tae the coffee table and took a billiard stick from the wall tae run the chalk over the end.

~

I played Quentin first, and then Lochinvar. Then Lochinvar played Quentin while I sat on the settee with m'feet up on the antique, near-priceless table. I had the leather-bound case open on m'lap and a whisky in m'hand. Haggis had jumped ontae the settee tae put his head on m'knee.

While they played I petted Haggis between the ears and held the photo up, gazing at the face of m'auld friend, rememberin' our long discussions about time and its path. *Twas a line or a wheel?* We had gone around and around, discussin' the merits of both. I chuckled.

Quentin said, "What are you laughing about?"

"Auld arguments between friends. I had forgotten him, almost, but it's all so clear now, as if twere yesterday that I was debating him. I was so certain I was right, but yet, everything that has happened since seems tae prove he was correct. I wonder if I ought tae admit it tae him."

Quentin took his turn, smacking the cue ball deftly against his solid color, dropping it intae the corner pocket. "Normally I would say you should admit it to set your mind at ease, but since getting back there would likely take a pound of flesh, I'm going to say no, just tuck it away."

I grunted in agreement. "What do ye think this Asgall is doing?"

Quentin said, "Could simply be a time traveler who wanted to be king. He picked a moment of turmoil, seized a throne, didn't affect much, we're all still here, same memories, as far as we know, and he's got his name in the history books. Maybe that's all it is."

He chalked up the end of his cue stick.

I said, "History is long though, there is a great deal of turmoil, yet here he is standin' beside my friend — dost ye truly think tis all it is?"

"Nah, Boss, I think he's fucking with you."

I chuckled.

I watched Lochinvar take his turn and asked, "What do you think, Lochinvar? What does Asgall want? Is he content tae be in the history books, or dost he hae a larger plan?"

Lochinvar leaned on the cue stick. "It's difficult tae say without more information. Ye ought tae see if the name Asgall comes up at any other points in history."

I flipped through the files and pulled out a few pages. "Lady Mairead has done it already."

"She is a wise lady."

I joked, "She inna here, ye can speak freely."

He laughed.

I said, "There are a few profiles for an Asgall flagged as possibilities, but this is a man who has been crowned a king, who goes by one name. Why would he want tae own a ranch in Arizona in the twentieth century? Tis not big enough." I

CHAPTER 31 - MAGNUS

flipped through pages. "Here is another Asgall who owns a farm in Spain, in the nineteenth century," I turned the page over and back. "It's not the same person, inconclusive, but it's not..."

Quentin said, "How long ago are those notes from?"

I found a date on the back corner of one. "Looks as if the search was from two weeks ago."

I called out for the room's computer tae change a projected image from the shifting forest images I had asked for when we entered, tae a search for the name Asgall through history.

A list of notorious Asgalls appeared, not many, a few with Asgall as the given name, a few with it as the surname, some with Asgall as the only name. Twas difficult tae see a connection. I scowled.

Colonel Quentin said, "This is why Lady Mairead uses AI to make the list, ask her for a new list tomorrow."

"And admit I am not capable?"

I scrolled through a couple and stopped on the next. "Here is an Asgall in the seventeenth century, listed as a landowner in Portugal."

Quentin took his turn, droppin' three balls in pockets. He did a wee dance. "Lots of landowners in the history of the world."

I said, "True." And scrolled down a bit more. There was a landowner named Asgall who owned a big chunk of land in Australia.

I asked the room tae narrow the list tae Asgalls with only one name. The list narrowed down and as I scrolled through most of them looked tae be landowners or farmers or ranchers.

Quentin beat Lochinvar at the game.

Lochinvar scowled. "We ought tae play again — ye need tae give me a chance tae win."

Quentin laughed. "Nope, you gotta let me have this. Next time you can ask for two out of three, but I won this fair and square."

Then they both turned tae me. Lochinvar said, "Och nae, what's goin' on, ye look staggered."

"Dost ye see it?"

Men named Asgall owned land in every century on most continents.

Quentin said, "Not conclusive." He asked the room tae project all images of all the Asgalls so we could compare them.

It came up with zero images.

"Maybe I didn't say it right." He tried wordin' the request in different ways.

Finally he found an article from 2035, headlined: The Secretive World's Largest Landowner. The subtitle said, Hint: He's named after Scotland's most famous King, Asgall I.

I said, "Och nae. Not only is he the world's largest landowner, they are callin' him Scotland's most famous king? This is heinous."

That article had nae photographs except for the paintings and sculptures of Asgall the king, many more than Lady Mairead had put in m'file. There were nae photographs of Asgall the modern landowner.

Quentin said, "Dude, after the fourteenth century he's a ghost."

Lochinvar said, "Seems as if this is the verra thing that Lady Mairead's fancy ChronoGuard ought tae be lookin' for."

I took a sip of m'whisky and said, "Aye."

I told the computer tae send the results of the search tae m'mother's room.

A moment later there appeared a projection of Lady Mairead in her robe, readied for bed. She looked frantic. "Magnus, did ye see? His power has grown since I last looked!"

"Aye, this is why I sent it tae ye."

She patted the side of her head with a trembling hand. "I just remembered something... and it has me disconcerted."

CHAPTER 31 - MAGNUS

"What is it?"

"Did ye ever hear about what happened tae yer Great Aunt Ariana? She was Donnan's father's sister?"

"Nae, I daena think I..."

"I had nearly forgotten the story and I daena ken how, it came tae me tonight verra clearly... when she was young, a man she was familiar with, stole her away."

I said, "Och nae, what was his name?"

"Asgall."

I exhaled.

"And she was never tae be seen again! It affected the whole family, they never forgave themselves for not protectin' her, but also... when she was taken, she had a vessel in her possession."

I looked down at the papers, shakin' my head. "Och, this is how he gained it, tis a tragedy. It must be the same Asgall."

"I tell ye, Magnus, I daena want tae exaggerate, but Asgall is going tae be a great deal of trouble."

"I daena think ye are exaggeratin' at all."

Then her look sharpened. "Why are ye still up? Ye were headed tae bed!"

"I am playin' billiards, but am headed there now."

"Is that dog on my settee?"

"I think tis *my* settee, and he is my invited guest."

"Fine, I will speak tae ye on this discovery in the morn." Her video ended.

Lochinvar said, "Magnus, afore we go, the more we think of it, can we look at Mistress Ash's future?"

I said, "Tae what end?"

"I daena ken, I am worried."

I said, "I daena ken how tae make ye understand, Lochinvar. I once looked up Kaitlyn's future and discovered that she had a different husband and had borne him a bairn. It confused and devastated me, almost destroyed me."

Lochinvar shook his head. "Ye ought tae hae known twas not true — Kaitlyn would never marry another."

"Aye, I later found out that twas an altered detail tae keep us safe, and it wouldna matter anyway — everything ye learn can be changed, Lochinvar, we prove it all the time."

"But couldna the case be made that ye were able tae change time because ye knew of it, even as disruptive as it was, ye were able tae act. If ye hadna known ye might hae allowed it tae happen."

I scoffed. "I suppose, but *listen* tae me, understand I am tryin' tae protect ye — daena look. And ye canna look anyway, the moment ye told Lady Mairead of yer relationship with Ash and showed her on the projection, she put up guardrails tae keep ye from looking."

"Really, she would do that?"

"Aye, because it is so dangerous."

"Fine, I winna look."

Quentin looked from one tae another. "Man, the mood got dire. Look on the bright side, Lochie, I'm grateful for the guardrail because I don't want my surprises spoiled."

I asked, "What kind of animal will Beaty be surprisin' with ye this time?"

He said, "I'm suspicious it will be another chicken, I overheard her whispering to Noah about it the other day. I will need tae practice my surprised expression." He smiled widely and pretended, "'A chicken! Awesome, we needed another chicken!' or I will disappoint her terribly."

We all laughed.

Quentin said, "Need anything else, Magnus, need help with your speech?"

"Are ye offerin' tae deliver it for me?"

"Heck no."

"Then nae, I winna need ye... In the morn when I deliver it

just be certain tae sit in the front row and give me enough applause tae wake up the audience who I will hae lulled tae sleep."

Quentin said, "Good, because speaking of being lulled to sleep, I am headed to bed. I'm exhausted."

I said, "Good night, Quentin, but Lochinvar, can ye remain for a moment? I need tae speak tae ye."

CHAPTER 32 - ASH

PALACE SALOON

I walked into work, "Hi Do—!" He subtly shook his head. And when the big man he was talking to looked my way, Don gestured very slightly, his fingers cutting across his throat. *Be quiet? Stop talking? What did he mean? Why?*

Don said, "Hey Joanne! Good to see you, hey, can you go check in the back if Ash is here? Great!"

I walked as fast as I could past the bar and through the door to the back storeroom. My heart was racing. *What the hell was that?*

There was something about that strange guy, something dark and threatening, the way he moved slowly as he turned and stared at me as I went by.

Don had purposely gotten me out of there, was he in trouble? Why did the man ask for Ash, was that dude looking for me? Was I in trouble?

Did I need to call the police?

Don called in, "Is Ash back there?"

I called out, "No, not sure, she's not on the schedule tonight."

I could hear Don speaking to the guy, "Yeah, man, sorry, forgot what her schedule was..."

CHAPTER 32 - ASH

I looked at my phone, it was too early for our security guard to get in.

I had a gun in my bag. I unbuckled it and had my phone in one hand, my gun in the other. I stood in the hallway, just inside the storeroom door, and waited, listening, for any clue what I needed to do.

After about five tense minutes. Don pushed through the doors and came to the storeroom, looking agitated.

I said, "What was going on?"

"I don't know, Ash, that guy was effing around all up in your business and got me all freaked out — you got enemies?"

I shook my head. "No, none, I'm the nicest girl in the world — what the hell?"

"Did you recognize him? Did you see how shadowy he was?"

I shook my head, "Yeah, totally, I never got what shadowy meant. As soon as he looked at me I wanted the hell out of there."

"Yeah," he ran his hand through his hair. "Jeez." He looked at his watch. "When does security get here? Who's on the shift?"

I shrugged, "Travis I think, not sure when he's coming."

He looked up and down the hall. "Yeah, right. Travis is coming in, right."

"Man, he really rattled you — what did he say?"

"I served him first, thinking he was just a dude, needing a beer. Made him pay upfront though, because he looked shifty. Then, all casual like, he asked if I had seen a man named Magnus around. They were 'old friends,' he said. I said, 'Yeah he was just here the other night,' then he said, 'good,' but kept sitting there. My spidey senses went up. I asked if he was going to call his friend, he pretended like he hadn't heard me. Then he just kinda said, 'What about a man named Lochinvar, you seen him?' I said, 'Is he a friend too?' He smiled a really sick grin and I knew he was trouble. I was trying to figure out how to get him out of there, then he said, 'What time does Ash get in?' A beat later, you walked in. I thought fast, banking on him not knowing what you looked like. It seemed to work."

"You did think really fast, thank you, but why is he looking for me?"

"I have no idea. When does Lochie get back?"

"Two weeks, he just left yesterday."

"Maybe you ought to call his sister."

I thought about that for a moment. "Yeah, maybe, my heart is racing. He's really gone?"

"Yeah, totally gone, I looked down the street, he got in a big SUV and rode away."

"Cool, cool. So yeah, it's probably fine, right? Maybe he is a friend — or wait, what if Buck sent him? Could he have been a biker he knows? Maybe he was here to scare Lochie, that seems like a Buck thing, right?"

Don shook his head. "I mean I guess but, I don't know, Ash, *maybe...?*"

"Yeah, that's what it is, and he's gone, right? So no worries. I feel weird calling her, she's like really rich and... you know, it's *awkward*. She gave me her phone number hours ago and already I'm like, 'Hey! Just calling to check in!' Let me think about it. I'll call her if it seems necessary."

Just then the security guard entered. Don filled him in on the weirdness and the guard went on high alert, checking the locks on the doors, and standing in the sidewalk looking up and down, but there wasn't much he could do.

Customers came in and it got busy, I almost forgot what was going on, except... at one point Don came around the bar to talk to me, something he never ever did. "I just thought of something!"

"What?"

"Remember I told you he got in an SUV? It was big and black, and nice and shiny, you know the kind — he got in the back."

I stood blinking.

CHAPTER 32 - ASH

He said, "Think about it, Ash, he was *driven* here. Then driven away. He paid for his beer in cash. He has a driver. Like he was in the *mob*."

"So he was rich—"

"He for sure wasn't a friend of Buck's, I doubt Buck could afford to pay him. That theory makes no sense. Think about it, if Buck was going to threaten someone, what would the criminal he hired look like? A criminal. Like a motorcycle club member, right? Rough and sinister. This guy's clothes were expensive, his hair trimmed, he was creepy but on a whole different level."

"Good point."

"I just think you ought to call Katie, she's Lochie's sister, she gave you her number, if she *is* in the mob, and that guy is here looking for her husband and Lochie and… she needs to know. That's how it works, right?"

"I agree, I'll call her as soon as I'm off tonight, but… how do you know how the mob works?"

He said, earnestly, "Movies, and speaking of movies, you drive here? I ought to walk you out."

"Man, you are completely rattled."

"Yeah, you didn't see the look in his eyes, that dude was serious trouble."

"I drove, you can walk me to my car."

"Good."

CHAPTER 33 - MAGNUS

Lochinvar sat on a chair across from me and sighed. He looked tense, leaned forward on his knees.

I said, "What are ye upset about? I just wanted tae discuss something."

"If this is more lecturin' I daena want tae hear it. All ye auld men hae done is lecture me: I am too young tae ken what I am doin', I am too dim tae understand Ash, I am too ancient tae ken how she thinks. I hae become weary of it."

I nodded. "Aye, ye are correct Lochinvar, there has been a great deal of it. I balk at ye callin' me auld, I feel certain I am just past thirty, but how can I keep track? There is nae way tae ken, and in what truly matters, my experience, ye are correct, I might as well be as auld as the hills. I hae lived many lifetimes."

"Daena mean ye ken all there is, ye arna always right."

"Tis true, and a bit of humility would do me good. On the other hand, I am a king, sometimes king's get tae lecture." I tapped the document case beside me, "Sometimes kings must give speeches their mother has written for them."

"So ye lecture me because yer mother lectures ye?"

"Aye, but this is an excuse, I am chagrined by yer accusation.

CHAPTER 33 - MAGNUS

We, the family, just want ye tae do well, we want ye tae win the lass, because we like ye, we want the best for ye."

"I ken. I am simply weary of it. And I tell ye, she is mine, I am nae wrong on it."

"Good." I leaned forward and opened and closed m'mouth.

He chuckled. "Out with it, I am listening."

"I just want... ye ken, this life is verra dangerous. The path ahead of ye is one of violence and war, ye are m'sword, ye hae already risked yer life for m'crown, ye... ye hae pledged that ye will help maintain my throne. There is a life of uncertainty ahead of ye. And taking a wife might keep ye warm at night, but ye will hae tae consider her safety. Ye will be pulled in many different ways, tryin' tae live up tae m'demands, while keepin' her safe... I hae been there, for long years I was m'mother's sword, then m'father's champion, and all the while I wanted tae keep Kaitlyn safe. Twas verra difficult, but I was driven because twas m'own throne, I had tae win it for m'son." I shook my head. "Takin' a wife, ye will likely hae sons, sons who ye will want tae protect, a wife ye will want tae keep safe, all while fightin' alongside me for *my* throne. I am simply wondering if ye hae thought it through?"

He nodded, quietly. "Aye, Magnus, I hae thought it through. I am yer brother, I..."

I said, "Tis often brothers who are the most dangerous tae a crown. Especially brothers who hae a family, who see themselves as worthy, who are capable of violence tae gain it."

"Ye are describin' a man verra different from m'self, Magnus."

"It seems so, but ye haena met yer son yet."

"Aye, but I hae met ye, Magnus, I hae fought alongside ye. I hae seen how heavy the crown sits, ye are auld, I am young, and—"

I chuckled again. "I believe there is a decade between us, perhaps less, ye make me sound ancient."

He teased, "Tis yer *experience*. I hae seen the gravity of yer throne, and I worry about Archie growin' tae become a man who will be king — he will hae tae fight in the arena? Would Ben be his sword?" He scoffed. "Ye are right, I haena met m'son yet, but I daena want him tae be a king in this world. Not if he must fight for it, but I am not selfless, I ken that Fraoch has chosen not tae hae sons. He has pledged his allegiance and daena want tae bring sons intae it—"

"Tis not the only reason; he lost a son, now he and Hayley hae chosen tae go without. But aye, brothers and nephews are a threat. Ye ken, it has always been that way."

His hands were folded between his knees. "But tis not my way, Magnus, ye ken this. Ye hae brought me intae yer family, I hold a sword for ye, but I ken ye would draw yer sword for me as well. I ken if I hae sons they would carry the bloodline of Donnan, but Donnan picked ye tae follow his line, and yer bloodline also carries the blood of Lady Mairead—"

"She is a formidable champion."

"Aye, if I decided tae claim yer throne who would I hae in my corner?"

"That daena assuage my concerns or set my mind at ease, Lochinvar, ye might make alliances."

"But tae what end?" He shook his head. "Ye hae given me a home and a family for the first time in m'life, and until all the lecturin' this week, ye hae given me respect, and because ye arna verra good at fightin' in the arena, I get tae be a hero as well."

I laughed.

He said, "I will hae ten sons, we will give them the titles of dukes, they will be rich and hae power, yet they winna need tae fight tae keep their throne. They will be raised alongside Archie and Jack, they will think of them as brothers, they winna want tae usurp him. We are a clan and we will fight taegether tae keep the throne safe."

I said, "It's just that history shows, brothers may decide on treachery."

"History is also full of brothers who hae fought alongside

each other for common goals, ye forget this because uncles and cousins hae fought ye, but treachery is the aberration, not the norm." He shrugged. "Ye are greatly overthinkin' the fact that I hae taken a wife."

"But that brings me around tae the beginning part, keepin' her safe is likely tae break yer spirit."

"Aye, I ken, but what good is a spirit that inna tied tae earthly love, Magnus? I deserve the warm bed, I will take the heartache in trade for a slice of her pie."

I laughed. And said, "Good, and I will do all I can tae help ye as ye keep her safe by yer side."

He said, "So how much of the speech hae ye memorized?"

"Near none. I ought tae get tae it."

He left tae go tae his rooms.

CHAPTER 34 - ASGALL

THE CHAMBER OF ASGALL I, SCONE PALACE, 1296

I was sitting in my medieval office, thinkin', when Bernard knocked on the door. "Come in!"

I nodded toward m'chamberlain, askin' him tae send the chamber boy in tae build up the fire while Bernard took the leather chair across from me. I wished the chairs were more comfortable, but I had tae keep the comforts of one time away from the comforts of another. This was the curse of time travel. Some might think the issue would be the relationships ye lost as ye jumped through time, living twice as long as another man, but people were replaceable. I could find a beautiful woman in the eighteenth century and bring her with me tae the thirteenth century, and wearing appropriate clothes for the time period, she could blend in enough. Nae, the curse was the inanimate objects that wouldna blend — a proper pair of boots, a water filter, a lightbulb, a cigarette. Och nae, how I missed cigarettes. I tapped my finger on the desk, irritated. I wanted tae smoke, but couldna until this meeting was done.

Bernard opened a leather folder and spread out some pale white sheets of paper. They were from the future, out of place, but he was cautious enough. "As your real estate agent."

We both laughed.

CHAPTER 34 - ASGALL

I said, "What hae ye found?"

"A parcel of land in what will become Los Angeles, for a good price."

"I am not verra liquid..."

"If you sell the Winterborne Estate in 2050, you'd have more than enough."

"Make it happen then. I did like Winterborne, but it is full of terrible memories ever since the debacle with *Ariana*."

He didn't look up from the binder of pages. "May she Rest In Peace."

"Aye. With that sale will there be enough left for the cobalt mine in Africa?"

"Yes, your lawyers will have those contracts ready by the end of the month." He added, "Speaking of, Your Highness, I think I came up with a solution for the other issue."

I raised my brow and steadied my gaze. "My other issue?"

"You know... the fertility issue, we discussed it last year." He squirmed under my gaze.

"I ken. Ye pried into my private business."

"I asked, with so many wives, why you had not had any, you know... issue."

I raised my brow. "My wives haena performed their duties." I chuckled, "Do I sound like an ancient king?"

"Yes, it was quite impressive how stern you sounded."

"Of the six wives not one has become pregnant, they haena performed their wifely duties, though at least two of them had performed *some* duties spectacularly, just not the crucial ones."

"That was Raquel and Tiffany?"

"Aye," I smiled, "ye remember Raquel and Tiffany? Were ye coveting m'wives, Bernard? Dreamin' of bedding the wives of Asgall?"

"No sire, not at all, they just seemed, um... prone to being um..." He shifted and squirmed, while I considered the ways I might kill him.

"...prone tae being, um... seductive, desirable? Ye looked with temptation at m'wives?"

I would need tae kill him soon as he had been useful way too long. He knew details about my business, enough for me tae be counting his days, and now he had just admitted tae thinking about how I hadna sired sons, and also had been coveting my wives. "Do ye hae any more thoughts on m'wives or my cock?"

"No, sire!" He looked horrified, heat reddening his cheeks. This used tae thrill me, but he was too easy. He perhaps knew his days were numbered. "Of course not. Never. May they Rest in Peace. I would never."

I chuckled.

"So what did ye discover when ye were thinkin' on m'royal cock, my sexy wives, and my lack of sons?"

"That a way to have a son would be to um... acquire one."

I nodded. "Go on."

"I found one. I mean, a son, a boy, who you can easily.... um, acquire."

"That's why you're the best in the business."

He flipped through his pages and spread a hand across one. Then turned the book and pointed. It was a photo of a very pretty young woman.

"That is not a son."

"She is the mother. I know when the son is born so I calculated when the child was conceived. The mother is not married at the time of conception."

"Why would this matter tae me? The history of the world is full of young pretty women having their lives ruined by spreading their legs for a man. Who is the father?"

"Lochinvar Campbell, son of Donnan."

"Verra interesting! I begin tae see yer point." I picked up the photo tae admire it again. "She has a fine look, and she is coveted by Lochinvar — verra verra interesting."

I leaned back in my chair and looked up at the ceiling and

CHAPTER 34 - ASGALL

mulled it over out loud. "I could wait until the son is born — but that is more complicated — ye say they are unmarried?"

"Yes."

"Verra interesting, if I married her... when the son is born he would be mine... Ye say she is fine stock?"

"She comes from a fine family. She was a soldier."

"Ha!" I looked at the photo shaking my head. "The sons of Donnan are so predictable, everything is about battle and strength. While they are fortressing their lands, thinking about their bloodline, they daena even see me coming."

"Yes, you're growing in power."

"What does that mean? *Growing* in power? I *am* all-powerful. I own all the land. And I already *am* a king."

"I only meant from when you started to now."

"You speak of me as if I am not the largest landowner in the history of the world. 'Growing'? Do ye think I am a child?"

He shifted in his seat. "That's not what I said, I—"

"So my son would be a descendant of Donnan—"

"Step-son."

I raised my brow. "If I disappear everyone who knows, then...who would *know*?"

He gulped.

"I claim him as my son, and then we take over the future, he is installed. Nae one can complain because he's a descendant of Donnan, but he is my son, he ushers in *my* Empire. Verra interesting idea, Bernard, ye hae come verra close tae makin' yerself useful. Ye hae a plan for acquiring her?"

"I'll hire the same security we used for the Dubai vault."

"Good, they were precise and kept it verra quiet." I looked out the window at the sky and asked, "Do you think he has noticed — I am not ready tor him tae notice yet."

"Who?"

"Magnus. I am so close. I plan tae take his crown, *then* he can notice when it is too late tae stop me."

"I can not tell if he's noticed or not... we have been very

cautious, I don't see how he could..." He was squirming again. He added, "I think if you decide to take Ash McNeil, you would have a son, your power would..."

"There ye go again — ye want tae say *grow*, daena ye, Bernard?"

"I simply mean, with caution, he will notice you once you have *all* the power."

"Good, good. I agree. Just not too soon. Bring her here, I'll set her up at the brewery in Fortingall."

"Excellent plan, hidden away in the thirteenth century, he would never find her even if he started to look. Will you meet her there?"

"I will visit, make her acquaintance, but I canna imagine why I would live there. I hate that century... but I will make certain she has what she needs while we will wait for the bairn tae be born."

CHAPTER 35 - ASH

DOWNTOWN FERNANDINA BEACH

*D*on walked me to my car, parked at the end of the block. He was nervous, kept checking around. He mumbled, "You're gonna call her? Or should I call her?"

"I promise, as soon as I get home."

"Cool."

I unlocked my car and climbed in. He closed the door and tapped the roof. Then rolled his hand.

I rolled down the window.

He said, "Hey, drive me down to my truck, then I'll follow you home."

"This is a *lot*. There's no one here."

"I know you hate being babied, I get that, but my gut is telling me—"

"Look, Don, I'm armed, my house is right there, I can take care of myself. I will call you as soon as I get home."

"And then you'll call Lochie's sister."

"I promise."

He nodded, tapped the top of my car, and then rolled his hand, a gesture that meant, 'go on then, drive on through.'

I pulled from the parking lot and drove toward home. I was muttering to myself about how it was only a few blocks away, *I could have easily walked this, instead Don wanted to follow me...? Sheesh.*

The streets were slow, residential, lots of stop signs... and kinda dark. I pulled to a stop at a sign, drove through the intersection, and in the corner of my eye saw a dark SUV turn on its lights and drive away.

Just a coincidence.

But it was ominous, my heart began to race.

Oh. Oh no.

It was only three blocks to my house and I kind of wished Don had followed me home.

It came to me that I needed to call Kaitlyn Campbell and tell her what was going on. I shouldn't have put it off — it was weird, it involved her, and frankly, I felt really frightened.

I leaned over, pulled my purse up from between the seats, and rummaged through it for my phone. I glanced in the rearview mirror as I pulled up to the next stop sign. Nothing back there. *This is fine.*

I pulled into the intersection and glanced down at my phone. I opened it with my face, glanced up at the road, then opened the contacts app and found:

Kaitlyn Campbell - Lochie's sister

Lights illuminated my car. A big SUV pulled in right behind me.

I swerved, accidentally drove up on the curb and jammed on my brake, jerking my car. I had almost driven into an oak tree at five miles per hour. *Calm down, Ash, freaking out is going to get you in serious trouble...* I pushed the call button, tossed the phone in my lap, forgetting to put it on speaker, and then dug in my purse for my gun, while I yanked my wheel left, drove off the curb careening back to the road.

My phone slid to the floorboards as Kaitlyn's voice very faintly said, "Hello?"

CHAPTER 35 - ASH

I yelled so she might hear me, "This is Ash, um..." I glanced in the rear view. "...someone is following me!"

The SUV was driving slowly down the middle of the road. I came to the side of my house and thought about continuing on, but pulled into my driveway, twisting to look out the back windows, as the SUV drove slowly by... Kaitlyn's voice said, "What's happen—?"

A loud bam! on the front hood of my car.

I shrieked — A man was standing there with his hand on my hood and a gun pointed at me. Kaitlyn's voice saying, "...Ash, are you okay?"

I ducked to the side, threw my car into reverse, and gunned the engine while I was pawing through my purse for my gun.

Kaitlyn's voice, asking what was happening, faintly, as I backed up and rammed into another SUV — smash. My airbag deployed, shoving me back against the seat. My purse dumped over on the floorboards. Kaitlyn's voice, "...what is going on, tell me if you're okay!"

I was fully panicking, dark vision, a roaring sound, a racing heart. A man was standing there, next thing, my car window was broken— I leaned away, shrieking, as a man's hands reached into the car, he violently opened my door. I was being dragged out, shrieking and struggling as I felt myself leaving my seat. A hand clamped across my mouth and then there was a sharp pain, that rose up my arms and across my shoulders and down to my heart, my breathing seized. I felt so much pain, every tiny little bit of my skin and bones and muscles and sinews were shocked by agony — *is this what it feels like to die?*

I didn't remember anything else.

CHAPTER 36 - KAITLYN

HOME

I had been asleep. I didn't know why I picked up the phone or answered it, not knowing the number, but it had been Ash, screaming. And now there was nothing, no sound at all. I clicked my phone to speaker in case... anything.

Had she gotten in a car accident? I threw off my covers, clutching my phone in my hand and rushed out of the bedroom and down the stairs. Whisper-yelling, "Fraoch! Fraoch!"

Zach was sitting on a chair in the living room, a PlayStation controller in his hand. He looked up, "What...?"

"Where's Fraoch? I just got the craziest—" I put the phone to my ear and listened, nothing. I said, "Ash, you there?" I shook my head.

Zach said, "Fraoch's out on the deck."

I raced out on the deck, Fraoch was at the end of the walkway, facing out over the dunes. He turned around, as my footsteps thumped down the decking. "Thought ye went tae bed!"

"Lochie's girlfriend, Ash, just called me — she sounded scared, she..." I was out of breath by the time I reached him. "She said someone was following her... she might have been grabbed. I... don't know." I held the phone up to his ear.

He listened, then shook his head.

CHAPTER 36 - KAITLYN

"She screamed, there was a struggle, I think..." I said into the phone, "Ash...?" Then said, "Nothing, she said, 'Someone is following...' We need to go check on her. You remember where she lives?"

"Aye, let me tell security tae step up their patrols."

He and I rushed up the deck to get ready to go.

Twenty minutes later, I pulled the truck up beside Ash's house. We could see a car in the driveway, the back bumper was askew. The driver's side door was open, the headlights on.

Everything was wet and dripping. "Damn, this looks ominous."

I pulled the truck to the curb and we both climbed out. We could see inside the car now: the airbag had been deployed, the engine was still running.

I looked at Fraoch, "Oh no, what happened to her?"

"I daena ken. Ye go knock on the door. I'll look around in the car."

I strode around the house and up to the front door and knocked, a few minutes later the curtain pulled back from the window beside the door. An elderly woman's voice screeched, "What do you want? It's the middle of the night!"

I called through the window, "Um... is Ash here?"

"No! She's not home! She keeps me up all night with her coming and going!"

"You didn't hear anything odd?"

"No, there was a terrible storm. It battered the house."

"She didn't come home tonight?"

"No! Get off my porch!"

"Of course, sorry to bother you."

I left the porch and returned to the car, saying to Fraoch, who was digging around in the floorboards, "The lady there said she's not home." I looked around at the lawn. "There are tire ruts on the grass, with puddles in them — it means missing cars, a missing person, and a sudden storm."

"Great, tis clearly time travel." He passed me out a purse, full of stuff, hastily shoved in.

"What happened to it?"

"Twas all over the floor."

"Is that all of it?" There was a handgun in it, her wallet, a makeup bag.

"Aye, except..." He had his tongue out while he twisted in the seat and jammed his hand between the seats. He dug up a phone and passed it to me.

I spoke into my phone and my voice came out of Ash's phone.

Then a truck pulled up behind ours. I peered, "Who's that?"

Fraoch climbed from the car.

The bartender from the Palace, Don, stepped out of his truck. "Hey Katie, hey Fraoch, what's going on — where's Ash?"

Fraoch said, "I was goin' tae ask ye the same thing."

He strode up to the car. "Jeez, she was in an accident? Where is she?" He put both his hands on his head.

I said, "I don't know."

"Dammit, I knew I should follow her home, oh man, did you check at her house?"

I nodded, "She hasn't been home."

"Shit. She promised to call me, she didn't call. She... Did that guy kidnap her, you think?"

I said, "What guy? We don't know anything, she called me and it sounded like something terrible was happening."

"This guy came by the Palace tonight, he was looking for Ash, he asked about Lochinvar... I told her to call you, Katie, I was sure he was going to be trouble."

He dropped his hands. "We gotta call the police."

I looked at Fraoch.

Fraoch said, "We canna involve the police, Don, tis a problem for us."

CHAPTER 36 - KAITLYN

"No, no, that's not good, what are you suggesting — that we just let her be kidnapped?"

Fraoch said, "Nae, we will get her back, we ken we will, but we canna hae the police involved."

Don huffed. "I knew this was all sketchy, all of it."

I said, "Did the guy say anything else?"

"He said he was Magnus's friend — are you sure we can't involve the police?"

I shook my head. "Look, we are going to get her back, Lochie won't rest until he does. Just, give us a few days, we'll find her."

"Am I going to get in trouble? If I don't call this in, is this going to come back to haunt me? What if she blames me for not calling it in?"

"She won't, I promise. Look, can I get your phone number? You can call me if anything else happens, I'll call you if we learn anything." I pulled my phone from my pocket and he gave me his number and I typed it in. Then I texted: Me, Katie.

His pocket beeped when he received the text and he nodded.

Fraoch said, "I will make certain she kens ye wanted tae call them. I will take full responsibility for decidin' not tae."

Don nodded. "Damn, this sucks. I wish I had been here."

Fraoch said, "They would hae taken ye as well. Trust me, ye daena want tae be involved."

Fraoch held out a hand and began sort of herding Don back to his truck. "We will get her back, I promise. We will all come down tae the Palace and hae a beer tae celebrate."

Don climbed in the truck. "Okay man, yeah... how many days?"

Fraoch had his hand on his door. "Give us three days, if she inna back we will go tae another plan."

"Okay, sounds good." He started his truck.

Fraoch said, "And daena tell anyone."

Don nodded, "Yeah, I get it. I do not want to be involved." He drove away.

. . .

I closed the door on Ash's car and locked it.

We took her purse and stuff and climbed into our truck to drive home.

He asked, "Dost ye think Don will be quiet?"

"Yeah, he thinks we're a crime family or something. He doesn't want to cross us."

Fraoch shrugged. "He is right in it."

"I guess he kind of is."

He exhaled, "I suppose our peace is over, there is time travel afoot."

I said, "Dammit, so what do we do?"

"We need tae move the family tae the safe house."

"I think we need to take everyone to Riaghalbane. We don't know what's going on, we need Magnus and Quentin to know."

"Aye, as soon as we are home we will pack tae go."

CHAPTER 37 - MAGNUS

RIAGHALBANE

I woke up and made my Dawn Address tae the nation. I spoke at length on the State of the Kingdom, then I laid out m'plan for the comin' year. I followed the address with a prayer, sayin' that with the dawn I prayed for peace for our kingdom, safety, and the wellbein' of the citizens of Riaghalbane. That, along with the rising sun, we must be filled with hope for the comin' day, our minds full of gratitude for our blessings and the peace reigning over the lands.

The speech was well received and in the applause I understood the importance of it. Quentin clapped a hand on my shoulder, "That was good, Boss, I think Lady Mairead was right."

"Aye, but daena tell her."

He said, "Never."

I met with Quentin, Lochinvar, Lady Mairead, and my advisors over breakfast. But once the meal was over, after a great deal of coffee, all the advisors had moved on tae other purposes and we were left tae speak.

Lady Mairead leaned back in her chair. "Och, I thought they would never leave, tis so tedious tae listen tae their dithering and pontificating when what we really need tae ken is did ye learn anything else?"

"Nae."

"This is madness."

I said, "Aye," then asked the room tae project last night's search.

The room's voice asked, "Would you like new search results, Your Majesty?"

"There are new results, since last night?"

"Yes, Your Majesty."

The results were projected up on the wall. Lady Mairead said, "Slow scroll," and the results went by, one after another, the results of Asgall, landowner, interspersed with headlines that read: 'Secretive...' and '...reclusive...'

I said, "What are we tae do?"

She scowled.

"I feel as if I hae a new nemesis and I had nae idea he existed."

Quentin said, "You're a king, you rule a kingdom, you have all the power in the world, but then check this guy, a secretive ass has been buying real estate and gathering power. While you're famous and your name is in the books, he's hidden."

"Hidden, except for that he is a king." I said, "And his power stretches verra far back tae the thirteenth century. Och nae, much farther back than I ever wanted tae go again."

Quentin said, "Yep, I'm far more comfortable with a bookend at the year 1557, when we go past that *everything* always turns bad."

"He has made great use of a Trailblazer, I believe."

Lady Mairead said, "It's infuriating." She looked around "Let this be a warning tae ye — we hae a cruel upstart and usurper, who we must contend with, *again*."

I said, "He began amassin' power back in the thirteenth century, yet he is an 'upstart'?"

She smoothed her skirts. "Ye know as well as I do that it

daena matter, in the circular nature of time, ye were king first and last, he would do well tae—"

I was watching the projection, the Asgall results scrolling by, noticed something and commanded, "Stop!"

She said, "Magnus, daena boss me!"

I said, "Nae, I dinna mean ye, I meant 'Look, there is an *Asgall Holdings* address, dost ye see?"

There was a result that showed an image of a Celtic knot. The words Asgall Holdings ran through the middle.

She read over the result. There was a description, a short history, a mention that the company was active in the early twentieth century. I asked for more information, but there were nae records of the company except when it appeared decades later. The computer seemed tae believe that the Asgall Holdings of the early twentieth century and the Asgall Holdings in other centuries were not connected, until Lady Mairead asked the computer tae compare and tell us the chance of it being the same company. It gave us a possibility of fifty-three point nine percent.

She said, "Good enough. I hae a home in New York in that time, I will go and research about him—"

I teased, "Ye could stay here and research on the computer."

She said, "Daena be ridiculous, Magnus, tis far better tae go like a civilized person, and ask the people who are involved in the markets. They will ken far more than this God-awful machine. This will be a trip of discovery. Besides I hae been needing a vacation."

I said, "Tis unlikely that a reclusive man will divulge secrets so easily."

"Ye are all missing the point." Her arm spread out toward the projection. "This is his first sign of weakness. He has made a mistake having a public company in New York in a century in which I dwell on my off days. I hae numerous friends who are verra well connected. If Asgall has made such a large mistake at this time, he will hae made more. The only question is after we discover where he is, what are we going tae do?"

"I suppose we will need tae deal with him. I haena decided if I will end his company with regulations, take his power by seizing his land, or tae battle him in the courts."

Lochinvar said, "Tis too civilized, we ought tae draw swords against him."

Quentin said, "He is a ghost. It's hard to draw swords on a ghost."

Lochinvar said, "But we ken he was a king in 1296, I ken where he was crowned. I can go right there and deal with him."

Quentin said, "Put that in your back pocket, it might get to that, but it is not that simple, we would have to test the path first, we are assuming he used the Trailblazer, but we don't know for sure. The last thing you want is to get stuck somewhere in the past. And you don't want to rely on *me* to use the Trailblazer to rescue you. I like you but it *sucks*."

Lochinvar said, "Colonel Quentin, are ye sayin' if I am stuck in the past ye winna rescue me?"

"No, of course I would, but I would complain the whole time. Let's do simple first."

Quentin was staring at the scrolling results. "Do you see that one?" He pointed at one that said: Asgall Holdings, ownership of Dunkeld Cathedral and surroundings.

I said, "Och nae, I haena seen that yet, he is buyin' land around Loch Tay? Did ye see it, Lady Mairead?"

"I am certain I would hae mentioned it. Until now there has been nae record of—" Her eyes went wide as she read the entry. "Look! They are calling him one of the most important landowners in Scottish history! And it says he was named after Asgall I, one of the most important Scottish kings! This is *unconscionable*, the most important Scottish king? Tis outrageous! Ye

CHAPTER 37 - MAGNUS

were king in 1290, ye hae been a lord, och nae, this is unbelievable!"

Lochinvar said, "But Magnus's time as king has been forgotten."

"I ken! I ken it is, but how are they listing this Asgall as important enough tae be called the most important Scottish *anything*. This is humiliating!" She raised her chin, "He is impersonating ye, trying tae overcome ye."

I asked, "Tae what end?"

"Tae *yer* end."

I sighed. "We hae arena battles. If he wants a battle he can come and fight me."

"He has nae claim tae yer throne. What if instead he just buys all the land, owns all the property, amasses power, then voila, he becomes king?"

"How?"

She leaned back and looked at the projection as it slowly scrolled through all of Asgall's holdings. "I am not able tae think like a diabolical madman, but I daena like the look of any of this."

I said, "Ye greatly underestimate yer diabolical madness."

She raised her glass toward me.

I said, "I think if ye put all that I own ontae a list and scrolled it as we ate our lunch, it would be much longer."

"But ye daena own a bit of land before the eighteenth century, Magnus! We need tae diversify!"

An urgent alert sounded, a warning that a storm had hit.

Colonel Quentin immediately contacted the commander on the west wing. But we could already see which vessel was in use.

I shoved my chair back as I stood. "Tis Kaitlyn."

The alert sounded in the room: "Your Majesty, the Queen and the Royal Family have arrived."

Lady Mairead asked, "Why, under the heavens, did they come?"

Colonel Quentin said, "They would only come if it's an emergency."

We left the dining room, rushing down the corridors toward the landing on the west roof.

I was met by a commander near the doors. I asked, "Who is it?"

"The Queen, the Princes and Princess, the—"

I threw open the doors to see my entire family, surrounded by my guards. Some of the kids were up sitting on stretchers. Isla was wailing. I saw Beaty holding Noah and most frightening of all, James and Sophie, holding her newborn. It must hae been terrifyin' tae move an infant who was only a few days auld.

Haggis bounded past me toward Archie and Ben tae jump at their feet, though Archie was slumped over lookin' verra injured. I pushed through the crowd toward Kaitlyn and swept her and Jack intae m'arms, holding ontae them both, then putting out an arm for Isla, with a "Wheesht, lass, ye are goin' tae frighten yer brother — Kaitlyn, what happened?"

"Something happened to Ash, it's connected to us, it's…" She said this with her face pressed against my shoulder.

I said, "Och nae," my eyes swept the landing, to see Lochinvar, giving a hand to Fraoch, helping him up.

Fraoch was talking, Lochinvar exclaimed, "Nae! What happened tae her?"

Lady Mairead behind me said, "Magnus! Look at all the bairns, whatever is goin' on?"

I said, "Tis the normal amount, ye forget yerself."

"But where will we put all of them? We daena hae a nursery!"

I asked, "Is everyone well? We hae physicians if ye need medical attention."

Archie said, "I hurt everywhere."

"Where is yer gold thread?"

Kaitlyn said, "We had to make sure Junior had one, Archie opted to go without."

CHAPTER 37 - MAGNUS

Lady Mairead said, "Good lord, the *Prince* went without? I hae heard *everything*."

I squeezed Archie's shoulder and kissed his head. "Och, I am proud of ye, ye are a brave lad."

He put up his arms and though he was such a large lad I kent he needed some attention, so I picked him up in m'arms without making a fuss. He put his head on my shoulder.

Fraoch picked up Isla and we all crossed the landing tae the door, then went down the long corridor.

Lady Mairead said, "We are headed tae our war room?"

"Nae, we will go tae the Gallery, there will be plenty of comfortable seats, a billiard table for the boys—"

"Think of the art!"

"I winna give them a football, likely."

"And the dog — there is now a pig and a chicken! I am surprised ye dinna drag the horses intae the palace."

"Aye, there are also a great many people who have fled their home out of fear." I held the door open for her, watching over the heads of m'family as Colonel Quentin was giving orders, putting guards at every door, sending m'military intae high alert.

He had Lochinvar helping him, which was good, or Lochinvar would be losing his mind while we got the bairns settled. I asked, "Lady Mairead, are ye goin' tae helpfully listen tae what has happened, or continue complaining? Because I am certain I can hae ye sent from the room."

CHAPTER 38 - MAGNUS

THE BILLIARD ROOM - RIAGHALBANE

As Sophie sat down, Lady Mairead asked, "When was he born?"

Sophie said, "He is three days auld."

Lady Mairead put her hand out and stroked his head, "He is a verra fine boy — his name is James Cook the second, but ye will call him Junior?"

Sophie said, "Aye, Lady Mairead."

"Good, he looks as if he will be verra strong." She plucked a hair from his head.

The bairn screwed his face up as if tae cry.

"Mother!"

Lady Mairead raised her chin and took the most expensive chair, the one that was covered in silk and near a thousand years auld. "I needed this for the genetic test. We must hae a record of all in the family."

James was furious, "Damn, you just yank hair right off a newborn's head?"

She said, "A little discomfort is necessary sometimes, even bairns must know."

Sophie soothed the baby. James shook his head, "Jesus, I forgot how absolutely insane it was to spend time with you,

CHAPTER 38 - MAGNUS

Lady Mairead."

She said, "Ye and I hae had tae come tae many agreements through the years, Master Cook, and this is one of them, as long as Junior is a part of the family, he is also my concern. I will take a hair if I need one."

I said, "Perhaps, and I am sayin' it with all due respect, if ye become inclined tae cause sharp pain and distress tae a bairn ye ought tae ask the mother first, so she might be ready tae sooth him after. Or ye might use scissors."

She rolled her eyes as she called for a servant tae take the hair tae be tested. We all settled on settees and chairs, the kids tucked into arms held on laps as they recovered from the ordeal.

Lady Mairead, tae make nice said, "Kaitlyn, remind me, I will give ye another thread so Prince Archibald winna hae tae go without."

"Thank you, Lady Mairead, that would be appreciated."

Colonel Quentin and Lochinvar rushed in and Lochinvar said, "What happened tae Ash?"

Fraoch said, "She called Kaitlyn and said she was being followed, she was frightened, then she screamed and—"

Lochinvar said, "Och nae!"

Kaitlyn said, "It was very hard to hear her, she didn't have me on speaker phone, so I don't really know what happened. Fraoch and I went to her house to check on—"

Lochinvar said, "What did ye find, is she alright?"

Fraoch looked uncomfortable, he shook his head.

Kaitlyn said, "Ash is missing, Lochie, I'm so sorry. She was pulled from her car. It looks like there was a struggle. And it was wet from a storm. The bartender from the Palace, Don, drove up to check on her, he was worried because a man had come by earlier, looking for her. He said the man mentioned you and Magnus. I don't know who it was, but it was definitely a time traveler who took her."

"Why would someone take her? What is happening? Och

nae, tis just like Magnus's aunt, ye ken, Lady Mairead? Tis like the story ye told."

Lady Mairead shook her head, "Och nae, this is dire."

Colonel Quentin said, "I really really don't understand how we're just now hearing this. We have all this tech. We're in the future, how did we not know?"

I said, "Tis difficult tae see a disappearance, there was nae police report, our program dinna pick up on it."

I asked the room tae turn on the projection and tae put it on information about Ashley McNeil. It was the same photos and information from the night before.

Lochinvar walked up to the projection and stood looking at her face. "There's nae mention of her disappearance? What good is this?"

I said, "Lady Mairead, can ye remove the guardrail on the information?"

She sighed, and asked the room, "Please turn off the guardrail I placed upon the records of the person, Ashley McNeill."

The voice in the room asked for Lady Mairead's security word.

She glanced around then said, "Fionn." She said tae me, "Daena remember it, Magnus, I will change it by the end of the day."

I nodded, "Ye say that every time, yet ye never do."

She raised her chin.

I said, "Daena worry on it, I winna remember it."

"Good."

The projection came up with no results for Ashley McNeil after the date she went missing.

Colonel Quentin stood near the results asking for addresses, phone numbers, and the names of Ash's family members. I said, "What are ye checkin' now?"

He said, "I'm seeing her military records and health reports, even pulled up her school grades."

CHAPTER 38 - MAGNUS

Kaitlyn stood beside him, asking the computer to show Ash's Facebook, Instagram, and X accounts. She scrolled through her Instagram profile, then said, "They all stop the night she was taken."

Quentin said, "Yep, she disappeared."

Lochinvar looked from Kaitlyn tae Quentin and back at the projection. Shaking his head, "She canna be gone! Did she die?"

I said, "I regret the guardrail now, if we had seen this last night we would already be searchin' for her... Lochinvar, this is where the trouble comes in, ye canna speculate — there are nae records, but we daena ken why — this daena mean she is lost for good."

He looked like he was in shock. "Ye think we will find her?"

I said, "Aye. I feel certain her disappearance is connected tae Asgall Holdings and King Asgall—"

Kaitlyn asked, "King Asgall?"

"Aye, we hae a new enemy, he owns a company in the twentieth century, he is a landowner all around the world, and he is a king of Scotland in the thirteenth century."

Her face went pale. "A king, like you were a king?"

"Aye, tis uncomfortably similar tae my own history, tis either mimicry or subterfuge, either way he is causin' a great deal of trouble." He glanced at Lochinvar, who looked agitated. "But we *will* find her."

"Like Donnan's father found his sister? He didn't, she was never found again! Lady Mairead said it, I heard it right here!"

I said, "Well, it wasn't our family lookin' for her. I will not rest. Are ye goin' tae rest?"

"Nae."

"Good." I asked the computer projection, "Shew me Asgall Holdings and any connection tae Ashley McNeil, or her nickname Ash."

The voice in the room responded, "There is no direct connection. The indirect connections are the Ash tree, represented as the Tree of Life on the brand logo of Asgall Holdings, one of the world's oldest and most esteemed companies."

There was a projection of a Celtic knot with a tree trunk in the middle, roots below, limbs above, knotted taegether.

The room's voice continued, "According to a New York Times article from November 7, 1912, entitled *The Reclusive Land Baron and the Ash Tree*, the branding of Asgall Holdings was designed to honor the wife of the Scottish King, Asgall I, who sat on the throne in the late thirteenth century.

Lochinvar had gone pale, he blinked. "I told her she was named after Yggdrasil, the Tree of Life, och nae, tis her."

I asked, "We daena ken this yet, Lochinvar, we must continue tae look, there are inconsistencies and—"

"Tis clear as day. Her name is Ash, like the tree, the tree in the Tree of Life. I told her she was the tree of life and she is calling herself —" His eyes went wide. "Dost ye think she is sending a message? She is telling us that she is there!"

I chewed my lip. "It might be, aye, I suppose..."

I asked the room, "Are there any marriage records for Asgall I or the founder of Asgall Holdings?"

The computer responded, "There are no known marriage records for Asgall I beyond a name, Ash, unknown surname. The records also show that the founder of Asgall Holdings had a wife and son."

I said, "Names?"

The projection changed to a photograph of a woman with a young boy on her lap, in the back of a limo. She had her arm up blocking her face. "Is this the only photo?"

The voice said: Yes.

Then there appeared an obituary: Ash (no known last name), deceased at age twenty-five. Wife of reclusive land baron Asgall, CEO of Asgall Holdings. She leaves behind an infant son, Dominion Mac Asgall.

Lochinvar said, "Is that Ash — we found her? Och nae, she's dead? I am too late?"

I said, "This is… this simply shows what *might* happen. This was announced in the twentieth century, but…" I asked the computer tae shew me her burial place and found nae results. "This is all inconclusive."

The kids ran around the room. The staff brought us drinks and snacks, those that had traveled were lying back on the cushions, recuperating. Lochinvar was up, pacing the room, filled with angst, while Quentin and I stood shoulder tae shoulder and I called out requests tae the computer.

Lochinvar asked, "How could she marry him?"

Kaitlyn said, "Are we even certain it's her? This is likely a coincidence. The female name Ash must be fairly common."

I had m'arms crossed on my chest and my mind spinning. I asked the room, "Shew me a photo of Dominion, son of Asgall," and, "Show me the birth certificate of Dominion…" and then back tae the photo of the woman in the back of the limo. "Can ye tell if this is her?"

Lochinvar shook his head.

I asked for more and more leads, but everything seemed a dead end.

Lady Mairead asked the computer, "Can ye compare everything ye ken about Ash McNeil, born in 2002 and Ash married tae Asgall of Asgall Holdings in the twentieth century, and give me a percentage of probability that they are the same person."

The voice in the room answered, "The probability is a 50.24% match."

She brushed her hands. "Tis the same person then. We hae solved it."

Kaitlyn said, "But it's very close to fifty-fifty."

"Aye, but think on it, without birth certificates, marriage licenses, burial grounds or photographs, and without the two people being alive in the same century, our computer believes it is more likely than not. This is good enough."

Emma said, "I guess so…"

"Tis clear!"

Kaitlyn said, "So we think Asgall definitely took Ash?"

I nodded.

Our eyes drew tae Lochinvar, standing, starin' at the projection, his face with an expression of deep sadness. "She is gone, nae more? I left her and allowed her tae be kidnapped and murdered? Or tae marry and hae a bairn with someone else and live and die without me? What am I tae do?"

Junior began tae cry.

Kids squabbled over the billiards game.

The room had taken on a chaotic energy and Lochinvar was feelin' despair.

I said, "We will get her back." I ran my hand over my face. "I promise ye, Lochinvar, we will. We need tae arm ourselves, we will go as soon as we gather our—"

Fraoch clapped his hand on Lochinvar's back. "Come with me tae the church, Og Lochie, we need tae clear yer mind before battle."

Lochinvar nodded.

I said, "Dost ye need me tae come?"

Fraoch shook his head. "Nae, rest for a bit, Og Maggy, I need tae speak with him alone."

As they walked from the room, I said, tae the rest of the group, my voice raised over the wailin' bairn, "I daena think there is anything else we can discern here, we must decide where we will look first — we need tae think, and we need tae collect ourselves. We will hae rooms assigned for everyone. I am certain ye are all hungry, we will gather in the dining room at five o'clock for dinner."

CHAPTER 39 - ASH

THE PAST

*E*verything hurt. I woke up in the dark, very dark, dark, total darkness. I said, in a whisper, "Hello?" No sound. Or rather, no sound nearby, I...I was under something very heavy. Like a weighted blanket... I inhaled. It smelled old and musty, thick and not laundered... a piece of it tickled my nose. A fur? The top of my head was cold in the air. Where the heck was I? I put out my hand and felt a cold wall beside me.

There was no hum. It sounded like I was camping in nowhere, just the sounds of night, and a... faintly, the lowing of a cow. The steps of an animal.

I felt blind. I concentrated, *adjust your eyes...* but I couldn't make out anything. I moved my head around, looking out different directions, and noticed a pale gray space. A window. I focused on it but couldn't determine anything outside.

I was in a cabin of some kind. Was I in the woods? *Oh my God, I was being trafficked.*

I started to panic, stomach dropping, heart racing, tried to draw in breath, but it was short and ragged. I was frozen, but wanted to look out that window. My eyes faced it, but I couldn't make myself move. It was like being separate from my body. I needed to see. I needed to look.

Go go go go.

If I was in Yulee or some other place in the county I needed to get the heck out of here.

Go go go.

I could get out the window. I could smash the glass.

Go.

I lay there staring at the square of paleness, thinking of nothing but the racing-heart horror of what might be happening to me. Sound was muffled, except I could hear my breaths and racing heart pounding in my ears.

But then I calmed myself. *Deep breath, in, then out.*

This was fubar, but I could handle it. *Go.*

I threw back the bed covers and scrambled up from the bed. I was in my boots, wearing my work clothes still, a long cargo skirt and a short sleeve shirt, and immediately started shivering. I rushed to the window, but it looked weird. I pressed my hands against it, and it felt like parchment paper over an open window with no glass. *Weird.* I pushed on it, and tore it away from the side. No wonder it was cold in the room — it was a cold night, brisk and chilly.

A cloud moved away from the moon and the landscape glowed. I could see a grassy lawn, and ringing that, high timber walls. Beyond, I could see the tops of dark trees, *a forest?* Did I recognize it?

I held the parchment up and looked to the right and left, seeing a few low buildings. I recognized nothing.

I tried to think of where it could be that there was a timber wall... nowhere?

I had explored a lot of Nassau county but didn't remember anything like this at all. Also, chillingly, the air felt different, the smells. It smelled disgusting, like I was on a farm, but not in the salt air Florida way. This smelled musty and old and blatantly gross and disgusting.

I would need to run.

I let the parchment flap down and felt toward the posts on

CHAPTER 39 - ASH

the bed corners, some kind of drapery hanging on them. I felt around on the bumpy mattress for anything to wrap around myself for warmth, finding in the heavy pile a wool blanket. I pulled it around my shoulders and felt along the wall opposite me, looking for a door. What felt like branches brushed the top of my hair. I pulled my hair free and my hands hit what felt like wood, rough wood, and I felt for a doorknob of some kind, finding just more wood. I pressed, it didn't move. I tried to pull, it wouldn't move. Maybe I was wrong. I felt more, heading to the right — banging my knee on a low wooden piece of furniture.

Ouch!

I rubbed it, trying to listen. *Did anyone hear it, was there no one here?*

No one came. I must not have had a guard.

This was good.

I would escape, run until I found a house with someone home and bang on the door. I ignored the fact that there were some big forests in Florida. I was capable of a long walk. This would be doable — if I could get out.

I tried for a few more minutes, but couldn't find a door so I returned to the window. I pulled up the parchment again and looked out, the ground seemed like it was right there, just a few feet down. I hoisted myself up, put one leg out, had to bunch my skirt up to get my legs spread enough to cross the sill, and quickly brought up my other leg to step down. I was out!

The sky above me was lightening by degrees... it made me think that dawn was on its way, maybe, but I couldn't be sure.

But there weren't any lights illuminating anything, and I sensed that I was surrounded by walls, buildings, and by the stench, some kind of stables nearby. Or a porta-potty. But also it smelled like fire. There was a fire somewhere near — which would mean heat and warmth, but also, guaranteed that was where the men who had...

It was hard to say it — I was kidnapped? What kind of

horrible nightmare was this? What evil? How had I let this happen, I had been armed! I should have killed that guy. All those guys.

But I couldn't dwell on it, I had to get out of here. I walked, as briskly as I could, forward, my hands out, going through darkness toward the wall. Stumbling over a bush, I crouched quietly and listened. Then headed to the left of that until I got to the blackness of the wall. I felt along it and my excitement built. I would get out, *just follow this fence.* I walked with my shoulder against it until I came to a corner, then I followed it in another direction, another corner. *How many?* I huffed. *Was I going in a circle?*

I abruptly came to a stone wall. I crouched and followed it around, but I couldn't tell where it was going and I was exposed with nothing to hide behind.

I had no idea where I was and was lost in a freaking circle. *Think, Ash. What do you do?*

I was shivering — *You can't figure out how to get out.*

Yes I can. I'm just cold, I will get out.

Crouched, with my back against the wall, I needed to calm myself. I breathed, in and out with my eyes closed, and then opened my eyes. I could see my hand against my knee. *Was dawn coming?*

If I just waited for a few minutes, it would be easier to see.

It would also be easier to *be* seen. I ran to the shadow of the timber wall and waited for the sun.

Ahead of me was a cluster of low buildings with thatched roofs. It seemed almost medieval — was I in St Augustine? Or what about north, was I in Savannah? How long had I been out?

My eyes swept the courtyard and then saw a young woman in a long skirt, looking Amish or something, oh damn, was this a cult? I pressed closer to the wall, trying to hide in a shadow, averting my head. If I didn't look at her, maybe she wouldn't see me. *Was there an east coast cult of some kind, had I been kidnapped into it?*

CHAPTER 39 - ASH

I wasn't hiding very well, because the woman saw me and rushed up, speaking very loud and very fast. The issue was…

I couldn't understand a word.

"Carson a tha thu an seo!" She repeated it again, "Carson a tha thu an seo!" Her voice sounded far away, everything was dark around the edges, the sound of my breathing crowded out everything else.

I was terrified.

She wasn't menacing though, she seemed to be trying to take care of me. *Just like a cult.*

She spoke in rapid-fire gibberish with guttural noises, pulling my blanket around my shoulders, tugging me away from the wall, hugging around my shoulders, she led me toward the buildings.

Her voice grew soothing and low. She did seem to want me to be okay, but it was hard to think— I was going to pee on myself. I couldn't think of escape or running, or… "Bathroom? I need to use the bathroom, I need a toilet." She looked at me blankly, shaking her head, leading me toward a low building with a thatched roof.

This had to be some weird dream, but it felt so real, the pain in my bladder really hurt, badly.

I reached up to touch the thatching as I ducked to go through the short door. *Lochie wouldn't fit in here.* The room was cold, she rushed to the fireplace and began shoving sticks and kindling in it. I heard a flint strike as she tried to build a fire.

This was the room I escaped from. It was very dark around the edges, as if there was a smoke filter on everything. There was the bed, a tapestry hanging on the wall, a rug on the floor, a table and a couple of chairs. A wooden chest at the end of the bed.

I said again, "I *really* need a bathroom."

She looked at me blankly.

I acted out, my hands waving down in front of my skirt. She nodded, stood, rushed to my side, grasped my elbow, and pulled me to a bowl in the corner.

My eyes went wide. "Here? Here in this bowl?"

She nodded her head, speaking fast and using her hands to mimic raising skirts and crouching. Then she rushed back to the hearth.

I pulled up my skirt, pulled down my underwear, and held it out of the way as I crouched over the bowl. I peed, feeling a great deal of relief, and then a rush of consciousness now that the pressing urge was gone — *where the hell was I?*

The door opened, another young woman entered with a tray of food she placed on a table near the fireplace. She set a place. *Whose meal was it, mine?*

I pooped. In front of the two women who were holding me hostage. I was usually not very regular, but here I was pooping at the worst possible time.

No freaking toilet paper.

I said, "I need something to wipe with."

They both looked at me, looks of confusion, then one rushed over, it seemed to be the way she moved, rushing around. She picked up a bit of moss from the nearby corner, and held it in front of me, speaking fast. She was muffled. My vision was effed up, it was like I was wearing sunglasses indoors. I wondered if I had been drugged.

I put out my hand. She dropped the moss into it. I wiped my bottom with moss and tossed it into the bowl.

One of the women gestured me over to a bowl to wash my hands. The water was scented pleasantly, and I was handed a piece of linen to dry them.

Then they both bowed and gestured toward the wooden plate with what looked like stringy meat and a hunk of bread. There was a pewter mug beside it, no utensils.

When I didn't go toward the table, one of the women gestured again. The other smiled pleasantly, and waved both her hands toward the table. I went closer, but when I didn't sit down to eat the first woman used her hands to gesture eating.

I sank into the chair. Behind them the door was ajar, I could

CHAPTER 39 - ASH

just pull it open, walk out and leave, but I didn't know where the outer door was.

I said, "Can you tell me what's going on?"

Both the women shook their heads, not as if they couldn't tell me, but because they clearly didn't understand me. They both bowed.

The heat from the fire warmed me. I looked over the unappetizing food. I was hungry but so scared that my stomach was upset.

I was in a medieval reenactment of some kind, or a cult, and the two women seemed nice enough: They were feeding me, they weren't causing me immediate harm, but they couldn't or wouldn't actually communicate. And none of this made sense.

But I calculated the steps to the door. There was a hiding place in the corner. There wasn't much that would make a weapon...

I gazed around the room as I chewed the crusty bread. The meat was poultry of some kind, gamey tasting, like a dark meat from a turkey. It all needed spice.

I could pick up this chair and swing it at this woman while her back was to me. I could knock them both out with the candlestick...

I drank from the mug. It was a dark ale, with a thick head. I was tense and frightened, but the warmth of the hearth, the bread, and the stout beer worked to calm my nerves. The mug had a bit of heft to it, I could use it as a weapon.

The women left, thankfully, carrying my poop bowl out to dump it, leaving me alone in this 'kidnap-house-of-horrors' to finish eating.

The men who had grabbed me had been dressed in modern clothes, I felt sure. They had been driving SUVs, they hadn't been old fashioned like this. These people were pretending to be in some ancient kind of land... I was wracking my brain for a memory of some kind of cult in the county — I grew up in a small town, I didn't understand why

I had never heard of any religious communes. How had this place been kept secret?

After I finished eating I stared into space. *How would I get out of here?* I needed to find a phone, a gun, anything to use to call for help.

The two women returned, one carrying a bundle of cloth, the other bringing a pitcher of water. They gestured for me to stand and came at me with a wet rag.

I shook my head. They made hand gestures for washing my hands and face.

I looked down. My clothes were gross, my arms were filthy, likely my face was equally bad. Fine. I stuck out my hands. One ran the cloth over my hands and arms, the other started washing my face. I spluttered, and tried to turn my head. I would not be manhandled, but they manhandled me anyway, holding my arms they washed me without my consent.

Then I pulled away and went and stood against the wall near the table with the mug. They both held up a dress and urged me with wild gestures to take my shirt off. They wanted to dress me.

Over my dead body.

I shook my head and held up the mug, menacingly.

They gave up, laying out the clothes on the bed and then bowing and leaving the room.

I looked down at what I was wearing and over at the clothes they had left out for me, they did look warmer, the fabric was pretty, but it would be a mistake to put it on — if this was a cult then putting on their uniform was the first step in joining.

I would not.

I approached the bed and felt the fabric and considered. The weird part was that this dress was prettier than theirs.

I still would not wear it.

Even though the dress had long sleeves and would definitely be warmer than the t-shirt I was wearing. There was a cape, but even that was a no.

The skirt I was wearing was dark gray, and had drawstrings

CHAPTER 39 - ASH

that cinched up the side, I loosened those, so that the bottom hem went straight across, covering my ankles, but that was all I could do to get warm.

I strode over to the door and found it unlocked. I pushed it open and stood in the doorway, looking around at the buildings and the timber walls. My sight was dark and dim, my hearing muffled. *What did they do to me? And who were they?*

I could leave. I could just go. Down at the end of the timber wall I could see what might be a gate. Would there be guards? I was so confused. *Where would I go?*

I would decide once I was out.

I kept the door ajar but returned to the interior of the room and noticed a piece of paper stuck in the folds of the dress. I pulled it free, unfolded it, and in a looping script it said:

Make yourself at home.

I dropped it to the ground, my hands trembling and looked around the room.

I was completely alone, kidnapped, and probably something terrible was about to happen. They wanted to dress me like some kind of princess. Why on earth would they give me a dress? I would not comply.

CHAPTER 40 - ASH

◈

THE WAY PAST

I needed a weapon.

I looked around the room, there was nothing good enough. I went back to the doorway and stood looking out, taking stock. I could see the gate in the distance.

Between me and the gate were numerous people, all dressed in this odd medieval way, dusty and dirty and drab.

A man walked by and bowed as he passed.

Weird.

I would find a weapon of some kind, then I would head toward the gate. I walked across the compound, my arms hugging my middle, shivering in the cold and came to a low building with horse stables and noticed, hanging on the wall, a long iron spike with the end hooked over. It was about eighteen inches long.

A weapon.

I strode up to it, but there was a sound behind me. I spun around. A boy was standing there with his brow drawn. He bowed.

I carried on, standing on my toes to reach it. "I'm taking this spike. Or what is it... a tent stake, or... I don't know, but I'm taking it. You can't stop me. It's mine, want it, need it." It

CHAPTER 40 - ASH

was heavier than I thought, about five pounds, and because I didn't expect it to be that weight, I grunted as I pulled it off the wall.

The boy didn't attempt to stop me.

I held it tight in my right hand, the pointed end down, turned, and stalked toward the gate, my teeth chattering.

A man who looked like a guardsman strode toward me as I neared the gate. I raised the spike, prepared to stab it if need be, but he bowed.

I said, "You need to let me pass."

He spoke. He didn't sound antagonistic, but of course I couldn't understand a word. I waved my hand toward the gate. He shook his head, *that* I understood.

"I want out! You have to let me out!"

People all around me bowed.

Then one of the young women from my room rushed up, carrying a wool wrap and talking non-stop. She wrapped the wool shawl around my shoulders and seemed honestly concerned about my wellbeing.

She conferred with the guard, and then the guard spoke loudly to some other men, and they opened the gate.

I looked around. *I'm free to go?* Everyone bowed.

Fine, good, thank you.

I walked to the gate and went through. I was out. They had let me go.

But the young woman followed me about seven feet behind.

I considered my options. There was a long dirt path that came to a fork. I had no idea which way to go once I got there. I could usually sense my direction, where the ocean lay, but I was completely lost. This landscape was ringed by mountains, I had never seen anything like it.

I trembled in fear. *How far away was I from Florida? How long had I been out?*

The spike wasn't so much heavy as cumbersome, and it didn't have a comfortable place to hold it. Carrying it for a long time was not fun. I switched the spike to my other hand, and opened and closed the hand that had been gripping it in fear.

Was I dreaming? Or completely out of my mind on whatever drug they gave me?

Scarier still.

I walked for a few feet, with the young woman at my heel. I stopped and gestured. "Stop. You stay here. Don't come with me."

Her eyes went wide.

I said, "No. Don't come."

I took a couple of steps then she took a step. I turned and told her again. "No, don't follow me. No."

I started to walk and looked back, she remained there, shading her eyes with her hand, watching me go. I walked down the wide path, surrounded on both sides by tall grass, it was warmer on my face than it had been last night, but still cool. I was grateful for the wrap. I looked back over my shoulder. She was still there.

I came to the fork in the road and tried to decide. By the shadows I was facing south. *East or West, Ash? You gotta decide.*

East toward the morning sun.

I set off down the road, glancing back once to see the woman still standing there.

I walked and walked, until I came to the edge of a forest and heard water moving nearby. A river, I could follow it to the next town. I entered the woods, it grew dark and trees crowded the path. What the hell was I doing walking aimlessly into the woods? I checked behind me, I could see my path, I wouldn't get lost. If I had to go back, I could. But I wouldn't, I was free. I was escaping.

CHAPTER 40 - ASH

I walked a bit longer until I emerged from the woods. Ahead of me a wide rocky bank and a gurgling river.

I looked up and down in both directions. Nothing. Damn it.

Would the water be safe to drink? Probably not. But I was very thirsty. Very very thirsty. I had to drink. The water was fast, it was coming from the direction of a snow capped mountain. It would be fine — probably. And besides, I didn't see any industry.

I went to the edge, and touched the water, it was cold, brisk, I scooped up some and drank. *Oh man, it was delicious.* I drank and drank more. And then sat on a boulder with the sun on my face and thought about what I would do next.

I was free.

I could follow this river, to the left or right, up or down. But the banks were rocky, there was forest beyond.

And no signs of civilized life. I let the sun shine on my face and took a deep breath. Why didn't I see any industry? Nothing, no wires, no roads — how common was this?

I opened my eyes and stared at the sky, blue with puffs of white. Not a stripe to be seen. I stood and gazed around. I heard no jet engines. I saw no planes.

That was weird, but was it? I felt like it was.

But was it?

Where the hell was I?

I needed to go up to get a view.

I followed the river as it bent north and then left the banks of the river seeing there was a slope up the side of a mountain. It was an easy dirt path, every now and then I would look back over my shoulder to look, seeing the compound that I had left, but nothing else. *I need to get a better view.* After an hour of walking I came to a boulder outcropping and climbed onto it in a blustering wind and took in the wide panorama of the valley.

The river wound through the valley, there was the

compound. Near it was a church. A few small houses, a tiny farm. No roads. No cars. No towns that I could see in any other direction.

My eyes swept the landscape, huddling against the wind, trying to determine where to go.

Finally, I decided to pray. I didn't pray often anymore, not in years, but if ever there were a time to ask for help it would be now. I got down on my knees and clasped my hands and began to pray. I asked for guidance. I begged for help. I prayed for a long time, until my knees ached, until I couldn't bear it.

Please help me find a way out of here.

Or if I couldn't find a way out, for someone to rescue me, or if not that, to finally wake up from this nightmare. *Please.*

Then a low voice filled my mind, like an exhale — *Where?*

I don't know. I don't recognize anything.

CHAPTER 41 - LOCHINVAR

THE CHAPEL - RIAGHALBANE

At the doors of the church, I was irritated, "Why did ye call me in here? I hae things I must be doin'."

Fraoch said, "Take a pew for a moment, I want tae speak tae ye."

I sat down in a pew and he heaved himself intae the seat beside me.

"Ye look like a man who needs tae calm his mind, ye hae a battle ahead."

"I need tae ride intae battle, not sit in a church because ye told me tae."

He exhaled. "Where is the battle, Og Lochie? Ye ken where ye are headed?"

I shook my head. "Nae."

He nodded. "Without a plan ye are likely tae lose yer life, ye must think afore ye act."

I glared, lookin' forward at the altar.

He seemed tae be choosin' his words. "I wanted tae speak tae ye alone, because Og Maggy inna goin' tae advise ye well on this, he is prone tae ridin' intae battle, riskin' his life without careful reflection first."

"He is right. What do *ye* ken?"

"Not much, but I ken the world is wide and time is long, like a loch it stretches before us, and the man ye want, he is a fish, he is holdin' yer maiden somewhere in the loch—"

I chuckled. "Och nae, ye are goin' tae tell a man a story about fishin' tae keep him distracted from battlin'?"

"Aye, and ye must wheesht because we are in a house of God and tis better tae speak on fish than war."

I nodded.

He continued, "So if ye are looking out over a loch and tryin' tae find one single, solitary fish what are ye goin' tae do?"

"I assume ye are goin' tae say tae clear m'mind and wait, but it would work tae detonate a bomb in it, I think."

He smiled. "But then where is the maiden?"

"She is nae more."

He clapped his hand on my shoulder. "Clear yer mind and pray, Og Lochie, ask God tae help ye find the path tae her. Then we will ride intae battle at yer side."

So I got down on m'knees and I pled for guidance in findin' Ash. I told God she was lost and that I was goin' tae rescue her, but that I needed his assistance and then I asked him tae offer her comfort, tae assuage her fears, and near the end, my brow sweatin', I repeated, *I am comin', daena worry, I am comin'. I will find ye, daena fear...*

Amen.

Then I stood and walked down the aisle toward the doors, Fraoch met me there. "Feel better?"

"Aye, I do, thank ye. I will pack and dress and then I will come up with a plan, and then I will go."

He said, "Aye, let me pack m'things, I am goin' as well."

CHAPTER 42 - ASH

I stood, brushed off my knees and shook out my legs. I was still lost, but I had found some clarity.

I knew there were two options: One, if you can escape safely, escape.

I had escaped, but this wasn't safe.

I had no food, no phone, and no idea which direction to travel. The woods looked endless. There was a large lake in the distance. I could be walking for days before I came to civilization.

The second option was to stay put and try to survive until rescuers found you.

Was someone coming, did they even know I was gone?

I had called Kaitlyn Campbell. Don had already been worried. For sure one of them called the police.

There was definitely a search for me.

But I couldn't go back to that compound, no way.

I decided to follow the river, I would definitely come to a town, eventually. Probably.

I walked down the hill and continued following the river east and then as it turned to the south east. I walked for a really long time.

Until I was hungry and exhausted.

My mind was complaining, *this is like some nightmare horror movie. The reason why they let you go is because there's no way you can leave.*

And, *I am going to die out here and no one will know.*

I collapsed down on a rock.

I was so tired of walking. It was hard to think of a worse fate than disappearing like this. I thought about my mom, what would she think had happened to me? She would never know.

Then the deep voice came to me again, and this time it was indisputably Lochie's voice. I was certain. He said, clear as day, *I am lookin' for ye.*

I'm scared, I don't know what to do.

I am comin', daena be scared.

I took a long deep breath. I felt the sun on my face, and watched the river streaming over rocks, a silvery flash of a fish as it followed the current back the way I had come...

I needed to be logical.

A man had come looking for me at the Palace. He knew Lochie by name. He was why I had been taken.

Because of Lochinvar.

This was some kind of dispute, I was a hostage, and likely there would be a negotiation of some kind. I needed to stay alive so I could be rescued.

The people in the compound were feeding me.

And I hadn't brought any food with me.

And it was growing colder.

It was dangerous to go back but I might not survive out here.

Then I wondered if there might be bears.

CHAPTER 42 - ASH

I scrambled to my feet.
I would go back.
I would gather food, put on more layers, and tomorrow I would walk out heading west.
In the meantime I had a weapon. I looked down at the spike in my hand. Hefted it into the other hand, and began walking back.

I wouldn't let myself think about it, until finally, exhausted, hungry, and scared, I thought, *did I remember where the path was?*
But then, one of the women from the compound was standing on the riverbank, watching in the direction I had gone.
She waved her hand.
As I neared, she headed into the woods.
I was tired, starving, cold, so I followed on the path.
Was I going back?
Yep. And I was furious with myself about it.
But I wasn't sure what else to do.

The other woman met us and they both walked with me back to the room. She set me in the chair and food was brought for me. I ate slowly a meal that tasted of gamey fowl and gravy. I drank two mugs of ale even though I knew I shouldn't drink. I needed my head about me, but I wanted to drink, I desired numbness. I stuck some of the bread aside for my next escape.
I was lonely and confused. I ate and watched the woman encourage the flames in the fireplace and slowly it grew dark. I kept my spike near me within reach, but no one wanted to harm me and then finally it was night. They bowed and left me to sleep.
I went to bed with the iron spike beside me, holding it in my fist.

. . .

I barely slept.

It was very quiet on the one hand, no hum of electricity or machines, and noisy on the other: wind howling, and when it stilled the sounds of animals moving, people talking, coughing, laughing, then more wind.

It was too dark, darker than I ever thought dark could be. I got up and used the pot, feeling my way to it, and the woman came in, spoke to me — it seemed as if she were asking if I was okay. I nodded, climbed into bed, and stared into the darkness again.

At dawn I didn't want to get up, so I stayed there. The women came in a little later and tried to nudge me to get up, but I just shook my head and pulled the pile of blankets up over my ears. I lay there, trying to decide what to do.

∽

Later, the door was open, the women were bustling around the room. One put a bundle of sweet-smelling lavender in the corner to dispel the stench of the piss pot. The other put a bouquet of flowers in a bowl on the table. There was bread and cheese set in front of my place with a blaze in the fireplace.

My first thought waking up slowly had been Lochie, the mystery of how he had come into my life and somehow now this — a flash in my mind of his smile, his jawline right beside my gaze, his cologne in my nose, his neck muscles as he raised his head to tease me. He had really liked me. I knew it.

He had told me that he did dangerous work. Did it involve the guys in the SUVs? Was he in the mafia and was I caught in some turf battle?

Except how was *this* the turf?

CHAPTER 42 - ASH

None of it made sense. If this involved Lochie, if it involved his work fighting for his brother's lands, then the story was magical, how were the lands like this?

And magic didn't exist.

This place seemed like something out of Game of Thrones — if a dragon landed in the courtyard I would be like, *yeah, of course it did.*

God, I really wanted a pizza. Followed up with a piece of chocolate cake, whipped cream on top.

I thought about Lochie's lips pressed against my forehead. Then when he walked across my apartment with his ass so freaking perfect.

He had been like a Roman god. A ginger Roman god, and he had adored me.

He thought I was bonny.

And he had eased into my life as if he were marrying me, as if we had settled it. When he said 'We hae decided,' putting down the menu, it had seemed like he meant so much more. He took it for granted we were going to be together. It was hard to describe, no one would believe me — I had known him for two days.

And now I was kidnapped. Hostage in a primitive foreign camp where people bowed when I passed.

∽

I got up. I peed. I sat at the table in my disgustingly dirty clothes with the wrap around my shoulders and ate breakfast. Drank some ale with it. I gestured and mimed that I really wanted water. They gave me more ale.

They brought in another dress. It was beautiful and in a different color, but I refused it.

No way. Even if it did look warmer. I was not joining this cult, not for a layer of clothes in a pretty shade of blue.

~

The wind was howling outside, so I didn't try to escape again. I stayed near the fireplace and the day was long and boring. I slept more because I was tired from the long walk yesterday. And I had raw blisters from carrying my spike. I was overwhelmed by all of this. I collected a bit more food.

If I collected bread tomorrow, the following day I would be ready to leave.

~

Another night passed. When I woke up the wind had calmed, so I explored the compound, looking inside the different buildings and stalls, getting the lay of the space. I left the spike leaned against a fence to climb up a ladder leaning against the outer wall and looked out over the landscape. I was going to go west. I peered out in that direction, my eyes following the path as far as I could see. There had to be a town out there.

A police department.

In the meantime I wanted a bag to take my food with me when I left. I climbed down the ladder, picked up the spike again, and began exploring the different buildings searching for gear. I found a long building, low and thatched, with a large fire going, smoke billowing up from the chimney. The interior was dimly lit, and smelled of earth and grains and yeast and smoke — casks were settled around, and a couple of vats. Big kettles boiled over a fire. It smelled like ale. Along the wall was a pile of empty cloth sacks.

There were about seven men inside, working. They paused

CHAPTER 42 - ASH

when I entered, and bowed, deeply. I gestured for them to go back to work then went over and made myself at home, picking through the sacks, checking them for rips. I found one that had a rope that would work for a shoulder strap.

While I was busy at this, one of the men brought me a stool and another brought me a mug full of ale. So, I held my new sack on my lap, holding my spike in one hand, drinking the ale, while watching them work.

Why was I here in a compound with a brewery? Who was holding me?

It had been days.

No one was coming, it was apparent I would have to escape. But not today, today was already growing long. I would put my collected bread in the sack. I had my spike, no one had taken it from me. Tomorrow I could hike out of here.

Heading west at the fork. That was what I would do.

I left the brewery to walk around the compound, counting: there were two large buildings, and about fifteen small buildings, including the one I was being held in. It seemed like there were ten guardsmen, but I glanced in a door and saw bunks inside, with men on them, so there might be double the number. I found a kitchen and counted four people inside. I looked in all the rooms I could access looking for an address, a map, or any weapons.

A boy was raking hay in the stable. There were women bustling by carrying full baskets. I stepped into a large room where about ten people were sitting at tables. They all turned, went quiet, bobbed their heads.

A really weird thing was that I couldn't find anything written down. No letters, no signs, no notes. I guessed there were about seventy people living here, and not one book. No one spoke a bit of English. And they all oddly hushed and bowed their heads when I entered rooms. I needed explanations, I needed anyone to understand one word of English.

. . .

The two young women were at the chicken coops, laughing. The sound of laughter was a relief.

One offered me a stool and I sat and watched them feed and chase chickens, laughing and talking about things, looking as timeless and ordinary as women through history. But then a deep melancholy grew in me and I stood and returned to my room to sit by myself in despair.

CHAPTER 43 - KAITLYN

THE KING'S APARTMENT - RIAGHALBANE

We were in our apartment. I stood in the middle looking around, it had been months since I had visited but it hadn't changed at all.

I said, "Wow, that is a lot to think about, huh?"

"Aye," Magnus looked down at a pen in his hand, then tossed it on the table near the door. "Tis remindin' me of when I lost ye in the past and had tae find ye."

"Which time?"

He chuckled sadly. "I tried tae warn Lochinvar, that the way forward with a wife is tae always be frantically trying to keep her safe."

"But he wouldn't listen?"

"Aye, he wouldna listen."

"Would you have listened?"

"Never. I wouldna hae changed a thing."

"Yeah, that's what I thought you'd say." I tilted my head, "Why did Fraoch take him to the chapel?"

"Because we are about tae ride intae battle and though tis m'nature tae raise m'sword, it might not be what is called for in this instance. We must find her, Fraoch is likely urgin' Lochinvar tae think it through and pray first." He exhaled. "Fraoch is wise in this. And while Lochinvar is in the chapel I wanted tae take a breath, tae ask if ye are well, mo reul-iuil, were ye frightened?"

I nodded. "Can we sit on the couch?"

He sat down and pushed the coffee table away. I climbed onto his lap, sitting astride, my arms tucked in, he wrapped his arms around me. I pressed my cheek to his shoulder. "This is what I needed, thank you..."

"Ye're welcome."

"I feel like I used to handle ten times this drama, but I think since we've had an easy time it got... I don't know, shocking."

"Aye, we are soft."

"Yeah. I was staring at her empty car, it looked like a struggle, and she is just gone, och nae."

He chuckled. "I like it when ye say it."

"It fits, this calls for a proper 'och nae'."

I sat up and looked down in his eyes. "She's been kidnapped. I think it's time travel. Imagine it, Magnus, she has *no* idea what is happening to her!"

"I keep thinking of ye, when ye were held tae be a wet-nurse, och nae."

I nodded and kissed the bridge of his nose. Then pressed my forehead to his. "So with time to think, what's our plan?"

He put his hands on my hips and pulled me closer, down. "We are thinkin'? I am becomin' unable tae think."

I kissed him. "I like that after all these years you're still incorrigible."

"I like that after all these years ye will still climb on m'lap and whisper Scottish sounding words in m'ears."

I whispered, "Och aye," in his ear and he moaned and his hands were rubbing up my shirt, and fondling around my breasts.

I said, "Aren't we supposed to be coming up with a plan?"

"I hae a plan right here with yer name on it."

"Och, I feel yer plan, Master Magnus, tis a verra big plan!"

He laughed as he heaved us both up from the couch, my legs

CHAPTER 43 - KAITLYN

around, his hands under my thighs, and walked me into our bedroom and tossed me on our bed.

In a few moments of frenetic activity we took off our shoes and socks, removed our clothes, and then he climbed onto the bed, crawling up my body, kissing my thighs and stomach, playing between my legs, as he trailed a tongue up my chest to my throat. There a nibble and a warm breath in my ears, that familiar scent and heat of my husband, the taste of him on my tongue as we kissed and licked, and the friction of my palms running along his planes and angles, the hardness of his form as I pulled him in and joined him and we rode to the climax of a midafternoon quickie.

It might have been an inopportune time, but oh so necessary sometimes to take a moment to love each other like this. To release our angst and worry. I ran my hand down his arm and kissed the spot on his shoulder above his scar.

His mouth against my neck, he said, "Now I can think."

"Me too." I ran my fingers through his hair, and twirled them in his curls. I said, "What do you think we're going to do?"

"We are goin' tae mount a rescue of the maiden."

I nodded. "Do you have any ideas where she might be?"

"Nae, but we hae a couple of places tae begin— there is Asgall's company in the twentieth century and his kingdom in the thirteenth century. We will need tae gather weapons and then we will go."

He exhaled. "Lady Mairead told me a terrible tale that has me verra concerned..."

I raised my head. "What was it?"

"M'great aunt, I had never heard her mentioned before. When she was young, a man named Asgall took her. She disappeared and was never seen again."

My eyes went wide. "Oh no!"

"Aye. This is how he got his hands on a vessel, we assume he has other machines as well."

"Like a Trailblazer?"

"Aye, it seems likely."

"This is horrible. Does Lochie know she was never seen again? He's probably freaking."

"Aye, he heard."

"Damn." I lay my head back, then raised it again. "If he's a king in the thirteenth century then he used a Trailblazer to open a path past 1557, right? That's probably why you are remembering your throne so well now."

"Aye, I daena ken for certain, but that seems likely." He rolled off me and lay on the side, looking down on me. "He is also mentioned as one of the most important Scottish kings, tis outrageous."

"Most important? Who voted? I don't remember being asked my opinion. He's a kidnapper, a thief, a possible murderer? The more I hear about him the more he sounds like an arse. Is he a cousin, or some other horrible relation?"

"Nae, it daena sound like it. This is a good thing, cousins are complicated. He has nae claim tae this throne, so at least he winna challenge me. But I also daena ken what his plan is... What game is he playin'?"

He exhaled. "But whatever is comin', we must begin looking for Ash."

"At least you won't have to do much Trailblazing."

"Aye, tis the one good thing. He has likely blazed a trail tae at least 1296. We will carry one just in case, but I doubt we will need it if we must go tae his kingdom. But we might not need tae go so far back, he might hae Ash any number of places. We might be searching for a long time."

He ran his hand down my chest, trailing his fingers along my skin, watching me tremble under his fingers. I wriggled closer.

"I remember the feelin' of havin' lost ye, and the desperation tae get tae ye as soon as ye were taken, afore anything terrible had happened tae ye. Och nae, Lochinvar will be frantic. I am surprised he haena left already."

CHAPTER 43 - KAITLYN

"He has grown up a lot, and he loves her."

Magnus nodded. "Aye, he will need that maturity and strength tae find her, and then he will need anger and violence tae make Asgall pay."

"...And you're sure it's Asgall? It isn't coincidence? Of course, as I say that, I remember your great aunt, it must be him."

"I am certain, he's got his sticky fingers all over it."

I stared at our ceiling, the filigree and crown molding, the intricate carving and details to make our room beautiful, a safe haven for us. "But what is his motive? Why did he steal Ash?"

Magnus raised his brow. "Ye daena see it yet?"

"No, what...?"

"Tis Lochinvar's son."

"Oh. How do you think...?"

"This is the only explanation for why they would take the woman who Lochinvar has a relationship with — they arna holdin' her hostage or they would hae sent me demands already. I think he chose m'great aunt for the same reason, he wants bairn who are descendants of the throne of Riaghalbane, ye ken, tis clear.'"

I said, "*Oh.* The baby would be Donnan's grandson. And on and on. He's stolen a possible prince of Riaghalbane? So Ash isn't even necessary, she's just a vessel?" I thought for a moment more. Then I said, "Ohhhh, is that why she died so young? Because she wasn't necessary once the child is born?"

Magnus pressed his finger to my lips. "Wheesht, mo reul-iuil, some things are better left unsaid. First we must rescue the maiden, afore any of that happens."

"I take it we shouldn't tell Lochie about this?"

"Nae, I need his senses homed on the task at hand, tae tell him of our speculations will only add tae his anger and grief, we will keep him focused — he wants tae rescue the maiden. This is enough."

"I agree."

Then I said, "So you're going with him?"

"I must. I am certain Fraoch is already packin'. Lochie will need his brothers."

I nodded again. "This all sounds like a plan, but I don't... I really don't want you to go again."

He rolled onto his back. "I ken."

His eyes looking back and forth on the ceiling he said, "I am uncertain how tae find her, and I am doin' this for Lochinvar, but tae risk my own life for the girl he just recently met seems tae be a fool's errand, but I owe him, and tis our kingdom that is ultimately responsible, and so... I must go. This is my duty. I am worried on Archibald though, will ye make certain he understands and daena worry? He is thinking on my death."

I nodded, "He's been clingy while you were gone."

"He is having the same dreams as I... I talked it through with him, tryin' tae set his mind at ease, but I can see it is still affecting him. The dreams feel verra real, tis difficult tae tell him that it is not real when it seems so... I am asking for ye tae take special care with him while I am gone, so as he is nae worried."

I nodded. "I will." Then I narrowed my eyes. "Do you think that the dreams you're having of being a king have become true? Have you checked the historical record? Are you listed?"

"Aye, Kaitlyn, I checked, and I am not listed, thankfully. Twould be a terrible thing tae hae an empire through time. It has been overwritten, this is a good thing."

I bit my lip. "So why are you remembering it so clearly? Why are the memories so insistent?"

Magnus said, "I daena ken. Tis almost as if tis *becoming* real. I hae tae keep myself from continuin' tae check the historical record, at any moment it might hae m'name listed."

"Ugh, then what, you'd be responsible for a kingdom in the thirteenth century and the twenty-fourth? You're right, that's an empire that wouldn't be easy to hold."

"Tis why I canna think on it, we hae things tae do, we must move ahead with the rescue mission."

"If you get stuck in the past will you um... let me know?

Somehow? We could come. Don't be stoic and decide to just live there, alone. I know it's hard to be in the past, but if you need me, if you need the kids, we will come. Being together is the most important thing."

"Aye, I will bring ye if I get stuck in the past."

"Please don't get stuck. Take lots of pens."

"Of course, now we ought tae get dressed, we hae tae discuss with everyone else."

CHAPTER 44 - KAITLYN

DINING ROOM - RIAGHALBANE

We met in the dining room at the agreed upon time, where they were serving a buffet table of finger foods for all of us. The little kids had napped, the bigger kids had explored, when we walked into the room we saw Lochie standing near the table, chewing some food he had been picking from the trays, completely dressed in historical garb, with a duffle bag packed beside his feet.

I said, "Ye are packed already, Lochie?"

"Aye, even if I hae tae go alone."

Magnus said, "Ye winna hae tae go alone, I will attend ye. I am mostly packed—"

Lochie said, "We hae a moment tae eat first and we must decide where we are goin'."

Magnus looked at Fraoch and back at Lochie. "Ye got clarity in yer discussion with Fraoch?"

"Aye, he calmed m'arse down, and I prayed on it. We need tae eat for our strength, we need tae discuss our plan, first, and we need tae make certain the family is protected while we are away, then we will go."

Magnus opened his eyes wide, "Good, I will dress as soon as we eat."

CHAPTER 44 - KAITLYN

"Thank ye, Magnus."

Fraoch was scooping chicken wings and fries onto his plate. "I am goin' as well. M'bag's packed. Og Lochie just needs tae tell me where we are headed." He plopped dipping sauce on his plate with a flourish. "Are ye impressed, Og Maggy, with his calm demeanor?"

"I am, I thought we would hae our swords unsheathed, tearin' through a Scottish forest in a long ago kingdom by now."

Fraoch tapped the side of his temple. "But is that where she is?"

"I daena ken. Tis why I am glad ye talked tae Lochinvar instead of me."

Lochie said, "The auld man has lulled me intae a stupor with borin' stories about fishing, but within the story was a seed of truth that I hae decided tae heed."

Magnus said, "And what is the truth?"

Lochie said, "If I do anythin' rash she is likely tae die."

Magnus put his hand on his shoulder and squeezed.

Quentin said, "I suppose if you three are going, then Zach and James and I are responsible for all the rest of these peeps?"

Magnus grinned. "Everyone but Lady Mairead she prefers tae—"

She walked in. "I think I heard my name, Magnus." She stopped short. "Och, look at the people teeming in the dining room, we hae become barbarians." Her eyes dropped onto the table. "Tis your idea, Kaitlyn? We must eat from the trough?"

I rolled my eyes.

Zach said, "I ordered this, I knew the kids would wake up hungry and—"

"If ye design your meals around the bairns, Chef Zach, ye will hae hungry adults and undisciplined bairns. Trust me, I hae raised a few barbarians myself. Ye must learn, a child is tae eat when, and what, he is told tae eat."

Zach pulled his collar from his throat. "Yes, ma'am."

Lady Mairead's eyes swept the room, she shook her head. "Och, I need tae go elsewhere."

Magnus said, "As soon as we eat we will discuss our plan, gettin' ye far away from the joyous bairns will be our top priority."

She raised her chin. "Tis not that I daena feel fondness for my grandchildren, tis simply that they are too much for hours on end and that they are accompanied by a menagerie of animals is unnerving."

Isla marched by, singing, "Too much! Too much!" Haggis trotting along behind her.

Magnus stifled a laugh.

We went down the buffet line, filling our plates. I helped Isla with Archie right behind me, he whispered, "Da is leaving?"

"Yes he is, but don't you worry, Archie, he will be back in a few days."

Magnus said, "Archibald, I will be gone for a few days, and while I am gone I will assign some jobs for ye and Ben tae keep yer hands occupied and your mind tired, dost that sound good?"

Isla folded her hands together under her chin, and batted her eyes. "Da, will you let me do a job with the animals?"

"I will make a list that ye will abide by, but I will take yer preference intae account."

He winked at me.

And then we both glanced at Archie. The color had left his face, he shook his head. "Nae, you can't go, Da, I won't let you! You can't! You won't come back. I know it. This is just like my dream! You'll be gone and they will make me take the crown!"

I glanced at Magnus's face — he was shocked, his mouth opening and closing.

Isla was watching, intent, thankfully quiet and not adding to her brother's outburst.

Ben looked frightened. Everyone was looking.

CHAPTER 44 - KAITLYN

Lady Mairead stood close, listening.

It all made me nervous. I talked more when I was nervous, so I said, lying, knowing that time travel trips were never easy, but saying it anyway, "Archie, that was just a dream, you don't have to worry about it. This is just going to be an easy trip. Right, Magnus? Just an easy trip, you'll go in and come back."

Archie leveled his eyes. "Da, will this be an easy trip?"

Magnus glanced at me, then shook his head slowly. "I am sorry, Archibald, but nae, it looks tae be difficult, this is why I canna take ye with me. But I will come home. And ye must wait patiently until I do, and ye canna be afraid. If ye are afraid ye canna let anyone ken. Except yer ma, ye can tell yer ma, but ye canna scare Isla. Ye canna show Ben yer weakness. Ye must raise yer head high and hae courage. Ye hae a job tae do. Dost ye ken what it is?"

He shook his head.

"Tis tae be the crown prince."

"Aye, Da. I will do my best."

"Good, Kaitlyn would ye like tae add tae it?"

"Yes, I love you, Archie, you can talk to me at any time."

Lady Mairead said, "I would like tae say, I ken I wasna asked, but I hae never been more proud of my grandson, Archibald."

"Really?" He looked around the room. "Basically everyone is staring."

"Of course they are. Ye behaved like a frightened lad at the beginning of the conversation but by the end ye gathered yerself up and straightened yer back and I could see the grown man in ye. Ye reminded me of yer grandfather, he was a horrible man in many ways, but when he needed tae do something dire, he set his mind. I see ye got it from him."

Magnus said, "I actually think he has a lot of his grandmother in him. I hae seen ye raise yer chin and ride intae battle before."

She raised her brow, and her eyes went far away. "Tis true, I once had tae lead a man tae the upper floor with the intent tae put in his drink a drop of—" She noticed everyone looking and finished, "I did what needed tae be done."

Magnus said, "That is my point. Ye must do what needs tae be done, Archibald, and I as well." He teased, "Daena worry on thrones, ye arna goin' tae hae a throne under yer arse, not yet, ye are too wee."

Archibald said, "I see it clear though Da, you are not there, they are saying, 'The king is dead, long live the king!'"

Lady Mairead said, "Tis yer dream, Archibald? Och nae, ye canna foretell the future! The future is being written, ye are going tae jump tae the end of the story? Only God will ken, the rest of us must be content with the living of it."

"It feels real."

"But ye see, it canna happen, not how ye are thinking on it, and do ye ken why?"

He shook his head.

"Because I am here. First, if something happened tae Magnus, ye are forgetting that I would seize power. Ye think I would let ye, a lad with only eight years of life, rule Riaghalbane? Ye think I will just step aside? Nae, grandson, I would seize power until ye were of age. So the crowd would be likely cheering something else, like 'All hail Lady Mairead, Queen of Riaghalbane and ruler of all time.'"

Archie chuckled.

"And then ye would hae tae wait for *years* afore ye could get the throne from me, think on how wily I am. If something happened, God forbid, ye are too young tae be king I would *hae* tae take charge. Everyone can see it."

I laughed. "What am I, just an afterthought? I'm the queen, why am I not the queen in this scenario?"

Lady Mairead said, "Ye could hae the title of Queen Mother, the sort of queen who spends most of her time at social functions."

I could see she was being humorous, so I didn't let it bother

CHAPTER 44 - KAITLYN

me instead I chuckled. "I suppose that does fit my personality better."

She said, "Of course, I spend many a night thinking it over. I will seize power, Colonel Quentin would assist me as m'Secretary of Defense, all would be well."

Magnus said, "Colonel Quentin, did ye ken ye were Lady Mairead's ally in a plot tae overthrow the kingdom?"

"I had no idea."

Lady Mairead said, "I require not one word of approval, Magnus, I will simply do it. Fraoch would be my Secretary of the Home Department and Lochinvar will be my Secretary of State. Dost ye see, Archibald, ye winna hae tae worry, yer grandmother will hae it all under control. Yer uncles will assist, yer entire family will help, and we will make certain that ye daena hae tae behave like a king until ye are ready."

Her brow went up, as if she were asking him tae think through what she said.

His eyes narrowed, "You said that I wouldn't have to behave like a king, but I would be a king, even if I were young, so my dream might be true."

"I am glad ye noticed this, as it means ye are astute, but it still daena mean that yer dream is true, yer dream is just that, a dream. Yer father will return, and the rest are just the feverish dreams of a wee prince and the well-laid plans of a grandmother in her quest for power."

Magnus said, "While I am intrigued and exasperated by learnin' of m'mother's plans tae wrest power, I agree with the main point, yer dream daena mean anything. Besides, ye told me yer dream was about the past, the kingdom is here in the future, it daena make sense as I am not a king in the past."

He nodded. "Ye were though, perhaps you will be again."

"Where did ye hear that I was a king in the past?"

"I remember it."

Magnus nodded, watching his son, then said, "Perhaps, but it still daena make the dream true. The important thing is that the crown prince kens that this is not tremendously worrisome, the dream he is having is wrenching but also unrealistic. I am goin' tae be here tae run everything, and when it comes time for him tae take the throne he will be so auld that he will be grateful that I am gone, finally."

Archie threw his arms around his da's waist and held on. Magnus patted the back of his head. "I ken, son, I ken."

After a few minutes, Archie released his grip and wiped his eyes and said, "Bug Man! Want to go explore?"

Ben put down a chicken wing. "Yep, coming!"

They ran off with Isla yelling, "Wait for me!" But they were already gone.

Lady Mairead was left muttering, "If they get chicken grease on my tapestries I will murder them and not give it another thought."

Magnus said, "Thank ye, Mother, for the help with him, ye set his mind at ease — mine however is fully tormented."

She smiled, "*This* was my plan. It will help ensure ye work verra hard tae return, as ye will be driven by fear of me. Ye will be taking the dog and pig and chicken?"

"I will be leavin' them tae guard the family."

"I thought twas worth a try."

We finished our buffet meal and I watched Magnus, looking thoughtful and concerned. He seemed distracted as if he were coming up with a big plan.

CHAPTER 45 - MAGNUS

RIAGHALBANE

The mindset of m'son was greatly concernin' me. I kept thinkin' on his recent question, *If I am king, are you gone?* And his dream that matched my own, *Long live the king*, and how that meant it must be a memory — if I was there, it ought not concern him much, but the fact that his dream included the chant, *The king is dead!* concerned him a great deal, and finally, most worryin', the fear in his eyes.

We were all settled in chairs. The kids had returned from their exploration. Lochinvar's leg was bouncing, he was ready tae go. "Where will we look first? Tis time tae make a plan."

I stood, "I agree. But first, I hae made a decision, I would like tae move the family tae Balloch while we rescue the maiden."

Lady Mairead said, "Wouldna it make sense tae leave everyone here — we have the computers, yer large military, yer castle?"

I glanced at Archie. He and Ben were sittin' on a chair, their legs swinging as they dinna touch the floor. "Nae, while I understand that there are positive reasons tae stay here, I think the Prince needs tae see his cousins. Runnin' through the halls of a musty castle in the eighteenth century will do him good."

Archie said tae Ben, "Bug Man, we're going to go see the cousins!"

They high-fived.

I said, "Master James, I will let ye choose whether tae move yer bairn or nae. Ye are welcome tae stay here, or ye can come with us tae Balloch."

James looked at Sophie. "What do you think, babe?"

Sophie said, "M'lord, I would like tae go with the rest of the family. That way ye might be of a help tae them."

James said, "Alright, we are decided, as long as Junior gets a gold thread."

I said, "That will be a priority. Everyone else is game?"

The group nodded.

I said, "Okay, then, ontae the matter at hand. We hae two possible dates. Tis yer decision, Lochinvar, where do ye want tae look first?"

Lochinvar ran his hands through his hair. "Tell me the two choices."

I said, "One is from a published article about Asgall Holdings, tis..." I flipped through the pages in the leather folder, finding the document and reading aloud: "November 7, 1912." I flipped tae the following page: "Here is the address for Asgall Holdings, in New York City."

Lady Mairead interrupted, "I ken where that is, I will go with ye."

"Good, that makes sense. We also ken that Asgall was crowned king in the year 1296. If we are fortunate, Ash might be found in either New York or Scone—"

Lady Mairead said, "Or neither of those places. Ye must be prepared, Lochinvar."

He scowled.

I said, "The only preparation Lochinvar needs is tae decide where tae begin."

Lochinvar shook his head and held out his hand for the

folder. He looked through the pages. Then shook his head. "This is a lot of words that daena help."

Fraoch said, "Between us all we hae a lot of experience with time travel, Og Maggy has run a few rescue missions, how many?"

I said, "About three hundred seventy two."

Kaitlyn said, "Everyone in here has rescued someone at some point."

Lochinvar nodded. "I want tae run off tae the thirteenth century and battle Asgall at the walls of a castle, but what if I am wrong? I want tae ken what the family thinks, I call a vote."

Zach said, "Hoowhee. I don't even let the family vote on dinner, you think this is a good way to plan a rescue mission?"

Lochinvar said, "I dinna say it would be bindin', I just want tae hear yer opinion on it."

Kaitlyn rushed tae the buffet and returned tae her seat with a notebook and pen. "I'll keep track."

James raised his hand. "So in all of time we are trying to decide whether to go to a certain date in 1912 or a whole year in the thirteenth century?"

Lochinvar said, "Exactly."

He said, "We got nothing else?"

"Nae, we hae only this."

James breathed out. "Okay, let's vote. Glad there's a lot of us, cause I would not want to be the one deciding this alone."

Lochinvar stood up and I sat down.

He said, "Mistress Ash is my lass, I will vote first."

He looked around at the other faces. "I want tae run intae the castle with m'sword drawn. I vote thirteenth century."

Fraoch said, "What if she inna there?"

Lochinvar scowled. "It remains m'vote." Then he said, "We ken Lady Mairead will want tae go tae the twentieth century."

She said, "Aye."

Then he asked, "How about ye, Fraoch?"

Fraoch said, "I agree with Lady Mairead, we ought tae go on a fact-finding mission first."

Hayley smacked him on the shoulder and whispered, "You're agreeing with Lady Mairead!"

He asked, "What would ye say?"

She said, "Fine, I also say the twentieth century."

Kaitlyn was writing furiously.

Lochinvar sat down in his chair.

I said, "Where ye goin'?"

"Don't know, I regret this stupid vote. Will ye run it?"

"Aye." I stood. "Quentin? Beaty?"

Colonel Quentin said, "Because we don't for sure know that the timeline goes back past 1557, we would need to test, we would have to be cautious, we might need to use the..." He shivered, "...Trailblazer. I opt for the simpler place, first. We should go to the twentieth century, find out what we are up against."

Beaty said, "I think ye ought tae pray on it first, Lochinvar, then ride intae battle with yer sword high. There is justice at stake."

I raised my brow. "Verra interesting. Zach and Emma?"

Zach said, "I agree with Beaty, swing that sword, Lochie."

Emma said, "I agree with my husband, Lochie should follow his heart."

Lochinvar's foot was jiggling, he drew his sword from its sheath and held it point down between his feet.

I said, "Lochinvar, I thought ye said it wasna binding?"

"Tis binding if it goes my way. And I am just ready — tis comfortable tae rest m'hands on my hilt."

I said, "James and Sophie?"

James let Sophie go first. "I believe Lady Mairead will be able tae learn what we need, and we must ken more afore we act. Please note that I am wantin' the men tae go with Lady Mairead tae the twentieth century first."

James said, "I'm thirteenth century, first. Do it, go team Lochinvar."

CHAPTER 45 - MAGNUS

I said, "Kaitlyn?"

She said, "I'm writing down my idea, that I am on the side of caution. It's always good to be on the side of caution. Twentieth century."

I said, "Generally, except when the villain has stolen yer maiden, then ye ought not be cautious, ye ought tae start swingin'. I vote for the thirteenth century. Will ye count the votes?"

Kaitlyn counted. "It's a tie."

"Och nae."

Lochinvar said, "Archibald, would ye like tae break the tie for us?"

He said, "I side with Fraoch and Colonel Quentin, it's safer—"

Ben said, "Ride into battle!"

I laughed. "Och nae, another tie!"

Lochinvar said, "Isla, would ye like tae break the tie?"

She said, "Side with Mammy."

Kaitlyn leveled her eyes at Magnus. "Your son and daughter vote for caution."

I nodded.

Lochinvar looked around at all of us, then at Archie. He exhaled. "Alright, this is what we will do. We will go check in New York first. It has been decided."

He added, "But we daena need everyone at once, Lady Mairead and I will go tae the twentieth century and discover what we can while the rest of ye move tae Balloch."

I said, "Ye are certain?"

"Aye, it seems likely the fastest way tae begin, or I will hae tae stand around waitin' for all of ye tae pack yer things for Balloch."

Zach said, "It's a lot like herding cats."

Lochinvar said, "Aye, tis. Lady Mairead, would ye be able tae go straight away?"

She stood. "I will be ready as soon as I dress."

. . .

We all withdrew tae make ready for the trip.

The Trailblazer was brought tae me. I wrapped it and put it in a messenger bag. We had three vessels for those of us on the mission, many more for the rest of the family. We had enough gold threads for the bairns. The horses were bein' saddled. I had bags of guns. Some grenade launchers, grenades, a drone. We were wearin' garb from the past, and had a bag of camping equipment for when we needed it. We had some food so we wouldna need tae hunt or bargain for every meal.

We had presents for the cousins. Fraoch and I had changes of clothes.

During our preparation Lady Mairead, dressed in early twentieth-century traveling clothes, strolled intae m'office as I was gathering paperwork for the trip. "I wanted ye tae ken, the lad and I are leaving now."

"Tis a kindness that ye are accompanying him."

"Well, he is a good lad, he is easy upon the eyes and kens his place."

"Ye hae always had a soft spot for him."

"He has enough of Donnan in him that I do feel rather softened toward him, but, ye ken, if he ever crosses me I will end him, just as I ended his mother." She turned on her heel and left for the twentieth century.

~

Later the rest of us gathered on the helicopter pad on the west side of the castle. Haggis was excited, we had our horses, a pig and a chicken, seven bairns, and a great many people tae be springing upon m'sister and brother. We packed and piled crates of food because the winter of 1709 had been the coldest on record and we wanted to provide sustenance. We piled the gear, held ontae each others' arms, wrapped around our bairns and jumped.

CHAPTER 46 - KAITLYN

1710 - BALLOCH CASTLE

When I woke up, Sean was standing above me. Beside me Magnus was sitting up, still dazed, looking up at his brother.

Sean said, "I ken I always say this, Young Magnus, but ye are lyin' in the dirt like a mucag, and ye hae an actual mucag with ye this time, or is that Fraoch?"

Magnus laughed and put out a hand. "Help me up."

Fraoch said, "I ken I say this every time, but must we awaken tae the ridicule of Sean Campbell every time we visit the cousins?"

"If ye want me tae haul ye and all yer things tae the castle, then aye, I get tae mock ye. Och, tis a good thing ye hae come in summer, we hae just passed the coldest winter I hae ever seen."

Magnus brushed off his kilt. "We brought more food, did everyone fare well?"

"Aye, mother has been sendin' supplies from yer kingdom, we survived."

Magnus said, "Ye might say that if the supplies were from my kingdom, I was the one sending it."

"The cards were signed, Lady Mairead."

"Of course they were."

CHAPTER 46 - KAITLYN

"And we are already grateful for the food and drink ye brought with ye."

"I dinna mention drink!"

"Och, ye ken ye never come without sodas and whisky and chocolate. The cousins are goin' tae be desperate for the sour candies."

"Then I am verra glad we brought them along."

Sean and Liam helped us all up and then we rode to the castle on horses and in carts with the men making trips with our gear and supplies for the rest of the day.

I remembered the last time we were here, though the details were fuzzy — Sean had dragged Magnus into the dungeon. I remembered the haze of looking down on Magnus wheeled in the back of a cart, the loss of people I loved, somehow... though now the memory seemed so far back that I couldn't remember why or how, just that keeping people you loved near was the most important thing.

I kissed Jack's head as I carried him in the sling on the path towards Balloch, relieved that the haze of memories were inside my mind only, and everyone else seemed blissfully unaware.

Sean had said, "Och, Jack is near full grown!"

I had laughed. "He's only ten months or so!"

"Has it been so long?" He turned to Magnus, "Ye must come more often, Young Magnus, the boys need their cousins!"

"Och aye, tis why we are here, Archibald needed the fine Scottish summer air."

Lizbeth was in the courtyard, her arms out. "Och, tis Kaitlyn and Madame Hayley and Sophie and Beaty and all the bairns! Sophie! Tis a new bairn?" She peeked in Sophie's sling.

She said, "He is just born."

"Aye, we ought tae get ye both tae bed. But what a handsome bairn, what is his name?"

"James Cook, but we call him Junior."

To James she said, "He is the spitting image of ye, Master Cook, ye must be verra proud!" Then she turned to Magnus, put a hand on each of his upper arms. "I am so verra pleased ye hae come. We hae had a long winter, we needed this blessing, Young Magnus. Tae see yer family has been blessed with a new bairn is enough tae brush away the cold."

He said, "It seems warm enough taeday."

"Aye, but this is August, Magnus, the first warm day of the year, och, it has been dreich and dire."

"Thank God ye made it through, Lizbeth."

She patted the side of his face. "If it haena been for the warm clothes and boots ye hae brought us through the years, and the supplies Lady Mairead sent from yer kingdom, we would hae been lost."

He said, under his breath, "Ye would never consider movin'? Comin' tae live in our kingdom? The weather is kept at bay by our machines, Lizbeth."

She shook her head. "Nae, Magnus, I winna consider it. This is my family, my home, the land of m'heart... nae." She turned, "We need tae get the bairns tae the nursery and the cousins tae—"

Her son and Sean's sons rushed by with Ben and Archie in chase.

"I see they hae found each other, good!"

Her eyes settled on the baby in Beaty's arms. "Och, Noah has grown big, strong and healthy, Beaty, ye must be verra proud."

She dabbed at her eyes. "Och, this is all so heartwarming."

Sean said, "And where is Young Lochinvar, has he finally driven ye away with his incessant braggin'?"

"Our Lochinvar has fallen for a maiden who has been absconded with by a villain, this is why we are here."

Sean said, "Och nae, Young Magnus, are ye bringing a villain tae our castle walls again?"

Magnus groaned. "I truly pray not, Sean — this is a new

villain, we daena ken what he is capable of. Lochinvar and Lady Mairead hae gone on an errand tae see if they can find where he is hiding her, then Fraoch and I will be traveling with Lochinvar tae rescue her. We brought the family tae keep them under yer protection while we are away."

"Aye, tis a relief ye will leave, we prefer the company of yer family tae ye, anyway."

Magnus laughed. "Och I missed ye, I needed the humility."

"Tis why older brothers are born, Magnus, tae teach their younger brothers their place."

CHAPTER 47 - ASH

SOMEWHERE UNKNOWN...

I was going to escape today, but it was just past dawn and I wasn't out of bed yet, when I was startled by the sound of horses, weird, lots of horses, enough for an army. The rumble of them was terrifying, something I had never heard before, but I knew in my bones. Horses. Probably a lot of men riding them.

I was going to escape, had I missed my chance?

I scrambled from the bed and stood at the far wall from the door with the iron spike in my hand.

It was a very tense ten minutes or so when my ears pounded. There were shouts of men outside, then my door shoved open and a large shadow appeared in the frame.

I held the iron spike up like a sword.

A strange man walked in and stood there, not looking at me, but peeling off his gloves. He was wearing a fur around his shoulders, a long dress-like outfit that went down to boots. He had belts around his waist, long hair, a thick mustache, tiny, menacing eyes, a weird-ass gold band around his forehead as if he was the dude at the Ren Faire who pretended to be a king.

He chillingly said, "I see ye hae made yerself at home."

"Who in the ever-burning hot fires of Hades are you?"

CHAPTER 47 - ASH

"I am goin' tae be yer husband, here tae introduce m'self."

"You get the hell away from me." My arms were shaking — I tried to hold them still, but the iron spike had grown heavy and I was weak with fear. I had been holding it up in front of me for a long time with my adrenaline pumping.

"Ooooh, frightening. The lady thinks she can scare me."

I thought, *I could charge at him, just fight him, get it over with*, but then what? My guess was there were at least twenty men out there now, that's what the horses had sounded like, and the village was already full of people, they didn't seem to wish me animosity, mostly they just bowed their heads when I walked by, but still... what would they do if I survived assaulting this stranger dressed in medieval garb?

Who was I kidding, he was big, I wouldn't survive it.

I leveled my eyes. "Tell me where I am."

"Ye are in my home."

"It's a crap home, you ought to have better furnishings, centralized heat and air. This is a hovel in the middle of nowhere. Is this some kind of cult? You the leader? I'm not joining your Kool-Aid cult, I'm a service member in the United States Army, I demand you let me go."

His brow raised. "Ye are delightful — I canna decide whether tae smack ye across the face or laugh."

"You come near me and I'm going to drive this spike through your vampire-heart. Then I'll feed you to the dragons outside. Where the hell are we?"

He turned the chair from the table and sat down in it, wriggled a bit to make himself comfortable, then crossed one leg over the other knee, leaning back as if he had not a care in the world. He smacked the gloves against the table and looked off out the window.

"Do ye smoke, Ash?"

"Smoke? What are you talking about?"

"Smoke cigarettes, I hae a habit of them..."

"I don't understand... no. I don't smoke."

"Not havin' cigarettes makes me irritable."

My eyes went wide. "Why are you telling me this?"

"I want ye tae marry me, I will make ye verra comfortable—"

"Bullshit. Where are we? Once I murder you and escape, and trust me, I know how to do it, I have a route planned. The worst part is choosing how to kill you: I know at least half a dozen ways just using this spike."

He smiled. "I see ye are verra overly confident. Some might find this a good quality in a queen, I find it tae be vexing. Find a way tae be more humble or I am going tae put a stop tae yer mouth."

I was so freaking scared I couldn't think of a word to say.

He glared at me, his eyes intense, his mouth smiling a menacing, terrifying smile.

"You are not going to lay a hand on me, I promise you that."

"Daena be so insufferable, I daena want tae touch ye, ye are not my type. Ye and I are going tae make an alliance, so I can get out of here and go to a reasonable place where I can buy a pack of cigarettes and smoke them freely." He pulled a paper from a leather pouch on his belt and spread it out on the table. He placed a pen on top.

"Sign here, and I will stay away for the most part."

"Will you let me go home?"

"In time. Ye will be my guest, first, then ye can return home."

"Not good enough. I want to go home now, I have people who miss me, who are looking for me. This is not okay."

"How will they ever find ye, Queen Ash?"

"Why the hell are you calling me that?"

"Because I am a king, and ye are my chosen queen."

"King of *what*...? You're a mental case, I am not interested in a dude in a dress with delusions of grandeur — you need a therapist."

"King of Scotland."

CHAPTER 47 - ASH

I blinked, my arms were so sore from holding the spike up in the air, my arms trembling, I was totally overwhelmed. "Scotland? How did I get to Scotland?"

I thought, *Does this involve Lochie?*

He tapped the paper. "I am not leaving this room until ye sign this contract. If ye winna sign on yer own, I will force ye tae. I daena see any reason why ye would want tae endure the pain, but I am a king and I am not used tae this much insolence; tis testing my already verra thin patience."

"I don't understand at all, this is Scotland? Do you know Lochie?"

He smiled knowingly, but he asked, "Who is Lochie?"

"Lochinvar, he's someone... I..." I wasn't sure what to say. I didn't know enough about him to be able to describe him. "He lives on Amelia Island."

"Aye, I ken of Lochinvar." He glared at me, long.

Then he tapped the paper again.

I said, "So what exactly does this contract say?"

"It says ye will become a queen. It *means* that ye will stay here for a bit longer, and then ye can go home. In the meantime ye will be clothed well, fed as ye wish, and ye will hae all ye need."

"I need a great deal more than this, this is like living in the dark ages."

He chuckled. "This is not a negotiation, ye will sign it." He exhaled. "I will make certain ye hae better food."

"Better bedding too."

He nodded.

Then he tapped the paper.

I let go of the spike with one hand and shook it out, then traded hands, shaking out the other. "You're being very vague about how long I will need to stay here."

He raised his brow. "I am being secretive because I daena need tae tell ye. Ye need tae ken, Queen Ashley, ye will either sign this and survive, with the deal I am offering, or ye winna survive. This is up tae ye."

I could see the shadows of other men outside the room. Waiting, guarding. My arms were screaming. I wanted the pain to stop. I was so scared. I wanted more than anything to get this evil dude out of my room.

And one thing was in my mind, my training: *survive the encounter.*

He hadn't hurt me, but I could see it in his eyes that he could, without a moment's hesitation.

And I had somehow been moved to Scotland without realizing it. How?

What had happened to me?

If I signed it I might survive.

It ran through my mind, *This contract will never stand up in a court of law.* I was signing under extreme duress, I could just do it. Just sign.

Also, maybe the contract would have some information on it: a date, an address, this guy's name, something I could tell the police as soon as I got away.

"You must have drugged me to get me to Scotland — what else did you do to me?"

He shrugged. "Nothin', we hae plenty of time tae get tae know each other."

"You disgust me, you better not have done anything to me."

I shook out my arms again, then said, "I'm not walking over there to sign while you're sitting there. You need to move away."

He said, "Of course." He got up and walked over to the door and stood there with his back to it. He was only about ten feet away. I knew it was dangerous, but I couldn't think of what else to do.

I went up to the contract, holding the spike in my left hand and looked down on the paper.

It said at the top in decorative script:

CHAPTER 47 - ASH

Marriage Agreement

and under it:

I, Queen Ash, wife of Asgall I, King of Scotland, agree to his terms.

"I can't sign this, it doesn't say anything. What am I agreeing to?"

"You are agreeing to live here for a time, tae be the Queen of Scotland. Then you get to go home. I already explained this."

"This is nonsense, you want me to live in this hovel pretending to be a queen? Is this some kind of Ren Faire? Wait, is this a reality show? Are you filming this? I am not giving permission to be filmed, under no circumstances. Is this porn? Is this an Only Fans? I will not be filmed. Period."

"I am not filming ye. *Sign.*" The way he said it. Short and clipped, like a command, set a chill up my spine. I picked up the pen, pushed the button on the back to expose the point. "How do you want me to sign this bull-hockey, with my full name, or this made up cockamamie 'Queen Ash' BS?"

"Sign it Queen Ash — ye hae high thoughts on yerself for someone named after the ash in a fireplace."

"I am not, I am named after the Ash tree, the Tree of Life, Yggdrasil."

He shrugged. "Sign."

"Where is this place? Usually when signing a contract, one signs the date and *place.*"

"This is my brewery."

"The name?"

"It daena hae a name, tis a brewery."

"That's stupid, you are a king, you have a brewery and you

haven't named it? What am I supposed to write for the place — The cruel king's stupid brewery in Scotland?"

"I daena care what ye name it, name it whatever ye want."

"Fine, as the queen I will name it the Tree of Life Brewery. In the divorce I will take *all* the proceeds."

I signed my name:

Ash

The Tree of Life Brewery, Scotland

I asked, ready to calculate how many days since I had been taken, "What is the date?"

He said, "May twenty-second, the year of Our Lord, twelve hundred ninety six."

I was leaned over the page, my hand poised, blinking. I stammered, "Wha— what did you say?"

"May twenty-second, the year of Our Lord, twelve hundred ninety six."

My hands shook as I wrote it, under the place.

May 22, 1296

I asked, "Are you claiming this is some kind of time travel?"

"Yes, it's time travel." He put out a hand for the contract.

"*Right.* You're a king, I'm a queen, we've time traveled to the year 1296. Got it."

He said, "Tis true."

I yanked it from the table and held it away. "If this is time travel, how will I get home?"

"Give me the contract."

His voice, cold and commanding, frightened me. I held it out, then thought better of being so close. I dropped it to the table and stepped back to the wall. I raised the spike again and glared.

He grabbed the contract and looked it over. He put it on the table, bent over it, and used the pen to scratch out the place and date I had written so it was indecipherable. "Why are you doing that?"

"So nae one will ken where or when ye are livin'. Ye canna be too careful." He folded the contract up and inserted it in his pouch. "Thank ye, ye were verra obligin'. Now I need tae return tae a reasonable age, a place with cigarettes and proper mixed drinks, where tis possible for a man tae enjoy himself. Ye will stay here." He looked around. "Enjoyin' my hospitality, verra far back in the past."

"I hate you."

He shrugged. "As ye might surmise, providin' what ye need for comfort in the middle ages is difficult. I am verra cautious about moving objects from one time tae another, I rarely chance it, so there is a degree of suffering ye will feel. I will do my best tae see ye fed and clothed well, considerin' the limitations of the place, but ye must keep yer origins hidden. The villagers grow frightened by strangers. This is why, up until now ye hae been guarded by men of this time, but after meetin' ye I see ye are determined tae cause trouble, I will be putting armed guards on the walls. Ye winna escape again." He smiled watching the color drain from my face. "And I would behave, if I were ye. If the locals think ye unusual they might declare ye a witch. I winna hae any power tae stop it, even if I were here. And I won't be."

"You said you were the king, doesn't that mean you'll be here...?"

"Nae, I daena like this time enough tae actually live here."

I shook my head. "I truly don't understand. This isn't real."

"Tis verra real."

"I can't speak the language."

"Ye will learn, ye will be here for quite some time."

"What do you mean—?"

He pulled open the door and left without answering.

I stood staring at the door, my heart racing, then I ran toward it and yanked it open, as I saw villagers with their heads bowed and the man I had been speaking to mounting his horse.

I couldn't let him leave, he was the only one who spoke English, who had answers, who could explain this, but he was also cold and cruel and I could tell he didn't care if I lived or died. I couldn't believe I had survived our encounter.

I ought to have been quiet, but instead I yelled, "Wait!"

He pulled his horse around, looked down his nose, coldly. "Aye?"

"Um, what am I supposed to do? What is the point?"

He chuckled. "The queen wants tae ken her point?"

"Yes."

"Yer point is tae give me a son for m'kingdom, the same as all queens."

I opened and closed my mouth as he directed five men dressed like mercenaries and armed with rifles up to join the other guards on the walls.

Then, without glancing back, he rode from the compound surrounded by men.

I looked around at the walls, men guarding me from leaving, then at the gathered people as they raised their heads, casting furtive glances my way. I looked down at the spike, still in my hand. People bowed then returned to work.

It looked like the Middle Ages, sounded like it, smelled like how I would imagine it would smell. *Was this what losing your mind felt like?*

Was I in a padded room somewhere with this story playing in my mind?

It was the only reasonable supposition, because time travel didn't exist.

CHAPTER 47 - ASH

He wanted me to have his son? Was he going to force himself on me?

Over my dead body. I was going to run.

I had my food, my bag.

This creep would never see me again.

I changed the spike to my other hand. It had been a good-enough weapon until the new guards showed up. I would need to get my hands on one of their rifles to get away — *How was this real? It had to be a dream, right?* I reached out and touched the low hanging thatch on the roof. Then I felt the white walls. It all felt real. There was a sprig of lavender on the window sill. I picked it up and smelled it. It smelled woodsy and floral as it should.

The young women approached carrying baskets, bringing me a meal, the scent of bread wafting by as they took it inside to my table. Their heads bobbed as they passed.

I followed them in and watched them unpack the meal.

Then I noticed my sack on the crate at the end of my bed. It had a hole chewed in the side. I opened the top of it, the bread I had collected was gone. Some beast had eaten my escape food.

I would have to collect bread again and steal another sack before I could escape. *If* I could escape.

What did he mean by you're going to have my son?

I turned to the two women and said, pressing my hand to my heart. "I am Ash." I repeated it, "I am Ash, Ash. Ash, Ash."

The two women said, "Ash."

I nodded. "Ash."

Then I pointed, "What is your name?" I repeated myself a few times, but they giggled, bowed their heads, averted their eyes, and kept saying, "Ash."

I tried more, "Ash," pat my chest, "what is your name?"

They said, "Ash."

And I gave up. I pulled out the chair, slammed the spike onto the table, and exhaled.

The young women began bustling around the room,

building my fire, taking away my piss pot, while I chewed a piece of bread, staring at the wall. There was some cheese, a bit of fruit preserves, the bread was good and warm. My mug had some milk in it, warm, odd, not to my liking, but the bread was sticking in a lump in my throat, I needed the milk to wash it down.

The lump was threatening a long cry.

I pushed the food away, pulled up the spike and went over to the bed, placing it beside my pillow. I climbed into the old bed and pulled the fur and wool and heavy linen blankets over me. Fully dressed, I lay on my side, focused on my hands.

The young women left the room quietly.

It was mid morning and I was done with this, all done.

What was I going to do?

I needed to gather my thoughts, come up with a plan... but first I needed to figure this out. Did time travel exist?

He said I had time traveled. I didn't know how, but let's just say I had.

This dude, the king, Asgall... absolute stupid name... had seemed to know Lochie.

Lochinvar.

Was he a time traveler?

...

...

...

That would explain a lot, actually.

Lochie's description of his life in Scotland had seemed kind of suspect.

His brothers all sounded like this king-dude.

Lochie's uniform had a sword, he said he regularly fought, he wouldn't say if he killed anyone... if I thought about his conversation from this perspective, a time traveler, his answers, his

CHAPTER 47 - ASH

inability to answer, his mannerisms, *oh my goodness*, I remembered the poem. He had recited a poem for the whole bar.

I hadn't been able to put my finger on the novelty of it, but that was... odd. It was the move of a guy who 'didn't grow up around here' as my uncle used to say.

Around here.

So if I was in the past, in the year 1296, holy cheese and crackers, how would I get home?

Was I just waiting for king creep to impregnate me, bear him a son, and then he would let me go? What a nightmare.

Or was Lochie going to come rescue me?

His sister-in-law had said, "...call if anything weird..."

I had called — maybe she knew. This for sure had been what she meant, right?

'Weird' was equal to time travel...

They weren't in the mob, they were time-traveling.

And I was seriously delusional, had read too many dystopian stories, had lost my mind.

Or this was all true.

CHAPTER 48 - LOCHINVAR

MANHATTAN, NOVEMBER 7, 1912

I had jumped and m'body ached, terribly. I blinked, my eyes adjusting, twas night. I looked right and left. Lady Mairead was already sitting up. "Ye are finally goin' tae rise?"

"Ye dinna give me a gold thread, everything aches."

"Ye arna a bairn, daena act like one, we must get up, there are beasts around."

I brushed off m'shoulders and back from the dirt.

She said, "As tis night, we will need a hotel."

"Och nae, Lady Mairead, I canna, ye daena understand — we must act, I canna sleep, I canna rest, it has already been long hours since I found out she was taken away. I am tryin' tae be reasonable, tae be a grown man who does sensible things, but I canna be reasonable on it anymore."

She looked at me long. Then she nodded. "I understand, Lochinvar, aye, I understand. We will go directly tae the address tae investigate."

"Thank ye, Lady Mairead."

"Ye are welcome."

I stood and put out a hand tae help her up. "If ye daena mind me askin', what did I say that made ye soften tae m'cause?"

CHAPTER 48 - LOCHINVAR

She raised her chin, the way she often did, lookin' much like her granddaughter, Isla. "Ye might nae believe it, Lochinvar, but I hae a soft place in m'heart for young men and the objects of their devotion. I was once such an object, and the young man would hae done anything for me, tae keep me safe. Ye remind me a bit of him, so I find myself inclined tae help."

I nodded and hefted our bags tae m'shoulders. "What happened tae him?"

She was quiet as we trudged across the grassy field tae the path. "He lost his life, long before he could rescue me from my fate."

I nodded then asked, "But would ye hae wanted a different life?"

We came tae the road outside the gates of the park and I walked beside her down the sidewalk.

"Nae, I suppose not, my son is a king, I hae founded a museum, I hae had my likeness painted by artists in many centuries. I hae been adored by one of the great geniuses of the twentieth century. It has been a grand life. But I do sometimes wonder if the simple life I had been promised when I was but a lass of sixteen might hae been the better."

I chuckled. "Tis difficult tae imagine the formidable Lady Mairead content with a simple life."

She said, "Ye ken, Lochinvar, tae be formidable inna always the best measure of a life, nor tae be threatening, or tae demand and wield power — I see my son and his wife whom he adores, and his family close around him. He has been fortunate tae hae both power and a family who admires him."

"He has been fortunate tae hae ye in his corner."

"Aye, tis my fate tae protect my son and his throne. I try not tae dwell on the other paths I might hae taken."

She added, "We are headed down that street, the address ought tae be on the left side. It looks tae be about nine at night, we will see if someone is occupying the premises."

I asked, "Are ye armed?"

"Of course. A handgun and two blades."

I chuckled again.

We crossed the intersection and made our way down the street and came tae a tall stone stair leading tae a front door.

"Och, here is the place, there is the sign beside the door." Twas a card with the words 'Asgall Holdings' in a small brass frame.

She said, "Remain here, watch for trouble. I will ring the bell."

She climbed the steps while I waited, looking up and down the empty street. Someone walked by at the far end, but continued on. As she pushed the doorbell, I heard the faint sound of it ringing inside the building.

I glanced over m'shoulder, she was peering in the glass window.

She sounded the bell again.

Her whisper, "Tis empty."

I nodded, chewin' my lip, mulling it over. Then I rushed up the stair, drawin' my dirk, pushed past her, and punched the window with the hilt, shatterin' the glass.

She furiously whispered, "Lochinvar!"

I glanced up and down the street, and dinna see any lights come on.

Usin' the hilt, I broke out the last jagged pieces of glass, then reached inside and fumbled at the doorknob. I unlocked the deadbolt above it, and nodded at Lady Mairead. "Done."

Wearin' pale white gloves, she turned the front knob and pushed the door open. We both snuck through the doorway and she closed it behind us, wipin' the interior handles and locks of my fingerprints.

It was verra dark inside, and clear that nae one was inhabiting the place. I walked down the main hallway, there were two doors tae the right. The first was empty but for a desk and chair that I could make out by the exterior streetlamp. The second was completely empty, I had tae walk in, allow my eyes tae adjust. Nothing.

I found a small room at the end of the hall that was also empty, meanwhile I heard the creaking on the stair of Lady Mairead climbing tae the second floor.

I returned tae the front room, the desk was lit from the street enough tae see twas barren except for an ashtray with a pile of cigarette butts inside. I pulled out the only drawer, seeing it was empty. Then I looked around and noticed a large dark stain upon the floor. I crouched beside it and touched it. Twas dry, difficult tae discern, but it had a look of blood — och nae.

I returned tae the foyer and climbed the steps following Lady Mairead.

She was in a front room with a small bedside lamp turned on, dimly illuminating an unused bedroom. The bed had nae bedding, everything looked as if it had been closed for a long time. She wiped her glove through the dust on the table, and put the fingertip in the light tae show me, twas yellow. She whispered, "They were smokers."

I said, "Did ye notice the blood downstairs?"

She looked shocked. "...where?"

"Beside the desk, dost ye think tis Ash?"

A momentary fear crossed her face, but she said, "Nae, it canna be her, I daena see any sign of her ever bein' here. This has been an office, tis all." She opened the closet door and bent over, looking inside. She pulled out a bottle and held it up, then went over tae the lamp for a closer look.

I looked over her shoulder. The label had a Tree of Life design on it.

She passed the bottle tae me and then went around looking in drawers. She found an ashtray inside a drawer with three cigarette butts in it, she placed them inside an envelope and stuffed it in her bag. Then declared, "This is all I can find. Nae sign of the maiden, we will hae tae look elsewhere."

She clicked off the lamp and we climbed down the stairs,

making it tae the hall just inside the front door, when there was a loud banging knock. "Hello! This is the police! Anyone home?"

Lady Mairead and I ducked intae the front room and pressed up against the wall just inside the door.

The police officers shoved the door open and with flashlight beams, swinging around the hallway, they entered the house. Their steps were heavy, they neared the room we were in and looked in, swinging the beam of light around. We pressed closer tae the wall.

They moved farther down the hallway toward the back rooms.

From the corner of m'eye I noticed Lady Mairead's movement, she was pulling a vessel from her bag. She put her hand on my arm and tapped, one, two... three. She rushed from the room and I followed — we ran behind the men, makin' it tae the front door as they called, "Stop...!"

We raced out the doorway, barreling down the steps tae the street, while Lady Mairead yelled, "Grab my arm!"

She was twistin' the vessel. I could feel the wind rise, and reached forward, clamping my hand tae her arm, mid-sprint, as the storm grew around us. I raised m'other arm tae protect m'eyes, and realized I was still clutchin' the beer bottle in my hand.

CHAPTER 49 - ASH

MAY 22, 1296 IN FORTINGALL

I was having a dream.

I was walking the grounds of the compound, my finger trailing along a wooden rail. It felt real, the area smelled realistic, yet there was a dark tinge around my sight. I was looking out on the buildings around me as if in tunnel vision, as if down a long path. The sound of my footsteps echoed in my mind.

I walked across the yard to the building near the wall, where the kettles were boiling, new beer being made. The men looked up, their heads bobbed in acknowledgement, then they went about their sweaty work.

I heard in my head, Lochie's voice, clear — *Where are ye?*
I don't know.
I looked right and left. *I can't tell. Help me, please.*

CHAPTER 50 - LOCHINVAR

THE CLEARING, NEAR BALLOCH, 1710

As the pain subsided, there was a voice — it was high and frightened, a whisper almost like an exhale—
...I don't know where I am...
Was it Ash?
Was she speaking to me?
...I'm lost... Can you please ask Lochie to look for me? God, please help me...
My mind filled with disjointed sensations, the heat from a flame, a blue sky with the edge of a thatched roof, the weight of a thick wool blanket, the feel of a rough-hewn plank as I ran m'finger along it, and the scent of bread, lavender, dirt, feces, and the prevalent aroma of hops within a bygone village.

CHAPTER 51 - LOCHINVAR

THE CLEARING NEAR BALLOCH CASTLE, 1710

Magnus was standing above me as I slowly gained consciousness.

He chuckled, "I will kindly ask ye tae unhand m'mother."

I mumbled and groaned and felt around, realizin' my face was on her chest. "Och nae," I pulled m'self up tae a sitting position.

She sat up, patting her hair. "Magnus, daena mock us. We hae been fleein' from the police, twas a frightening prospect. We barely escaped"

He smiled. "I think tis always frightening, rarely are we at peace when we jump — Did ye find out anything?"

"Nae, naething of use, the business office of Asgall Holdings is closed up and—"

I said, "There was a pool of dried blood upon the floor."

Lady Mairead said, "A murder was committed, it has naething tae do with us in *any* way."

"How do ye ken?"

"That office in Manhattan would be the worst place tae hold someone, ye saw how quickly the police responded — Asgall took her somewhere else, I am certain."

Magnus nodded, "Then we will hae tae begin searching in 1296."

I exhaled and shook my head. "Aye, tis what we ought tae hae done in the first place, I fear we are verra far behind."

He said, "I ken ye are concerned, Lochinvar, but we are closer tae findin' her—"

"I think I heard her voice, she was beggin' God for help. This is a thing that can happen?"

Magnus nodded. "Aye, ye can sometimes hear, ye can sometimes feel their presence. Kaitlyn calls it bein' entangled."

I said, "It bothers me greatly, she daena ken I am lookin' for her."

"In yer prayers today, ye could tell her — set her mind at ease, perhaps she will hear."

I nodded.

He asked, "Did she tell ye anythin' that might be helpful tae figuring out where she is?"

"Nae, I daena remember it clearly, naething but her voice, calling tae me."

Magnus helped me tae stand and I glanced down at the bottle. He asked, "Did ye bring me a beer?"

"Tis mine, I found it."

Lady Mairead raised her brow. "I found it, but ye might hae it as I daena like beer much."

Magnus said, "Tis likely bad, it looks verra auld."

"Ye forget we were in a place that *was* verra auld."

"Not as auld as *this* place."

"Och, right, I forget sometimes. The land here seems younger compared tae the tall buildings of the city and then which is young or auld? Tis all a confusing mess — when will we go?"

Magnus said, "I thought ye might want tae be fed first, unless ye went tae a fine restaurant in New York?"

CHAPTER 51 - LOCHINVAR

Lady Mairead said, "I was given not one minute tae see my friends or do any visiting in Manhattan. Aye, we are hungry."

I said, "Famished." I held the bottle up. "It has a Tree of Life on the label, and that seems auspicious."

CHAPTER 52 - KAITLYN

THE GREAT HALL - BALLOCH CASTLE

As soon as Lady Mairead arrived we had been told by messenger that the Earl was planning a large meal to welcome his sister.

We had to be presentable. The lady's maids bustled around, grabbing clothes and jewelry from every chest, because we had to dress five women: Hayley, Beaty, Emma, and Sophie, and me, all without enough time to prepare.

I had my hair up and wore an ornately patterned pale yellow dress with embroidered flowers. Magnus was wearing a coat and kilt, very clean and handsome, and when he saw me emerge from my dressing, his eyes lit up. "Och, ye are stunning!"

He pressed close and looked down at my cleavage. "Tis a fine sight, verra fine." His finger trailed along the edge of my dress, on the skin of my breast. "Tis goin' tae cause me distress tae watch the draw of yer breath..."

I breathed in and sighed.

He leaned down and pressed his lips to my breast.

I tilted my head back and he drew his lips up my throat. He whispered, "May we undress ye?"

I laughed, "You are a scoundrel, Magnus, no, you will need to suffer, because it took hours to get dressed!"

CHAPTER 52 - KAITLYN

He had laughed, "What if I only touched ye, right here..." He kissed my breast. "And right here..."

He grasped the front of my skirt and began pulling and bunching it up, more and more, until there was a pile of fabric at my waist. His hand found my next under-layer. "Och nae, there is more!"

I laughed.

He allowed the hem of my skirts to fall back to the ground and hung his head in joking dismay. "I canna even locate yer gardens, I am lost."

"It was a valiant effort, King Magnus."

"I hae been foiled by the queen's undergarmies."

"It's just as well, we are expected downstairs."

He put out his arm to escort me down.

We were all collected down in the Great Hall, having a drink, milling about, dressed in our finery, waiting for the Earl and his son, John, to arrive. Sean had whispered to Magnus, "It has been many visits since ye and John hae been here at the same time. He is afraid of ye—"

I chuckled. "Afraid of *me*? I am the nicest person in the world."

Sean laughed.

Fraoch said, "Og Maggy looks at him the wrong way and he scurries off."

Sean said, "If ye bow out yer chest and tower over him, perhaps he will depart for Edinburgh and leave us in peace."

Fraoch laughed. "Och, good plan, I would like tae see it."

Sean said, "Aye, me as well, his current visit has lasted for a month or more; tis time for him tae share his temper with the good people of Edinburgh, we hae had enough of his charms."

Lizbeth sipped from her wine. "While this is a good and entertaining thought, please be on yer best behavior, Young Magnus, and daena upset John or we will all hae tae endure his temper. We are going tae put ye at one end of the table, John at the other, well away. Tis not out of disrespect for ye, but tae keep ye out of harm's way."

She patted his arm, "Daena let it bother ye, I hae been told that he and the Earl hae been called verra early tae Edinburgh, so we will soon hae Balloch tae ourselves. The rest of yer visit will be less fraught."

Magnus said, "I could just buy the place, throw the Earl and John from it."

Lizbeth raised her brow. "I doubt the Queen would agree tae a peer, even a *Scottish* peer, being so rudely treated."

Magnus asked, "Lady Mairead, what dost ye think?"

She raised her chin. "I winna answer. Tae air it would be tae sound conniving."

"Ye want tae worry on yer reputation now?"

She said, "Leave me from yer conspiring, Magnus. *Although*, I am rather put out that I am standing here waiting while John inconsiderately takes his time." The corner of her mouth went up. "I hae always thought that Sean would look verra fine at the head of the table."

Magnus jokingly shrugged. "I could buy the whole country, throw the Queen from the throne."

Lizbeth's eyes went wide. She batted his arm. "Tis treasonous!"

Magnus winked, "Tis only treasonous if I meant it. Nae, I would never." He spoke loudly, "I daena want any extra thrones, nae more kingdoms tae rule, I want tae go on the record, twas a joke. I daena want tae overthrow any *more* crowns."

James and Quentin and Fraoch laughed.

Magnus clapped Sean on the back. "But what if we found ye a title, what if I bought one for ye? We are Campbells, there must be three castles within a day's ride that are empty and need a laird tae rule over the lands."

Sean said, "Ye could do it?"

"Aye, let me see what I can do."

Lady Mairead said, "We daena want tae alter history, we hae long considered that all ought tae remain in their place."

Magnus's brow went up. "But it is becomin' near impossible tae bear the Earl and his son, and m'family's place under them, and twill only get worse. Tae continue on like this means my place is tae be disrespected by my uncle — is it my place tae be seated below the salt in the Great Hall?"

Lady Mairead scowled. "That is unconscionable."

I admired them all. Lady Mairead was stunning, in the finest dress of deep red, ornately decorated, her hair up, a very expensive diamond necklace ornamenting her neck, with pale makeup and dramatic rouge.

Lizbeth was beautiful, her dress was a shimmery silver. Hayley, Beaty, Emma, and Sophie were wearing dresses that were more simple, but their hair was up, decorated with fancy pins, and they were wearing makeup. Emma and Sophie both had fine lace wraps around their shoulders, with elegant brooches securing them.

They all looked really gorgeous.

The men were wearing dress coats and kilts, their hair natural, combed and curled. Fraoch had his slicked back from his face. They all were looking very handsome.

The tables were set with fine tablecloths and napkins, china, silver tableware, and wine glasses. Finally, the Earl entered with his son beside him, steadying his arm as the Earl was quite old by now.

They were both wearing wigs. The Earl's was very high. They both had rouged cheeks and looked ridiculous beside the natural faces and hair of Sean and Liam and the men traveling with Magnus.

It took a long time for introductions and welcomes. The Earl and John moved and spoke slowly, used to taking their time, methodical and stately, and expecting all around them to hang on their words. They went around the circle, meeting all. We were very hungry, but had to listen to John say, "Lord James, ye are an architect, ye say?"

"Yes, a builder."

John nodded. "Good, good." A long breath. "Hae ye seen the cathedral in Edinburgh?"

"No, is it grand?"

"Verra." Then he asked, "Hae ye seen the shipyard in Glasgow?"

"No, is it big?"

James had a look on his face, 'rescue me!'

Lizbeth deftly diverted John's attention to Zach and then Zach found himself nodding while John said, "Lord Zach, ye are a chef, hae ye studied in Paris?"

Zach said, "No, never been."

John said, "Good, good." And opened his mouth to ask another question, when Lizbeth intervened, "Should we sit?"

We all moved to the very long table, the men all stood behind their chairs while the ladies were seated. Then the Earl sat at the head, and all the men sat down. John sat beside his father, and they both immediately began comparing the table to their settings and fine dinners in Edinburgh.

Lizbeth, sitting near them, rolled her eyes.

The Earl and his immediate family sat at the high end of the table, then Lady Mairead; Sean and his wife, Maggie; Liam and Lizbeth, with Magnus beside her, sat across from Lady Mairead. All the rest of us were positioned down the table by social standing. James whispered, as he moved down the chairs to sit with Zach, Emma, Quentin, Beaty, and Sophie, "We're the fun end."

I whispered, "I'm jealous."

Lochie, Fraoch, and Hayley sat between us and the fun end.

Lady Mairead gazed up and down with her chin raised, a wee bit of a sneer.

I could tell she was irritated at the affront to her son, Magnus, the king, sitting so far away from the Earl.

But Magnus shook his head. "Tis fine, Lady Mairead, nae worries. Ye daena need tae mention it."

She huffed and whispered, "The more and more I think of it, the more I want tae buy Sean a title. A small barony would be well done, I think."

Magnus said, "Aye, we ought tae do it first thing, his sons are growin', they need a placement."

CHAPTER 53 - LOCHINVAR

BALLOCH CASTLE, 1710

I was torn between bein' famished and wantin' tae go. A bowl of chowder was put in front of me, I said, "Och nae, it smells so good, I am hungry, and yet, I am ready tae go, ye ready tae go, Fraoch?"

"Ye ken ye ought tae finish yer chowder, ye never ken when ye will get another warm meal."

Magnus said, "We will go as soon as dinner is over, Lochinvar. Ye said ye were hungry, fill up."

"Fine," I ate the chowder, then the poached salmon with two slices of eel pie, wishin' twas peach. Then I ate stewed grouse, followed by custard with brandied cherries on the side.

I leaned back in my chair, patting my full stomach. "Och, I am full, can we go now?"

Fraoch was puttin' a bite of custard in his mouth. "Let a man finish his dessert, Og Lochie, we will go as soon as the meal is over, tis still light outside, we hae plenty of time."

Magnus said, "We hae all the time in the world."

I was impatient. I patted my stomach once more, and decided tae drink from the beer bottle that I had kept beside me at m'place. The lid was one of the ceramic stoppers, held on by a metal wire. I popped it open and swung the stopper off.

Fraoch said, "Ye are goin' tae drink it — how auld dost ye think tis?"

I sniffed it. "Smells good." The scent in my memory, the dream, flashed in my mind. The boiling of hops... *It had smelt similar tae this.* I took a swig. I grimaced. "It turned."

They all laughed.

John called down, "What did ye say?"

Lady Mairead said, "We are speaking on a family matter."

"Good, good." He asked, "Hae ye been tae Edinburgh lately, Lady Mairead?"

"Nae, but I hae been tae London. I met with Anne, she is embroiled in war, as ye ken. I was asked my advice."

The Earl leaned forward, "Ye met with the Queen?"

"Aye, she was keen tae ken m'opinion on the colonies."

The Earl whispered tae John, "Ye ought tae go hae an audience with the queen, give her my thoughts on the matter."

"Aye, father."

Lady Mairead straightened her back haughtily, having won the conversation. She whispered tae Magnus, "That ought tae hold their attention, so they will leave us alone."

She turned tae me, "Ye ought not pick up odd things and drink it, ye never ken what might hae been placed inside."

My eyes wide I said, "Like what, like poison?"

Magnus said, "There inna poison in it, tis just auld."

Fraoch said, "Aye, I told ye the beer was auld, but ye drank it anyway, and there inna a good hospital for centuries."

Lady Mairead said, "He daena need a hospital, he has a fine constitution. Twill give him the belches, possibly a case of parasites. He will likely survive it."

I said, "Worms?"

Magnus said, "I remember once when Auld Ian-Morgy had the wee-writhing beasties, dost ye remember Sean?"

"Och aye, his stench-emittin' flatulence filled the castle. Lizbeth said if we smelled it the worms might get in our nose."

She shrugged. "Tis true enough, ye ought tae run, nae harm comes from caution."

I was looking from one tae the other then down at the beer. "I daena want worms."

Fraoch said, "Nae, Og Lochie, use yer brain, the worms would die in the beer, ye daena need tae be concerned. Ye drink it down, yer stomach might pain ye, but ye will grow from the experience."

Kaitlyn said, "My grandmother used to say, you have to eat a peck of dirt before you die."

I looked down intae the neck of the bottle. "Nae dirt." I took another big swig. Stuck my tongue out and smacked my lips. "Och, tis growin' on me."

James said, "Hopefully nothing is growing *in* you."

"Verra funny." I leaned back in my chair and held the bottle up and admired the label.

Kaitlyn said, "What does the label say?"

I spun it around, there was the image and the words, Tree of Life. I read it aloud. "Tree of Life." In verra small print I read, "Founded in Fortingall." I asked Magnus, "Tis nearby inna it?"

"Aye, just north of the loch, near the auld tree. Could be what the tree is about. We hae a good jump spot there we use sometimes."

I peered at the number below it, "Est. 1296." "Twelve ninety-six? Inna that the date for—?"

Magnus grabbed the bottle and pointed at the label. "See in the trunk twists? It says, Asgall. 1296 was when Asgall was crowned king."

I grabbed it back and looked, "I daena ken why I dinna see it before."

Quentin said, "So Asgall has a brewery in 1296?"

Fraoch said, "Och nae, that is a verra auld beer."

Kaitlyn whispered, "He's a time traveler. The beer's probably not so many centuries old."

Lady Mairead said, "Probably. Though if ye kept a bottle of

CHAPTER 53 - LOCHINVAR

beer for five hundred years it might make ye a great deal at auction."

I said, "So I might be drinkin' Asgall's auction beer? Now I *will* finish it." I chugged a bit then gagged and belched. "It grows worse."

I banged it down on the table, causing a sharp look from the Earl and John at the other end of the table.

And then a vision flashed in m'mind — the scent of hops, a kettle boilin' over a fire. "Och nae." I looked at the label again.

Magnus said, "What is happening?"

"I am seein' where she is — there is a brewery. I can smell it and sense she is there."

"Ye think he is hidin' her in a brewery?"

"Aye, here." I tapped the label on the bottle. "In Fortingall in the year 1296. It has come tae me with certainty, this is where Asgall is hidin' her."

Magnus' brow drew down, then he called down the table. "M'lord, is there currently a brewery at Fortingall?"

The Earl shook his head, "Nae, there once was, but nae more."

I said, "She's there, I ken it."

Fraoch leaned forward. "But how do ye ken?"

"I prayed and waited for an answer, just like ye told me, Fraoch, and now I hae this beer bottle with a place and a year, and I can sense it, the aroma of hops, when I close m'eyes I see the kettles boilin'. Tis because of Ash that the brewery is called Tree of Life, I can see her there, Fraoch, tis clear in m'mind."

Fraoch said, "That is good enough for me." He wiped his mouth with a napkin.

Lady Mairead said, "Tis verra far back, he must hae used theTrailblazer — but, make certain we carry one along in case."

Magnus raised his brow, "This is the royal we, Lady Mairead?"

She smiled, "Aye."

Magnus said, "I doubt we will need tae use it, but I hae mine with me. Did ye bring yers?"

"I dinna bring it, and I winna tell ye where tis, but I can get my hands on it verra easily."

"Alright then, good, if we somehow get stuck make certain ye hae yers ready tae press intae service for our rescue."

I pushed out my chair. "Tis time tae go."

Magnus glanced at Kaitlyn for a moment, then nodded. "Aye." He pushed his chair back and stood.

Fraoch stood up. "Looks like we are goin'." He kissed Hayley goodbye. "Love ye."

"I love you too, safe travels."

"Aye."

Quentin said, "We are still waiting here, Boss?"

Magnus said, "Aye, we will return promptly or ye will be in charge of our rescue."

The Earl said, "What's that ye say, Magnus — ye are leaving in the middle of the meal?"

"Aye, sire, we must attend tae an important matter—"

"In the night?"

Magnus looked at the window, twas light outside still, and would be for an hour more. "Tis early still, but aye, we must go... my regrets and we will return in four days."

The Earl said, "Well, we winna be here, we are removing tae Edinburgh tomorrow, there are plenty of people here, more than can be accommodated comfortably..." He continued on while Magnus stalked toward the door leading us away.

CHAPTER 54 - KAITLYN

BALLOCH CASTLE

I stood, bowed, gave my regrets, and rushed after the men as they left the Great Hall. In the gallery I called after Magnus, "Love, I'm going to get the kids, I'll meet you in the courtyard."

I ran to the nursery where all the kids were having a heck of a raucous time.

"Archie?"

A woman there said, "He has gone explorin' with the cousins."

"Great." I picked up Jack and gathered Isla and we went to the courtyard sending a messenger to hunt for Archie but he was already there by the time we arrived. He had a pensive look on his face as he watched his father gather his things, yet again.

Quentin had collected bags of weapons, Magnus had them loaded onto their horses.

We watched as there was a lot of activity and we didn't want to get in the way. But finally they were ready.

Magnus said tae Archie, "Wee man, I am goin' tae help yer uncle rescue his maiden, I will be home in four days."

Archie nodded. "Where are you going, Da?"

"I am goin' tae the thirteenth century, tae a village called

Fortingall, tis right there over in that direction, not far away, ye hae been there."

He said, "It's a very old village?"

"Aye, but this is not yer dream, Archibald, I promise — I am not, nor hae I ever been a king in 1296. It inna the same."

To Isla he said, "In four days — can ye count them?"

She said, "Yes, Da, I will keep track."

"I will make sure tae bring ye a good present."

I gave Magnus one long last lingering goodbye hug. He kissed Jack's head.

Lady Mairead rushed across the courtyard from the stair, wavin' a book.

"Magnus, I hae an idea!"

When she approached, Lochie and Fraoch gathered around. She said, "Magnus, if ye run intae any trouble in the thirteenth century, ye will go tae the library at Stirling and find this book!" She had a hand on the top and bottom cover.

"Tis the psalter ye found with the M on it?"

"Aye."

"How will I hae access tae the library in Stirling castle?"

"Ye were once a king there, twas yer castle at one time—"

Magnus glanced at Archie, who was biting his lip.

Magnus said, "Archibald, I wasna a king in 1296, *ever*, and though I might hae been a king in 1290, there are a whole six years between the two — tis a long time."

Archie nodded.

Lady Mairead said, "What I mean is, if it comes tae trouble, ye ought tae figure it out. Go tae Stirling, get yer hands on this book. And ye will make a small note upon this page." She gingerly opened the pages to the middle. "Dost ye see this art? And the blank spot here? Ye will write the month and year using yer best pen—"

Archie's eyes went wide. "Da! Do you have a good pen?"

"Aye, son, I never leave home without at least one." He

pulled pens from his sporran and passed one tae each of the other men for their own.

Lady Mairead said, "Ye will write the date here. I will send someone tae get ye."

Fraoch said, "Ye winna tarry?"

"Of course not, someone will come promptly."

Magnus said, "Are ye certain the book is there?"

"Nothing is a certainty, Magnus, but if tis not there ye can bind and publish another, put it on the shelf of the library, and I will find it. But as ye can imagine, that will take a bit longer and will draw more attention tae yer plight and tae time travel."

"If I need ye I will write the date on this page. But look through the entire book, just in case."

She sighed. "Tis a verra auld and fragile book, daena rely on my flipping through all pages, instead, try tae follow directions, and I canna urge this enough, Magnus, ye must write it verra small, this is not a time for making a spectacle."

"Aye, if I am havin' an emergency and need a rescue I will make certain tae not ruin the book."

"It is *priceless*."

Archie said, "If Da writes in it, we would see it in this one?"

Lady Mairead said, "That is what I suspect."

He had his eyes on it, chewing his lip.

Lady Mairead looked at him, looking at the book. Finally she said, "I suppose ye want it, Archibald?"

He nodded.

She said, "This book is priceless and I will only give it tae ye if ye promise ye will be verra careful. Ye canna fondle it, nor put yer grubby paws upon it. I want ye tae promise tae be *clean*."

He said, "I will be verra careful."

Magnus said, "I trust him, twill be in good hands."

Lady Mairead thrust the book forward and Archie clutched it to his chest.

Lady Mairead pulled a small book and a pen from her

pocket. She opened the book at a ribbon bookmark on a clean page. "What is the exact date ye are going tae?"

"We are goin' tae start at January first of the year and begin tae check from there."

She said, "That is a senseless idea, ye will waste time and energy, ye ken as well as I that the easiest twist of the vessel is tae change the year, keeping the month and day intact. I always assume, unless I hae been given information tae the contrary, that the person will go tae the same date that they hae left. What was the date she was absconded from?"

Magnus looked at me.

I said, "May nineteenth."

Lady Mairead said, "Then I would add three days for the buffer and go on May twenty-third."

I said, "Do they really need the three days?"

"We always need at least the three days, tis sensible."

Magnus said, "Alright, Lady Mairead, I will do as ye suggest."

"If I am wrong ye can begin on January first, but I am never wrong."

Magnus looked at me with a bit of a smile, we just allowed her declaration to stand without argument. Fraoch said, "And with *that* I will go and say another proper goodbye tae m'wife." He strolled away.

I asked Magnus, "You have everything you need?"

"Aye, we hae been packed, we are ready tae go." He put his arm around me and pressed his lips to my ear. "Be cautious not tae frighten Archie, he is on the edge of overwrought."

"I know, I will. Please promise me you'll come home, highlander."

"I promise, I will be home in four days, ye will barely miss me."

He looked down at Haggis, wagging his tail. "Ye stay with Archibald."

Haggis sat down.

CHAPTER 54 - KAITLYN

. . .

The three men climbed on their horses, Magnus on Dràgon, Fraoch on Thor, and Lochie on Cookie, and turned them toward the gates. Magnus said, "Goodbye, bairns, see ye in four days."

Jack raised a hand, "Ba-ba!"

Magnus smiled. And then their horses thundered away, into the pale dusk of the summer night.

∼

After saying goodbye, we all headed to our rooms.

It took a long time to get out of the fine dress, and to take my hair down to sleep. It was still fairly early, and barely dark, but it had been a long day and I was tired, overwhelmed by Magnus leaving again, and unsettled by the look on Archie's face.

He was terrified.

He was still clutching the book. He had put it down briefly while he undressed for bed, but clutched it again now. He was haunting my room. I had to pointedly ask him to leave so I could pee and change out of my dress, but he waited right outside the door, and came back as soon as I gave him the all clear.

Jack was already asleep on the wee bed by the fire, Isla was looking at a picture book with a flashlight on her bed. She often slept in the nursery these days, but because Archie couldn't let me out of his sight she was going to sleep here too; anxiety was spreading.

We climbed into bed, and Archie held the book on his chest.

I lay on my side, watching his pensive face, not unlike his father's sometimes.

Isla sat up in bed and looked across the room at us, then climbed out of her bed to come toward us. I called, "Bring your pillow, Isla."

She turned and went back for her pillow and drew near, tossed it on the bed, climbed up and over me to sleep against my back.

She had forgotten her book and flashlight so she climbed back over me, went to get them, returned, climbing back over me, and tossed and turned getting comfortable. She opened her book and turned on the light, illuminating her side of the bed.

I teased, "Comfortable?"

She missed my joke. "Yes, are you comfortable, Mammy?"

"Yes."

I was watching Archie when he turned his head and looked at me. "I can't stop it, Mammy, it is going and going."

"The chant?"

He nodded, his face screwed up, a tear spilled out. "They're saying 'The King is Dead!' That's Da, isn't it Da?"

Isla sat up. "It's not Da, Da is not dead."

"I know that, Isla, that's not what I mean." He huffed.

I brushed his hair off his forehead. "I'm sorry, little man, I'm not sure how to set your mind at ease. Isla is right, though, that is not Da, he's not dead. Nothing is going to happen to him—"

"How do you know?"

I thought for a moment. "Because he has done really dangerous, death-defying things in his life, and this is just a small thing, I can't believe he would come to harm doing this small thing. Also, he's doing it to help his brother, how unfair would it be if something happened to him when he was trying to help? Those are two reasons why I think nothing will happen. And I know they're not perfect reasons, but if you remind yourself of them they will set your mind at ease, I think."

He nodded.

Isla sat up again. "Archie, want to use my flashlight to look in the book?"

He sat up, his wee shoulders rounded over the book in his lap. He carefully turned to the page and Isla climbed on me, her knobby knee pressing into my side as she peered down in the directed flashlight beam at the page. She whispered, "Is it there?"

"No. Nothing."

I said, "This is good news. I for one hope he doesn't send us a note asking us to help, but if he does, we will know what to do, right?"

Archie said, "We'll go get him."

"Yes. Now I think it's time to go to sleep. Think you can?"

"I'll try."

I leaned up on my elbow and took the book from his lap, closed it, put it under his pillow, and smoothed it down. He curled on his side. I lay back down. Isla turned off her flashlight and put it and her book under her pillow.

Jack called. "Ma-ma!"

I called back, "Jack, coming!"

I climbed from the bed, pitter-pattered into the other room, and lifted him from his bed, cooing, "Did Jackie wake up? Mama is sleeping, want to come sleep in bed with Mama?"

He tucked his head to my shoulder and I climbed us into bed. He squeezed in between me and Archie. I lay down.

And exhaled.

Archie sniffled.

I asked, "You want to twirl my hair?"

He nodded. And looped his fingers in my hair, like he used to when he was really wee, and he began to twirl a lock, a sniffle that sounded suspiciously like crying, until he finally fell asleep.

He woke twice that night. Both times in fear. The second time he cried, "Mammy, they won't be quiet, they say he's dead." I held onto him, soothing him, digging Isla's flashlight from under her pillow, and helping him check the page once more. Before slowly getting him to fall asleep again.

. . .

The next day he wouldn't put down the book. He wouldn't leave my side.

Lady Mairead found me in the corridor, just as I was mid-yawn because it had been such a rough night. She whispered, "What are ye going tae do with him?"

I said, "Archie, go stand over there, let me talk to your Grandmother." I asked, "What do you mean?"

"He is fitful and anxious!"

"He's having bad dreams, so is your son, by the way. It's like an echo and it's freaking him out, frankly, both of them, freaking out. Magnus keeps hearing chants of Long Live the King and—"

Her eyes settled across the room on Archie, "What is happening in yer dream now?"

He said, very quietly, "They are chanting, 'the king is dead.'"

"I canna hear ye."

He raised his chin, and said it again, "'The King is Dead.' And I am there, they are yelling it at me."

Lady Mairead said, "*Who* is saying it?"

"The people, I don't know."

"Archibald, those are just words, spoken by villagers, by the *peasants*. Ye canna believe a word they say. Tis a turn of phrase, they are welcoming a new king, and braying about the auld king, it could be *anyone*." She looked at him. "Come closer. Hae ye checked the book?"

He walked over, shaking his head as he pulled the flashlight from his pocket. A momentary look of displeasure crossed Lady Mairead's face, when he opened the book where his finger had been holding the page and shined the light down on it. "No, nothing."

"This is good news, Archibald. And if something appears there, ye come and find me, first thing. I will solve it. I canna abide by such a dour face. Did ye ken, once, I was locked in my

CHAPTER 54 - KAITLYN

room and forced tae endure incredible privations. Did I look dour and sad? Nae, dost ye ken what I did?"

"I don't know."

"I picked myself up and I fought and I won and now I am the mother of a king, the grandmother of a future king. Dost ye think I will allow for anyone in my family tae fail or tae lose? Nae, I winna. And I absolutely will not stand for the peasants tae chant at me. Ye raise yer chin and ye ignore them, they are nothing tae ye. Ye are goin' tae be a king, ye daena hae time for pouting."

She nodded at me. "Dost ye need anything else, Kaitlyn?"

"No, thank you."

She turned on her heel and walked away.

I looked at Archie and gave him a smile. "Feel better?"

He twisted his mouth, "She makes me feel better because she's kind of scary."

I said, "I absolutely agree and I'm always relieved she's on our side."

We walked to the nursery to look for the cousins.

CHAPTER 55 - MAGNUS

FORTINGALL - MAY 23, 1296

We arrived at midmorning, waking up in a puddle of rain as a cart rolled by, driven by a farmer. He was movin' slowly and peering closely. I met his eyes and then remembered, we had time-jumped with a great deal of weapons and wealth.

I lumbered up as he continued on down the path, and then I splashed around diggin' through the horse packs making sure it was all still there. Lochinvar and Fraoch began tae stir.

I said, "Tis time tae be up, ye are rollin' in the mud."

"Ye sound like Sean."

I chuckled. "And ye look like Mookie."

Lochinvar said, "Mookie is usually cleaner than this." He climbed tae his feet and wrung out the bottom of his tunic. "Tis good we dinna need tae use the Trailblazer."

I said, "Aye, we were fortunate he blazed the path already, and now we ken more, he used the Trailblazer back tae 1296 and somehow he became king."

Lochinvar said, "Why are you going through our things?"

I said, "There are travelers on the path, a farmer takin' an interest, but our gear looks tae all be here. We might want tae get hidden afore word gets out that strangers are journeyin' through."

I buckled the side of a pack. "Tis mid-morning, we need tae look around and come up with our plan."

Fraoch said, "Och nae, I just woke up and ye are harrassin' me like an irritated squirrel."

I remembered comparin' Kaitlyn tae a squirrel, a verra long time ago, I had called it majestic. "I am more inclined tae think on m'self as a bear, we need tae rise out of hibernation — get tae yer feet. Let's go."

Fraoch rose tae his feet, wiped off and wrung out his cloak and tunic, and we mounted Dràgon, Thor, and Cookie tae ride closer.

~

We were on our stomachs on a ridge looking out over a valley and we each had binoculars tae our eyes, scanning the landscape.

There was a large walled compound, many buildings within a tall timber wall. I counted and said, "Sixteen buildings."

Fraoch said, "Great Hall beside the north wall, the guard barracks are near the gate." One chimney was emitting a large amount of smoke, the fire was large. We werna certain of the work within, except for a cart goin' through the gate with lumber piled on the back.

Fraoch said, "Dost ye think tis a brewery?"

I said, "Likely..."

Lochinvar said, "Aye, tis the brewery, I ken it. I count six guards on the east wall, two are dressed in modern gear."

I said, "Och nae, they are carryin' rifles."

Fraoch said, "Aye, rifles, they are time travelers."

I said, "I count ten guards on the west and north walls, I see three wearin' gear and carryin' guns. See anymore?"

Fraoch said, "Nae, but we ought tae assume there are. Dost ye see anymore weapons?"

I said, "Most of the guards hae bows and swords — why dost they need so many guards?"

Lochinvar said, "Because they are holdin' Ash inside and they ken I am comin'."

The wind switched and the smell of hops blew toward us. Lochinvar said, "Aye, told ye, tis the brewery, she's in there, somewhere, I am certain..." He swept the binoculars back and forth over the cluster of buildings. "Do we need tae ken what building?"

"Aye, if we go in at night, we will need tae ken exactly where she is. Just keep watchin'. Tis a fine day, she's likely tae come out."

I put my binoculars back tae my eyes. We watched for a long time, with nothing much happening.

Fraoch finally said, "Og Maggy, ye are worried on Archie?"

"Aye, he is tormented, but then so am I..."

"How so?"

I put down the binoculars and explained, "When I close m'eyes I see and hear, verra clear, a wide crowd yelling, 'Long Live the King,' it haunts me... I daena ken how tae explain why, tis relentless, I canna turn it off. Tis one way that it bothers me, but more pressin', it is not a celebration but... how tae describe it...? Tis pointed... the voices are tellin' me, that 'Long Live the King,' and I feel certain I am the king they mean, but tis medieval and as ye ken I *was* a king, crowned in 1290."

Fraoch said, "This is 1296, there is a new king."

I said, "Aye," I rolled ontae my back and looked up at the blue sky with the rolling clouds. "Tis like a rift in time has been torn open."

Lochinvar said, his eyes still focused on the compound through his binoculars, "I am new around here, how did you become a king back then?"

CHAPTER 55 - MAGNUS

"A man named Sir Padraig used the Trailblazer tae forge a path verra far back. Ormr and Domnall, who ye remember—"

"I helped kill them in the arena."

"Aye, they became kings through time. They were growing in power, I had tae fight them and in doing so I seized the throne and became the Scottish king in the thirteenth century. I lived there for... twas a year or more, I believe. Dost ye think, Fraoch?"

"I canna remember except I was soul weary from the battles tae win yer crown."

"Och, I remember being on the edge of a field, and the rain comin' down, Haggis was beside me. Meeting Haggis was the best part of becomin' king."

Fraoch said, "Aye. Tis true.'"

"I had a tenuous grip on the throne though, time was shiftin', and James was screwin' it all up—"

"How?"

Fraoch and I both said, "Loopin'."

I said, "This is around the time when we met ye, Lochinvar, we used the Bridge and I wasna listed as a king of Scotland anymore. History was settled as it ought tae be. The memories of my kingdom were all but gone. We wove a new pattern tae history."

Lochinvar said, "Until now."

I said, "Aye, now we are rememberin'. Our weaving has been torn."

Fraoch said, "Asgall has used the Trailblazer tae go back tae the year 1296. This is why the memories hae come back because ye were a king, it *happened*."

I narrowed my eyes. "But we over-wrote it. We made a new weaving, tis *woven*."

"Not anymore, Og Maggy, just because ye keep saying 'we wove it' daena make it true. Time was changed, ye forgot what happened. Now ye remember again. If twas a weaving, the weave has been torn asunder by Asgall the Arsewipe."

"Och nae, so ye think it likely that the timeline has returned tae one where I was the King in 1290?"

"Aye, tis the best, simplest explanation, tis always the simplest explanation that is true."

Lochinvar asked, "But if that is true, then how did Arsewipe become king? If you were crowned king in 1290, how did he take the crown in 1296? Did he kill ye?"

I chewed my lip.

Fraoch said, "Tis highly unlikely as Og Maggy is sitting right here."

I said, "Archie is tormented by the chant 'The king is dead, long live the king!' His chant is different than mine."

Fraoch said, "Of course he is tormented, he's just a young boy, he haena even grown auld enough and haena done anything embarrassing enough tae get his name — he's a nephew of Fraoch and still gets called Archie? Tis an embarrassment." Then he put down his binoculars as well. "But, all kiddin' aside, he looks verra frightened."

"Aye, he thinks he is a witness tae the death of a king, his father, and that he is bein' called tae lead a kingdom — och, tis dismayin', he is only a wee lad."

"And these both started at the same time?"

"Aye, it started near the same night. Like a time rift, exposin' us tae an echo."

"I bet twas when Arsewipe used the Trailblazer, he broke the world."

Lochinvar said, "But again, I wonder, how did Asgall become king if ye were king in 1290 and ye are still alive and he dinna kill ye?"

I said, "What dost ye mean?"

"Ye are thinking on it like tis a memory, or a rift, like a mistake in time, but perhaps tis a warning, or a message — a sign that ye ought tae be doin' something. If ye were king in 1290, how is he a king in 1296?"

"Tis a verra good question." I watched a hawk swirling in the bright blue medieval sky. "I was a king — what happened tae my throne?"

"Another man is wearin' yer crown, pretending tae be the king, ye hae been usurped."

I said, "Maybe the chant is telling me I still live, I am still king — och, I daena want tae be, seems an awful responsibility tae be a king in the thirteenth century, but..."

Fraoch said, "Ye bowed yer head and the crown was placed upon it. Ye accepted the responsibility, tis yers. What did ye do, Og Maggy, walk away from it? Lived yer charmed life, full of ease? Ye hae been livin' in exile and now another man is sitting upon yer throne? It daena seem like something our brother, Og Maggy, would allow tae happen. Does it, Lochinvar?"

"Nae, ye let a man take yer throne and now he has taken m'maiden? He is growin' in strength! Perhaps the fact that ye haena put Arsewipe in his place is frightening yer son. Perhaps Archie senses yer weakness—"

I raised my head. "Careful, Lochinvar."

He shrugged. "I mean, he is fearful that he is alone and needs tae take the throne, ye canna deny he feels weak and ineffectual—"

"As he ought, he is only eight."

"Aye, he should believe ye tae be stronger, tae be able tae protect him."

I growled. "Be *verra* careful."

Fraoch said, "Og Lochie has a point, if Asgall is a king, then ye are dead, that is what yer son is feeling. But ye are not dead, so are ye weak? Did ye allow yer throne tae be usurped? Ugh, I daena like the sound of it."

I watched the clouds and the birds ridin' the high winds, the chant in m'mind, *Long Live the—*

Lochinvar said, "I see her!"

I flipped tae my stomach and pulled up the binoculars, directing them toward where he was looking. There was Ash, ye could tell because she was wearin' modern clothes, walking from one of the buildings. We watched her as she took a circuitous route through the courtyard.

He said, "Tis her, och, we found her. Lady Mairead was right about the date, but how long has she been here, should we come at another time?"

Fraoch said, "I daena ken, she looks unharmed."

Lochinvar said, "She's wearing modern clothes, she canna hae been here for long."

She paused at a few places, for a time, then she returned tae the building.

Lochinvar said, "Did ye see! When she went in, through the door, I saw a bed. That is the room where she is staying."

I said, "There is smoke from the chimney there, we can guess that is where she spends her time and sleeps."

Fraoch said, "Tis odd, she is not captive. She just walks freely."

"What can she do? She has nae where tae go." Lochinvar added, "We will go get her soon, right?"

I nodded and sat up.

Fraoch opened one of our packs and passed out some of our food. while I opened a weapons bag and divided the guns.

Fraoch said, "What is our plan?"

I said, "We are goin' tae toss the flash-bangs, create smoke, carry guns, shoot the arseholes, rush in, and rescue the maiden."

"Ye sound like Colonel Quentin."

"Aye, he's the one who designed the plan, he told me tae flash-bang-smoke-shoot. He calls me the boss but he's the one callin' the shots."

Lochinvar said, "We counted at least sixteen guards."

"We ought tae assume there are more."

"What about the drone, we could send it over tae see."

I mulled that over.

He said, "It would signal that we are comin', but tis verra quiet and if we distracted their attention in another direction we could send a drone in through the window tae tell Ash that we are comin'. She was a soldier, if she kens help is on the way she winna be as frightened, and she might be able tae help from the inside."

I said, "Alright, let's do that." I drew on the ground with a stick. "Fraoch will go around here and explode a smoke bomb, divertin' their attention here." I marked an x.

"I will fly the drone over the wall on this side and in through the window, here. If all goes well Lochinvar will be able tae speak tae her through the radio."

Fraoch wiped his hands of his sandwich and said, "Good plan, give me thirty minutes." He pulled on his bullet-proof vest, put on his helmet, grabbed a satchel with the flash-bangs and grenades in it, and mounted Thor tae go.

CHAPTER 56 - MAGNUS

FORTINGALL - MAY 23, 1296

Lochinvar and I checked our watches, I unpacked the drone and used my knife tae carve intae the paint on the bottom.

Lochinvar said, "What are ye writing?"

I showed him. It said:

Tae Ass-gall, from Magnus I

He said, "Och, tis verra grand, that might be the best thing ye hae ever done."

I laughed. Then said, "Let's suit up, in case, as Colonel Quentin would say, this goes South."

Lochinvar said, "What does it mean?"

"Not entirely certain, but I daena argue, if he says tae suit up, I do it." We put on our bullet-proof vests and our helmets.

Then when twas time I flew the drone from the woods, hovering a distance away.

Lochinvar watched through the binoculars. "Hold, hold... hold..."

Then tae our right, a verra loud explosion. Lochinvar yelled, "Go!"

CHAPTER 56 - MAGNUS

Using the screen I flew the drone forward, I was not verra good. I had practiced before, but not in a long time. It swept tae the left and right, staggering as it approached the wall. I asked, "How does it look, Lochinvar?"

"They are still looking at the smoke cloud."

He called Fraoch on the radio, "Count tae three then do another."

I flew the drone up the wall and over. "All good?"

"All good, nae one noticed."

I flew the drone down the other side and along the ground. Lochinvar said, "Halt."

I pulled it up short. "Someone is looking. Hold, hold."

Then there was another explosion.

He said, "Hold!" Then, "Go!" I flew straight toward the building, around the corner, skirting it, and I was behind the building where I hoped there would be a window. There was... I flew the drone in, there was Ash, lookin' directly at m'screen.

I said, "Lochinvar, come speak!"

He scrambled over tae where I held the screen. "How do I?"

She looked frightened, looking at the drone.

I pushed the microphone on. "Speak."

Lochinvar said, "Ash, I am coming—"

"Lochie? Oh my God, Lochie? You're here?"

"How long hae ye been there — should I come now—?"

"Come right now, Lochie, now!"

Lochinvar said, "Aye, I am comin'."

She startled and turned to the door, "Someone's here—"

A man stormed through the door. He was yellin' in Scottish Gaelic.

I dove the drone tae the floor, but it had already caught his eye.

Our screen showed Ash's shoes. Her voice emitted from the speaker. "Nothing, I don't know what it is, leave it alone!"

The drone was picked up. A man's face peered on the screen

as he twisted and turned the drone around. Her voice. "I don't know what it is!"

Lochinvar spoke intae the radio tae Fraoch, "They found the drone."

Fraoch's voice, "Och nae."

I asked, "Dost we give them time tae relax, or attack now?"

Fraoch exhaled, then said, "...attack now."

I pressed my finger tae the microphone on the drone. Lochinvar said, "Ash, get tae a safe spot. We are coming."

I tossed the monitor intae my weapons satchel and strapped on my gun.

Lochinvar said, "Colonel Quentin was right, tis a good thing we had our armor on already."

"Aye, we are ridin' intae battle." I mounted Dràgon. Lochinvar had already jumped on Cookie.

We left our camp and rode at a tear down the hill towards the village. Across the grassy valley I could see Fraoch on Thor barreling from the trees, so he would arrive at almost the same time.

Gunfire sounded.

Lochinvar and I turned our horses out of range.

I said intae m'radio, "Fraoch, fire at the east wall near the chimney." He jumped from his horse and yanked the grenade launcher from his bag. I jumped from Dràgon and aimed my rifle. I began shooting at the men on the walls.

Fraoch fired a grenade, knocking the wall down, sending up smoke and fire. Men were coming from the gates. Lochinvar and I shot them as they came, Fraoch fired on the section of wall behind it, and shot again farther along. The section of the east wall was in rubble.

Lochinvar and I left Dràgon and Cookie there in the field and began tae run toward the gates. There was nae gunfire, Fraoch's explosions had moved them back from the walls, and once I made the gate, we had cover, but next we had tae go intae the compound and fight man tae man.

CHAPTER 56 - MAGNUS

I said, "Ye ready for this?"

Lochinvar said, "Aye, I am ready, follow me."

I heard another of Fraoch's explosions on the southern wall. "Good, go go go!"

He rushed through the gate. I followed with my gun up, made it tae the gate, then raced behind him across the courtyard toward the main building — a flash of gunfire. I dove behind a wall. Lochinvar crouched behind a rail. He and I both had our guns up, I scanned the buildings with m'scope. I said intae m'radio, "Fraoch, ye see the chimney on the west wall?"

"Aye — one two three." The roof of the building exploded and burst intae flames. Lochinvar scrambled tae his feet and raced toward the door.

CHAPTER 57 - ASH

FORTINGALL, MAY 23, 1296

The man had me around the neck, with a hand clamped on my mouth.

Across the room I could see my spike under my bed, where he had kicked it — I had been so shocked by the drone that I had dropped it and now it was too far away. *Fine.* I could actually get away from this guy, with an elbow to his ribs, because he was holding me poorly, but I wasn't sure what waited for me outside and he had no gun for me to steal.

With the battle raging outside, I was safer in here, for now, but then a loud explosion, closer than the last, happened. Men were yelling, and then the rat-a-tat-tat of gunfire — footsteps outside as men ran by, an even louder explosion, a man running, a yell, and then the door of my room shoved open and Lochie, gun drawn, aimed right at the man. "Let go of her!" I was so freaking glad to see him.

I swung my elbow back, hard, and as my captor doubled over, brought his head down and connected it to my knee. Lochie said, "Och, well done!"

It hadn't really been well done, my knee was bound by my skirts, but when the dude weakly tried to grab my legs, I shoved

CHAPTER 57 - ASH

him back. He stumbled against the wall and held his hands up cowering.

Lochie passed me a gun. "Take this!"

My heart was racing. He took his helmet off and jammed it on my head. "Follow me!"

I fell in behind him and we emerged from the building. I saw men on one side of the yard, behind a wall, firing at the other side — in the direction we were headed. Lochie yelled into his radio, "Cover us!"

His brother Magnus stood and fired behind us as we raced that way and then directly behind us, another explosion and the firing stopped as we scrambled to Magnus's position.

He said, "We good?"

I nodded.

Lochie said, "Aye."

Magnus asked, "Where is Asgall?"

I shook my head. "The man who visited me...? He... I don't know, he's not here — he came once, yesterday, and I haven't seen him since."

"Och nae, we arna goin' tae get him!"

Lochie said, "Ye'll hae tae confront him elsewhere, for now we need tae get from this hellish place." Gunfire sounded, Lochie ducked.

There was an explosion. The gunfire ended. Magnus said, "We're headed tae the gate, then our horses."

I nodded. "Let's do this."

Lochie patted the top of my helmet. "In front of me."

Crouching, we ran toward the gate, I kept my eyes scanning the yard and the walls, keeping up with Magnus, hearing the bursts of air coming from Lochie's nose as he ran. I saw a man on the wall. "Wall!"

Lochie turned and fired three times. I wished I had given him back the helmet. He was tall, and looked exposed, it freaked me out, but then an explosion hit that section of wall, and a board flew toward us, hitting me, hard. I screamed and dropped my gun, stumbling to the ground, dislocating my shoulder — *That was going to hurt.*

Lochie scooped up my gun and nudged my back, "Up, go, Ash, run!"

I raced toward the gate, making it there, holding my arm. Lochie rushed up, then Magnus said, "Go!" He turned, and bolted out the gate as an explosion hit the opposite wall. We ran. Lochie caught up to me and ran alongside me, occasionally looking back over his shoulder, slowing and firing, then catching up again. Until we made it to the two horses. I had never ridden a horse before. Magnus mounted his and brought it around behind ours. Fraoch rode up on another horse and, with Magnus, blocked our horse from the walls as Lochie swung his rifle to his back and put his hand on his horse's reins. "Up!"

I tentatively grabbed a strap, and jumped but didn't come close. I grabbed the saddle, but my hand slipped. With one arm I frantically tried to jam my toe in the stirrup — Magnus yelled, "Guards're coming through the gates!"

I felt Lochie's shoulder on my ass heaving me up and over, I flopped onto the saddle — the pain in my shoulder making me see stars — I put out my good arm to keep from sliding head-first off the horse, but then there was a strong hand on the back of my thigh, holding me secure. The saddle shifted as Lochie lowered himself beside me. "Ash, hold ontae m'thigh, we hae tae go!" I gripped my arm around his thigh, my face pressed against his tunic, my legs dangling on the other side, and Lochie spurred the horse into a gallop. I shrieked as the horse rumbled under me, my ass in the air as I bounced up and down on my stomach. I clamped my eyes tight, Oh no, oh no.

Lochie held onto me with a forearm clamped across my back. All around me I could hear a rumbling of horse hooves as we raced across the fields. I raised my head to see — we were headed into the woods. Then we were in the trees, the shade making it cool and dark.

Magnus said, "Ye hae a vessel, take her tae Balloch! Take

m'horse with ye." He jumped from his horse and began pulling packs from the side.

Lochie said, "Where are ye goin'?"

Magnus said, "As we discussed, I need tae go take m'throne."

"Tis what we discussed?"

"Aye, tis my throne, he canna hae it."

"But ye will need yer horse—"

"I might need tae use the Trailblazer, I doubt Asgall used it past 1296. I canna put Dràgon through it — Fraoch ye comin' with me?'

Fraoch dismounted his horse. "Och nae, we hae tae use the Trailblazer?" He grabbed a bag off his horse. "Fine I will come, stop beggin' me."

Magnus placed the horses' reins in Lochie's hand. "Men are coming, go go go!" He and Fraoch slung bags over their shoulders and scrambled up the hill, deeper into the woods.

Lochie said, "Let go m'leg, Ash, I'm slidin' ye down." He directed my feet to the ground, gently, but I still stumbled when I hit land and fell back on my ass, holding my arm. "What is happening, Lochie! What is going on!"

My arm hurt. I was so scared — "Are they coming?"

"Aye, they are right behind us."

He dropped to the ground and wrapped all the reins around his forearm. Crouched right in front of me, he pulled a small device, about the size and shape of a Red Bull can, he held it, and looked at me. "I ken ye are frightened, Ash, but we are goin' tae jump, hold ontae my arm."

I shook my head. "Don't want to."

"Hold on!" He twisted the machine.

I shook my head again, he dropped his knees on both sides of my hips, sitting on me, pinning me down, put an arm around the back of my head, holding me to his chest and said, "Hold on, daena be frightened..."

And then there was the worst pain I had ever felt rolling up my arm and spreading down my back — I began to scream.

CHAPTER 58 - MAGNUS

We made it tae the woods and scrambled up the rise tae the spot where we had been hidin' earlier.

Fraoch watched down the path, as the storm carryin' Lochie and Ash slowly dissipated, while I looked around tae make sure we had all our gear.

He said, "Och, my heart is pounding in m'chest, that was a drastic chase."

"Aye, but we got the maiden."

He said, "But we dinna kill the king."

I growled. "He inna a king, the more I think on it, *I* am the king. This inna over." The chant in my head had reached a fever-pitch, *Long live the king! Long live the king!*

I shook my head, trying tae calm it.

"So now ye are a king in this God-forsaken place?"

"Aye, I hae decided that I hae tae be, I must be, tis my throne. I took it in 1290. Asgall canna hae it in 1296, I winna stand for it."

"I am pleased, as this means ye are listening tae me for once."

"I always listen tae ye — daena I listen tae ye?"

"I would say rarely, but tis just as well as I rarely ken what is

CHAPTER 58 - MAGNUS

happening, except now, there are some things that are evident — ye were the king first, Asgall canna hae yer throne. I hae tae piss, can ye take the guard?"

"Aye." I traded places with him and watched down the path, while Fraoch pissed in the bushes.

He called over, "So we are goin' tae go back and take yer kingdom again, but dinna we go back once tae get Haggis? Will we be loopin'?"

"Did we?"

"Aye, I remember... I think. Tis hazy."

I shook my head, staring off intae the distance. "I hae memories that are hazy and some that are clear. I think the hazed ones are from shiftin' and turnin'. Nae, we are returnin' tae a different time. Tis clear, I believe we will overwrite it."

He reemerged from behind the tree and said, "Nae one is coming?"

"Nae, we lost them."

He was movin' weapons from one pack intae another. "Do ye want me tae bring the sandwiches?"

"That goes without sayin'."

He shoved our food intae his pack.

I continued, "I remember a day verra clearly, I am king, I had been king for almost a year. Tis the year of our Lord, 1291. There are nae time shifts, tis verra calm. I will return tae the verra next day. I believe we will be safe from looping."

"How certain are ye?"

"About fifty-fifty."

He chuckled. "I suppose I hae tae be okay with those odds, as I decided tae remain behind and help ye, though twas while being chased, under duress."

"Ye want tae change yer mind?"

"Nae, I suppose not, it has been a while since we had a Fraognus adventure, I am in the mood. Though I daena like the idea of bein' without our horses."

"We ken Asgall opened time back tae 1296 but we daena

ken if he has gone farther back. I doubt it, so this part of our adventure involves the Trailblazer. I daena want tae put the horses through it."

"They would hate that God-forsaken machine."

"Exactly."

"Though I see ye daena hae the same consideration for yer brother, Fraoch."

"M'brother, Fraoch, could hae gone home with the horses, instead here he stands."

"Aye, tis my way, selfless and mad."

We stood beside each other and I pulled the Trailblazer from my bag.

He said, "What made ye decide tae go back and claim yer kingdom?"

"The things ye were sayin'— ye are right, it does seem as if there has been a rift, a resurgence of that timeline. My history is callin' me." I tugged at my ear. "Relentlessly."

I looked over the Trailblazer, checking the controls — difficult tae concentrate with the repeating chant: *Long live the king, long live the king.*

He said, "Och, I hate this machine."

"We hae another vessel, ye could return tae Balloch."

"Nae, daena be ridiculous. I can hate it and still do it, I am a complicated man, this is a thing I can do." He rolled his neck and pounded a fist against his biceps and then his thighs. "Remind me again why we are doin' it?"

"I am goin' tae rewrite the history of Scotland, and I am bettin' that twill be more stable once I do. I will secure m'throne for m'son and make certain that Asgall canna gain it. I will stop him afore he can become a king."

"Och nae, I hope we daena hae tae war and battle for your throne again."

"I hope nae, but we might..."

"Ye goin' tae walk in like ye never left?"

I held the Trailblazer out, he grabbed hold of the side. "I

think that is m'plan. Walk up, say hello, demand they bow, and assume the throne."

He said, "Ye sound pretty confident for someone about tae use the Trailblazer, ye ever done it before?"

"Nae, but I ken the basics, hold on."

He started laughing as I started it up.

CHAPTER 59 - KAITLYN

BALLOCH CASTLE

*A*rchie was beside me on a bench in the courtyard, we had come down there to help with the market activities of the day, but he had been morosely standing beside me, holding my hand, hiding his head against my side, and people, especially his cousins, were giving him looks of disdain.

An entire reputation he had built up was being lost in a few days of clinginess — what kind of weird rite of strength and bravery would he have to do to get his coolness back?

I had drawn him toward the bench and sat down, enjoying the warm sun on my skin. Archie sat beside me, his finger inserted in the book, his head against my shoulder, and we were quiet together. I understood.

He knew I understood. I had been in this position so many times before.

Not knowing was so difficult.

He opened the book and looked at the page and then closed it and sighed.

I said, "I know."

Lizbeth found us there. "Enjoyin' the sun?"

"Yep."

CHAPTER 59 - KAITLYN

She sat down beside Archie. "Has a message appeared from yer Da?"

He shook his head.

She said, "Och nae, tis verra awful tae wait for a letter."

We sat quietly, then she said, "Yer cousins were telling me about yer troubles. What does it sound like, Archibald, in yer head?"

"Like a million people are yelling at me."

"Och nae! That sounds dreadful!"

He said, "Tis. And they are saying that Da is dead."

"Ye hae been beset by monsters."

He nodded.

"I pray when I am beset, but sometimes it takes a few days before my mind clears." She patted the back of his hand. "I will bring ye a poultice for yer temples and give ye an extra dessert this evening. Ye must hae sweets tae help clear it."

He said, "Thank you, Aunt Lizbeth."

"Ye're welcome. I will tell the boys that ye are busy for now, but they will want extra fun on the morrow when ye are all better, and ye will be better, Archibald. The monsters canna live in ye for so long, they grow bored, they will move ontae someone else tae torture."

"You think?"

"I know. Tis the thing I know more than anything. This terrible time ye are havin' it canna last."

She stood and squeezed my shoulder.

"I will see ye at dinner."

She left across the courtyard and then it dawned on me, I had a terrible headache, and the hairs on my arm were standing on end.

Quentin was on the wall and he glanced down and pointed at his arm.

I nodded.

He looked around at the sky as if that might explain it.

Then he jogged down the steps and crossed toward me.

"You feel it, it's the Trailblazer, right? I'm not losing my mind?"

"Nope, that's what's happening."

He narrowed his eyes. "I guess that's good news, they're working on something."

I glanced down at Archie. "You feel it?"

"Yeah, it hurts behind my eyes."

He checked the page in the book again.

CHAPTER 60 - MAGNUS

USING THE TRAILBLAZER

AAAAGGGGGHHHHHH. The feelin' was so intensely painful that I let go and shoved the Trailblazer as far away as I could get it. *Nae nae nae.*

Fraoch groaned beside me.

I vomited in the grass, I was on m'hands and knees. *Och nae. Long live the king, long live the king, long...*

I winna live for much longer.

"What did ye say, ye're mumbling..."

I daena remember. I retched, but m'stomach was empty, I sat, spent, head hanging, weakened.

How far did we go? Are we there? I couldna tell if I spoke out loud or in my head which was already clogged with the endless chant.

I heard Fraoch slide the horror machine closer. He said, "I canna read it, m'eyes are unfocused."

"Ye are useless." I was jokin' — I rolled back so that I was lyin' on the ground.

He kept staring at it, then said, "We hae gone further back by two months."

"Och nae, wheesht, I daena want tae ken."

"There is only one rule of Trailblazer, ye canna let go."

"Aye, I see that now, tis unbearable. I am glad I dinna bring Dràgon, he daena deserve this."

"Yet here lies Fraoch, long sufferin' brother tae the merciless king."

I pulled myself up. "Ye ready tae try again?"

He wiped his hands up and down on his face.

"This time we go until we canna bear it."

I growled in answer, because I couldna form words.

We both held the Trailblazer and began again.

∾

I shoved the Trailblazer away.

Nae nae nae nae.

I was lyin' on m'side, m'face wet from my sick or tears or both.

I groaned.

Fraoch's foot was near m'face and I thought, *he has died.*

It seemed clear that one or both of us had, *there was nae way we survived that.*

I pulled my hand up, wincing, and poked his shoe.

He moaned.

This wasna like using the vessels, those caused a great deal of intense pain, but this wracked yer form, felt as if ye were tortured. Time jumping with the vessels felt as if ye needed tae rest tae recover, ye felt weak. With the Trailblazer it felt like ye might never survive.

I said, "Tis dark."

Silence.

I lay there, starin' up at the tree limbs dark against the lighter glow of a night with a moon, somewhere. The chant was louder still, *Long live the king, long live the king, long live the king...* And I almost wished I would die tae shut it from my head.

. . .

I woke at dawn with Fraoch sitting up, leaning against a tree.

"How far did we go?"

He said, "I canna bear tae look, the disappointment might kill me."

I looked over at the machine, about ten feet away, but couldn't imagine how tae get tae it.

He said, "I changed m'mind, I daena want tae get ye yer throne, this is a terrible idea."

"Tis a terrible idea, I daena want the throne. Ye are right, I changed my mind as well."

"Then we go home, ye will hae tae be content with havin' a kingdom at one end of time."

I sat there quietly. "I agree, yet... can ye hear it Fraoch?"

Fraoch shook his head. "Nae, just the infernal birds, singing their joyous wee hearts out, payin' little mind tae us dyin' here."

"I am surprised ye canna hear it."

Fraoch said, "Louder?"

"Aye, and more insistent. Dost ye think it has grown worse for Archibald as well?"

"I daena ken, but we ought tae continue as if it has."

I said, "Ye are a good uncle."

He chuckled. "If I die here, I want it on m'stone, Fraoch, he was a good uncle."

"Who is diggin' the hole, Fraoch? Ye are imaginin' a better scenario than this, I daena hae the strength tae dig yer grave so ye canna die. If ye do I will lay a stone upon ye that says, Fraoch, he was an arse." I raised up on one elbow with a groan and reached out and with a trembling hand dragged the Trailblazer close. I peered down at it. "We went two and a half years."

He dragged a bag that was slung around his leg, closer and opened it up, "Twas better. But I need tae rest afore we can go again. Want a sandwich?"

I nodded and put my hands out, but said, "Aim for m'lap, I canna trust m'eyes and hands tae work taegether."

He lobbed the sandwich intae m'lap.

We both ate quietly, then napped for the rest of the day.

Then we ate our last sandwiches and fell intae a fitful sleep.

The next morning, Fraoch said, "I am not perfect, but we can try once more."

"We hae eaten our last food. If we daena make it we might be so weakened we become stranded."

"Then we ought tae go when I hae the perfect balance of hunger and will."

We shuffled together, with our bags in our arms, and held the trailblazer between us. I said, "Daena let go."

"I winna, not until we are there."

~

Och nae. It was pouring rain down upon us.

I was wet through. I looked around blearily, there were trees a bit away. I shoved Fraoch's shoulder. "Come on."

He pushed his head up. I dragged myself and our bags toward the trees.

He began draggin' himself after me.

Twas a big pine, with broad branches, dry enough under it, but the lower branches were low, we had tae lay under them for the shelter. I dropped down ontae my stomach and slept tae the chants.

I daena ken how long we were sleeping, but when we woke up the chants were still going. I begged them tae stop. I prayed they would stop.

CHAPTER 60 - MAGNUS

We pulled ourselves into a huddle by a tree deeper intae the forest. He said, "I am famished."

"Hae we entered the complainin' part of the trip? Because with the yellin' in m'mind I am in nae mood."

"I hae been on m'best behavior, but aye, tis all complainin' from here on out. Until I am fed. Ye ken how it goes."

Long live the king, long live the king. We both stared bleary eyed out at the relentless rain until I said, "I am famished."

He chuckled.

He said, "I daena want tae, but we ought tae see how far we hae gone."

I dropped my head back on the tree trunk. "Och nae."

He crawled intae the rain and grabbed the machine and looked at it.

Long live the king, long live the king....

"What does it say?"

He smiled, a weakened smile. "We hae gone further back, past the date, Og Maggy, we are in 1285, we did it."

"Thank God." My eyes misted with the relief. I drew a muddy arm across my face.

We sat as if in a daze. "Now what?"

My stomach growled. "Dost ye hae the strength tae jump tae the right day? We need some food."

"As long as I daena hae tae use the Trailblazer again, I can do anything."

It took me a long time tae get the Trailblazer stored away and longer still tae find my vessel in my sporran and tae decide how tae set it. "Come here."

"I canna, ye come here."

I rolled over so that we were side by side and put out my arm. He wrapped his arm around it. "Ye got yer bag?"

He kicked his leg and dragged a bag closer and laid his thigh across it. "Got it."

I pulled my bags close, held ontae Fraoch's arm, and worked

the vessel on my stomach, pantin' from the effort of raising my head tae look down on it.

I laid my head back in the dirt. "Fraoch, we are jumpin'."

"When—?"

"Now — hold on."

∼

I awoke first, damp and cold, and nudged Fraoch's ribs. "Wake up, Frookie, yer snorin' is infuriatin' me."

"I am not snorin', I daena snore," he mumbled with his eyes closed.

"Then ye ought tae awaken, there is a buzzsaw cutting logs under yer head."

"Hayley shoves me over, tis the polite thing tae do."

"I am not yer wife, I daena hae tae be polite."

He grumbled as he sat up.

"I am grateful ye came, thank ye. We hae survived it. I am verra hungry."

"Yer welcome, I am hungry as well."

A verra faint bird twittered.

He said, "Dost ye want me tae hunt it for breakfast?"

I chuckled. "Nae, we daena need songbird, we need tae get up and begin walking t'ward Stirling castle."

"We ought tae stop in at the first pub we see, I daena want tae be disgusting *and* hungry when we arrive at the castle. I will be argumentative."

"Tis Scotland, we ought tae be able tae find a pub within a stone's throw and someone tae argue with so ye will be spent of it."

∼

We came upon a village almost as soon as we left the woods, twas verra small, but there was a tavern. We had stopped speaking and were trodding, exhausted and weak, and Fraoch mumbled, when we were just yards away. "Och, I daena ken if I will make it. If I collapse, go on without me."

"We are too close, I would hae tae drag ye, cause I winna return for ye. We will both die out here within sight."

"Och, ye are bellyachin', *fine.*"

We continued until we came tae the door and entered intae the dim room.

The man said, "What ye want?"

"Two drinks, and some food, sire."

He grumbled as he drew ale intae mugs.

I said, "Tis too cold tae sit inside."

The man waved his hand at us. "Och, tis warm enough!"

"Even so we will sit outside in the sunlight."

Fraoch and I both chugged down our ale. I asked for more and passed him a silver coin.

"Tis crucial that we are fed, verra quickly, or I winna be able tae stand."

"Alright, alright." The man went tae the back of the room and Fraoch and I went outside tae sit on a bench in front of the tavern, with the sun warming it.

We watched a farmer working on a plot of land before us, and a cart being pulled in the direction of the castle.

The man appeared a few minutes later with bread and cheese and a bit of meat. I paid him three pieces of silver, too much, but I felt verra generous. I stuffed a piece of bread in m'mouth and chewed. He held up a coin, and said, "Long Live the King!"

I blinked and swallowed the bread. "What did ye say?"

"God save him — the king, with a long life."

Fraoch said, "And this king is...?"

"Mag Mòr—"

Fraoch leaned forward. "Och, that is right, Mag Mòr, yet dinna I hear he was dead, that another was eying his throne?"

"Nae, he has been away from Stirling, but I haena heard anyone tryin' tae take the throne."

Fraoch said, "Och, this is verra good." He smiled at me, "See Og Maggy, there inna a usurper eyeing Mag Mòr's throne."

"Aye, I see."

Fraoch said, "Tis verra good — pray Mag Mòr will return soon, and set all our minds at ease. In the meantime, I think we will need more ale, it has been a long night."

The tavern keeper left tae get our drinks.

Fraoch ate a hunk of meat. "This is good news, Og Maggy, if there were a usurper, the tavern keeper would be one tae ken." He chewed and swallowed. "How's the chantin'?"

"Still fillin' my mind."

"Maybe tis because we are in the shadow of the castle, perhaps when ye get tae the top of the hill twill silence."

"Again, we can only pray it will."

CHAPTER 61 - KAITLYN

BALLOCH CASTLE

Zach was running down the corridor as Archie and I were going up to the room to get ready for dinner. "The monitor! Someone is coming, the men, a storm!"

I hugged my arm around Archie, and smiled down at him. "This is good news!"

Zach jogged down the stairs, "Going to tell Quentin!"

Archie and I got Jack and Isla from the nursery and followed him down, making it to the courtyard as Quentin, Liam, and Sean were riding horses out the gate headed towards the clearing.

I said, "Well, this is great, want to wait here until they come?"

He nodded and sat back down on our bench, putting the book down beside him for the first time in days.

My ass was worn from sitting so long. I refused to do it any longer.

I paced around, carrying Jack, talking to him, smiling at Archie and Isla, remembering now that it would take a while, more than an hour at least.

. . .

Ben came and met us and he and Archie surprised me by deciding to go up on the wall to watch out for Magnus, Fraoch, and Lochie, and hopefully Ash, as they returned to the castle.

Jack and Isla and I waited near the door, Hayley coming to keep me company.

CHAPTER 62 - LOCHINVAR

THE CLEARING NEAR BALLOCH CASTLE

Wake up, wake up, ye hae Ash with ye, ye must wake up. I woke with a start, I had tae get up, she would be frightened. I was lyin' beside her m'leg thrown over her hips. I pulled my leg off, she moaned. I forced m'self up and kneeled beside her "Ash, wake up, ye ken tis me, Lochie, I am so sorry, ye must wake up."

I placed my hands on both sides of her face. "Mistress Ash, please, please wake up."

Her eyes fluttered, then opened and focused on me, then her mouth drew down. "Owie owie, owie, Lochie, it hurts."

"I ken it does, Mistress Ash, I am so sorry. I ken."

She grabbed her left arm. "I dislocated my shoulder!" Tears spilled from her eyes. "I didn't want to do it — I told you I didn't want to. It hurts everywhere."

I said, "Someone will be here for us in just a minute, all will be well."

She became aware of our surroundings, looking all around at the trees. "We're surrounded by woods — what woods are these? Where are we?"

"We are in Scotland, Ash, at Balloch castle, the home of the Earl of Breadalbane."

She looked directly at me, "What year?"

"The year of our Lord, 1710."

Horses were coming up the path.

I scrambled up and stood over her, with my hand on my gun and waited.

Twas Quentin, Sean, and Liam.

Quentin said, "Dammit, Lochie, where's Magnus, is he okay?"

I said, "He's good, Fraoch is good, they helped me get Ash."

"Why the hell didn't they come back with you?"

"Magnus thought he could solve everything by taking his throne once more."

Sean said, "And *why* do you have their horses?"

I shook my head, "I daena ken... I think... Magnus said they might hae tae use the Trailblazer, but I canna remember the details. We were bein' chased. They tossed the reins at me and told me tae jump."

"So you don't *really* know where they are?"

"The last thing we talked about was his throne, I am certain they are returnin' tae..." I glanced at Ash, she had gone pale. "More pressin', Ash is injured."

While Sean and Liam began gatherin' our horses taegether. Quentin dismounted his horse and crouched beside Ash. "Hey, Ash, how's it going?"

Her hand gripped her shoulder. "Where are you from — you sound normal."

"Fernandina Beach."

"Island local... okay, you explain it, what the hell is going on?"

"Damn, you're all the way back at 'what the hell is going on'? That's not good, jumping sucks, especially when you have no idea what's going on. But... welcome to Scotland."

Ash winced. "Sucks so far."

Quentin said, "Where does it hurt?"

CHAPTER 62 - LOCHINVAR

"I dislocated it. I did it once before, about four years ago."

Quentin said, "So... you know it's going to hurt, right? The next few minutes are going to be awful." He helped her sit up. "Did you do this part in the hospital?"

"Yep."

Her face was in a grimace of pain. I hated seein' it, I stood up and began pacin' around them.

Quentin said, "You're cool, Lochie?"

"Tis hard tae watch, I daena want ye tae hurt her."

She blew out air, "Owie owie owie."

I asked, "Dost ye need me tae hold yer hand?"

She nodded.

I crouched down beside her and held her good hand. But then I looked at her palm. "Yer hands look verra painful, Ash."

She nodded. "Blisters from carrying my weapon."

I said, "What kind of weapon?"

"An iron spike, about five pounds, about twenty inches long. It was not great, but it was all I could find."

"Och nae..."

Quentin said, "I hate to be the bearer of bad news, but we don't have a hospital, Ash, so you're just going to have to buck up while we get this joint back, can you do that?"

She nodded.

He took her hand and gently raised it up and over her head.

She breathed in bursts, puff puff puff. "Owie owie owie," she choked out, "I suppose there's no pain meds either?"

He folded her arm down. She was panting.

"No no, we have lots of pain meds, we got all the pain meds, just no doctor. We're going rogue. Now scratch your back. Back and forth." She winced, holding her breath as she shifted her hand back and forth until there was an audible pop and her shoulder went back intae place.

She let out the air and said, "Oh thank gumdrops and Easter candy, sweet, sweet relief."

Quentin helped her bring her arm back around to her front. He said, "Lochie, check my side pack, there's a first aid kit."

I raced over tae the horse and dug through the pack for a big red box with a cross on the side. I brought it back and he said, "Ash, I'm going to give you a rudimentary field-wrap, we'll do it better when you get to the castle."

He unwound a bandage and bound it around her shoulder and arm, holdin' it close tae her side. Then he cleaned her palms and wiped the skin with an ointment, and wrapped them with white bandages. She said, "Feels better already."

Quentin opened a jar of medicine and poured three pills intae her palm. He passed her a bottle with water.

She said, looking down on the pills, "I don't know, I might get pretty loopy, seems like I might need my wits about me."

Quentin said, "I know you've been through an ordeal and this is all scary, but we're going to a really nice castle, you'll have a bed and a warm meal. Take the medicine."

She popped them in her mouth and drank a long draft of water tae wash them down.

I said, "We hae a cart or a horse, both are likely tae cause ye discomfort."

"I'll take the cart, if that's okay, the horse is kinda... It's all a lot for me to get used to." One of the horses stamped and snorted. Her face drew down.

I helped her up and with an arm for support brought her tae the cart. She was covered in dirt. I brushed a twig from her hair and got her sittin' in the middle on a burlap sack. I dug through one of the packs on my horse and found a plaid tae wrap around her shoulders, fussin' with gettin' it tight and tucked in so that her arm was stationary. We were verra close while I worked and then I said, "I am sorry."

She blinked and looked as if she might cry.

"It winna be a long ride, Mistress Ash, I will do my best tae keep ye comfortable."

Sean and Liam checked the harness for the horse and then we headed toward Balloch castle.

CHAPTER 63 - ASH

BALLOCH CASTLE

*P*opping my shoulder joint back in place improved the pain immensely, but all the rest of this situation was insane. I was lying in a cart, being dragged around by horses. I had been in a shootout, Lochie had done something to me that scared me and hurt terribly, and now we were going somewhere — where were we going?

To a castle.

None of it made sense, but there was a Florida boy here. That was weird. Did that mean this was a dream?

None of it seemed real.

I realized that the cart was metal, and the wheels had rubber tires. Near me was a nameplate — TuffCart. It was bouncing me, but they were pulling me slow, trying to keep the bouncing to a minimum. I was actually getting lulled to sleep, probably the effect of the drugs, too. Watching the trees go by, an endless woods, what woods? I was definitely feeling, loose. Looser. Looserer.

The cart rolled, the movement shifted side to side. I looked up at Lochie, he was up on a horse, riding beside me, backlit by sun, hot, straight backed and competent, gosh he was hot. Roll shift, shift roll.

CHAPTER 63 - ASH

He looked down, his expression was really concerned about me.

Yeah, well me too.

"Ye well, Ash?"

I raised my good arm, my hand wrapped in white bandage, and pointed at him, "You are not real, m'laird." I giggled.

His jaw clenched.

None of this is real. Do you hear me? None of it.

CHAPTER 64 - KAITLYN

BALLOCH CASTLE

Finally Archie yelled down, "Mammy! They're coming!" Jack and Hayley applauded, I stood in the open gate watching down the causeway, but there was something off about the scene. It took a few moments of watching, the group in the far distance, before I realized that two of the horses didn't have riders. Magnus wasn't with them.

I heard a loud scream from the walls and turned as Archie collapsed on the parapet.

I passed Jack to Hayley and raced up the steps, *Oh no oh no oh no oh no.* Ben was pale in fear. There were men surrounding Archie. I shoved past them. "Baby, are you okay?"

He was passed out cold. I pushed his hair off his forehead. "Archie, honey, come on, wake up."

I looked at one of the guards. "Do you see them coming? Is Magnus with them?"

He shook his head, "Nae. Only Lochinvar."

I smoothed and caressed Archie's face. "Come on, wake up, little guy, you need to wake up. I know your dad isn't here, but I'm sure it's fine. Uncle Fraoch is with him, nothing will happen to him if Fraoch is there. You know this."

CHAPTER 64 - KAITLYN

Archie's eyes fluttered open, he said, "I think he died, Mammy."

James came up behind us, "Is everything okay, Katie?"

I shook my head. "Can you help me get him down to our room?"

James picked Archie up, and Ben and I followed them down the steps. We met Isla, who was carrying Archie's book, and Hayley passed me Jack.

I said, "Find out what's happening, come tell me, okay? As soon as you know,"

Hayley said, "Of course, Katie, as soon as I know."

Holding Isla by the hand, carrying Jack, I followed James up to my bedroom, so worried about Archie, limp in his arms, and terrified that something horrible had happened to Magnus. I wanted to be down in the courtyard to hear what had happened, but Archie needed me more.

~

Isla sat quietly on the bed beside Archie who was curled up around the book kind of sleeping, in and out of consciousness.

James said, "Do you mind if Sophie comes in? She would like to sit with you while you wait."

"I would like that."

So Sophie was nursing Junior sitting on the couch, nearby, a comforting presence.

Beaty rushed in, "Dost ye want me tae take Jack tae the nursery?"

Jack put up his arms to go with her.

She said, "Send someone tae tell me, as soon as ye ken."

"I will."

But then Hayley rushed in and sat down beside me. "Okay,

here's the thing, Archie, don't be worried — your dad is okay, he's just not home *yet*."

I said, "Explain it, what happened?"

"They found Ash, she's here, Quentin is so sorry he forgot the radio, he wasn't thinking, he feels terrible."

I glanced at Archie, his chin trembling.

I said, "Just tell me what happened, Hayley."

"They rescued Ash, and they were being chased, so Lochie left fast, but Magnus and Fraoch needed to do one more thing first."

"What could that possibly...?"

Her eyes flitted to Archie and she jerked her head.

He said, "You can say it, Aunt Hayley, they went to go get Da's throne?"

She was quiet then said, "Yep, they went back to 1290 or probably 1291 because of time that passed."

I glanced at Archie, he was counting on his fingers between 1291 and 1296.

I asked Hayley, "Is that why I felt the Trailblazer?"

"Yeah, that's probably why."

He said, "Five years between."

I said, "Yes, it's a long time."

Hayley patted Archie's hand. "This is good news. Uncle Fraoch and your Da are not going to let anything happen to each other, they are going to solve this problem and I have never known them to not be able to solve something. They are completely competent in solving things."

I said, "Thank you for letting us know, can you go hear more?"

"Yep, I'm your eyes and ears. And Archie, they are coming home, Uncle Fraoch will not let us down."

She got up, kissed Archie's cheek, kissed Isla, kissed my forehead, and then kissed Sophie and Junior and rushed away.

CHAPTER 65 - ASH

BALLOCH CASTLE

I was lifted from the cart by someone. I opened my eyes, a blurry Lochie swam into view. "Hi!" I giggled. "You're not real."

"I assure ye I am."

I looked around, faces swimming around me, all looking weirdly old-fashioned, wearing skirts. The men had weapons and beards and, I pointed, "You're not real. You're not real. You're not real." I swung my good arm around. "All y'all not real."

Lochie began striding across the... where were we? Stone walls, like a castle. Funny, they said castle and now we were in a castle and it all seemed real, but couldn't possibly be... but I had been in the longest most realistic dream of my life.

There was a woman walking ahead of us, "Ye can take her tae the east room on the third floor, Lochinvar, the chambermaid has it readied."

His deep voice returned, "Aye, Madame Lizbeth, thank ye."

We started up a stairwell and I reached my hand out and felt the stone wall as we climbed. "None of this is real." There was a draft, the air was cold, I tucked my head against his chest. "Warm." I sighed. "I like you even though you're just a dream."

Lochie said to the woman, "She is overly weary and overcome from the injury."

The woman said, "I understand."

We went down a long dark corridor and I faded in and out of consciousness until a heavy door was opened and the temperature and light changed. We were in a room. I looked around and said, "Old bed, old table, old fireplace, old walls..." Then forgot what I was talking about, happily it was warm, there was a fire roaring in the hearth.

I was placed down on a lumpy mattress, in a bed with a canopy, a small bed, not much more than a twin.

Lochie fluffed the pillow under my head and said, "Tis comfortable?"

My face was heavy, my lips felt like they were sliding down off my face into the down pillow. "No, but that's okay, Lochie, you did your best. It's all a figment, a weird figment of my..." I couldn't remember what I was saying again, so I stopped.

The woman, Lizbeth said, "I will leave ye — dost ye need aught, Lochinvar?"

"Nae, I will stay here until she comes back tae herself."

It grew quiet in the room. Lochie pulled a chair up beside the bed.

I fell asleep.

I woke up a little while later, on my side, my sore shoulder up, with the sound of Lochie's voice muttering though I couldn't understand what he was saying.... "What...?"

He brushed my hair off my cheek. "I was prayin'."

I chuckled, looking at my bandaged hands, "You don't have to pray for me — I feel great!"

He smiled down on me. "Ye hae been out of yer mind."

I said, "Did I say something stupid?"

He shook his head, with his eyes cast down.

"Ugh, I'm so sorry. I didn't mean it, whatever it was. I don't know, I feel sane, but this all seems maddening. What is happening, Lochie?"

"I am a time traveler."

I narrowed my eyes. "Time travel doesn't exist."

He shrugged. "Then how dost ye explain that ye hae been in the thirteenth century, that now ye are in the eighteenth century? What is yer explanation, Ash?"

"I don't know."

"I'm a time traveler, the brother of a king."

"Who was the man who kidnapped me?"

"His name is Asgall, we daena ken much about him, but he is tryin' tae outmaneuver Magnus."

"Why me?"

"Because I love ye, and—"

"You love me?"

"Aye, I promised tae protect ye and I... dinna."

I was looking at my bandaged hand on the pillow beside me. "You didn't promise me anything."

He said, "I did in m'heart. When we did the thumb oath, I swore I would never—"

"You swore you would never beguile me, Lochie, you *promised*." A tear spilled down my nose. "And you have done *nothing* but beguile me, so much beguiling, everywhere, beguiled."

"I am sorry, Ash..." He shifted in his seat. "I dinna ken how tae tell ye. Ye wouldna believe me if I had. Tis a fanciful tale and I hoped that if ye fell in love with me first, ye might believe it later."

"Exactly. That is beguiling, Lochie."

He nodded.

Then added, "In m'defense, I hae been lost since I met ye and dinna ken how tae behave. I wasna certain what tae tell ye."

"So you didn't tell me — I could have died." My eyes went wide. "Is everyone worried about me? Where do they think I went?"

"I daena ken, but ye can return tae the next day, most people winna ken ye were gone... twas good ye called Kaitlyn, tis how we kent ye had been taken."

I relaxed my head back to the pillow. "So you're a time traveler, and you have beguiled me, and now I'm caught up in it too?"

"Aye, Ash, I am verra sorry. I dinna mean tae draw ye in, I will take ye home as soon as ye are well enough tae travel, and then I will leave ye alone and ye can go back tae yer life. I winna bother ye again. I promise ye will be safe from harm once I am gone."

I watched him speak, marveling at the planes and angles of his face, his jaw, with its newly grown beard.

"I don't want you to go. Why would you leave me?"

"Because I am dangerous, I am the brother of a king, and I daena ken how tae keep ye safe. I am an orphan, ye can see that yer bed is small, and this is beyond what they would ever offer me, because ye are a guest ye are given yer own room, with a small bed, but when I come tae visit I am made tae sleep with the men in the barracks, tis all I am, an orphan who was found by Magnus, his half-brother by blood, but he dinna ken I existed until he was forced tae take me on. I grew up fightin' for my life, being beaten when I dinna fight well enough. I hae given Magnus my oath tae be his sword, and in exchange I hae the treatment of a lord, but not the respect. I daena hae vast armies, I canna command others tae my bidding, I only fight. I am verra good at fighting, Ash, but that also means I attract battles, what kind of life does this mean for ye? Tis not a good enough life, ye deserve more."

My mouth drew down. "That is the saddest story I ever heard."

He nodded. "Tis true."

"It's not really true, what I hear is you are a knight, you fight for a king, you saved yourself by being the best fighter around,

CHAPTER 65 - ASH

and you are young but already when you have a guest at the — what castle is this?"

"Balloch, the Earl of Breadalbane's castle."

"When Lord Lochinvar the Great invites a guest to stay at Bally, the Earl of Breadelywhoo gives her a very fine bedroom, one of the best—"

He chuckled, "Twas his niece who gave us the guest room, we ought not tell the Earl, and this inna a good room, the bed is verra small."

I said, "You, my love, are not seeing the worth of yourself."

The corner of his mouth turned up. "Ye called me 'my love'."

I sighed. "I have been hopelessly beguiled. You're better at that than you give yourself credit for, too."

"If ye see the worth of me, tis good enough—"

There was a knock on the door. Lochie said, "Enter!"

The woman named Hayley came in. She said, "I'm sorry to interrupt, I just really need to hear more about what was going on. I really need to know if you think Fraoch and Magnus are okay."

"Aye, Hayley, I am certain they are well."

"Thank God, I mean, I thought it was okay, but I just needed to hear you say it. I felt the Trailblazer."

"Aye, they must be usin' it. They dinna want tae subject the horses tae it, and I needed tae get Ash home. She was injured, but as far as I know they are well."

"That is a relief, thank you."

"Would ye sit with Ash for a moment? I need tae relieve m'self."

"Of course. Would you go talk to Kaitlyn too, Archie is freaking out — they really need to be reassured."

"Archie is upset?"

"Yeah, he's not doing good."

"Och nae." He squeezed my hand. "I will leave ye with Madame Hayley, I must speak tae m'nephew, he is worried on his Da."

I nodded. "I understand."

CHAPTER 66 - KAITLYN

MAGNUS AND KAITLYN'S BEDROOM CHAMBER

*T*here was a knock on the door and Lochie entered. "Hello, I came tae see ye — tae speak tae Archie."

Archie was crying, his hands over his ears, having just told me again that the chanting wouldn't stop — he was breaking my heart.

I offered Lochie a chair, but he said, "Nae, I daena want an uncomfortable seat, I want tae perch on the side of a bed." He shoved Archie over with his hip and sat on the edge of the mattress. "Hey, wee man, what are ye doin'?"

Archie kept his hands clamped on his ears and shook his head.

Lochie said, "I was just with yer Da, he is well. I am sorry I scared ye when I returned without him, but he told me tae tell ye that he will be home soon. He had one thing tae do first."

"He is dead, they are telling me, the king is dead."

"He was verra concerned about it, Archie. He went tae go see if he can solve it. I told him I thought that ye were hearing it because he haena held ontae his throne, so he's gone to secure it, tae take back Scotland for his own, then ye will see..." Lochie's voice trailed off. Archie was just watching him, his body tense, his hands clamped tight.

"I am verra sorry, wee man."

Archie said, "Nothing you can do though, this is what happens — a throne gets passed to a son, even if he doesn't want it. I don't want it. Not if Da dies." He rolled over on his side, picked up the book and pressed it over his ear and closed his eyes tightly.

Lochie shook his head.

Then said to me, "I am sorry Kaitlyn, I wish I could set his mind quiet."

"So what happened?"

"Fraoch and I spoke with Magnus at length about how we believe that all of this," he gestured toward Archie, "is unsettled, because he gained a throne in the year 1290, but dinna hold it. He allowed it tae be usurped by Asgall. We were advisin' Magnus, but at the time I dinna ken if he agreed, he was grumblin' that I was disparagin' him and his actions."

I said, "Been there."

"Aye, it dinna seem like he was takin' our advice, but then we rescued Ash, and as we were fleeing, and I can't stress this enough, we were being chased, Magnus said he was going to go take his throne. Tis a part of his plan tae fight Asgall." He shook his head. "If he had known the state of his son, I think he would hae come home first, but he *will* come home."

"Thank you, Lochie, I'm really glad you got Ash back, I'll come visit her once we figure this out. I can't leave his side."

"Daena worry on it, she will understand. Hayley is speaking with her now."

"That's good, she'll be able to commiserate, she's been trapped in the past before."

CHAPTER 67 - ASH

BALLOCH CASTLE - GUEST CHAMBER

Hayley said, "So how are you doing?"

"The pain meds are wearing off, the soreness is coming back. I was just kidnapped, held for days, *that's* going to need some therapy, and my surroundings look ancient... this is not normal."

"You're in the past."

"So this is real? I'm not losing my mind?"

"This is absolutely real, you are not losing your mind. I was jumped into the past once, stuck, it was terrifying, but that's how I met my husband so I guess it wasn't all bad."

"When did we invent time travel?"

"Someone else invented it, we've just stolen the tech, and now we're using it."

"Like... *aliens*?"

"I don't know, honestly, could be. We sit up discussing it all the time, some of us think yes, aliens, but the vessels don't take us off-planet."

"Yeah, that's weird."

"The fact that it stays on-planet makes me think it's a group of us from the future-future."

"Or humans that descended from aliens in the past-past, the same alien-human-hybrid who built the pyramids."

Hayley chuckled. "I can see you'll be a good addition to our discussions. Zach will enjoy having someone in his camp."

I said, "A question... when I was in the compound, Lochinvar sent a drone into the room, he asked if he should come now — what did he mean?"

She said, "I think he wasn't sure when you got there, you might have been there for months, he might have wanted to try to rescue you earlier."

I thought that through. "He could have done that?"

She nodded. "Yeah, time travel, but note I said, 'try to', he would have had to leave you to do it, and a lot could go wrong. Time could shift. Things might change. There would be a chance he might lose you again."

"Ugh, then I'm glad I didn't understand the question — I'm glad he didn't try." I took a deep breath. "So I'm not going to wake up and this will all be over?"

"It's been years, no, there's no waking up — this is your reality now, unless of course you want to go back to your regular life and never see Lochie again."

"No, that's not what I want." I blew out air. "Jimminy Jehosophat, this is a mind mucker."

"*Exactly.* And I don't want to freak you out, but this is dangerous. Sometimes it's insane how dangerous it is — you have soldier skills? You'll need them.*"*

"I don't know how to ride a horse."

"You'll learn. Katie didn't know how and she figured it out. She didn't have any soldier skills, she was kidnapped once, here in the past, it took Magnus a couple of days to find her, and somehow she survived."

"Damn, what did he do?"

She leveled her eyes. "He killed all of them in front of her."

I gulped. "Oh... and Lochie has killed people before?"

CHAPTER 67 - ASH

"Yes. It's safe to assume he's killed a *lot*. There's an arena in Magnus's kingdom where men fight to the death—"

"In front of an audience? Did Lochie kill someone in front of an audience?"

"Yeah... but it's like war, you know? Kill or be killed."

"Yeah I know. So how many people are Magnus and his brothers at war with?"

Hayley pretended to count on her fingers then said, "We've had peace for a while, no enemies. It was blissful, but here we are, Asgall is new."

"I want to kick his ass."

"Then welcome to the family."

I took a deep breath, my shoulder was beginning to hurt. "How is everyone related to Lochie?"

"Fraoch, Magnus and Lochie have the same father. They're half-brothers. James, Quentin, and Zach are as good as brothers. They would all fight for each other. They all do. Fraoch and Lochie argue like crazy, but don't let it bother you, Fraoch really cares about what happens to him. When Lochie said he needed to go find you, Fraoch and Magnus just packed their bags to go. That's how they feel about each other, and you're part of that now too. I guess what I'm saying is, he's a good boy."

I chuckled.

There was a knock on the door, Lochie stepped in.

I asked Hayley, "Do you know where there're more pain killers? My shoulder is aching."

Hayley found the bottle on the side table and gave me two with some water in a mug. Lochie helped me sit up to drink it. Then she left us alone.

I said, "You relieved yourself? Where does that happen?"

"There is a garderobe down the hall or a chamberpot in the corner."

I joked, "Och nae, another pisspot."

He smiled.

"I also went tae see m'nephew. He is not well, I am concerned for him."

I put my good hand out and he held it, looking down on it. His thumb moving back and forth across my fingers.

"What do you mean by not well? He's sick?"

"Nae, tis more like he is anxious. He feels he has seen the future, where his father dies and he becomes a king. He is haunted by it."

"Poor kid."

"Aye, tae be a prince is a hard thing."

I looked up at him and he met my eyes.

Then he averted his eyes. "I hae been wonderin'..."

"Wondering what?"

"If ye meant it when ye took the thumb oath, if ye still mean it... ? I never meant tae beguile ye, Ash, or bring ye intae danger. When ye were taken I felt verra lost..."

I watched his face, his eyes cast down, handsome and yes, seeming lost, worried...

I said, "You have a heart as big as the world, Lochie. I am so grateful that you're in love with me, and yes, I meant the thumb oath." I put my thumb in my mouth and held it out, covered in slobber, because I was getting pretty loopy again.

He sucked on his thumb and then pressed it to mine. "From this day forward, I winna beguile ye."

I giggled, sleepily. "Good, because I would kick your hot, sexy butt. "

He laughed.

I said, "Will you come get in bed with me? I'm starting to feel loopy. You love me, you have to hold me while I sleep, part of the deal."

He pulled off his shoes and socks and said, "Sorry tis a frightful stench." He moved them away.

I said, my voice kind of slurring, "I'm a frightful stench... been wearing these clothes for years." I giggled.

CHAPTER 67 - ASH

He said, "Ye are a wee bit odiferous."

"My breath or my pits?"

He climbed onto the bed behind me. "Tis yer pits, they smell as if ye fought a battle in the thirteenth century."

I said, "Ugh, I guess we're moving right past looking beautiful for you, to you telling me I stink."

He jokingly pulled up his own arm and put it near my nose. "Ye are always goin' tae smell better than m'own stench. We must grow used tae it, there inna any smeary sticks of deodorant anywhere near here." Then he pressed his nose to my arm near my pit. "Yers smell of battle that has been fought and won and a bit of onion, so it calms me and makes me hungry. These are good things."

I laughed. "And you still love me."

"Aye. Even more." He spooned me with an arm draped around my side. "Does this hurt yer shoulder?"

"No," I wriggled closer, so his face was right behind my head, his deep breath near my ear.

He asked, "Did he hurt ye?"

I shook my head. "No, he didn't even touch me. He made me sign a contract, Lochie, claiming it made us 'married' but I didn't even sign my last name. I don't think it would hold up in a court of law in any year or in any time."

"Aye, ye signed under duress. Also ye already pressed yer spit-covered thumb tae mine, he canna hae ye, ye pledged yerself tae me first."

I smiled. "It was so important. I didn't know it at the time, but I am very glad I pressed my spit-thumb to yours."

"Twas important, especially after holdin' my hand and servin' me yer pie."

He exhaled. "I am glad he dinna hurt ye. I am still goin' tae kill him, but this means I can revenge upon him more methodically, with more thought."

"Revenge is a dish best served cold."

"Aye, tis verra wise."

"I can't take credit for it, it's a quote from someone..."

We lay there for a few minutes and then he said, very close to my ear, "I *am* real."

"I know you are, Lochie, I'm sorry I said it. I didn't mean it."

I turned and he kissed me on the corner of my mouth. But then twisting hurt my shoulder. I went back to lying on my side and his arm went back around me, his hand right in front of my mouth. I kissed his thumb.

I said, "So this is what we are going to do, time travel together?"

He said, "Aye. Twill be a good life, Ash, although twill be dangerous, I winna lie—"

"I don't mind a little danger, but if we can go anywhere, in any time, m'laird, we ought to make sure there are better mattresses."

He kissed me right behind my ear. "I will take ye everywhere in the world, tae every time. I will give ye a soft bed whenever I can, I will be a lord of time and ye will be m'lady."

I giggled, "The Lady Ash of Lochie's Soft Bed."

He said, his voice low and rumbling, "Aye."

And then I slowly fell asleep.

CHAPTER 68 - ASGALL

NEW YORK, NOVEMBER 2, 1912

I swept my arm across my desk sending papers flying toward Bernard. We were in the office, at Asgall Holdings.

"Explain it!"

"She was removed from the brewery."

I narrowed my eyes. "Ye assured me this plan was goin' tae work, this was yer idea, we followed yer execution."

He shifted and squirmed.

I leaned on the desk, enjoying the sight. Then smiled. "You like it here, Bernard, it's comfy in the twentieth century? You like Manhattan and the parties?"

He nodded.

I took a last long drag from a cigarette and blew smoke toward his face. I jabbed the cigarette out in the ash tray. "I am glad ye hae been enjoyin' yerself — I hae been building my empire, but Bernard...? He is havin' fun in Manhattan." I smiled widely, malevolently. "Good for ye."

I pulled out m'pack and pulled another cigarette out, lit it and took another drag, watching him thinking of all the ways I could kill him. "I really shouldna smoke, it makes it verra difficult tae go back tae the past without them. I ought tae quit — how did Magnus find out where we hid her?"

"I am not certain, sire."

"Until we kidnapped her, he had nae idea I existed. I was safe and my plans were unimpeded. Twas a good thing, was it not?"

He nodded, "A good thing, yes sire."

"Then how did he find out about me?" I took another drag of the cigarette, and punctuated the air as I spoke. "You came up with a plan. You arranged its execution. And you allowed Magnus to discover where we were holding her. Ash escaped, Magnus now knows about me, years of effort, destroyed."

I watched him glance around the room as if looking for an escape route.

"What am I supposed tae do now — daena answer it, ye see that ye must die for it, tis treasonous."

"If you give me a moment to formulate a new plan, I will advise your next—"

I raised my brow.

"My *next*? After yer disastrous *last* idea?"

He gulped.

I jabbed out the second cigarette and considered pulling a third from the box, lingering over the idea, making him wait and suffer.

"I could kill ye, but it takes time tae find someone new tae do the work, ye hae me over a barrel here, ye are well trained and ye owe me a great—"

He dropped tae his knees. "Please sire, spare me, I will do whatever ye need. I thought we had hidden her, her full name was not on any documents, there were no photographs, your connection to Fortingall was hidden—"

"Until it wasna."

"Yes, sire."

I folded my arms across m'chest and tapped my foot, thinking. "I want a list of the Campbell cousins, the ones with direct or indirect claims tae the throne—"

"Would you like the two lists separate or with a note beside them that says..."

I gave him a withering look.

His voice trailed off. "I will figure out how to compile it for you."

"First, I want the woman back. The plan was decided, I daena like losing. This is our priority. I want the child. While ye figure out how tae make this happen, I will return tae 1296 and strengthen and fortify m'throne as I..."

Bernard lost color in his face.

"What?"

"Magnus has taken the Scottish throne in the year 1290, they call him Mag Mòr —"

I shoved the last of the papers off my desk. "Yer incompetence will be the end of me!" I pulled a cigarette from the pack and lit it, puffed from it. "How did he become king? Did he take it from Balliol?"

"I am not certain, Sire—"

"Get me a meeting with William Wallace, I need tae shore up m'alliance. Do I still have a throne?"

"I am not... I daena ken."

I dumped my cigarette intae the ashtray, ripped open a drawer, grabbed my pistol, and shot him.

He grabbed his chest and collapsed tae the ground. Och nae, twould be an irritation tae cover this up.

I tossed the gun back tae the drawer and slammed it shut.

He gurgled his last breaths.

I sat down in the chair and thought over what I needed: A list of the cousins. Tae complete my purchase of the land in two more centuries. The woman and her child. The more I thought about it, the more I wanted tae be in control of one of Donnan's grandsons. And I had tae retake m'thirteenth century throne. All of it would be easier if Bernard hadna forced me tae kill him.

I pulled the cigarette from the ashtray, leaned back in my chair tae decide where tae begin — first, I would hae tae close down this office because of the blood upon the floor.

CHAPTER 69 - KAITLYN

MAGNUS AND KAITLYN'S CHAMBER - BALLOCH CASTLE

I was sitting beside Archie, singing him a lullaby, smoothing the hair from his sweaty forehead. I had hidden his book under a pillow and wouldn't let him touch it. I had prayed. I had made him repeat a prayer. I had asked him to repeat everything he heard inside his head.

He recounted it, his voice shaky, his lip trembling, "The king is dead! The king is dead!"

The visual description he gave me seemed familiar, crowds, fluttering white flags against a blue sky. I wasn't sure when I'd seen it before but it felt old to me. He said it felt old, but what did he know? He was only eight times around the sun.

Lizbeth sent food to the room. Ben came by to visit. Emma joined me, bringing Jack for bed and I snuck in and out of the room to use the chamber pot.

When I returned Archie had the book in his arms again.

I was done arguing.

It had grown dark outside, the day long gone. I sat down with Jack sleepy in my arms. "Did you check the page while I was in the bathroom?"

He nodded.

"Was there a message?"

"No, want to see?"

"Sure, show me."

Jack's head was heavy as he drifted away to sleep. Archie sat up, opened the book to the page, and clicked on his flashlight to shine the light right on the tiny place where his grandmother had told Magnus to put the mark. He looked at it carefully. Then whispered. "Do you think you see something, right there?"

"I don't love, if your Da wanted to send you a message it would be much more prominent than that tiny smudge, a fleck of dust really. He would make sure it was easily seen, you know how much he loves his pens, right? Have you ever seen his signature? It's big with lots of loops. He would make sure you could read it, he wouldn't want us to miss it."

"Grandmother told him to make it small though…"

"I doubt your father will listen to that."

He yawned.

"I think you're sleepy."

"I'm afraid to go to sleep, what if something happens?"

"I'm your night guard."

"Will you check the book?"

"Yes." I stood and put down Jack in the middle of the bed between Archie and Isla, who was already almost asleep.

I sat back in the chair and placed the book in my lap. I held the flashlight on top of it.

"Check every hour, Mammy, wake me if something happens. I'll go get him."

I kissed his temple. "I will."

He clamped his hands over his ears and curled up on his side, and tightened his eyes.

I sighed, watching his little body as it slowly relaxed and fell asleep. He was dealing with life and death, the pressure of being the first born son. On his slight shoulders he carried the weight of a kingdom. It terrified me that he might be telling the future.

I opened to the page, and shined the light on it to see… but there was nothing there.

CHAPTER 70 - MAGNUS

NEAR STIRLING CASTLE, 1291

We approached from the southeast, marveling at the sight of the grassy slope risin' tae the timber walls of the castle. Twas a familiar approach, the thick wooden gate and timber walls ahead of us enclosing a few stone buildings: a stone chapel, a low stone building for kitchens and storerooms, and the King's house, the three-story stone building that held the royal bedrooms and offices. The Great Hall, the barracks for the men, the stables, and a few other buildings were all built of timber.

I had barely remembered this place, but now it all seemed familiar, and as I always thought in this approach, I wished that m'walls were higher and made of stone.

As we neared we were spotted by my guards. Four men rushed forward, bowing and filing around us. Two other men rushed away. I knew they were going to find Cailean, tae tell him I had returned.

Fraoch said, under his breath, "Tis as if ye never left."

"Aye."

Fraoch looked across the courtyard tae the King's house. "Until we walked through the gate I dinna remember this place, now tis familiar. I even hae a room, daena I hae a room?"

"I daena remember. But more importantly, do *I* hae a room? I think mine is there." I pointed at the upper window.

Cailean rushed tae the courtyard. "Magnus! Fraoch! M'apologies, Yer Majesty, m'apologies." He bowed. "I wasna expecting ye, Yer Majesty, until later in the week. Did ye hae good travels? Ye ought tae hae taken yer guard!"

I dinna remember what I had told him, so I said, "I ken, Cailean, sometimes a man daena want a guard. They are a great deal of flatulence and not much in the way of good conversation."

Cailean grinned, chuckling, and said, "Tis true."

"But aye, my travels were verra fruitful."

"Good, and I daena mean tae insult ye, but ye hae the stench of the road upon ye, Yer Majesty."

I laughed. "I assume I do, I ought tae wash and dress."

"While ye do I will ask the guard tae raise yer standard on the walls, and inform the kitchens — I canna promise a feast, but we will do our best, we werna expecting ye!" He turned tae Fraoch, "I will give ye a room on the second floor, tis under my room. I hope ye will be good with the arrangement. Magnus has allowed me the best room because I am stiff and achy with my age."

Fraoch said, "Of course. I think that is the one I always hae...?"

"Ye haena been here, Fraoch. I would hae remembered!"

Fraoch winced, "Aye, ye are right, Cailean, on our travels Magnus told me so many stories that it seems as if I lived here all m'life. M'point, Cailean, is that Magnus talks a great deal."

I said, "Tis better tae be known as a great talker, than as ye are, filled with flatulence."

Cailean laughed. "I had forgotten how ye both speak in jest with each other. Ye are reminding me of yer bickering in the tent in the battlefields, when we were gaining your crown — how is Haggis by the way?"

"He is verra good, he is guardin' the bairns at home, a verra cù math."

"I look forward tae meetin' yer bairns."

"I will bring them soon, how are yer sons?"

"Verra well, I will send word that ye hae returned, they will want tae come celebrate."

"I look forward tae it."

He led us up the stairs. "Fraoch, I will shew ye tae yer room."

I followed him up, but continued on tae the third floor, and my room, I now remembered it well.

CHAPTER 71 - MAGNUS

THE KING'S CHAMBER, STIRLING CASTLE

There was a chambermaid readyin' the room as I entered. She bowed and left hastily. A boy built a high fire in the fireplace tae cut the gloom, as the room hadna been used in a few days.

I removed my clothes and bathed with a rag and water from the pitcher and dressed in clean, more royal clothes that fit the time. My shirt was tight across m'shoulders, I had been working out regularly in Florida. I stretched, tryin' tae give m'self more room.

Then I put on a tunic, with a fur-lined collar and cuffs. I buckled a belt around m'waist, and m'cloak, pinned with a large brooch around my shoulders. I sat down on the settee tae put on m'boots.

The sight of the fire gave me pause. I remembered sittin' here, my hand on Haggis's head, while I was fretting over Kaitlyn bein' trapped on another timeline, long hours, worrying and praying — what of that was real and what was lost tae time?

I couldna say, but I did ken this, that my kingdom was here. The throne was mine. I was goin' tae hold it and keep it, and most important, I ought not keep it by m'self, because it had

CHAPTER 71 - MAGNUS

been a lonely endeavor last time. I wouldna make that mistake again.

After dressing, I left my chamber with guards falling in around me.

I went down the steps and crossed the courtyard, tae the doors of the small royal chapel. I entered through the thick wooden doors, enclosed by stone walls and high arched ceilings. Afternoon light filtered through the small stained glass window, across the floor and pews. And I was reminded again, I needed tae replace the window with a larger more brilliant one.

The air was cool and still, perfumed by the aroma of incense.

I heard the rustle of robes as the priest realized I had arrived and approached tae greet me.

He insisted on a prayer, but then when he wanted tae continue conversing, I interrupted tae ask what I needed, "Dost we hae a library?"

"A collection of manuscripts, Yer Majesty?"

"Aye, bound books; I am lookin' for one in particular."

"I hae the Bible, twas a gift from ye, as ye remember, the rest of the books ye keep within yer chancery."

"Och, there is a shelf in my chancery...?" I repeated him, because I wasna certain what he meant.

"Aye, Yer Majesty, ye hae given me leave tae look through them, I am honored by yer kindnesses."

"Ye mean in m'office, the room beside m'chamber?"

"Aye sire, ye hae oft spoken of it as yer chancery."

Och nae, I had nae memory of having books there, I couldna remember what the interior of the room even looked like, but I took my leave and climbed the steps toward my chamber once more.

. . .

I went through my sitting room and through a smaller door intae the office. There was a table, with three chairs, and I suddenly remembered sittin' there, with Cailean opposite me, discussin' the news of the kingdom.

It was odd that I hadna remembered it before. And there was a table with a row of books. I stood looking at it for a time — I dinna remember putting them here, perhaps they had been added by Cailean? Though as I ran m'finger down the titles they seemed added by m'self.

Another sign of a timeline, that had been twisted.

I had a book of poems by Rabbie Burns, the *Complete Works of Shakespeare*, my copy of Sun Tzu's *Art of War*, and a bible I recognized. I pulled it from the shelf and found the name Lady Mairead Campbell written in her hand on the inside page. Beside that was a verra auld copy of the Iliad, and at the end of the row, the psalter. My finger paused there and I considered it. I had been looking for it, but hadna believed it would be here.

I pulled it from the shelf and a memory hit me. Cailean had given it tae me, tae celebrate my accession tae the throne. He had ordered it created with the ornate M on the cover and had given it tae me with the words, "I ken ye are parted from yer family, I hope this will bring ye solace."

I flipped through the pages tae the chapter Lady Mairead had shown me.

I closed the book, tucked it under my arm, and returned downstairs for a meal.

I saw Fraoch leaning against a wall in the courtyard.

"Ye waitin' for me?"

"Aye, bored, nae one wants tae see me, ye go everywhere with a guard. How many men dost ye need tae relieve yerself?"

"Four, apparently."

"Och nae, ye are full of yerself tae need four men tae hold yer cock when ye piss."

I shrugged. "I am a king, tis a majestic cock."

We entered the Great Hall. All bowed deeply as I passed. There werna many guests, as I had surprised Cailean and the kitchen staff, but there were about twenty people there who wanted tae welcome me on my return.

I was famished by the time I took a seat at the head of the long table, with Fraoch and Cailean tae m'right and left.

The meal was good, four courses, with a main dish of venison with gravy, followed by a verra pleasing dessert of rhubarb crumble with vanilla custard. We drank many glasses of wine.

After the meal Fraoch leaned back and patted his rounded stomach. "Och aye, twas grand."

I said, "Twas *verra* grand, Cailean, thank ye for organizin' the meal, we were famished."

"I am pleased I could welcome ye home, well." He stifled a yawn. "M'apologies, yer majesty, I am weary from the day."

"How hae ye been Cailean, well?"

"Och, I hae the aches and pains of age and battle."

"Ye are lonely as well, hae ye considered taking a wife? Someone tae smooth yer brow and warm yer bed?"

He chuckled. "The ones who are warm and smoothing daena want an auld man like me."

Fraoch said, "But ye are the right hand man tae the king! If I had been so powerful it would hae been easy tae win m'wife! Instead I had tae win her with rose-scented grease in m'hair and m'charmin' personality."

"True... perhaps on another night, ye can show me how tae use m'personality and power tae win a lady."

Fraoch said, "...and on the night of the feast, I will advise ye on how tae grease back yer hair so ye smell like a garden, the ladies do love it." He said, "Och, we ought tae introduce ye tae Lady Mairead, she would find ye dashing."

Cailean said, "Lady Mairead is...?"

I said, "My mother, and she is too much trouble for ye,

remember I said ye needed someone tae smooth yer brow? Lady Mairead is prone tae wrinklin' a man directly intae his auld age."

Fraoch laughed.

I said, "But speakin' on m'mother, at her urgin' I would like tae give a Dawn Address on the morrow."

"This is new, ye hae never given one before."

"Lady Mairead advises me tis important for a king tae make a Dawn Address after he has been away tae properly announce that he has returned."

Cailean said, "I think tis a verra good idea, would ye do it in the courtyard or the chapel?"

"The courtyard would be good, I think, can ye spread word that all are expected? Then all can break fast."

Cailean said, "Aye, I will. And Magnus, tis good tae hae ye home."

"Thank ye, Cailean."

"Let us begin with an announcement."

He banged on the table, pushed back his chair and stood. He held up his glass. "Yer king, Mag Mòr, will be gracin' us with a proper Dawn Address in the morn. Ye are all expected in the courtyard. Just before dawn."

He raised his mug tae a man sitting at the side table. "Even ye, Ian — daena be so drunk ye sleep through it. Whether ye are up all night, or sleepin' like a bairn, ye must attend." The people dining in the Great Hall laughed.

Cailean raised his mug tae me. "And, Yer Majesty, I welcome ye on yer return tae Stirling, slainte!"

I raised my glass and said, "Slainte!"

Cailean put down his mug. "And now I need tae go tae m'chamber tae rest for the morn. Good evenin', Yer Majesty."

He limped from the room.

I said, "Och nae, I daena like tae see him in pain."

Fraoch said, "I will go get him some medicine as soon as we are able."

"And heatin' pads and a good mattress, did we get him a

good mattress? Are there good mattresses here? I forgot tae check m'bed."

"I napped all afternoon, m'bed daena hae a good mattress. If Cailean's mattress is the same, tis surprising he can walk upright at all."

"Ye napped? Och nae, ye are auld too."

"Or young like a bairn, bairns nap all the time! What did ye do while I was sleepin'?"

"I worried, and contemplated."

"Like an auld man."

I chuckled.

Then we both drank from our mugs. I asked, "What dost ye think, Fraoch, about all this?"

"I think ye hae won yer kingdom, handily. Ye sit upon the throne of Scotland, and ye are in a good position tae protect the realm from the ascendance of Arsebunkle the Aggravatin'."

"Och, that is a good name, did ye just come up with it?"

"Aye, verra proud of it. I am, as m'wife would say, on fire tonight. I am not certain what it means but I think it means m'glory warms me from the inside."

"So I am a king at two ends of time?"

"Aye, and ye must hold both these thrones. I hate tae be the one tae say it, Og Maggy, but ye will need tae be here for a time, tae make sure this one is held strong."

"I agree." I nodded. "I absolutely agree. Dost ye think I hae changed anything else, dost ye think Archie still feels it is dire?"

"Ye are worried on him?"

"Verra worried."

He took a sip of wine. "Life is short, ye ken, Og Maggy, yer son is worried about yer impending death from auld age, he can see ye witherin' afore him—"

"I am at most thirty-one."

He chuckled. "I forget sometimes I am older than ye."

"If he is seein' the future, I daena ken how tae help him, tae set his mind at ease."

"Maybe ye hae tae just be the king — ye rule, ye take charge, and if he is frightened, perhaps seein' ye be in charge will give him strength."

I nodded. "Aye."

He yawned. "I am exhausted. What a few days we hae had! We rescued the maiden, worked the Trailblazer, and took yer throne. Och, Og Maggy, we are heroes."

I said, "I am verra weary as well and I hae a speech tae deliver in the morn."

"Dost ye ken what ye are goin' tae say?"

I patted the book. "I hae the speech that Lady Mairead wrote for me, folded in the pages, here, tis a good speech, and I can speak extemporaneously if I need tae."

"If there is one thing Og Maggy can do, he can talk on and on about his greatness."

I laughed as we stood. People all around the Great Hall bowed as I left the room with Fraoch following.

CHAPTER 72 - MAGNUS

DAWN AT STIRLING

I went tae my room, warm from a built up fire. I undressed and climbed intae bed. Fraoch was right, I had a mattress that wasna good enough. I would bring new. I would bring bedding. I would bring comfort for Cailean — I was asleep almost as soon as my head hit the pillow.

There was a knock a few hours later.
"I am up!"
Fraoch's voice, "Daena sound like it, ye are generally taller, yer voice is comin' up from near the ground."
"Och nae, ye are a trial and tribulation." I tossed my heavy blankets off and climbed from bed.
"Tis the nicest thing ye ever said. Dress, Yer Majesty, the Dawn awaits."

Two attendants helped me dress in a fine tunic with a fresh cloak with embroidered details along the edging. My brooch, holdin' the cloak at my chest, was verra fine, with a large red stone. My gold crown was brought in and placed upon my head.

We left my chamber and met Fraoch in the hall. I passed him m'leather bag that contained m'pens and the book.

He said, "I am tae carry the king's handbag?"

"Aye, ye must, it winna go with m'fine long dress."

He laughed and slung it on his shoulder and then he walked with me, surrounded by my guard, down tae the courtyard where we met Cailean, already there, arranging the crowd.

I climbed up ontae a rough platform. There were a couple hundred people there, a verra grand crowd for such a spontaneous event. I was filled with gratitude, similar tae the feelin' I had when I made the Dawn Address in Riaghalbane. I also felt surety, this was what I needed tae do — twas the Dawn of my Empire, I had tae mark the moment.

The crowd cheered and I raised my hands, askin' them tae quiet.

Then I unfolded the speech.

I looked down on it, and somehow, suddenly it dinna seem right.

I looked out over the crowd, there was a dim light, a cold chill, tae the east a glimmer of light, I began...

"Welcome tae m'first Dawn Address. I wanted tae speak tae ye about the battles we hae waged and the challenges that the kingdom has faced in the past. It has been a dark time, but ye are resilient and determined. We, the people of Alba, hae overcome adversity and we stand here now, in the heart of Stirling, the seat of power for our kingdom, and we are determined and strong. There inna an army in the world that can defeat us, for we are the mighty lands of Scotland, and bow down tae none."

The sun began tae rise, castin' a warm glow over the gathered crowd.

There was cheering, and as the sun emerged over the timber walls, I began tae pray, sayin', as I had in Riaghalbane, that with the dawn I prayed for peace for our kingdom, safety, and wellbein' of the subjects of Scotland. That along with the rising sun, we must be filled with hope for the comin' day, our minds full of gratitude for our blessings and the peace reigning over the lands.

I added, as the sky was clear, with my standard flying against a sky becoming blue, "This is a dawn of a new era, a prosperous and peaceful future, and when, someday, my son takes the throne—"

A man from the front row yelled, "Ye hae a son?"

I smiled. "Aye, I hae two sons, the eldest is Archibald, a good strong name for a leader, ye will meet him soon enough. Though I warn ye, he is young. I hae years left as yer king."

The crowd began tae chant, "Long Live the King! Long Live Mag Mòr! Long Live the King! Long Live Mag Mòr!"

∼

Fraoch and I were sitting at the high table enjoyin' a large breakfast. He said, "Now with this good meal and the meal last night, my lack is almost filled."

He shoveled eggs in his mouth. "Ye did well this morn, yer wee speechy was inspirin'."

"Thank ye, Fraoch."

"Course ye could hae said more about strength and kickin' the arse of yer enemies, but I get what ye were doin' tryin' tae give the people hope and meanin'."

"Aye, but I am still goin' tae kick the arse of m'enemies, as soon as I find him."

"Good, I will draw m'sword alongside ye. Onward tae a hopeful future, slayin' our enemies, Long Live the King!"

I chuckled. "Ye were inspired."

"Aye, it came tae me that I was right, ye had tae come take the throne here tae fix the timeline. Yer subjects werena callin' ye dead, they were yellin' Long Live the King, I am the hero here."

"I think Lochinvar agreed with ye, he helped convince me."

"Og Lochie is a man-child without sense. He only agreed

with me because he kens I am his better. Nae, twas all me! I am the hero! Ye are crowned king of Scotland with my help."

"We walked in through the front door."

He chuckled. "Ye ken it took a great many battles tae gain it."

"I ken. It might take a few tae keep it. We shall see."

I finished m'plate of food and pushed it away. "In the meantime, I daena like bein' without Kaitlyn and the bairns, if I am tae remain here, holdin' the kingdom, we need tae bring our family."

"Ye are assumin' that I am goin' tae live here as well?"

"Ye would leave me here in the thirteenth century tae hold a kingdom on m'own?"

"Of course I winna leave ye, but ye ought tae ask."

"Fraoch would ye stay here as m'hand?"

"Och nae, I canna believe ye think ye hae tae ask! What kind of brother dost ye take me for?"

"The kind who needs an arse whoopin', as James would say."

Fraoch laughed.

I opened the bag and pulled out the book and the pens, passin' one tae Fraoch.

"What's this for?"

"We are goin' tae send a message tae Archie, tae set his mind at ease and askin' him tae come."

Fraoch pushed his plate away.

I turned the book so it was open between us. "Ye draw on that page and I will draw upon this one."

I uncapped the pen and wrote beside an illumination of a man walkin' upon the flourish of an A:

All is well.

CHAPTER 72 - MAGNUS

Under it I wrote the date.

June 15, 1291

Under that I wrote:

Please come.

Then I signed it:

Magnus

Fraoch began tae draw on the edge of the facing page. He wrote:

Fraoch is here.

Under it he drew a man holding a fishing pole.
"What is that for?"
"So Hayley will ken tae bring m'fishing pole."
"Och tis a verra good idea." I flipped the page.
I drew a dog.
"So they will bring Haggis."
"Awesome, but Lady Mairead told ye tae mark it verra small on only one page."
"Tis my book, I was given it. Besides, when hae I ever done what she asked of me? I think it would be unsettlin' tae her if I were tae become obedient now."
Fraoch drew an orange tree that filled up the facin' page. "Tae keep away the scurvy."
"Verra good idea."

I drew three horses, but had tae continue the horse rear on the followin' page.

"Och, Lady Mairead is goin' tae murder ye."

He drew a PlayStation controller.

"What can I ask for that will make the food taste better?" I drew a portrait of Chef Zach.

He laughed.

I drew four forks. "So we winna be barbarians when we eat."

"This is a fun game."

"Aye. We need tae fill every page." On the first page I drew a sun and wrote:

Tis dawn, we are beginning.

Fraoch drew a roll of toilet paper.

After we filled the book with drawings upon every page, he said, "Will they receive the message ye think?"

"I daena ken. Tae be considered, we will send ye tae go get them. Kaitlyn and I ended up on different timelines once, I daena want anything tae go wrong. Ye go get them, bring them here."

"Good plan. That way if Hayley daena understand m'entreaties tae bring the fishing pole, I can tell her directly." He flipped through tae the page and looked over the drawing.

He drew an arrow toward the pole. "Nae, there is nae way she winna understand. Tis a perfect drawing of m'self holding the pole. But I will still go. Who else dost ye want me tae bring?"

I thought for a moment. "Anyone who wants tae come is welcome. I daena think we can return tae Amelia Island for a time... but Lady Mairead will return tae Riaghalbane. If some would like tae go tae the kingdom with her, they can, or they may remain at Balloch. Tis their choice."

CHAPTER 72 - MAGNUS

I flipped through tae the last page and wrote:

Tha neart againn mar aon.

Meaning, 'We hae strength as one,' and underlined it with a drawing of a sword.

Fraoch said, "Who is that for?"

"For whoever needs tae hear it."

Fraoch nodded. "I will gather m'things tae go."

"I will ride with ye tae the woods in m'park. Ye will return in three days and we will hae the feast Cailean promised me."

CHAPTER 73 - KAITLYN

DAWN AT BALLOCH

"Mammy? Mammy, wake up!" My face pressed into the pillow, deeply asleep, I felt a nudge on my shoulder.

What?

"Mammy! Da sent us a message!"

I sat up, "What do you mean, what...? You're smiling!" He had a grin across his face.

"I woke up, Mammy, and it stopped."

"It stopped... you mean the chanting? It's not happening?"

"It's not, it's all just... nothing,"

He clamped his eyes shut as if to show me, and said, "There's a clear sky and I can see the flag against it, and I can hear the chanting too, but it's just 'Long Live the King!' then 'Long Live Mag Mòr!'" He opened his eyes. "Is that Da?"

I nodded. "Yeah, Mag Mòr is your father, it means Mag the Great."

"He is."

"I know."

"...and I don't have to listen to it, it stops. And it doesn't scare me, it sounds good. They're saying it to Da right now, I think."

CHAPTER 73 - KAITLYN

"This is great, this is amazing."

I ran my hands up and down on my face to wake up.

Archie said, "Isla, wake up, Da sent us a message!"

"A message?"

Isla woke up and crawled sleepily onto my lap. Jack woke up, sat up, and said, "Da!"

"What message?"

He said, "Look!" He opened the book to the page, there was Magnus's handwriting:

All is well.
June 15, 1291
Please come.
Magnus

Then he pointed at a drawing of a man holding a stick.

I pointed at the words under it.

He said, "Fraoch wrote that so we would know he is there too and he's okay."

Isla said, "Why is he fishing?"

"That's so we can bring his fishing pole."

I laughed. "Oh my gosh, this is amazing, Archie, your Da wants us to come."

"Lady Mairead is going to be so mad, Da wrote all over the book. You want to see, Isla?"

She nodded.

Jack banged his hands. "Eee! Eee!"

Archie flipped the page and pointed. Isla said, "Haggis!"

Haggis ran in from his spot by the fireplace with his tail wagging. Archie said, with so much excitement, "Want to go see Da, boy?"

It made me laugh and cry the way Haggis rushed around the room looking for Da.

Isla clapped.

Archie said, "And here's three horses, that's Dràgon, Thor, and my horse, Mario."

He flipped a couple more pages. "There's a PlayStation controller, some forks, why are there forks?"

I shrugged. "Maybe they don't have forks, wow."

Archie said, "Weird, that's... really weird." He flipped the page. "And a drawing of a man.... I don't know."

I said, "I think that's Chef Zach."

Isla clapped again.

Archie showed me the first page, a sun, and my husband's writing: Tis dawn, we are beginning.

And I clapped. And my children beamed up at me and I said, "I am so excited, who wants to go see Da?"

Everyone said, "Me!" And I threw my arms around them and hugged them close.

"Okay," I wiped my eyes and climbed out of the bed. "We have to pack, we have to tell everyone."

Archie shoved his feet into shoes. "Let's go tell everyone!" We all peed first, and Isla and I put on our shoes.

My lady's maid helped me pull a bodice on and I wrapped a plaid around my shoulders, while Archie was begging to go, but I didn't want to miss anything. Then we all rushed from the room and down the hall. We passed Hayley's room first, and banged, then barged in. Archie said, "Aunt Hayley! Uncle Fraoch sent a message, he wants us to come!"

She said, "But he's okay, right? Everyone is okay?"

Archie nodded. He showed her the page. She said, "Let me guess: He wants me to bring him a fishing pole?"

Archie said, "Yep! We're going to tell everyone!"

We left Hayley's room and continued down the corridor. Zach stuck his head out from his room, Ben rushed out. I said, "Magnus sent a message, he wants us to come!"

Zach said, "To the thirteenth century?"

CHAPTER 73 - KAITLYN

"We can all talk about it over breakfast."

Quentin's door opened, "What's up?"

"Magnus wants us all to come!"

"Awesome, good, alright." He ran his hand over his hair. "What time is it?"

Archie yelled, "It's dawn! It's a new beginning!"

We went down the corridor and down the steps to James's room. We knocked quietly, he stuck his head out, his hair was sticking out everywhere. Over his shoulder I could see Sophie walking with the baby on her shoulder, soothing him. He said, "Baby was up a lot."

I whispered, "Magnus wants us to come, he's good, meet at breakfast to discuss."

He nodded. "Awesome." He started to turn away but then remembered, he turned back, and put out his fist to Archie, "Man, I am happy for you, dude, you good?"

"So good, Uncle James." They fist-bumped and then James went back into the room.

We all went to Lochie's door and knocked. Lochie said, "Come in!"

All the kids and I, even Ben and Zoe now, crept in. Lochie was up, Ash was still lying down in bed. Lochie said, "What is happenin'?" Looking from Archie to me and back.

Archie said, "Uncle Lochie, Da sent us a message."

"Tis a good message?" He sank into the chair.

Archie nodded and put the book open on Lochie's lap. "Look."

"Och aye! They are well, they want us tae come?"

Archie said, "Yes, and we are supposed to bring a fishing pole, Haggis, the horses, forks, and the Playstation."

"Tis all the most important things. How are ye, wee man? Ye well? I was worried on ye."

"I am well, Uncle Lochie, remember the chants in my mind? They're gone." He swiped his hands out, emphatically. "All gone.

Or the bad parts are gone, they are saying 'Long live the King' now and it's about Da, I'm sure of it."

"Och, that is verra good." He said, "Hae ye all met Ash?"

Ash said, "I am sorry I am not up, my shoulder was disjointed."

Zoe frowned. "Boo-boo."

Ash said, "Exactly."

I said, "How are you, Ash? I've been meaning to come talk, to welcome you—"

"I am doing really well, I totally understand, Lochie has been talking to me about what's been going on."

I had been watching her looking from Lochie to his nephew and I could see the love in her eyes. It made my heart swell. Lochie was going to be okay. Lochie said, "Ash, this is Archibald and Ben, the nephews, and Jack one of the bairns, and this is Isla and Zoe."

Isla said, "I am Isla the *niece* and this is Zoe."

Ash said, "I have heard so much about all of you. Where are we going?"

I said, "We have a lot to talk about, I'm calling a meeting downstairs, but Magnus has asked us to come to the thirteenth century and so we're going we need to um..."

Her eyes settled on Lochie. His eyes settled on her.

He said, "We need tae discuss."

I said, "Absolutely, of course, there's a lot to consider." I herded all the kids to the door. "Will you be at breakfast?"

Lochie said, "Aye, we will meet ye down there."

CHAPTER 74 - ASH

BALLOCH CASTLE

*L*ochie left and a maid helped me undress from my disgusting clothes into a dress that resembled the dresses the other women were wearing. This style had a bodice and a skirt and with my hair up, I felt pretty. My injured shoulder felt a lot better. I could almost do without a sling, but wore embroidered fabric around it just to remind myself not to reach with my arm.

Lochie returned. "There has been a storm, Quentin, Sean, and Liam hae gone tae see who tis."

"What do you mean, storm?"

"Och, I forget ye are new tae it. When ye time travel there is a storm. A storm means someone is coming."

"Weird."

"Aye, unless tis an actual storm. If ye hae been time traveling long enough ye begin tae see the difference."

He cocked his head to the side. "Ye look verra beautiful."

I blushed. "Thank you, Lochie."

"We'll go ahead and go down tae breakfast."

. . .

He walked me along the corridor, and down the steps and through the doors into a large room he called the gallery. *Wow.* One wall had large windows, the other wall was lined with paintings, there were marble sculptures along the wall, and a few sitting areas, with lovely antique furniture in intimately arranged circles for conversations. It was really fancy and expensive looking, I was gawking at it all. "It's like a museum."

"Wait until ye see Lady Mairead's collections! This gallery belongs tae her brother, her collection is many times more grand. But I warn ye, she is a conniving, deceitful, ornery auld broad, daena trust her generally. We are on Magnus's side though, which means she will do anything she can tae help us. As long as ye never cross her."

I said, "Wow she sounds like trouble..."

"Madame Hayley will barely speak tae her, ye must be cautious."

"Okay, anyone else I need to worry about?"

"Nae, everyone else are good people, she is the only one ye must watch."

Guards drew open double doors and we entered a large Great Hall. I was awestruck by the soaring ornately carved and painted wood ceiling, and the intricate tapestries adorning the walls. At one end of the room the morning light was shimmering through large, arched windows. And there was a long table down the room, with smaller more intimate tables along the side.

There was a fire in the large fireplace, and the scent of smoke filled the air, competing with the smell of baked bread — I was famished.

We made our way to seats but had to stop first near the head of the table. Lochie said, "Lady Mairead, I would like ye tae meet Ash McNeil. Ash McNeil, the Lady Mairead."

I bobbed my head. "Pleased to meet you."

She pushed back her chair, stood in front of me, and looked

me over. "So ye are the maiden who has been the cause of all this turmoil...?"

"Um, not really, I... it wasn't my fault. I..." I glanced at Lochie, he sort of winced and shook his head.

"Did three Campbells, including a king, hae tae rescue ye?"

"Yes, but in my defense, I had no idea about time travel, I—"

"Were ye armed?"

"Yes, I had a gun, I was just caught unaware. I had no idea I was in danger until—"

She interrupted me and turned her attention to Lochie. "Lochinvar, heed this, if ye daena give a woman enough information, how is she tae protect herself?"

"Aye, Lady Mairead, I hae learned a lesson."

"Good. We winna hold this against *anyone* but Asgall." She asked me, "Ye met him?"

"I did, briefly." My stomach growled, loudly. "My apologies."

The woman named Lizbeth said, "Mother, Mistress Ash has been injured and unable tae come tae meals since she arrived. Let her sit, we can ask her questions once we hae properly fed her."

Lady Mairead said, "Fine." And sat down in her seat.

More people were filing through the doors, I recognized many of them as members of Lochie's family, and then a plate was placed in front of me. A poached egg with a piece of bacon, a slice of heavy bread, and a bowl to the side of my plate with oatmeal in it, swimming in fresh milk.

I had a dish of jelly in front of my plate, a small plate of butter, and there was some honey for the oatmeal.

It was all delicious. I barely spoke while I ate.

Then, as if she had been waiting, Lady Mairead said, "So ye met Asgall, did ye ascertain how tae find him?"

I wiped my mouth with a napkin. "I have no idea, honestly."

She sighed, irritatedly.

Lochie squeezed my hand.

She said, "I suppose we will hae tae focus on the thirteenth century."

It came to me then, something Asgall had said, "Actually no, I don't think that's where he'll be — he told me he hated that um... time, he said he needed a cigarette. He wanted to smoke freely somewhere. I also know how many buildings were in the compound, how many people and weapons, the escape route, and can tell you that he had a thick mustache that pointed up on the sides."

She raised her chin. "So which is it, ye daena ken *anything* or ye ken a great deal?"

"I suppose I know a great deal."

Lady Mairead smiled, "I see we will get along nicely."

Kaitlyn sat down beside Lizbeth and Hayley and others took their seats farther down.

Kaitlyn said to Lady Mairead, "Did you hear the good news?"

Lady Mairead said, "Of course we heard, Archibald and Benjamin came tae m'rooms earlier and told me all about it, ye will be going tae meet Magnus?"

"Definitely, as soon as breakfast is over."

She sighed again. "I suppose I will return tae Riaghalbane."

The doors of the Great Hall opened once more and there was a loud booming voice. "I am home tae get ye!"

It was Lochie's brother, Fraoch, and when he entered everyone laughed and cheered.

Lady Mairead said, "Dear Lord, there is always a disruption, we will hae indigestion."

CHAPTER 75 - KAITLYN

THE GREAT HALL - BALLOCH CASTLE

Fraoch went up to Lady Mairead and said, "Good morn, Lady Mairead."

"Good morn, Fraoch, did ye wash up for breakfast? We daena want rowdy men shakin' and slingin' their filth upon us."

"I washed up, Lady Mairead, and while I did it I thought tae m'self, best get the grooves between the fingers, Frookie, ye want tae be clean afore ye give Lady Mairead a kiss upon the cheek."

He leaned in fast and pecked her on the cheek. She looked shocked, but then raised her chin and brow and settled as if she enjoyed it.

Fraoch turned to the rest of us. "I hae *also* returned from far away tae get the family. We used the Trailblazer." He glanced at Lizbeth and Sean and Liam, "If ye daena ken what tis, ye daena need tae ken, but we used it, and Magnus is safe. He bids ye come."

Lizbeth said, "Ye can speak freely, Fraoch, we hae heard all the tales."

Sean said, "There is always some kind of fanciful story. I just let it wash over me, like the waters Tay."

"Fine, I will tell ye, we used the Trailblazer, we hae gone tae the year 1291, there we hae found that Magnus is king. He is named Mag Mòr, and—"

Sean said, "Mag Mòr? Mag Mòr is *Magnus*?"

Fraoch said, "Ye hae heard of Mag Mòr?"

"Aye, I ken the list of kings, he is king after Alexander III. Twas a time of turmoil, the next king was Robert the Bruce. The Earl has a book with the list in it."

Fraoch said, "Yer list daena include Asgall?"

"Nae, never..." He looked at his fingers and pointed and folded them down as if he were counting, then said, "...never heard of an Asgall."

"Och, tis verra fine, verra fine."

Fraoch was standing while the rest of us were sitting with plates of food in front of us. He put his boot up on the seat, and leaned on his knee, but Lady Mairead said, "Och nae."

He pulled his foot down quickly. "M'apologies, Lady Mairead."

A servant brought him a plate. "Nae, I just ate dinner. I am not—" Then he seemed to change his mind, he sat down, and pulled the plate closer. He said tae Zach, "As ye always say, best eat if tis in front of ye."

Zach said, "It's true, right Ben?"

Fraoch said, "Archie, while I eat, how about ye stand up and address the table, ye tell everyone what the book says."

Archie stood. He looked for the first time in weeks, truly well, happy and healthy. He had the book in his arms but you could tell it wasn't out of desperation, it was out of delight. He stood beside his chair, then Lady Mairead said, "We canna see ye, Archie, ye are too short, stand upon the chair."

Fraoch muttered, chuckling, "Och nae."

She leveled her eyes on him, "He is my grandson and heir tae the throne of Riaghalbane and Scotland, his boots are never too dirty tae stand upon a chair." She waved her hand, "Now speak, Archibald."

Archie said, "This is the book. Grandmother gave it to me, it

CHAPTER 75 - KAITLYN

is verra old, Da has the same book where he is." He opened it to the first page and held it up. "See the sun? Da drew it." Jack on my lap clapped his hands. "Da!"

Archie said, "Exactly, Jack."

Fraoch, shoveling eggs in his mouth, said, "I was sitting right beside him, in the Great Hall—"

Lady Mairead said, "What Great Hall?"

"Stirling castle."

Lady Mairead said, "Och, this is verra good. Almost good enough that I will forgive the mess ye hae made tae the important and ancient book. *Almost.*"

Fraoch continued, "I drew the roll of toilet paper."

Archie pointed at it. "I think you meant, bring toilet paper."

"I did, if we hae some, we ought tae bring it, there inna any for near seven centuries."

Archie said, "Da wrote this about the dawn too." Then he flipped the page to another. "This is where he said to come." He showed that page all around the table.

Fraoch said, "That's my drawing of a fishing pole."

Hayley said, "You were telling me to bring it."

He kissed her on her cheek. "Magnus dinna think ye would ken what it meant."

Archie said, "We all know what you meant, Uncle Fraoch."

He showed another page and another. Then finally he showed the sword with the Gaelic words. He said, "I don't know what this says."

Sean said, "We hae strength as one."

Archie looked down on it, nodding, then he tucked the book back to his chest, while we applauded for his show and tell. Then he put the book down on the table while he climbed from the chair and he and Ben raced off with the cousins, leaving the book behind.

Lochie glanced at the book and met my eyes, he nodded. I nodded.

Beaty offered to take the rest of the kids to the nursery, and said to Quentin, "Whatever ye decide, Quennie, I am good with, as long as Mookie and Saddle can come."

She put Noah on one hip, Jack on the other, and Zoe and Isla followed her out of the Great Hall.

Fraoch said, "So we ought tae discuss if all are coming with me."

Lady Mairead took up a piece of bread and began to butter it. "Asgall is still at large, and menacing. I am verra pleased he has been removed from the line of kings, but he has still gained a lot of power and has amassed a good deal of land—"

Sean said, "Mother, if Asgall is amassing land and power, Magnus ought tae amass land and power first."

Lady Mairead punctuated the air with the butter knife. "Exactly, Sean. Asgall is behaving as if he is the first person tae *ever* think of buying up property, tis infuriating. He is slighting us. I hae been collecting art since before he first placed his grubby paws upon a vessel, how dare he? That in *itself* requires I buy everything."

Quentin said, "Everything?"

"Aye, all the art, the land, the gold, the *everything*. He canna be first. I am verra glad ye advised Magnus the way ye did, Fraoch, taking the throne before Asgall could take it was verra well done."

Fraoch said, "Og Lochie advised him as well."

She nodded to Lochie. "Ye have both proven yerselves verra helpful advisors tae Magnus." The corner of her mouth went up, as she joked, "When I buy the world I will gift ye a land somewhere."

Lochie said, "Thank ye, Lady Mairead, ye can give me Skye, where I grew up, I would like tae walk in tae Dunscaith as the owner."

She scowled and shook her head. "Ye rose in my estimation, Lochinvar, until ye asked for something so diminutive. This request makes ye sound like a poor orphan, wanting revenge upon a lord who is long dead. Ye hae won that battle already, ye

CHAPTER 75 - KAITLYN

want Dunscaith? A pile of stones on the edge of Skye? Fine ye can have it, but the men who advise Magnus ought tae hae the wisdom and fortitude tae ask for a much larger piece of the world — let us begin again. I am the mother of a king, founding an empire, and I hae told ye I am grateful for the advice ye gave my son, the king, and ye would like a gift of land — what land would ye want?"

"Och, in that case it ought tae be France?"

"Good boy, if I gain France, tis yers." She smiled.

Quentin said, "So, Lady Mairead, will you head back to Riaghalbane?"

"That seems the best place for me as I assume my place in the battle." She gestured toward Ash, "Ash McNeil has given me some details that perhaps ye ought tae hear, Colonel Quentin."

Ash cleared her throat tentatively. "I only spoke to Asgall once, he was a real jerk, just horrible. He didn't really tell me anything, nothing too useful, but he really hated the place. He said he was desperate for a cigarette and he wanted to go to a place where he could smoke freely."

Quentin nodded. "Narrows it down a bit. He's in the nineteenth or twentieth centuries, maybe."

Lady Mairead said, "Or Paris in any century."

Lochie chuckled, "Then let me handle it."

Quentin said, "You know French?"

Lochie said, "Lady Mairead just offered tae give me France!"

Quentin laughed. "Oh, right, I forgot already. We're dividing up the spoils before we've even met the enemy."

Fraoch said, "We hae narrowed it down, tis good that he inna in every century, there are verra many centuries. Narrowin' it tae two is good." He grinned, and said, "Lady Mairead, ye dinna ask me which piece of land I would want."

"I daena need tae ask, Fraoch, I will give ye the United States."

Fraoch grinned. "I daena need the whole place, just a few states with good fishing."

"Consider it done."

Fraoch said, "Back tae the decision — Lady Mairead will go tae Riaghalbane."

James said, "So my choice is stay here or go to the thirteenth century? Can we return tae Fernandina?"

Quentin said, "I think we can go in and out for supplies and to get some of our things—"

I said, "Ash needs to return to let the bartender at the Palace know she's okay."

Ash said, "And my family."

James said, "Good, but overall I think I'd like Sophie and Junior to remain here, I don't relish the idea of moving the baby again."

Quentin said, "I agree, it's comfortable and safe here. There's the nursery."

"And just til the baby gets older."

Quentin said, "I get it. That sounds good. Maybe you and I can go to Fernandina on a supply run. "

Ash said, "I don't really understand how this works, I need to tell Don I'm okay, do I need to go now? Because I don't like the idea of using that tech again."

I said, "You can wait a bit, until you're ready, and then go to the day after you left—"

Quentin said, "Usually we give a three day buffer. But in this case you want to set Don's mind at ease, we can make an exception. But when you go to the Island you need to be *really* cautious. I know this goes without saying to the rest of us, we are back on high alert. Extra security, all the precautions. We got another madman — no playing around."

Ash nodded.

I said, "What I would recommend is wait here until you're ready, then go."

Lizbeth said, "Ye are welcome here as long as ye need, all of ye are welcome tae stay."

Quentin said, "Beaty and I will stay here, but James and I

CHAPTER 75 - KAITLYN

will go on some supply runs. Then Beaty and I can go meet up with Magnus."

James said, "Damnit, now I want to go too. I don't want to miss out on seeing Mags with a crown on his head in ancient Scotland. Sophie, Junior, and I are a maybe, we're going to stay here until we're ready but we might go, too."

Quentin said, "So Beaty, Noah, and I are 'going later'. James and Sophie, and Junior are 'going maybe later'. What about you, Lochie? After Ash goes to Fernandina to check in?"

Lochie looked at Ash shaking his head. "We discussed that she will stay with me. We haena discussed what that means."

She was holding Lochie's hand on her lap, she leaned in and Lochie kissed her forehead.

Emma and I looked at each other and smiled.

Quentin said, "So you're an 'undecided maybe going later' — you'll stay here while you decide."

Lochie nodded, looking down at her. "This is a big question tae ask someone tae go tae m'brother's castle in the thirteenth century..."

She shook her head, her eyes wide. "I mean, what in the world kind of question is this? I just left there, *apparently* — I was in the thirteenth century... I don't even know what to think about this — can I be armed? I need a gun to protect myself."

Lady Mairead said, "Ye just rose in my estimation. Aye, ye must be armed well."

"Good... but I still don't know how to wrap my head around this."

Lochie joked, "Tis easy, ye just hae tae accept that tis a place with nae toilet paper."

Fraoch tapped the book. "There will be toilet paper, I put it on the list."

Quentin said, "James and I will get more. But this is a good point, how long is Magnus going to be there?"

Fraoch said, "I think he will need tae be there for a long time, he needs tae hold the throne."

Quentin said, "That answer doesn't help me know how much toilet paper to get."

James said, "How about we'll get a buttload?"

He and Hayley high-fived. All of us laughed.

I said, "The kids and I are going, Haggis, the horses, Hayley and Fraoch..." We all turned and looked at Zach and Emma.

Zach put his hands up. "Don't look at me, I'm decided. My face is in the ancient book, got no fucking choice, a king is calling me to come."

Emma said, "We can't split up the Ben and Archie duo, either. It'll be like Kilchurn, just more dire, but we're in it together. Yes, we're going."

Zach said, "...as long as a buttload of toilet paper is trailing behind us."

James laughed. He and Zach high-fived.

We were all laughing and didn't notice Sean push his chair away from the table — he leaned forward, his elbows on his knees. He said simply, "I want tae go meet Magnus there. Tha neart againn mar aon. We hae strength as one."

We all stopped talking and looked at him.

Lady Mairead said, "Ye never wanted tae time travel before."

"I hae been considering it, and it seems like Magnus needs m'help. The writin' with the sword was directed at me, I ken it. And I hae never been able tae help before, it has always been beyond m'abilities, but I would like tae lend my sword."

James said, "Hoowee, Sean, this might be the worst possible time. You could go to the future and have all the food, video games, flushing toilets, but you decide to go back in time instead?"

Sean shrugged. "I daena ken what half those words mean, Master James, but I think I ought tae go, it seems time. Liam can watch over Balloch. Maggie is well, I spoke tae her, she kens I must go if m'brother requires m'assistance, and m'boys are strong and healthy, we are well guarded. I can return when I am needed."

CHAPTER 75 - KAITLYN

Quentin said, "And James, Lochie, and I will be here with Liam watching over Balloch, Sean."

Fraoch slapped his hands on his knees, "This is a good plan. Gather yer things, family, we leave after lunch." He looked around. "Tis time for lunch yet?"

We all got up to gather our things, and I pulled Lizbeth aside. "Are you okay with Sean leaving?"

"Aye, a few months ago he spoke about it, I knew he wanted tae, and he told me, 'If I am asked I will go next time.' Tis funny, he wasna asked directly, but he considered the Gaelic line and built up his strength and offered tae go. I find it courageous." She said, "Please tell Young Magnus, he must make certain Sean is safe. We need him."

"I will, and he will understand."

"Good, thank ye, Kaitlyn."

CHAPTER 76 - KAITLYN

THE CLEARING, NEAR BALLOCH CASTLE

It was mid afternoon, Jack was exhausted, sleeping in my arms. Zach and Emma and their kids were packed and ready. Sean was stoic, holding the reins of the horses. He had been quiet, just asking where he needed to be and then watching and following.

Fraoch, on the other hand, was running the enterprise like he was the CEO. He ordered where everything and everyone ought to go.

Lady Mairead had already left, headed to Riaghalbane.

She left Archie's book here, James was the keeper of it. If we needed anything we would leave a message inside.

Quentin and James accompanied us to the clearing. After they saw us off they were going to go to Fernandina to get supplies. Everyone had a plan, a place, something to do.

Mine was basic: get to Magnus.

I tried not to think of all the times the 'get to Magnus' had happened under duress, completely frantic, fleeing something horrible. Or the time that I ended up on an alternate timeline and had been stuck there... that time had been Stirling Castle too.

CHAPTER 76 - KAITLYN

I gulped. I had been trapped in that castle, completely alone, no chance of escape.

It had been terrifying.

But, I told myself, this was a different situation, a very different circumstance. Everything was going to be okay—

Emma said, "You know what this is like? It's like we're with our family on the docks, getting ready to get on a ship, headed to the new world. Except it's a very very old world."

"It does seem like that. We're all in our best clothes, gathered with a very small amount of our worldly possessions, babes in arms, Sean looks seasick already."

We glanced at him, he looked very nervous.

Fraoch said, "How is everyone, ye ready tae go?"

I looked down on Archie and he looked up at me. I said, "Ready?"

"Yep." He scratched Haggis behind the ears. "Ready to go, boy?"

We all gathered in a circle and held on, arm to arm, and Fraoch twisted the vessel and the mighty storm began. Sean said, under his breath, "Och nae."

I said, "Hold on." And the vessel grabbed hold, hard.

CHAPTER 77 - LOCHINVAR

BALLOCH CASTLE

I took Ash up tae the high walls tae watch the storm, so she would ken what I meant.

We stood side by side looking out over the grass tae the forests in the distance and the bens arranged around our view. She said, "This is such a beautiful place, breathtaking."

"Aye."

"If you had told me, three weeks ago, that I would be standing on a castle wall in Scotland, I would have never believed it." She leaned against the stone. "I really can't go live in Fernandina, can't go to work next week?"

"Nae, not until we solve this."

Then I saw the trees in the direction of the clearing begin to whip around. I pointed. "Dost ye see the storm, beginning tae brew?"

"Oh wow."

A large bank of black storm clouds billowed intae the air.

She grabbed hold of my arm. "Oh no, are they going to be okay?"

"Aye, they are likely gone, they winna notice the storm, and when they awake on the other end twill be wet, possibly, but the storm will hae dissipated. Tis most brutal for the bystanders."

She nodded, but watched with a look of fear on her face.

"I am sorry I showed ye, I thought it might give ye more confidence, and I promised not tae keep things from ye."

"I understand. I'm glad you showed me. It's just daunting to imagine deciding to get in that storm. But I suppose I will have to eventually."

"Aye, we daena hae tae go yet, but we will hae tae tell Don ye are well, and then if ye are willing, tae meet with Magnus."

She smiled, "And your nephews."

"Aye, and even Fraoch, he will miss me greatly while I am away."

She watched me speak. Then said, "You don't think you matter much, but I was watching them, they see you as being important. I definitely don't want to keep you away from your family for long..."

I took her hand.

"What I mean is, thank you for staying behind, giving me a chance to figure this out, learn what is happening. I think I will be able to decide to go soon."

"Take yer time, we will catch up, we hae a time machine. We can stay here for a couple of weeks and arrive there a day behind."

She squinted her eyes. "You could mess with your age, cheat death."

"Ye canna cheat death, ye canna fix it. Tis looping, and we canna loop on ourselves. We can live longer than most, ye see Magnus calls himself thirty years auld but he has lived many years beyond it, some he remembers, some he daena. I call him auld because it bothers him, but tis also true."

The storm had grown violently, but now was folding in on itself, collapsing, and the winds were calming.

I said, "Ye are saying that ye will travel with me when tis time tae go?"

She nodded. "Even though I am afraid."

"Ye daena hae tae be afraid, I will take care of ye."

"Good, I just... I'm not sure what I'm offering to do. Not exactly." Her eyes swept the landscape. "Usually the way I talk myself into doing something is by, asking, 'Am I necessary?'"

I squeezed her hand, "Ye are verra necessary tae me, and I ought tae go, verra soon."

"You need me?"

"Aye."

"What if I said no, would you stay with me? Would you move back to Florida and live in my tiny apartment with me?"

I thought for a moment. "Aye, if I had tae, I would. Twould be at a cost, but I would, I need higher ceilings though."

She smiled. "Then I will go with you, Lochie. Let's do this thing." She exhaled. "As soon as I let Don and my family know, we will go live in the thirteenth century, something I thought was impossible only last week is now a decision I've made, but the strange thing is that I feel like I made the decision the night you spent the night."

I said, "Aye, we hae been decided since that night. I told ye the thumb oath was important."

CHAPTER 78 - MAGNUS

STIRLING CASTLE

*T*was after dinner, the third night. Cailean was in m'chamber, sitting with me, enjoyin' a whisky near the hearth.

"I ken ye are thrilled, Mag Mòr, that yer family will come on the morrow."

"Aye, I look forward tae showing them the castle and grounds. Stirling will reverberate with their high spirits, I canna wait."

"Ye hae been verra lonely without them."

"I hae, I daena like tae be too far away. As the wheel of time rolls, it seems we ought tae be ridin' alongside our family."

He chuckled. "Och nae, Mag Mòr, this again? Will ye once again argue the merits of a time*line*?"

"Nae, ye hae won the argument, Cailean. I lay down m'weapon, I hae lost. The line of time was a laughable idea. I hae been convinced of the notion that tis a wheel. All ye must do is see the sun comin' up on the day, descending in the West, and comin' around again on the next. Time canna march, it must roll. Dawn tae dusk."

He sipped his whisky. And stared at his glass. "Unless..."

I said, "Och nae, ye hae changed yer mind?"

"Tis less that I changed m'mind, more that I am not so settled in it that I will crow at having won. Who am I tae tell the mighty Mag Mòr, who uses time travel tae rule the world, how it works?"

I narrowed my eyes. "Ye ken about the time travel?"

"Ye told me of it months ago!"

"Och, tis right, I had forgotten. The rolling confused me."

I watched him as the light flickered on his face.

"Have ye ever met another time traveler, Cailean?"

He looked deep in thought, not choosing his words so much as searching his mind. He said, "I hae a vague memory, tis of a man named Asgall. I met with him, seems certain twas at Scone..." He leaned back in his seat as he often did, his hands clasped across his stomach. He could ruminate and plod along in conversation for hours. I was verra used tae his pace, and it dinna bother me, I was willing tae wait, because his journey often ended in wisdom. "...I remember the sky, it had the paleness of winter, and the trees were darkly etched on the sky. I was wearin' m'finest tunic, I can see it, the turquoise, dost ye ken the one I mean?"

I nodded.

He continued, "So twas an important meetin', I suspect, and m'knees ached, so twas winter and m'age was settled, I am an auld man, ye ken, Mag Mòr, verra auld, and I canna remember why I was called tae Scone but... as I passed through the gardens, there was a glisten upon the snow, and I thought tae m'self, tis like a jewel, I ought tae tell the king of this, so he might add it tae his speech, that the lands around his Abbey are like a jewel of Scotland... Dost ye remember me tellin' ye of the glistenin' snow on the gardens of Scone?"

I said, "Nae, I daena remember..."

"But in my memory, I want tae tell ye, Mag Mòr, but instead there stands a man, I vaguely remember his name, Asgall... and *he* is the king but I canna tell him the story of the snow...."

"Why nae?"

CHAPTER 78 - MAGNUS

He paused, his eyes traveling across the ceiling. "Because he is cruel, I hae learned tae remain quiet."

"Och nae."

"Aye." He exhaled, "But twas a dream, I haena met anyone named Asgall. And I canna place the time or how I got there."

"I ken Asgall, and ye are correct, he is a time traveler and it sounds as if ye hae met him once, though the wheel has continued turning on."

"Och, tis the work of demons. I am nae settled in it." He picked up his whisky glass and sipped from it again. "I would like tae travel, though..."

"Would ye? Where would ye like tae go?"

"Tae m'youth in Galloway, I would tell m'self 'Daena make the contract with the Earl, tis goin' tae cause ye trouble.'"

I chuckled. "The only problem with this idea is ye canna loop on yerself. I could go back there and warn ye."

He waved his hand. "Och nae, I would never listen. I had the dimness of youth, the folly of strength. I believed if I wanted tae do it, it must be right."

"Och aye, I ken a man who was just like that."

He laughed. "Yer young self?"

"And m'brother Fraoch, and Lochinvar, Quentin, James, and Zach... tis not possible tae be young and not be full of trouble for yer older self."

He nodded. "Will ye be able tae sleep waiting for yer family?"

"Nae, I am goin' tae be worried and watchful."

"Would ye like me tae sit up with ye?"

"Nae, I think I need tae be alone with my thoughts. I hae been worried on my son, he was havin' nightmares, worried that I might die and he would be forced tae ascend tae the throne. It caused him tae grow fearful."

He leaned back and looked up at the ceiling once more. "My eldest son feels the weight of responsibility as well, and I am but a hand tae the king. I can well think of the immense pressure it must be tae be the son of a king. It will take strong broad shoulders tae bear it."

"He is but eight circles around the sun."

"Och nae, he ought tae take tae the drink." He finished his whisky, and banged the glass tae the table. He belched. "Ye are young, yer son inna goin' tae be king for many long years. Tell him ye hae a kingdom of subjects who pray on yer behalf, *that* will keep ye living! On the morrow I will ask all tae chant Long Live the King when yer son arrives, so he will ken ye are protected." He patted my arm.

"Thank ye Cailean, that would likely do it."

"I look forward tae meeting him, we hae the rooms all readied."

"Good, thank ye, I will be gone in the morn. I plan tae be up before dawn. I will go tae the park and wait for them."

"With the dawn comes a new day."

"Aye."

He rose, took his leave, and left me alone with m'thoughts and worries.

My family was goin' tae travel more than four hundred years, and with the time twists and turns, the rift that had opened up, changing the timeline from settled in one way tae another, and another traveler usin' the machines, I couldna be comfortable believing it would go as planned, but there was nothin' I could do but wait.

CHAPTER 79 - MAGNUS

KING'S PARK - STIRLING

I rode away from the castle in darkness. M' guard ought tae hae accompanied me, but I ordered them tae stay behind. Twas purely selfish on my part: I wanted tae use m'lantern as I rode through the woods, the King's Park. Twas a huge tract of land set aside for huntin' and m'pleasure in general.

There was a dim light from the moon and stars castin' a soft glow on the surroundin' landscape. The night air was cool on m'cheeks. I raised the plaid higher around m'shoulders tae cut the breeze.

Ahead of me were silhouettes of ancient trees signaling m'park — how auld must those trees be that they were ancient in the thirteenth century? Their branches reachin' up toward the sky were like long fingers lifted in prayer.

In the quiet darkness I heard the rhythmic sound of m'horse's hooves, and the gentle rustling of leaves as the wind blew through the upper canopy.

At the edge of the woods I switched on a lamp, a curse and a blessin' how it lit the way, yet blinded me tae all else.

I watched ahead of us at the pool of light, the forest dark around us, and allowed the horse, a long inhabitant of the castle, tae guide me tae the clearing.

. . .

We emerged out of the forest in an open field and I switched off my lamp and dismounted the horse.

I gathered some fallen sticks, and a fire log I had brought from the castle, and crouched tae build a fire beside a low boulder. I raised the flames and sat and warmed my hands in the heat.

I looked out over the dark land. From ground level this was a view I dinna take verra often at night. I was usually up on the walls. I breathed in the scent of smoke and burning wood, and beyond it, the earthy scent of the woods and field. I listened tae the creaking and clacking of the branches as the wind blew low in the field and rose at the woods, and behind me was an owl, hooting, soundin' irritated that I had built a fire where he was tryin' tae hunt.

I felt warm, inside and out, at home. Twas a good land, it would provide well for as long as we needed tae be here.

The flame burned down as the sky began tae lighten, and then the wind rose. Above us were banking clouds. I grabbed the reins of m'horse and pulled him intae the woods, safe from the winds, and tied him tae a tree. I drew as near as I could before the whipping winds kept me from goin' any closer.

And when the wind rose even higher, I ducked behind a tree and clamped my eyes shut and huddled against its rage.

And then twas done.

I rushed out of the woods tae see m'family in heaps on a drenched ground. Three horses. Haggis raised his head, his tail shifted back and forth in the mud, as he slowly woke up. I

CHAPTER 79 - MAGNUS

located Kaitlyn and the bairns and crouched beside her with my hand on her shoulder and as dawn broke I made out Chef Zach and his family, Hayley and Fraoch, and... Sean.

Och, how did that happen?

Isla blinked her eyes first. "Hi Da."

"Hi wee one, ye good?"

She nodded. Archie opened his eyes, looked up at me confused, he said, "Da?" And then he scrambled up and threw his arms around my neck and held on tightly, burying his face in my shoulder, almost pushing me off my feet.

I finally pulled his head up and with a hand on each side of his face and looked in his eyes, "Archibald, did yer dream go away?"

He nodded. "It changed, Da, to Long Live the King."

"Aye, twill be a long life, a good life. Ye got m'note in the book?"

He nodded. "It was amazing, you fixed it — Grandmother was furious you wrote all over the pages."

I said, "Here's the thing about me, Archibald, I always do what I say I will do, and I rarely follow Lady Mairead's instructions, especially if twill ruin m'fun. Let it be a lesson tae ye."

He laughed.

Jack raised his head.

I pulled him intae my arms. And then Kaitlyn began tae stir.

I whispered, "I am here, I hae the bairns, ye are safe."

She went quiet again.

Jack looked at her with his brow down.

I said, "Mammy sleepy."

I stood with Jack in the crook of my arm. Archie and Isla, Zoe and Ben were climbing on a boulder, unfazed by the jump.

Sean began tae stir.

I said, "Hey brother, why are ye lyin' in the mud like a mucag?"

He groaned and threw an arm over his eyes tae block the morning sun. "What kind of demonic enterprise is this?"

"Ye hae traveled upon m'ship, I am welcomin' ye at port — how was it?"

"Terrible." He sat up and looked around. "It looks like Scotland."

"Aye, tis. Why did ye come?"

"Ye sent the message tae me."

"The message...?"

"Aye, 'Tha neart againn mar aon'. Twas meant for yer brother, Sean. As soon as I read it I knew ye needed m'service tae yer cause."

I nodded. "Aye, Brother, thank ye, I am glad ye understood it, and that ye came. It means a great deal tae me." I put out my hand tae help him tae his feet.

Fraoch lumbered up. "I told ye, Sean, dinna I tell ye?"

"Ye did, and somehow tis worse than ye said."

"But it inna endless scurvy-inducin' weeks upon the Atlantic Ocean, at least."

I said, "How are Lochinvar and the maiden? Where are Quentin and James?"

Fraoch helped Hayley up and counted off on his fingers. "James and Sophie are going tae stay at Balloch for a time, so the bairn is older before they travel. Quentin, Beaty, and Noah will come soon. In the meantime James and Quentin will be goin' tae Florida on supply runs. Og Lochie has tae convince the maiden tae travel. He says he will be here soon."

Hayley said, "He will need tae be persuasive. We are a million years in the past. I don't know if Ash is ready for this much fun."

Zach and Emma got up. He joked, "You called for me?"

I chuckled. "Ye ken it inna a proper home without Chef Zach."

He shook his head. "I'm going to guess that cooking now is going to be even more difficult since we're another four hundred years further in the past?"

CHAPTER 79 - MAGNUS

"Aye, we daena hae a good fork tae eat with — did ye bring some?"

He said, "Yep, a few. Quentin's bringing more. Don't want to change time, but holy shit, gotta have forks to eat. We aren't barbarians."

Emma said, "He's also bringing more toilet paper and orange and lemon trees."

Fraoch said, "And m'good fishin' pole, with the blue tackle box."

I helped Kaitlyn up, and embraced her. Holding Jack between us, she said, against my shoulder, "Were you waiting for us?"

"Since the middle of the night."

"You were worried we wouldn't make it? That we would end up on some alternate timeline?"

I nodded my head against her cheek. "It crossed m'mind."

She smoothed my hair back from my head. "We made it."

"Aye, and all are well. Thank ye for coming so far back in time. I ken tis selfish, but if I hae tae hold this throne I daena want tae be alone."

"I don't want you to be alone back here, this is just another place, like all the places before. This will just be where we live now."

Her eyes drew across to the boulder where the kids were all marching in a circle, laughing.

I smiled at her. And she smiled up at me. "I really liked how you drew the dawn in the book, and here we are."

"Aye, mo reul-iuil, here we are, a new beginning."

CHAPTER 80 - KAITLYN

STIRLING CASTLE

*A*rchie and Ben were each on the horses, Mario and Thor, Zoe and Isla were sharing Dràgon. The rest of us were on foot. Haggis bounding and rushing around sniffing the new world. Sean was looking around, taking it all in as Fraoch was talking happily about the landscape, explaining it all. Hayley said, "How long have you been here, my love?"

He chuckled, "I daena ken, we arrived a few days ago," then he and Magnus said at the same time, "It feels like we hae been here for a long time."

Magnus said, "I canna remember this park, yet it all feels commonplace, the kind of familiar that means I hae spent many a day ridin' through it."

I wore Jack in a sling on my front, my hand held by my husband as he guided us down the path towards his old home, our new home.

Then we came to our first glimpse of the castle up on the rocky crag, towering over the landscape. I remembered it, from my shifting past, the timber walls, the upward slope of the grass and the path to the front gate.

As we climbed, Magnus turned and swept out his arms

CHAPTER 80 - KAITLYN

toward the view. "Allow me tae introduce ye tae our kingdom, Alba."

Isla kindly said, "Wow, Da, it's beautiful."

"Aye, bairn, tis. Archibald, dost ye see the flags upon the walls?"

"Aye, Da, they are ours."

Magnus smiled. "That they are."

I glanced up at his face. "How you feeling, highlander?"

He said, "Verra satisfied, ye are here." He drew my hand up and kissed the back of my fingers. We turned toward the gate as it was being raised.

Magnus's friend, Cailean, who I had met briefly, somewhere, some time ago, was standing with his arms out, "Welcome!" Armored guardsmen filed out, and lined up along the path, so we would pass between them as we approached the gate.

Sean said, "Och, tis verra grand."

I said to the kids, "Watch how they bow, it's like a wave." As we passed the guards bowed their heads and only lifted them after we had gone by.

Archie whispered, "Cool."

Jack waved, "Ba-ba!"

Cailean said, when we stood before him, "Och aye, Mag Mòr, here is yer family!"

He clasped my hands in both of his, warmly and fondly, "Queen Kaitlyn, welcome tae Stirling, tis a pleasure, I feel as if I hae met ye before as Mag Mòr speaks of ye so kindly and often."

Magnus said, "Tis a jest on how much I talk, Cailean?"

He laughed, "Nae, tis a remark on how lonely ye hae been."

Fraoch said, "Nae, ye are too polite, Cailean, ye ken he talks too much."

We all helped the kids down from the horses, and then Magnus stood with a hand on each of the children's shoulders. "Cailean, this is my eldest son, Archibald. My daughter, Isla, and m'son, Jack." Jack waved, grinning, then tucked his head into my shoulder.

Cailean said, "Tis a beautiful family Mag Mòr."

Magnus said, "There are still more! Sean, m'brother," he clapped him on the shoulder, "has come, this is Fraoch's wife, Madame Hayley, and we hae Chef Zach, ye hae heard me speak about his food—"

Cailean teased, "Endlessly and exuberantly."

"And his lovely wife, Madame Emma, and their children, m'nephew Ben, and niece, Zoe."

Cailean said, "Finally I meet them all."

Fraoch said, "Except for the many who hae yet tae arrive. We will fill the castle once they all come."

Cailean said, "But for now, I meet the Prince! Og Archie, ye are the spittin' image of Mag Mòr! Follow me, I want tae shew ye something!"

He led us all through the gates, the morning sun warm on the walls, and our eyes were greeted with a full courtyard, a hundred people or more, and they began to chant, *Long Live the King! Long Live Mag Mòr! Long Live the King!*

Cailean said, "Tis good?"

Magnus said, "Aye, tis verra good." He looked down on Archie. "Tis good, Archibald?"

And Archie looked up at his father and said, "Aye."

I clutched Magnus's arm and kissed his shoulder. "You fixed it, my love."

CHAPTER 81 - MAGNUS

OUR CHAMBER IN THE KING'S HOUSE

We planned tae meet outside the Great Hall in a couple of hours so I could give everyone a good tour of the castle but in the meantime all were shewn tae their rooms tae rest after the journey.

I led my wife and bairns up the stairs tae m'chamber tae shew them where we would be livin' for a time.

Jack had fallen asleep, Isla and Archie were worn out from the travelin', we all sat on the settee in front of m'fireplace, and I had m'arms around them.

"I hae sat here many a night alone, mo reul-iuil."

Archie said, "It's funny that you know this place and we've never seen it before."

"Aye, tis like being torn asunder, now I feel mended that ye are here."

Isla said, "Da, you never be alone again, we will always be here." Then there was a knock on the door.

Ben and Zoe entered and Ben said, "Want to come see our room?"

Archie and Isla jumped up and followed Ben and Zoe out to go see their chambers.

Kaitlyn laughed. "That was very quick how she swore she would never leave you and then she did."

"Aye, I must grow used tae it." I kissed her on her temple.

She reached up and stroked the side of m'face. "You missed us while we were away?"

"I ken it wasna long, but—"

"It was over four centuries."

"Aye, there is somethin' about being this deep in the past that gives me a melancholy, mo reul-iuil. I miss ye and the bairns deeply. I am uneasy, ye ken; I hae experienced it many times before, and I ought tae be used tae it, but I canna be. I am in the past, the sun has set upon me. I brood that I might be lost in the depths of time—"

"You are being very dark."

"Aye, when I am in the past alone, the nights are long."

She stood and took my hand. "Have I said to you, Master Magnus, good morning?"

"Nae, I daena think ye hae yet."

She wordlessly drew me up from the settee and through the room tae our bed.

∼

The End.

THANK YOU

I see this story as a new beginning of Magnus and Kaitlyn's story, the dawn is here...
Which means there must be more to tell.
Magnus needs to hold a throne. The family has to come together. Lochinvar and Ash are beginning their lives together. We have new babies and older kids to grow up.
We have a bad guy to deal with.
The next book will be #20. The Empire

If you miss Magnus and Kaitlyn already, there is a Facebook group here: Kaitlyn and the Highlander
I would love it if you would join my Substack, here: Diana Knightley's Stories
Thank you for taking the time to read this book. The world is full of entertainment and I appreciate that you chose to spend some time with Magnus and Kaitlyn. I fell in love with Magnus when I was writing him, and I hope you fell in love a little bit, too.

As you all know, reviews are the best social proof a book can have, and I would greatly appreciate your review on this book.

ACKNOWLEDGMENTS

Thank you so much Cynthia Tyler, for your bountiful notes, your menu help, for reading through twice as you do, your edits, thoughts, historical advisements, and the proofing. I was thrilled that you want to know what happens next, me too.

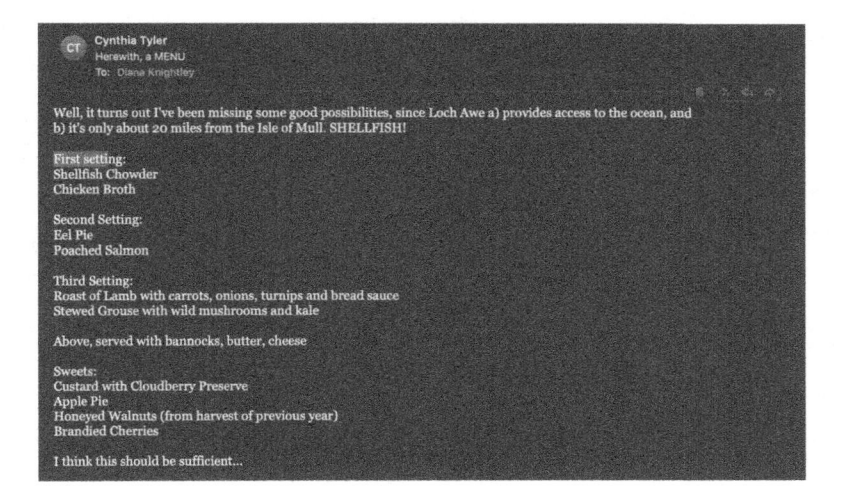

> **CT** Cynthia Tyler
> Herewith, a MENU
> To: Diana Knightley
>
> Well, it turns out I've been missing some good possibilities, since Loch Awe a) provides access to the ocean, and b) it's only about 20 miles from the Isle of Mull. SHELLFISH!
>
> First setting:
> Shellfish Chowder
> Chicken Broth
>
> Second Setting:
> Eel Pie
> Poached Salmon
>
> Third Setting:
> Roast of Lamb with carrots, onions, turnips and bread sauce
> Stewed Grouse with wild mushrooms and kale
>
> Above, served with bannocks, butter, cheese
>
> Sweets:
> Custard with Cloudberry Preserve
> Apple Pie
> Honeyed Walnuts (from harvest of previous year)
> Brandied Cherries
>
> I think this should be sufficient...

∽

Thank you so much David Sutton for your abundant notes and helping me find all the inconsistencies, my favorite this go around was when I left Fraoch behind in Fishtown, but then had him in Riaghalbane cracking jokes. I was pretty certain I hadn't done it, but here you were leading me through:

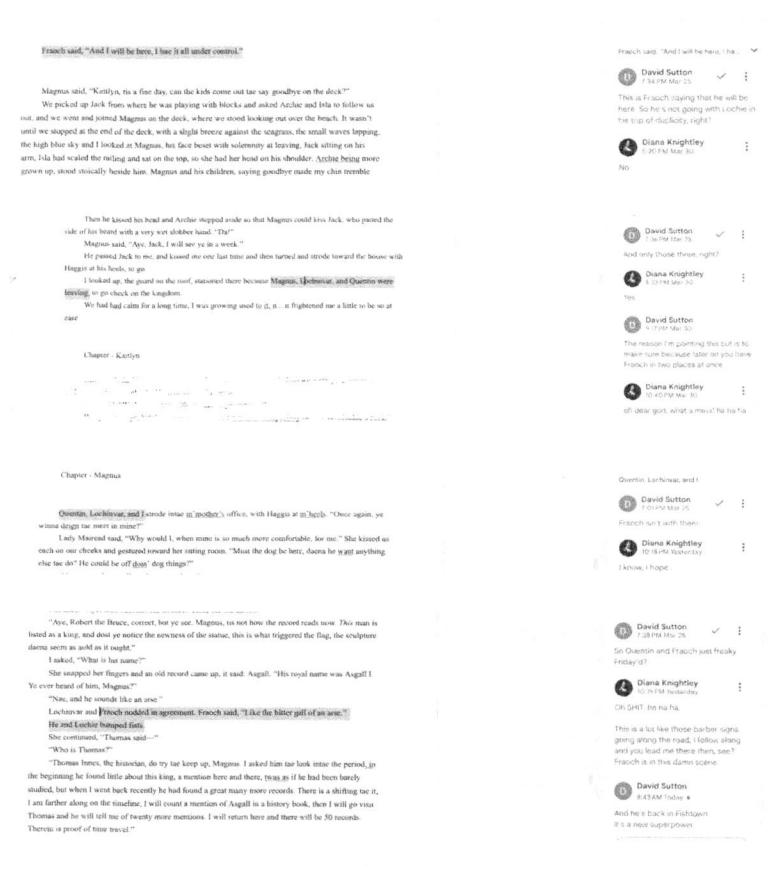

I'm so grateful you see this stuff.

~

Thank you to Kristen Schoenmann De Haan for your notes. You gave me clarity on the weight of the spike, reminded me to use Sean's wife's name (Maggie! I did it again, ha!) and leaving me hearts and smiles when you liked it... I appreciate it so much.

"Aye, tis my way, selfless and mad."

Thank you to Jessica Fox, for your notes, you found five different continuity problems that I hadn't even noticed. And you said this: "I liked the growth of the family both new baby and new character... I laughed and cringed at the scene of Lochie flirting with Ash... I loved the evolution of the family dynamics, the Fakiversary, how Lady Mairead manages to be likable while still being Queen B$#@&... Also loved the term Fraognus..."

Thank you, me too, I want more Fraognus adventures!

Thank you to *Jackie Malecki* and *Angelique Mahfood* (the admins) for your tireless excitement and exuberant energy around the group. All of your games and plans, you make it such a wonderful place, thank you for all you do.

And Angelique, thank you for your notebooks, keeping track of all of the details, I'm so grateful that you know who is related to whom and when they were born and when they were last seen and... etc. I couldn't keep it straight without you.

And thank you to Keira Stevens for narrating and bringing Kaitlyn and Magnus to life. I'm so proud that you're a part of the team.

And thank you to Shane East for voicing Magnus. He sounds exactly how I dreamed he would.

And more thanks to Jackie and Angelique for being admins of the big and growing FB group. 8.5K members! Your energy and positivity and humor and spirit, your calm demeanor when we need it, all the things you do and say and bring to the conversation fill me with gratitude.

You've blown me away with so many things. So many awesome things. Your enthusiasm is freaking amazing. Thank you.

~

Which brings me to a huge thank you to every single member of the FB group, Kaitlyn and the Highlander. If I could thank you individually I would, I do try. Thank you for every day, in every way, sharing your thoughts, joys, and loves with me. It's so amazing, thank you. You inspire me to try harder.

And for going beyond the ordinary and posting, commenting, contributing, and adding to discussions, thank you to: Dawn Underferth, Rena Sapko, Tonja Degroff, Tina Rox, Stacey Eddings, Nadeen Lough, Debra Walter, Dianna Schmidt, Bev Burns, Julia Burch, Lori Balise, Joleen Ramirez, Diane Cawlfield, Jenn E Pleaz, Anna Spain, Ginger Duke, Debra Bolton, Maureen Woeller, Joann Splonskowski, Mitzy Roberts, Barbara Baker, Retha Russell Martin, Kathy Hansel, Cynthia Tyler, Julie Dath, Alisa Davis, Darlene Sciarra McCormack, Elaine Brown, Kristen Schoenmann De Haan, Kalynne Connell, Jessica Blasek, Julie Chavez, Rita Johnson Small, Brianne Echard, Bonnie Elaine Gray, Cheryl Rushing, Tina McCoy, Katie Carman, Marcia Coonie Christensen, Liz MacGregor, Sandra Barlow Powell, Harley Moore, Margot Schellhas, Marie Smith, Lupe Skye, Wanda Jo Burroughs-Taylor, April Bochantin, Sonia Nuñez Estenoz, Alana K Mahler, Carol Wossidlo Leslie, Cindy Straniero, Crislee Anderson Moreno, Rebecca Bush, Nancy Josey Massengill, Carol Stevens Owen, Diane McGroarty McGowan,

Debra Arbed, Janice Hall Lewis, Shannon McNamara Sellstrom, Enza Ciaccia, Christina Rowley, Jackie Briggs, Kathleen Fullerton, JD Figueroa Diaz, Liz Leotsakos, Dorothy Chafin Hobbs, Maxine Sorokin-Altmann, Linda Wildman, Ruth DeVera Meyers, Denise Carpentier Sillon, Paula Flynn, Stacy D. Johnson, Cindy McLaughlin, Deborah Carleton, Kate Simon, Lisa D Yasko, Julie Lazaro, Liz Dayton Bowman, Christine Todd Champeaux, Lisa Lasell, Ellen McManus, Linda Grilli, Sue Miller, Eileen Kiehn- Dole, Melissa Harper Rasmussen, Karen Lessley Ingersoll, Karen Hixon, Tina-Maria Lopreiato Altiero, Helen Ramsey, Janice Wayman Hall, Susie Jones, Linda Jensen, Deb Maholm, Fay Burnett, Tracy Price Branham, and Jenny Bee

---

When I am writing and I get to a spot that needs research, or there is a detail I can't remember, I go to Facebook, ask, and my loyal readers step up to help. You find answers to my questions, fill in my memory lapses, and come up with so many new and clever ideas... I am forever ever ever grateful.

This round I needed to know:
 1. Would you say Magnus has used the Trailblazer before?
 2. Also what year was Lochie living when Lady Mairead rescued him? and Where?

Thank you to Kathy Hansel, Jo An Olson, Ericka French, Carol Stevens Owen, Alana K Mahler, April Bochantin, Angelique Mahfood, Harley Moore, Lupe Skye, Marie Smith, Laura Pozo, and Debra Arbed for answering, #1. No he hasn't used it. And #2, 1589, Dunscaith Castle.

and

When Mags was back in the year 1290, who else was there with him?

Thank you to Deb Maholm, Rena Sapko, Alana K Mahler, Patricia Howard Burke, Mitzy Roberts, Harley Moore, Angelique Mahfood, Andrea Gavrin, and Alison Caudle for your answers.

And when I ask 'research questions' you give such great answers...

∼

I asked for a list of the books on Magnus's bookshelf in 1296. I got so many amazing answers and chose:
1. book of poems by Rabbie Burns
2. the *Complete Works of Shakespeare*
3. Sun Tzu's *Art of War*
4. a bible
5. the Iliad

Thank you to Maureen Woeller, Michelle Bain, Michelle Lisgaris, Crislee Anderson Moreno, Darlene Sciarra McCormack, Debra Duncan Woodward, Dee Mecklin, Dev Daniel, Erika Meyer, Fiona Johnson, Harley Moore, Janet Close, Janice Hall Lewis, Jen Bement, Jennifer SepulvedaVandegraft, Joann Splonskowski, Kathy K Cox, Leah Krakowski, Lindsay Ames Gibson, Liz Rains Johnson, Lora Martin, Lupe Skye, Maro Andrikidis Hogan, Patricia A. Neuendorf, Patricia Howard Burke, Paula Flynn, Rena Sapko, Rita Johnson Small, Robin Holland Hagenbeck, Ruth DeVera Meyers, Stacey Eddings, Sue Miller, Tempe Garriott, Teresa Weeks Andrepont, Tonja Degroff, Tonja Townsend Owens, Angelique Mahfood, Tracy Abbott, Vickie Foree Burgin, Vicky Faherty, Anna Spain, Bonnie Elaine Gray, Carol Stevens Owen, and Carol Wossidlo Leslie for suggesting all or some of the books I chose.

∼

I asked for Lady Mairead's security word and chose: **Fionn**

Thank you Bev Burns, Cheryl Rushing, Harley Moore, Amanda Chestovich, Carol Wossidlo Leslie, Terri Marken,

Stacey Eddings, Lisa Hogan Sanabria, Melanie Hotovcin Lambie, and Susan O'neill Mottin.

～

And Archie and Ben got to name the Auld Warrior's horse...
    Amy Ply Miller picked Mario which I thought was perfect. Thank you.

～

In the very beginning of writing, I wanted the book to open with an event the gang hasn't experienced yet. There were some great ideas, but I decided to send most of them rafting on the Ichetucknee River...

～

Thank you to *Kevin Dowdee* for being there for me in the real world as I submerge into this world to write these stories of Magnus and Kaitlyn. I appreciate you so much.
    Thank you to my kids, *Ean, Gwynnie, Fiona,* and *Isobel,* for listening to me go on and on about these characters, advising me whenever you can, and accepting them as real parts of our lives. I love you.

SOME THOUGHTS AND RESEARCH...

Characters:
Kaitlyn Maude Sheffield - Born December 5, 1993
Magnus Archibald Caelhin Campbell - born August 11, 1681
Archibald (Archie) Caelhin Campbell - Son of Magnus and Bella born August 12, 2382
Isla Peace Barbara Campbell - Daughter of Magnus and Kaitlyn, born October 4, 2020
Jack Duncan Campbell - Son of Magnus and Kaitlyn, born July 31, 1709
Lady Mairead (Campbell) Delapointe - Magnus's mother, born 1660
Lochinvar - A son of Donnan, Half-brother to Magnus and Fraoch. Found living at Dunscaith Castle in 1589.
Hayley Sherman - Kaitlyn's best friend, now married to Fraoch MacDonald
Fraoch MacDonald - Married to Hayley. Born in 1714, meets Magnus in 1740, and pretends to be a MacLeod after his mother, Agnie MacLeod. His father is also Donnan, which makes him Magnus's brother.

Quentin Peters - Magnus's security guard/colonel in his future army
Beaty Peters - Quentin's wife, born in the late 1680s
Noah Peters - Son of Quentin and Beaty, born June 1, 2024
Zach Greene- The chef, married to Emma
Emma Garcia - Household manager, married to Zach
Ben Greene - Son of Zach and Emma, born May 15, 2018
Zoe Greene - Daughter of Zach and Emma, born September 7, 2021
James Cook - Former boyfriend of Kaitlyn. Now friend and frequent traveler. He's a contractor, so it's handy to have him around.
Sophie - Wife of James Cook. She is the great-great-granddaughter of Lady Mairead, her mother is Rebecca.
Junior - Son of James and Sophie, born May 16, 2025
Sean Campbell - Magnus's older half-brother
Lizbeth Campbell - Magnus's older half-sister
Sean and Lizbeth are the children of Lady Mairead and her first husband, the Earl of Lowden. They live in the early 18th century, in Scotland, at Balloch Castle.

The horses:
Sunny belongs to Magnus
Osna belongs to Kaitlyn
When Magnus and Kaitlyn were in the 16th century they rode Cynric and Hurley.
Hayley and Fraoch have the horses Gatorbelle and Thor
Lochinvar now has a horse named Cookie
Magnus now has Dràgon
Archie and Ben have a horse named Mario

SOME THOUGHTS AND RESEARCH... 439

The Kings of Riaghalbane from the Scottish Duke:
Normond I - 2167
Maximillian - 2196
Niall - 2221
Artair - 2249
Birk - 2276
Graeme - 2306
Donnan I - 2331
Donnan II - 2356
Magnus I - crowned August 11, 2382 the day before the birth of his son, Archibald Campbell, next in line for the throne.

(Because of Time Travel dates and names are subject to change...)

∼

Some **Scottish and Gaelic words** that appear within the book series:
dreich - dull and miserable weather
mo reul-iuil - my North Star (nickname)
osna - a sigh
dinna ken - didn't know
tae - to
winna - won't or will not
daena - don't
tis - it is or there is. This is most often a contraction 'tis, but it looked messy and hard to read on the page so I removed the apostrophe. For Magnus it's not a contraction, it's a word.
och nae - Oh no.
ken, kent, kens - know, knew, knows
mucag - is Gaelic for piglet
m'bhean - my wife
m'bhean ghlan - means clean wife, Fraoch's nickname for Hayley.
cù-sith - a mythological hound found in Scottish folklore.

cù - dog

~

Locations:
Fernandina Beach on Amelia Island, Florida, present day. Their beach house is on the south end of the island.

Magnus's homes in Scotland - **Balloch**. Built in 1552. In the early 1800s it was rebuilt as **Taymouth Castle**. It lays near Loch Tay near the River Tay

The kingdom of Magnus I, **Riaghalbane**, is in Scotland. Its name comes from *Riaghladh Albainn*, and like the name Breadalbane (from *Bràghad Albainn*) it was shortened as time went on. I decided it would now be **Riaghalbane.**

Magnus' castle, called, **Caisteal Morag,** is very near where Balloch Castle once stood, near Loch Tay.

Fortingall is a small village on the north side of Loch Tay.

The Palace Saloon. The oldest bar in Florida and the last American tavern to close during Prohibition. Once a favorite haunt of the Carnegies, the Rockefellers and other socialites, The Palace Saloon is still operating today.

Stirling Castle is in central Scotland and is one of the largest and most historically and architecturally important castles.

The Ichetucknee River flows from northeast to southwest for six miles or so in north central Florida. Its average depth is five feet, and it's cold!

~

Real People:
The **Earl of Breadalbane** (1636 - 1717) and his son John (1662 - 1752).

Thomas Innes (1662 – 28 January 1744) was a Scottish Roman Catholic priest and historian.

True things that happened:

First interregnum (1290-1292)
The death of Margaret of Norway began a two-year interregnum in Scotland caused by a succession crisis.

Then, **John Balliol** was crowned, ruling from 1292–1296

John Balliol abdicated in March 1296. That same month Edward I of England invaded Scotland. And there was a

Second Interregnum (1296–1306)
A set of guardians were appointed by Edward I and they ruled from 1296 to 1306, until the election of Robert the Bruce as the king of Scotland who ruled from 1306 - 1329.

∽

Theme of this book, finding the right time, beginning at the beginning, being first, dawn.

∽

There's my thumb, I'll ne'er beguile thee.

THE SCOTTISH DUKE, THE RULES OF TIME TRAVEL, AND ME

The year is 1670 and a young Duke has ridden out to explore a mysterious gale. He finds, in the center of a clearing, a strange apparatus.

He reaches for it and—

In Florida, 2012, a young storm-chaser has gone to investigate a storm — lightning arcs, the winds howl, trees whip around her, but when the storm clears she sees it: a small weird piece of tech jutting out of the sand.

She reaches out and—

The portals — active in two different times, in two different places — vibrate, grab hold, and rip them both through time.

They have just learned the first rule: Don't touch an active portal.

THE KAITLYN AND THE HIGHLANDER SERIES

Kaitlyn and the Highlander (Book 1)

Time and Space Between Us (Book 2)

Warrior of My Own (Book 3)

Begin Where We Are (Book 4)

Entangled with You (Book 5)

Magnus and a Love Beyond Words (Book 6)

Under the Same Sky (Book 7)

Nothing But Dust (Book 8)

Again My Love (Book 9)

Our Shared Horizon (Book 10)

Son and Throne (Book 11)

The Wellspring (Book 12)

Lady Mairead (Book 13)

The Guardian (Book 14)

Magnus the First (Book 15)

Only a Breath Away (Book 16)

Promises to Keep (Book 17)

Time is a Wheel (Book 18)

Long Live the King (Book 19)

BOOKS IN THE CAMPBELL SONS SERIES...

Why would I, a successful woman, bring a date to a funeral like a psychopath?

Because Finch Mac, the deliciously hot, Scottish, bearded, tattooed, incredibly famous rock star, who was once the love of my life... will be there.

And it's to signal — that I have totally moved on.

But... at some point in the last six years I went from righteous fury to... something that might involve second chances and happy endings.

Because while Finch Mac is dealing with his son, a world tour, and a custody battle,

I've been learning about forgiveness and the kind of love that rises above the past.

◊

We were so lost until we found each other.

I left my husband because he's a great big cheater, but decided to go *alone* on our big, long hike in the-middle-of-nowhere anyway. Destroyed. Wrecked. I wandered into a pub and found... Liam Campbell, hot, Scottish, a former-rugby star, now turned owner of a small-town pub and hotel.

And he found me.

◊

My dear old dad left me this failing pub, this run down motel and now m'days are spent worrying on money and how tae no'die of boredom in this wee town.

And then Blakely walked intae the pub, needing help.

The moment I lay eyes on her I knew she would be the love of m'life.

And that's where our story begins...

ABOUT ME, DIANA KNIGHTLEY

I write about heroes and tragedies and magical whisperings and always forever happily ever afters.

I love that scene where the two are desperate to be together but can't be because of war or apocalyptic-stuff or (scientifically sound!) time-jumping and he is begging the universe with a plea in his heart and she is distraught (yet still strong) and somehow — through kisses and steam and hope and heaps and piles of true love, they manage to come out on the other side.

My couples so far include Beckett and Luna, who battle their fear to search for each other during an apocalypse of rising waters.

Liam and Blakely, who find each other at the edge of a trail leading to big life changes.

Karrie and Finch Mac, who find forgiveness and a second chance at true love.

Nor and Livvy, who are beginning a grand adventure.

Hayley and Fraoch, Quentin and Beaty, Zach and Emma, and James and Sophie who have all taken their relationships from side stories in Kaitlyn and the Highlander to love stories in their own right.

And Magnus and Kaitlyn, who find themselves traveling through time to build a marriage and a family together.

I write under two pen names, this one here, Diana Knightley, and another one, H. D. Knightley, where I write books for Young Adults. (They are still romantic and fun and sometimes steamy though because love is grand at any age.)

DianaKnightley.com
Diana@dianaknightley.com
Substack: Diana Knightley's Stories

Made in United States
Orlando, FL
26 May 2024